PsF
GK

THE BRIDE'S HOUSE

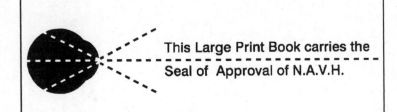

This Large Print Book carries the
Seal of Approval of N.A.V.H.

THE BRIDE'S HOUSE

SANDRA DALLAS

WHEELER PUBLISHING
A part of Gale, Cengage Learning

GALE
CENGAGE Learning

Detroit • New York • San Francisco • New Haven, Conn • Waterville, Maine • London

GALE
CENGAGE Learning˙

LIBRARY OF CONGRESS CATALOGING-IN-PUBLICATION DATA

Dallas, Sandra.
    The bride's house / by Sandra Dallas.
       p. cm.
    ISBN-13: 978-1-4104-3709-9 (hardcover)
    ISBN-10: 1-4104-3709-4 (hardcover)
    1. Young women—Fiction. 2. Triangles (Interpersonal relations)—Fiction. 3. Family secrets—Fiction. 4. Social classes—Fiction. 5. Georgetown (Colo.)—Fiction. 6. Colorado—History—19th century—Fiction. 7. Domestic fiction. 8. Large type books. I. Title.
    PS3554.A434B75 2011b
    813'.54—dc22   2011003005

Published in 2011 by arrangement with St. Martin's Press, LLC.

For the cousins, one family's future
Dana and Kendal
Aaron and Brendan
McCamie and Collier

PART I
NEALIE

CHAPTER 1

Something caused men to stare at Nealie Bent, although just what it was that made them do so wasn't clear. Her body was more angles than curves, and her face, too, had all those sharp planes, far too many to be pretty. She was too tall to suit, and with her long legs, she took strides that were more like a man's than the mincing steps of a young girl. The dress she wore, one of only two she owned, was faded yellow calico, threadbare at the wrists and neck and of the wrong color to complement her pale skin. Her second dress was no better.

Still, men turned to look at Nealie Bent, for there was no question that the tall, thin girl was striking, or at least peculiar-looking, with her eyes the color of the palest blue columbines late in the spring, her hair such a pale red that it was almost the hue of pink quartz, and her face as freckled as a turkey egg. It could have been her youth that drew their attention. After all, Georgetown itself was still young, and youth was highly prized. Most of the young women there were already old, worn out from the work a mining town demanded of them and from childbearing. The Alvarado Cemetery was full of babies, with here and there a mother buried beside her newborn in that forlorn spot. Like all the mountain towns, Georgetown was a hard place, and folks there had a saying: Any cat with a tail is a stranger.

The same might be said in a slightly different way for a young woman, because any female with youth, such as Nealie, was new in Georgetown. But she would age quick enough. Still, for now — and for a few years hence, perhaps — the girl's youthfulness matched the spirit of the town, a place that was mightily attractive to those seeking to make their fortunes.

If it wasn't Nealie's youth that drew glances, then it might have been her air of innocence, and innocence was in even shorter supply in Georgetown than youth. But in that, the girl's appearance was a sham, for Nealie's short life had been a hard one. Though she knew more about the dark side of life than most her age, there was not even the hint of those hardships on Nealie Bent, and she appeared as fresh and guileless as a newborn.

So no one could put a finger on exactly what it was that made men take another look at Nealie, not that anyone in that town bothered to analyze. But no one doubted that they turned to stare at her as she passed them on the broad board sidewalk or paused in her rounds of shopping to peer into store windows at the delectable items she could only dream about buying.

Will Spaulding was no different from the rest of the men in his admiration. He'd seen the girl as she filled her basket from the bins of apples and onions and potatoes. And now, as Nealie stood at the counter of the Kaiser Mercantile store, talking quietly with Mr. Kaiser, Will measured her with his eyes. She was five feet eight inches, only two inches shorter than he was. Will's eyes wandered over Nealie, taking in her slender build under the shabby dress, until he became aware that Mr. Kaiser was watching him and clearing his throat.

"I said, 'What can I do for you, young man?'" the storekeeper repeated. The girl had placed her purchases in her basket and was turning to go, not sending so much as a glance at the man standing next to her.

Will cleared his throat, but he didn't speak immediately. Instead, he stared at the girl as

11

she left the store and walked past the large glass window, leaving behind her soapy scent and the tinkling of the bell that announced customers. "Who is she?" he asked, as if he had the right to know.

"Oh, that's Nealie Bent," the older man replied, a look of bemused tolerance on his face. "You're not the first to ask. Did you come in for something or just to stare at the ladies?"

Without answering, Will turned away from the door and looked at the shopkeeper. He removed a list from his pocket, laying it on the counter and smoothing it with his hand. "I'm working up at the Rose of Sharon, and I'll be needing these things." He turned the list so that Mr. Kaiser could read it.

"We take cash," Mr. Kaiser said, which wasn't exactly true. He extended credit to those in town who needed it, as well as to good customers such as Nealie's employer, but he did not extend the courtesy to strangers.

"I'll pay it." Will's voice sounded as if he was not used to his credit being questioned. The older man moved his finger down the list, tapping a broken nail beside each item as he pronounced it out loud: "Three pair work pants, three work shirts, cap, boots, jacket, gloves, candlesticks, candles." He

12

droned on, and when he was finished, he said, "Yep, you work at a mine, all right. You a trammer?"

"Engineer. For the summer."

The young man's voice carried the slightest bit of authority as he corrected the misimpression, and Mr. Kaiser looked up and squinted at him, taking in the cut of his clothes, which made it obvious that Will was too fashionably dressed to be an ordinary miner. "You somebody's son?" he asked.

Will appeared taken aback at the impertinence, but he replied pleasantly enough, "Grandson. I'm William Spaulding. My grandfather's Theodore Spaulding. He owns half of the Sharon."

"Owns mines up in Leadville and Summit County, too," Mr. Kaiser added. Like everyone in the mountain towns, the shopkeeper was caught up in the mining fever and was as sure of the names of prominent investors as he was of those of his own customers. And well he might be, because outside capital was the lifeblood of the mining industry. Without development money, the gold and silver deposits were all but useless. Theodore Spaulding was not only a man of wealth but one respected in mining circles for his understanding of ore bodies and extraction methods. That did not make his

13

grandson anything more than a trifler, however. "So you thought you'd see what goes on underground, did you?"

"I've already seen what's underground. I have an engineering degree, so I know about mining, you see, at least theoretically. The old man thought I ought to get some practical experience for the summer. I've only just arrived."

"You'll get it." Now that he seemed satisfied about his customer's identity, Mr. Kaiser returned to the list. "I reckon we got everything you need." He moved around behind the counter, taking down boxes and holding out shirts and pants for sizes. He told Will to try on the heavy leather cap, then nodded, because the fit was right. Then he handed the young man two pairs of boots and told him to see which ones suited. Will sat down on a kitchen chair propped against the cold potbellied stove and removed his fine shoes. He clumped about on the floor in the stiff boots, and settled on one pair. Then he set his shoes on the counter and said that with all the mud on the streets, he might as well keep the boots on.

"Socks. You'll need plenty of them, because the Sharon floods, and you don't want to get your feet wet. Worst thing there is, wet feet in a mine. If the water doesn't rot your feet, it'll give you pneumonia." Mr. Kaiser placed four pairs on top of the pile of clothing. He checked the list again, then pulled a dark blue bandana from a drawer and set it on top. "Present," he said.

"Splendid! It will look grand."

"It's not for looks, Mr. Spaulding. You'll need the handkerchief to wipe your face when it's slashed with muck and cover your mouth and nose after a dynamite blast so's you won't get the miner's puff."

"Then I thank you, sir."

Mr. Kaiser licked the tip of the lead pencil he kept behind his ear and wrote the charge next to each item on the list, totaled the amount, and turned the paper toward Will, who pulled the money out of his pocket.

"There's one other thing I'm needing," the young man said, as he watched Mr. Kaiser wrap the purchases in brown paper and tie the bundle with string. "A boarding-house. I'm staying at the Hotel de Paris until my cottage is ready. Once I move in, I'll need a place to eat, because I don't fancy cooking for myself. Nor do I want to dress up every night for supper at the hotel."

"Georgetown's got a plenty of eateries."

"Somewhere clean where the food is good."

"That narrows it some." Mr. Kaiser

15

thought a minute. "You might try the Grubstake up on the hill. The bosses prefer it, since it's a good bit tonier than the others. Ma Judson's place is up on Main. She sets a good table. Then there's Lydia Travers's house on Rose Street. If I was you'd, I'd board with Mrs. Travers — Lidie, she's called."

"She's the best cook?"

"I didn't say that."

Will waited.

"Fact is, when it comes to cooking, Mrs. Travers's second to Ma Judson and not much better than the Grubstake."

"Cleaner, then?"

"Not so's you'd notice."

"Then why should I take my meals there?"

Mr. Kaiser studied the young man a minute and chuckled. "That's where Nealie Bent works."

Will reddened, and the shopkeeper added, "You wouldn't be the first to pick Mrs. Travers's place because of Nealie. But I ought to tell you she's all but spoke for by Charlie Dumas. He'd marry her in a minute if she'd have him."

Will took his bundle and started for the door, ignoring Mr. Kaiser's last words.

"Best you take no notice of her, Mr. Spaulding," Mr. Kaiser called after him.

"It's certain she took none of you."

The young man grinned and turned back to the counter where Mr. Kaiser stood fingering the canned goods.

But in fact, Nealie Bent had taken considerable notice of young Will Spaulding. She had caught sight of him as she ran her hands through the bin of potatoes to find ones that were firm, with no rotten spots. She had glanced up and observed him through her pale lashes, taken in the young man's face, which was strong with no soft places, a little like a good potato. He was clean shaven, a nice thing, because Nealie was not partial to whiskers. Will's eyes were a deep brown with flecks of gold the color of aspen leaves in the fall, and his brown hair fell across his face in waves. He might have been the handsomest man she had ever seen, and certainly, he was the best dressed in a town where few wore anything but faded work shirts and rusty overalls.

She admired Will's jacket, a thick corduroy the color of a mountain sheep, that was handsomely tailored to fit his shape, not store bought at a place like the Kaiser Mercantile. He wore tight-fitting trousers that were better suited to a big city than a mining camp, and his shoes — Nealie had

17

to keep herself from smiling — were of leather as fine as a glove and wouldn't last a day in the muck of the Georgetown streets.

The man was a stranger and a well-fixed one. And not for the likes of you, Nealie told herself as she pushed so hard at a soft spot in a potato that she broke the peel. She hastily placed the spoiled potato back in the bin, hoping Mr. Kaiser wasn't watching her. He was a bad one to tease, and she would die of mortification if he remarked on the way she had appraised the new fellow.

Such a man wasn't likely to notice her, she told herself. Nealie was not aware of the effect that she had on men, and if she had been, she would have been bewildered. Still, she wondered, as the young man came up to stand beside her at the counter while Mr. Kaiser wrote down her purchases on a piece of brown wrapping paper, what it would be like to be courted by such. Her mind wandered to thoughts of carriages and roses in the winter and diamond rings. But not for long. She could more easily find a gold mine than attract a man like this stranger, and so she turned her attention to Mr. Kaiser, double-checking his addition in her mind, because she was smart with numbers. Nealie considered questioning one of the figures so the young man would turn and look at her and maybe wish her a good morning, but she blushed at the thought, and without a word, she signed beside the amount entered in the ledger on the page that bore Mrs. Travers's name.

Then wishing that instead of her sound-less cotton shift, she owned a satin petticoat with a ruffle to wear, a garment that would create a soft *whish* as she moved, Nealie turned to the door, shifting the basket from hand to arm to free her other hand for the handle. She went out then, forcing herself not to turn around for another look at the young man, and walked past the big window without so much as a backward glance. She would think about him later, for what was the harm in dreaming about matched horses and diamonds as thick as stars?

At the corner, she confronted the mud, slick as treacle, that was the street. The runoff from the snow had turned the dirt streets into a wet mass as thick as fudge. Although it was May, spring — or what passed for spring — had not quite reached the high country. Houses bore bare spots where the wind had scoured off the paint, and yards were covered with patches of late snow. But the drifts high up on the peaks were melting, and water cascaded down the gullies and through the streets. Although

Nealie wore serviceable boots instead of slippers, she did not care to dirty them. It was an unpleasant chore to scrape off the mud that clung to them like glue and to oil the leather. She looked for dry spots in the muck or a board placed across the street for pedestrians, but such was not available. Nealie sighed and was just about to step into the brown stew when a man grabbed her arm.

"I'll carry you across, Miss Nealie," he said.

Remembering the man in the store, Nealie felt a wave of disappointment at the voice. Yes, Charlie Dumas could carry her as easily as if she was a feather. Charlie was a giant of a man, with the strength of a mule, and he could have picked up her and Mr. Kaiser and the stranger all at the same time and transported them across the street. But Nealie didn't want Charlie, who stood there with the neck buttons of his union shirt unbuttoned and his baggy pant legs tied to his boots with fuse cord. He snatched off his wide-brimmed hat, which had been rubbed with linseed oil to make it hard, and grinned at her. Charlie was altogether too familiar, and for reasons she didn't quite understand, she did not care to see the stranger come out of the store and find her

20

in Charlie's arms. But it was that or muddy her boots and maybe her skirts, too. Besides, if the stranger had not noticed her in the store, he surely would pay no attention to her on the street. So Nealie said she was obliged and let Charlie lift her as easily as she did her basket and ferry her through the muck.

He walked slowly, furrowing his brow as if thinking of a way to prolong the trip through the mud. Then his face lit up, and he stopped in the middle of the street. "Did I tell you I saw a man down by Taos Street in mud up to his neck? I told him that was deep muck." He grinned at Nealie to make sure he had her attention. "That man told me, 'Stranger, it wouldn't be so bad if I wasn't sitting on a horse.' " Charlie guffawed as he watched Nealie hopefully, to see if she found the joke funny, and she laughed politely, although she'd heard the tale two or three times already.

On the other side of the street, she escaped from Charlie's hold and struggled to stand up, putting as much distance as she could between herself and the big man.

"I'm grateful to you, Mr. Dumas," she said formally.

"Aw, won't you call me Charlie?" he

asked. "You did last week. Do you remember?"

Nealie remembered all too well, because it had been a magical time, and she was beside herself with joy. The two of them had sat together on chairs in the balcony of the opera house, watching a traveling troupe of performers. Charlie hadn't exactly thought to invite her, but Nealie had hinted so obviously that she wanted to go that he finally understood and bought the tickets. He sat restlessly on a chair that was too small for him, but Nealie was captivated by the performance and especially the star, an actress from Denver, who pranced about the stage, her satin dress and paste diamonds shimmering in the glow of the gaslights. Nealie grabbed her companion's arm and said, "Oh, Charlie, I never saw anyone so lovely." She smiled at him as if he were an actor himself, not a miner whose fingernails were black with grime and who smelled sour in his ill-fitting black suit.

"I don't remember that I did," Nealie told him now as she stood on the street corner, straightening her skirts.

"Well, I do. Besides —"

Nealie didn't want to hear the "besides," because she knew it meant "Besides, you know how I feel about you." "No besides," she said brusquely. "Thank you for the escort, Mr. Dumas. I'll see you at the supper table." She pulled away.

"I could carry your basket."

"It's not heavy," she said, not thanking him.

"No bother. I'm going that way."

"No," Nealie said forcefully, and walked away. She did not look back but knew that he did not follow her, because she no longer felt the stifling presence of the big man.

Charlie Dumas was a nice enough fellow, probably the nicest she had met in Georgetown — in her life, even — and she could do worse than marry such a one as he. After all, Charlie worked hard setting charges in the Bobcat Mine, and he didn't drink or gamble away his wages. Instead of spending his spare time in the pool halls, he prospected a little, and there was talk that he had a bit of money put away from a silver strike he'd made in Leadville. In fact, it was said that Charlie had discovered the Black Mountain Mine and sold it to H.A.W. Tabor, the silver king, but Nealie paid no attention to the gossip. Similar was told about everyone in Georgetown. Besides, a man who was well fixed wouldn't work underground if he didn't have to, would he?

She had to admit that Charlie was generous, buying tickets to that opera house performance when he didn't want to go himself, and she had been flattered when he began to court her. Except for his nose, which had been smashed in a mining accident, he was not such a bad-looking fellow, either, with his thick blond hair and deep-set blue eyes. Charlie was easygoing, too, slow to anger, and he was liked by the other boarders.

But Nealie had grown tired of his presumptions, the way he followed her on her walks, pretending to come across her by accident. When there was an amusement in town, such as a boxing match or a band concert, he'd announce to the table at the boardinghouse that he was escorting Nealie, discouraging the other men from asking her out, not that there was anyone else among the boarders with whom she'd care to associate.

Charlie's table manners were against him, and Nealie couldn't imagine eating in a fine restaurant such as the dining room of the Hotel de Paris with him. He drank his coffee from a saucer and stirred everything on his plate into a mess before shoveling it into his mouth with a spoon. He was kind in his way, bringing her specimens of ore that he found in his wanderings in the mountains or presenting her with a special oil to waterproof her boots, but he knew nothing about presents that appealed to a young girl's heart — hothouse flowers, books of poetry, kid gloves as smooth as custard. Not that anybody had ever presented her with such gifts, Nealie thought, smiling to herself. And what would she do with a book of poetry anyway?

Nealie wondered then if Charlie could read. She herself had worked so hard to get a little schooling that she couldn't abide a man who couldn't read. But he must, because in Georgetown, Charlie Dumas was not considered stupid. In fact, men had a way of seeking him out and asking his advice on mining.

Nealie mulled over the big man as she made her way back to Mrs. Travers's boardinghouse. She'd given Charlie a good deal of thought already, but now she pondered whether she ought to encourage him, not that he needed it. She didn't love him, and at times, she came close to detesting his ways. Although she had no right to expect anything more than Charlie, she did dream of better, and in an odd manner, she thought she deserved it. She couldn't have said why, because she didn't even know she thought that way. If Charlie were the best she could find, then she might just as well have married one of her pa's friends in Hannibal, Missouri. She hadn't run away just to hook up with a miner and live in a one-room log cabin with a dirt floor. She wasn't going to wear herself out scrubbing clothes and butchering hogs and caring for a bunch of squalling babies, an old woman at thirty. There had to be something else for her, although she wasn't sure just what it was.

Nealie had a vague sense that life had more to offer her than work as a serving girl in a boardinghouse. It was not a thought fully formed, however, and if it had been, Nealie would have been surprised at it, for she was of humble and penurious origins and had no cause to think so highly of herself. Had she been more conscious of the effect she had on men, she might have used her freshness and unusual good looks to advantage. But she was not aware that men turned to stare at her and wouldn't have believed it if someone had told her. After all, her father had said savagely that she was as ugly as a pig's foot and had proclaimed her curious pale red hair to be the mark of the devil, and he'd whipped her for it. Whipped her and worse. No, Nealie Bent considered herself no better than plain. And although youth and innocence were marketable commodities, she did not consider that she possessed them and could use them to her benefit.

The girl paused then, her hand on the fencepost of Mrs. Travers's boardinghouse, and looked back over her shoulder to see if Charlie was trailing her, but he was gone. And of course, there was no sign of the stranger. Nealie doubted that she would see him a second time, and she put him out of her mind.

"You're dawdling again," Mrs. Travers called out from the back porch, and Nealie straightened up and hurried into the house through the back door.

"It was muddy," Nealie explained, setting down her basket on a table whose wooden top had been scrubbed until it was smooth and almost white. The kitchen was neater than the yards outside that were stacked with piles of lumber and cordwood. A black cookstove occupied one wall of the kitchen, a kindling bucket beside it. Across from it was a dry sink painted bright orange and a walnut pie safe whose tin panels were punched with hearts and the initials *ET.* A wooden icebox stood next to a door that led into a tiny pantry that was filled with dishes and platters and foodstuffs — sacks of dried beans, tins of flour, cones of sugar

27

wrapped in blue paper, a bag of coffee beans.

"I was all right early on, but by the time I came home, the street wasn't froze anymore, and the mud was deep enough to swallow me up," Nealie explained. "Charlie told me a story about a man in the street in mud up to his neck."

"And he was sitting on a horse." Mrs. Travers waved her hand dismissively. "They tell it every year during runoff. It's 1881, and Georgetown's been here for twenty years. You'd think we'd have decent streets by now." She paused. "So you waited on the corner until Charlie Dumas came along. Am I right?"

"You are." Nealie didn't look up, although she knew Mrs. Travers was staring at her. The widow had taken a personal interest in Charlie's courtship and had told Nealie she'd best make up her mind soon or Charlie would find himself a girl who was not so particular. "I'd be real sorry to lose you, but I have to admit he's a good man. He treats you like the Queen of Turkey," she'd said.

"Then marry him yourself," Nealie had retorted.

"I would, but he's not partial to a woman old enough to be his mother. Besides, he means to marry *you* if he has to tear the

28

stars out of heaven."

Nealie had laughed, since she was good-natured and fond of the woman who was almost a mother to her.

Nealie wouldn't have left home if her real mother had been alive. They had protected each other. But her mother had died, and after a year, Nealie had fled the farm in Missouri. She could have gone up the river to Fort Madison, Iowa, or even Galena, Illinois, but her pa likely would have found her and fetched her home — dragged her back was more like it, because she wouldn't have gone willingly. So instead of running off to one of the neighboring towns, Nealie had saved up the coins she'd earned scrubbing for neighbors and working as a hired hand during harvest, supplemented them by stealing the money her father had put away for next year's seed, and one day when she'd been sent into Hannibal for supplies, she'd purchased a train ticket to the place everyone was talking about — Denver. And then because she was afraid her father would follow her even there, she'd bought a ticket to go forty miles farther to Georgetown. She'd never heard of the place, but she'd always been partial to the name George. She'd thought it was a sign.

When she reached Georgetown, Nealie

was bewildered. The depot was crowded with bearded men in muddy boots, talking and gesturing, noisy as schoolboys. Here and there stood frightened women, their hair covered by dirty squares of cotton, clutches of crying children clinging to their skirts. Those women babbled in languages Nealie didn't understand. She saw men in tailored suits and starched shirts, soft felt hats on their heads, and she turned her face from them, because she had seen such in the gambling halls in Hannibal. And she knew to stay away from the women who were dressed in flashy clothes cut low in the front, their hair arranged in fanciful swirls. One of them looked over the girl and smiled through lips that were tinted an unnatural red, but Nealie didn't smile back. She knew well enough about prostitutes, because her father had prophesied that if he didn't beat the devil out of her, Nealie would become one of their sisterhood someday.

And then there was Lidie Travers. Nealie hadn't noticed her, although the woman had seen Nealie as she climbed aboard the train in Denver, probably taken by the young woman's odd looks. The woman had watched the girl, who looked like someone's daughter or perhaps a bride. She saw Nealie step off the train in Georgetown and look

30

around, lost, because until that moment, Nealie had not considered what she would do once she reached her destination. Her plan had been just to get away. The girl wondered if she could afford a room for the night, and she removed from her pocket the little string bag that served as a purse and began to count her money.

Just then, a man who'd been looking over the crowd spotted Nealie and moved toward her, all but hidden from her behind a fat woman who was shoving her way through the throng. As the man reached Nealie, his long fingers grabbed her purse, and he slid away through the disembarking passengers. Nealie was too startled to cry out, and the crook was nearly gone when a strong hand grasped his arm and wrenched it behind his back. "Thief!" Mrs. Travers called in a loud voice. "He stole this woman's purse." She held him, because Mrs. Travers was a strong woman; lifting iron pans and carrying trays of food had toughened her arms as much as if she'd worked with a hammer and drill. Within seconds, the purse snatcher was surrounded by a crowd of men, because even in that rough town, a robber was despised, especially one who preyed on women.

Two of the men hustled the thief off to jail, and Mrs. Travers returned the purse to

Nealie. "It's best not to be so public with your money," she warned. "A place like this attracts the worst men there is." Then when the girl looked alarmed, Mrs. Travers added, "The best men, too, but sometimes you can't always tell the difference."

Nealie thanked her. "Georgetown sounded so nice, the name and all."

"You're here because you like the name?"

"I was always partial to 'George.' "

Mrs. Travers laughed. "Some are here whose reasons for it aren't any better. You don't have kin in Georgetown? Friends?"

Nealie shrugged, watching the woman, who was not pretty. She wasn't even handsome and never had been. But she had a strong face.

"Are you running away?"

"I'm seventeen. I can do as I please." Nealie wasn't seventeen, but she would be in six months.

"Oh, don't you worry. I'm not for sending you back if you don't want to go. I'm just asking. Do you have a place to stay?" Before Nealie could answer, Mrs. Travers said, "I didn't think so. Well, I've got a room off the kitchen. You could sleep there a night or two till you get your bearings."

"I'll pay," Nealie said. "I've got a little money left."

"Save it. But if you're of a mind to, you might help me cook supper."

"For your family?"

"I run a boardinghouse." She looked Nealie up and down. "I don't suppose you came here to cook for a bunch of miners, but if it suits, I could give you room and board and something besides. You could help me until you figure out why it is you're here." It was doubtful that until that moment, Mrs. Travers had ever considered hiring a girl, but Nealie appeared strong and good-natured, and Mrs. Travers was a capable judge of character. She was practical, as well, and undoubtedly, she knew that a young girl waiting on the table would attract business. It was possible that Mrs. Travers also believed the girl might be good company for her. The woman was a widow with no children, and Georgetown was a lonely place, with few females and those who were there too overworked to sit down for a chat.

Lydia Travers had come to Georgetown five years before, after her husband died, the brute. She'd run a boardinghouse in Kansas City, not just an eatery like the Georgetown boardinghouses, but a place that provided beds as well as meals. She'd run it with Lute Travers, worked her fingers

33

to the bone, while he drank up the profits and fisted her, to boot. She was not yet forty, but she looked ten, fifteen years older, thanks to the poundings Lute gave her. Then he died, passed out in the street and drowned with his face in the mud, and Mrs. Travers sold the boardinghouse and moved to Georgetown, vowing she'd never take another husband.

Nealie thought over the proposition for so long that Mrs. Travers said, "Well, come and stay anyway. You don't want to get mixed up with the likes of her, a sorry girl, if you take my meaning." Mrs. Travers nodded her head at the woman in the fancy dress who'd smiled at Nealie.

"I know about such," Nealie said. She added quickly so that Mrs. Travers wouldn't think she was acquainted with them, "Their kind was at home. And I'd be obliged to accept your offer, missus."

"Travers, Mrs. Lidie Travers," the woman introduced herself. By then, the crowd had thinned out. Mrs. Travers picked up her bags and looked around for Nealie's luggage.

"Oh, I don't have anything but my extra dress, and I'm wearing it under this one," the girl explained. "If Pa had seen me leaving with a box, he'd have tied me up in the barn and switched me good."

"How did you think you'd manage without so much as an extra handkerchief?" Mrs. Travers asked.

Nealie laughed at the idea. "I never had even one handkerchief, so I guess I can get along just fine without an extra. I didn't think about packing, not that it would have made a difference. I never had much. I had to get away is all, just had to."

The girl was so fierce that it was obvious she carried some secret. Perhaps she'd been beaten, or even worse. But Mrs. Travers only nodded and didn't ask questions, because she had never been one to pry into what wasn't her business. Perhaps she thought that in time, the girl would tell her where she'd come from and why, but until then, Nealie's past was hers to keep.

Without a word, Nealie took one of Mrs. Travers's bags from her, and the two walked out of the station into sunlight bright enough to hurt Nealie's eyes. The sun warmed her back, and the air was so thin and dry that Nealie felt as light as a blade of grass. Sounds of hammering swept down from the mountains, and the distant boom of a dynamite charge made the girl jump. A fog of smoke from the smelters hung over the town, but that did not bother Nealie, because it brought only a little haze. She liked the bustle, the sense of importance.

And now, just two months after her arrival, Nealie felt more at home in Georgetown than she ever had on her parents' farm.

CHAPTER 2

"What did you think of him?" Mrs. Travers asked after the boarders were gone and the two women were in the kitchen, cleaning up the supper mess.

Nealie didn't answer. She lifted the cast-iron kettle off the cookstove and filled the dishpan with hot water, tested it with her elbow, set the kettle back on the stove. She picked up one of the chunks of soap that the two of them had made from lye and bacon grease just the week before and made a lather. Then she filled the pan with heavy white cups and saucers and began scrubbing them with a dishrag.

"Well?" Mrs. Travers asked. She was used to the girl ignoring questions she didn't want to answer.

"Who?" Nealie asked.

"The new boarder. Mr. Spaulding."

"Oh, him. I barely noticed." In fact, Nealie had almost dropped the pot of stew she was carrying into the dining room when she saw Will Spaulding. Since she'd spotted him in the Kaiser Mercantile a few days earlier, she'd looked for him in town and had finally given up, thinking he was only passing through. Her heart had beat so fast at the sight of him sitting at the supper table that she'd thought the others could hear it.

"Like Hades!" Mrs. Travers said. "I saw you looking at him out of the side of your eyes like you do when you think nobody can tell. He's a looker, pretty as a new-laid egg. I'll grant you that."

"He is," Nealie admitted.

"And he seems plenty taken with you." Mrs. Travers, sitting on a kitchen chair, finished scraping off the plates into the scrap bucket, and stood up, her hands on her waist, stretching her back to get out the kinks.

"He didn't pay the slightest attention to me," Nealie said.

"Oh, he didn't, did he? And I wasn't the only one who saw it. I don't suppose you noticed Charlie Dumas stomping off the minute he finished his pie? I believe Charlie's jealous."

"He has no right to be," Nealie replied, slamming a cup down so hard on the drainboard that it chipped. Nealie looked at Mrs.

Travers, who shrugged. Most of the dishes were chipped or cracked. "I'm not his girl any more than you are, and I'm plain sick of the way he's around all the time, acting like he's entitled. He makes me tired."

"Now, don't you go chasing him away, Nealie. He pays his board on time and never a complaint about the food. He's a sticker, too, steady as any man I ever met." Picking up a dish towel, Mrs. Travers began drying the cups. "Here's a warning to you: Don't get to thinking too much about Mr. Spaulding. He's awful fine-haired for us. I'm surprised he boards here instead of the Grubstake with the rest of the highborn. You don't suppose he came here because he saw you someplace in town and followed you, do you?" When Nealie didn't answer, Mrs. Travers added, "No, I didn't think so."

"Nobody follows me except Mr. Dumas. He's generally always around, it seems." Nealie went to the back door and threw the dirty dishwater onto the flower bed, then put the pan back into the dry sink and filled it again with hot water from the kettle. She dropped handfuls of silverware into the pan, scrubbed the forks and knives and spoons with a brush, and laid them on the drainboard.

The two worked silently until the dishes

and utensils, the heavy pots and cast-iron pans, were dried and put away. Then Nealie took the bucket of scraps outside and threw them into the pig trough. The pig was penned in the far side of the yard, and Mrs. Travers had laid narrow boards across the mud as a sidewalk so the two women wouldn't get their boots dirty. Nealie watched the pig waddle to the trough and take huge bites of the garbage, reminding her of the way some of the men in the boardinghouse ate — Charlie Dumas, for one. As she balanced herself on the board, she caught sight of Will Spaulding leaning against the fence and stared at him in astonishment. She felt the blood rise to her face. Blushing easily was a burden she carried.

"Hello there, Miss Bent. It is Miss Bent, isn't it?" He removed his hat. "Mrs. Travers introduced you only by your first name, so I'm not sure."

"It is." Nealie was pleased that he knew her name and that he called her Miss Bent instead of Miss Nealie. It sounded refined.

"You hardly looked at me at dinner, and I was afraid you were angry that I've added to your burden. If that's the case, I hope to make it up to you, for I've never liked to cause unpleasantness. So I waited here, thinking you might come out. I'm new in town and don't have many friends yet. I'd like to consider you one."

It was the prettiest speech that Nealie had ever heard, and she was so taken with it that she couldn't think how to reply. So she stood mute, teetering on the board, the slop bucket gripped in her hand.

As if muteness were the proper answer, Will continued. "I'm told there is a drilling contest being held on Sunday afternoon, and I wonder if you would give me the pleasure of escorting you to it."

Nealie only stared.

"I'm being awfully forward, but Georgetown doesn't seem like a place where conventions matter much. In the East, you'd meet a girl at church and get to know her parents and then after a month or two, you'd ask to walk her home. That's such a bore. Georgetown isn't half so stiff. It's one of the things I like about the place — the lack of conventions." He stood up straight and put his hands on the top rail of the fence, and when Nealie didn't respond, he said, "I apologize if I've given offense. Perhaps you're spoken for."

"No. There's nobody I care about," Nealie replied. If she had been worldly, Nealie might have flirted a little, dropped a hint

41

that she had many suitors, turned down Will's first invitation while suggesting he might ask her out another time, made the man anxious. But she had none of those wiles. So tightening her grip on the bail handle of the bucket, she said, "You bet I'll go. I mean, I'd be pleased to accept, Mr. Spaulding." She wished her reply could have matched his fine words.

"It will be *my* pleasure," he said. "I'll say good evening then and see you at breakfast in the morning."

Nealie watched him place his hat on his head, turn gracefully, and disappear into the night.

"Oh, good evening yourself," she called, not sure he heard her. She stared into the darkness for a long time. When she turned to go back into the house, she found Mrs. Travers at the door, watching.

"Mr. Spaulding talks like a gentleman," Mrs. Travers said in what was not entirely a compliment.

"He asked me to go to the drilling contest come Sunday."

"So I heard." Mrs. Travers stepped back to let Nealie enter the kitchen. "What about Charlie Dumas?"

"What about him?" Nealie's tone was defensive.

"Wasn't he planning to take you?"

"I'm not obliged to him. Besides, he never asked."

"He probably thought he didn't have to. He'll be mighty hurt."

"Well, I don't see why. I've never encouraged him." Nealie poured hot water into the bucket and scoured it out. "He presumes."

Mrs. Travers studied the girl for a moment. "I wonder if Mr. Spaulding is all vine and no potatoes," she said, so softly that Nealie asked her to repeat the words. But the woman held her tongue, maybe because it wasn't her place to tell Nealie what to do. If the girl wanted a bit of fun, she wouldn't stand in her way. It was clear that Nealie hadn't had much of it in her life.

At supper later in the week, the men talked about the drilling contest and who was likely to win. There were three events that Sunday: single, double, and triple jacking. A single jacker gripped a four-pound hammer in one hand. In the other, he held a drill — a steel rod with a pointed tip — against a slab of granite. The jacker turned the drill each time he hit it, some fifty times a minute, until he'd drilled a hole deep enough for a charge of dynamite. Two men made up a double-jack team, one holding and turning the drill in the granite, while the other hit it with an eight-pound hammer. With triple jacking, two men took turns hitting the drill, which was held by a third man. The winner was the man or the team that drilled farthest into the rock in a given amount of time. A good jacker was much admired, because the mines needed efficient drillers to make the holes for the dynamite charges.

"You going to enter?" one of the men asked Charlie Dumas.

"Naw, it's not much of a contest, not like the Fourth of July," Charlie replied, looking at Nealie, who was handing around a platter of ham meat.

"You afraid you'll lose," the man taunted.

"I wouldn't lose," Charlie replied. "I'd just rather watch, that is, if somebody'll watch with me." He tried to catch Nealie's eye, but she refused to look at him.

"Charlie's getting soft," another man said. "Maybe he's lost his touch."

"I'm as good as I always was. I'd just rather stand by Miss Nealie while some other miner gets up a sweat." Charlie grinned at Nealie and said, "I'm going to put a bet on Jonce Kelly, and if he wins, I'll treat you to dinner at the Hotel de Paris,

Miss Nealie." He pronounced the hostelry's name *Pair-is,* instead of *Pair-ee.* "How'd you like that, Miss Nealie? I bet you never been there."

Nealie blushed and fled into the kitchen with the empty platter. She returned with a bowl of mashed potatoes in one hand and a pitcher of gravy in the other.

"You're going with me, aren't you, Miss Nealie?" Charlie looked at her, a little uncertain.

The girl set down the gravy so hard that it slopped onto the table. "No. I don't reckon I am, Mr. Dumas," she told him.

"Aw, you'll like the drilling contests. Won't you go with me?" Charlie said, as the other diners stopped eating to watch the two.

"I got plans," Nealie said. "I got other plans."

Charlie stared at her. "You don't want to go with me?" he asked, his mouth half filled with food. The other diners stared at him, and he shifted in his chair.

"You should have asked me before. Like I said, I got plans."

The dining room, which had once been the tiny house's parlor, was small, barely big enough for a table and nine chairs, and the air was always close, as if the miners around the table used it up. But it seemed even stuffier than usual, what with the window closed against the cold. Nealie wanted to flee to the kitchen to escape the curiosity of the boarders. One or two of them had hoped to court Nealie themselves, but they'd seen how it was with Charlie, and they'd kept silent. Now they listened with interest, looking from Charlie to Nealie, hoping she had quit the big man.

"Miss Bent is going with me," Will said quietly.

Charlie stared at him, his mouth open.

"It is my understanding she's not spoken for, and I invited her. She accepted."

"You got no right," Charlie said.

"Yes he does. You don't own me, Charlie Dumas. You never asked. You presume. I guess I'll step out with anybody I please."

"We got an understanding," Charlie persisted.

"Not with me you don't. I never agreed to anything with you."

Charlie's face turned red and he looked at his hands. Nealie hadn't wanted to embarrass him that way, but he shouldn't have asked her out in front of the other boarders. He should have known better.

Mrs. Travers came out from the kitchen then, her face flushed from leaning over the cookstove, her hands wrapped in her apron.

"Nealie, would you help me?" she asked. Nealie bolted from the dining room, and Mrs. Travers followed, telling the girl, "You dish up the apple crisp. I'll finish serving."

Nealie went to the bucket of water and splashed the cool liquid onto her face, then turned to the dessert and scooped it into bowls. She stayed in the kitchen until the boarders finished their suppers, talking little to each other, because they were all a bit embarrassed at what had happened. They left as soon as they had eaten their desserts, all except for Will. Nealie found him waiting for her when she went back into the dining room with a shuckbroom to sweep the carpet. She was startled, and a thought came over her that Will was going to tell her he'd made a mistake in asking her out. She couldn't blame him, of course, not after the scene Charlie had made. Will had been embarrassed, and he might think it her fault. Perhaps he had reconsidered asking her out and he was glad to have an excuse not to escort her. Maybe he'd decided she wasn't good enough to be seen with him.

"If you would like to be released from our commitment, I understand, although I would be greatly disappointed," he said. "I didn't mean to bring you complications, Miss Bent. It seems that Charlie Dumas has

47

a prior claim."

Nealie looked at him a moment before she said, "Mr. Dumas doesn't have any claim on me. Pay you no attention to him, Mr. Spaulding. He means no more to me than a horsefly. I said I was walking out with you on Sunday, and I intend to do it." She added, "If you still want me to."

"I do. Of course I do." Will smiled at her.

"That's splendid then. Since I met you, I've begun to like Georgetown more and more." As he picked up his hat, he added, "If you will pardon me for saying so, I believe you deserve better than a man who takes you for granted."

Nealie mulled over the remark after Will left and liked it.

The girl was close with her money, because she had known nothing but poverty and had a great fear of being caught up in it again now that she was on her own. Nonetheless, the next day, Nealie took a five-dollar gold piece from a tobacco sack she kept hidden in the toe of one of her Sunday shoes, which she'd purchased with her first wages, and tucked it into the basket when she went to market. After she had picked out the comestibles for supper, she asked Mr. Kaiser to take down a bolt of bright green cloth sprigged with white flowers that had caught her eye.

He unrolled the bolt and let the fabric spill across the counter. Nealie grabbed the loose material and held it against her face, then picked up a hand mirror to see whether the color suited. It was difficult to tell with the small looking glass.

"My, that's pretty with your coloring. I'd look just like a green tomato in it," a woman said, fingering the cloth. She was the wife of a miner who lived near the boardinghouse, and she and Nealie had exchanged pleasantries on the street.

"You think it suits?" Nealie asked. She wished she'd brought Mrs. Travers along for her opinion since her employer was not one to flatter, but Nealie hadn't wanted Mrs. Travers to see how excited she was about attending the drilling contest with Will Spaulding.

"I do, and if you don't like it, bring it to me, and I'll make a quilt of it. A quilt that color would be like sleeping under spring."

"You don't think it's too . . . ah . . . brassy?" Nealie liked the brightness, because she had never had a dress made from new cloth. Her clothes, even when they were new to her, had always been faded and worn.

"It's bold, but brassy? No," replied the

woman, who was herself dressed in a blue bright enough to make nature blush.

Nealie wasn't yet reassured. She looked up at the bolts of yellow and red. She'd never had choices like this before. Nor had she ever looked at herself in a large mirror to see which colors were right on her. She did like the green better than the other material, however, and so she bought the fabric and thread and packets of pins and needles and took them all back to the boardinghouse.

Mrs. Travers spotted the fabric before Nealie had emptied the basket. "Somebody's going to wear a new dress on Sunday, I'd say."

"Do you like it?" Nealie asked.

"You'll be as bright as a willow tree," Mrs. Travers said. She might have told the girl she'd look better in something more muted, but the fabric was already bought. She added, "Not many women can wear the color. I daresay you can."

Nealie breathed a sigh of relief. "Now, all I've got to do is sew it."

"If I help you with the stitching, we should have it done in no time."

"You'd do that? Even though you think I ought to step out with Mr. Dumas instead of Mr. Spaulding?"

"That's your business." Mrs. Travers pinched the fabric between her fingers. "This will take some work."

"If we had a sewing machine, we could finish it before supper. I saw a sewing machine once. You just put the fabric under a needle, and it sews a seam all by itself."

"And drips oil on it and chews up the material, too. I believe we'll do just as well by hand."

After they finished preparations for supper, the two women sat down at the dining room table, and using Nealie's second dress as a pattern, they cut out the green. Mrs. Travers pinned the pieces together, then Nealie tried on the dress. Mrs. Travers checked the fit, moving pins in and out, until she was satisfied. By the time the two quit to begin cooking, the dress was ready for stitching.

They finished their sewing on Saturday, Mrs. Travers doing most of the work, because Nealie was too restless to sit with a needle. She tried on the dress a final time, and then she looked at Mrs. Travers in dismay. "Buttons. I forgot to get buttons. I hope they have them at the store."

"I've got some you can use." Mrs. Travers went to a trunk and pulled out a box. She removed a set of black buttons, tied together

51

with a string, and another string of dull brass buttons. "You take your pick." The black would tone down the green a little.

"Brass. I never had brass buttons, although I found one once, a soldier button. I'll rub them with salt to make them shine." She didn't see Mrs. Travers frown as if she shouldn't have given the girl the choice.

Mrs. Travers did not serve meals on Sundays, so Nealie had hours to ready herself for her engagement with Will. She heated water on the cookstove and washed. Then she scrubbed her long hair, letting it dry by sitting with her back to the hot stove. She brushed the hair to get out the tangles, braided it, and wound the braid around the top of her head in a crown. She looked at herself in the small mirror over the dry sink, and dissatisfied, she took apart the braid and fashioned a bun at the nape of her neck. But she wasn't happy with the way that looked, either, so she tried wearing her hair down, then finally, at Mrs. Travers's suggestion, she pulled it back and tied it with a black ribbon. "I wish my hair was smooth," she complained to Mrs. Travers, not realizing that the curls that escaped around her face softened her features and gave her a childlike innocence that was more appealing than any sophisticated hair style.

Nealie put on the new dress, then took it off for fear of spoiling it and sat in the kitchen in one of Mrs. Travers's old wrappers, talking to the older woman. Every few minutes she jumped up and checked the clock in the parlor. Finally, a half hour before Will Spaulding was to call for her, she put on the green dress and went into the parlor, standing instead of sitting so as not to wrinkle the skirt.

Mrs. Travers came in then with a piece of lace wrapped in tissue. "Here's you a collar. I wore it to my wedding, and as I intend never to have another one, I've got no use for it. It will look pretty on the green and frame your face."

Nealie looked at the older woman with astonishment, for no one had ever given her such a wonderful present before. In fact, she'd never received a real present at all, only the ore specimens that Charlie Dumas had found and the dynamite box he gave her that she used as a trunk. She had lined it with a bit of calico to protect her possessions from the rough wood. "I couldn't," she stammered. "It's too fine for me."

"Nonsense. The collar's not doing anybody any good lying in a trunk where it'll turn yellow." Mrs. Travers reached up and placed the collar around Nealie's neck, then fastened it with a breastpin. "I'm only loaning you the pin," she said.

Nealie went into the kitchen and viewed herself in the mirror. "Why, I look as fine . . . as fine as frog's hair." She went back into the parlor, posing a little with her hand on the back of a chair, rehearsing what she'd say to Will when he arrived.

When she heard the knock on the door, she hesitated, however, for she knew she shouldn't appear anxious. She waited until there was a second knock, and Mrs. Travers called from the kitchen, "Are you froze into a statue, or can you see to the door?"

Her chin held high, just like the highborn ladies she'd seen in Hannibal, Nealie opened the door, but the smile on her face quickly became a frown. "Mr. Dumas, what are you doing here? I told you I wasn't going with you."

"I am. He came for me," Mrs. Travers said, nudging Nealie aside and motioning for Charlie to enter. "I wanted to see the contest myself, and Mr. Dumas offered to take me. I'll just get my wrap."

She left the room, and Nealie and Charlie stared at each other. At last, Nealie said, "That's real nice of you to go with her." She meant it, too, and felt not one bit of jealousy.

Charlie struggled for a reply but didn't make one, because at that moment, Will stepped onto the porch. When he saw Charlie, he stopped, confused.

"Mr. Spaulding, come right in," Nealie said quickly. "Mr. Dumas is taking Mrs. Travers to the contest."

"I see," Will replied, holding out his hand to Charlie, who shook it reluctantly.

"Come along, Charlie. We don't want to be late," Mrs. Travers said, returning to the room, where the two men stood awkwardly. "Nealie, there's a shawl on a hook in my room for you."

Nealie didn't want to wear a shawl, because the day was fine, but she did not care to leave with Charlie and Mrs. Travers, either, so she went into the bedroom, waiting until she heard the couple go down the walk. Then she returned to Will and set the wrap on a chair. "I guess I won't need this, after all. Besides, it will spoil my dress." She ran her hands across the skirt. "I just made it. Do you like it?"

Will stood back and looked at her critically, taking in the bright green, the brass buttons. "I'll never lose sight of you. That's for sure. Neither will anyone else."

Nealie smiled at the compliment, for

surely it was a compliment. Who could help but admire such a pretty dress?

Will held out his elbow to Nealie as they walked to the street, and when Nealie took it, Will put his hand over hers. Although he worked in the mine, his hand was smooth — and clean, Nealie noticed. With a thrill of excitement, Nealie realized she felt like a lady instead of a hired girl.

Neither of them had ever seen a drilling contest, although Will knew all about mining and explained the drilling to her. "It takes skill and strength, and when you're working with a partner, you surely do have to trust him."

"What if he misses with the hammer and smashes his hand?" Nealie asked, as she watched the first single jacker pound the drill into the rock.

"He hardly ever does."

"I guess he'd have to find another job of work if he did. Maybe be an engineer like you."

Will chuckled. "I'm hoping it takes more than bad hands to be an engineer. Some miners think engineers have smashed brains."

"No! You've got more brains than all the other boarders put together," Nealie said, then looked away when she realized Will had been joking.

"There's plenty about mining I don't know. I might understand the theories of ore geneses, and I know how to raise capital, but I'm not much good with the practical workings underground yet. In a cave-in, the miners would rather be with your friend Charlie Dumas than they would with me. So would I." He chuckled.

"Not me," Nealie said, then turned away at having made such a forward statement. But Will tightened his hand on hers, and she decided she might have said the right thing.

They watched the drillers, Nealie so caught up in the rhythm of the hammering that she paid no attention to Charlie Dumas, who stood in the crowd across from her, staring. She picked out the men she wanted to win, and her choices had nothing to do with their drilling ability. They included a miner who had once said good morning and taken off his hat when she passed and a jacker she knew had come from Fort Madison. When Will said he wanted to place a bet and asked her to choose a team, Nealie picked the team that included the husband of the woman who'd helped her choose the green fabric. When they won, Nealie jumped up and down, clapping her hands in excitement, and Will said they'd celebrate with dinner at the Hotel de Paris.

The streets were muddy still, although they were not as bad as they had been when Nealie had first glimpsed Will in the Kaiser store, and they were easier to cross because the miners had placed boards across the muck. "It's a good thing for that lumber. I'd hate to have to carry you," Will said. "We'd both be in the soup." Nealie laughed at that, although she would have liked to be ferried across the street in Will's arms as she had been in Charlie's. They went to the other side of the street, then walked along the wooden sidewalk, Will stopping to greet people, because it was known in town who he was now, and many were anxious to make his acquaintance, some of them women. Nealie knew one or two people herself, and nodded at them, hoping they noticed she was with Will, and they did. There was wonderment in Georgetown about Will Spaulding escorting a hired girl.

When she wasn't looking at the crowd, Nealie stared into the shop windows. She admired a plum-colored bonnet, thinking how nice it would go with her new dress. And she lingered as she looked over a cameo that was pinned to a black ribbon. It was just what she needed to go around her neck. And there were shawls as fine as cobwebs. But she was too happy to pay much attention to adornments and quickly forgot about them.

"I must say those men are artists with the drill and hammer," Will said, as Nealie paused to stare at a pair of red boots in a window. She dismissed them, because even she knew they were meant for a certain kind of woman. "I've never seen such work."

"I never heard of a drilling contest before I came here," Nealie told him.

"I never attended one, although I've seen plenty of drilling underground."

"Can you do it?"

"I doubt it." He cocked his head. "Could you?"

Nealie thought that over, not realizing Will had made another joke. "It can't be much harder than pounding in a spike. I might could do it with a four-pound hammer but not an eight-pounder. And not fifty times in a minute. That's certain." As her parents' only child, Nealie had helped her father construct some of the outbuildings on the farm. And she was used to lifting cast-iron pots and kettles in Mrs. Travers's kitchen and chopping kindling. So she was strong.

"You are full of surprises, Miss Bent. I

wouldn't think a woman could do such a thing."

"I can't think of a woman who couldn't." Nealie realized then that her answer had been unladylike, but she did not know how to take it back. "I'd never work underground," she said, knowing that wasn't the right thing to say, either.

"Well, I certainly hope not. They say women underground are unlucky, but I never believed in all those superstitions."

"You don't believe in tommyknockers?"

Will frowned. "I don't know tommyknockers."

"They're spirits that live in a mine and cause trouble, although you don't ever see them. The miners say they make a big racket to warn you when there's to be a cave-in."

"Then I hope I never meet one," he said.

"I believe in them. Mr. Dumas said he saw a miner rush out of a drift and quit the Bobcat, because a tommyknocker warned him with his little hammer. And not ten minutes later, the roof fell in. And another time, a miner's candle went out three times, and the man quit the mine and went home and found his wife entertaining another man, just like the candles told. So you see, they're true."

"Superstitions are the beliefs of ignorant

people," Will insisted. "That's not to say there isn't a little truth to them, but it's mostly common sense."

Nealie didn't agree. She believed in all kinds of signs. She knew for certain that if it rained into an open grave, there'd be another death in three days, and that a man who planted an evergreen would die before the tree cast a shadow his size. After all, her pa had refused to have evergreens on the farm, and he'd lived to be a cussed old man. But she held her tongue for fear Will would find *her* ignorant.

The pair turned in then at the Hotel de Paris, a fine two-story building whose exterior was scored to look like cut stone. Iron cresting decorated the exterior, and lace curtains hung in the windows. Nealie had seen traveling people come and go at the hotel, but she had never gone inside herself. "Have you been here?" she asked Will.

"I stayed in one of the rooms before my little cottage was ready," he replied, leading her into the dining room.

Nealie looked around in wonder. The tables, which stood on a floor that was striped with alternating boards of walnut and pine, were set with crystal and sterling silver. A polished walnut sideboard dominated one wall, and looking in a large mirror set in a gilt frame, she caught sight of herself standing beside Will. She'd never seen her reflection in such a big mirror, and she stared, wishing she had a tintype of the two of them as they looked at that moment, framed in just such a solid gold frame. The girl did not know the difference between gilt and gold.

A gentleman speaking in an accent that Will told her was French greeted him by name and led them to a table, handing them menus. Nealie didn't know what a menu was; she'd never eaten any place that had a choice of dishes. In fact, she'd never eaten in a restaurant at all, let alone one as fancy as the Hotel de Paris. Seeing her confusion, Will said, "Why don't I order for both of us."

"I can read," Nealie said, "if that's what you're thinking. I can read."

"Of course you can, but can you read French?" Will looked contrite at the remark and added, "I've eaten here before and can recommend the best dishes."

"Oh," Nealie said. "Well, I don't care what it is. I'm hungry enough to eat buzzard bait."

"I don't believe the Hotel de Paris serves buzzard bait, but there is fish and venison and ptarmigan."

"Not ptarmigan. I couldn't eat a ptarmigan. They're such pretty birds, all white in the winter. I saw one when I first arrived. And they take care of their chicks real good," she said.

"No ptarmigan," Will told the waiter. "Venison, then." He ordered other foods, and Nealie was glad he did, because she didn't recognize their names and would have been shy about asking Will to explain every offering.

In a few minutes, the waiter brought them special plates with oysters on them. "I'm not acquainted with those. What are they?" Nealie whispered, after the man left.

"Raw oysters. You eat them like this." Will picked up a tiny fork and speared an oyster and ate it.

Nealie imitated him, balancing an oyster on her fork and putting it into her mouth. She swallowed the oyster but didn't like its taste and made a face. Then suddenly the oyster popped back up, and she spit it out into her hand. "He's a slimy fellow," she said, staring at the round white object.

"Put it back onto the plate then. You don't have to eat them. Oysters are an acquired taste."

"But that man won't like it."

Will reached over and patted her hand. "He won't mind."

Nealie looked doubtful, but in a few minutes, the waiter removed the plate without so much as a glance at her. He returned with a bottle of wine, removed the cork, and poured a small amount into Will's glass. Will tasted it, nodded, and the waiter filled Nealie's glass. "It's a light wine, but you don't have to drink that, either, if you don't like it," Will said.

Nealie did like it, however. In fact, she wanted to gulp it down at once as she would a glass of water. But she had glimpsed the other ladies in the restaurant sipping their wine and imitated them.

When the food arrived, Nealie gripped her fork as if it were a hammer. Then she noticed how Will held his fork, gracefully. She looked around the room and saw that other people ate the way Will did. So she held the fork between her fingers and she picked at a vegetable she didn't recognize. She started to saw her meat into pieces, the way the miners did at the boardinghouse. But again, she watched Will, who cut off a single piece, then picked it up with his fork. Nealie thought about the way Charlie shoveled his food into his mouth and decided she would study Will to improve her manners.

"Where did you learn to read?" Will asked her. He picked up a salt shaker and offered it to her, but Nealie had salted her food when it arrived. She wondered now if she was supposed to taste it first.

"At school. I'm the only one in my family that can read. I guess my pa's in a pickle now without me. He said a girl that could read was as useless as a dog that could count. Well, I can cipher, too, better'n most. I bet my pa misses me for that, too."

"Do you miss them?"

Nealie shook her head. "Ma's dead. I ran off."

"Does he know where you are?"

"No, he does not." Nealie looked up at Will. "You won't tell him, will you?"

Will laughed. "Cross my heart. If you hadn't run away, I never would have met you." He leaned across the table and lowered his voice. "And I'm awfully glad I met you, Miss Bent." He leaned back, waiting for a response.

"You're the nicest person I'm acquainted with in Georgetown," Nealie said, "except for Mrs. Travers. If it hadn't been for her, maybe I would have ended up with those sorry girls on Brownell Street."

"Why, Miss Bent!"

Nealie blushed and said defensively, "Well, there isn't much choice for a girl like me."

"If you had gone to Brownell Street, then I might have met you there."

Nealie looked at Will in astonishment, because even she knew he had gone too far. "I'll thank you not to talk like that," she said. Then she spoiled the reproof by laughing.

"I suppose you've saved me from their clutches, for where else could I find a woman to talk to? And one who is so unpredictable. I've never met a girl like you."

"Oh, there's a plenty of ladies here."

"None so fetching as you are."

"Mr. Spaulding, I think you overspoke," Nealie replied, because his remark was obvious even to her — not that she didn't like it.

"Would you call me Will? I'd like that so much better." When Nealie nodded, he asked, "And may I call you Nealie? It's a prettier name than Bent. I suppose it's short for Cornelia, isn't it?"

"I guess you could. And Nealie isn't short for anything. It's just Nealie. I never liked it, or Bent, either."

"Why didn't you change it when you ran

away? It would make it harder for your father to find you."

Nealie had never thought of that. "What name would I pick?"

"Evangeline or Gertrude, maybe Mary or Pearl. I always favored Pearl."

"What about George? I'm partial to it. I could call myself George."

Will, who had taken a sip of his wine, sputtered. He wiped his mouth with his napkin and replied, "And would you have changed your last name from Bent to Straight?"

"Why, that's the funniest thing I ever heard!" She began to laugh, too, until she realized that people had turned to stare at them and looked down at her lap. "I guess I'm too loud. Well, I had to be to get heard over the hogs," she said.

"I don't care. I haven't had this much fun since I arrived here. You keep me from loneliness. I didn't want to come here, you know."

"Did your grandfather whip you to make you come?" Nealie asked, because of course, she knew old Mr. Spaulding controlled the Rose of Sharon.

He looked at her curiously. "Whip me? Hardly. My grandfather would never whip me, nor my father, either. My family is not that barbaric. They convinced me that firsthand knowledge of the Sharon would help my career. They're right, of course. It's just that I thought I wouldn't like it here. But I do." He smiled at Nealie.

Then Nealie asked him what name he would have chosen for himself. Will thought that over and replied, "General Ulysses S. Grant." They laughed again, not stopping until the waiter removed their plates and set down silver cups, and Will explained, "Raspberry ice."

"This time of year?" Nealie thought she had never tasted anything so fine. But when the waiter set down coffee in demitasse cups, she frowned. "You'd think they'd give you a decent cup of coffee. This isn't any more than a sip."

"You can have all you want, but you may not like it. This is strong."

Nealie sipped and decided the coffee was indeed strong — too strong. She could tell the waiter a thing or two about making coffee, but of course she didn't. She put the coffee aside and sipped the last of her wine. It made her feel fine, and she wished the day would last forever. In fact, it already had lasted far longer than she had expected, and when the two of them left the dining room, the sun had gone behind the mountain range. The mud in the streets was hard again, and the air was chilly. Will took off his coat and put it around Nealie, asking if she wanted to go home or walk a bit.

"Walk. I like to look at the houses," Nealie told him. So they climbed the mountainside, then circled around and walked back past the hotel, down Taos Street, stopping to see a house that was under construction. "My, I'd like to live in a house like that, with an upstairs and a tower and a yard that's all grass and flowers instead of a pigpen."

The site was deserted, and the two of them circled the house, whose back door was on Griffith Street. "It's a splendid house," Will observed. "A bride's house."

"Oh," Nealie breathed. "So it is. Fit for a bride. It's just about perfect." The girl tried to think of herself as a bride coming home to that house with its tall windows and big veranda and fanciful gingerbread trim, a house as white and fine as a bride's cake, but she couldn't. She couldn't imagine herself in something so nice. "If you lived in a house like that, everybody in town would take off their hat to you."

"Then it's just the house you should have. Who's to say you won't live here someday?"

And then Nealie saw herself standing at

69

the front door of the house on an early evening, watching a man come up the steps and kiss her on the cheek, then follow her inside where children waited. The man looked a great deal like Will Spaulding.

They walked back to the boardinghouse then. "I don't know how long I'll be in Georgetown, but I'm sure it will be through the summer, maybe longer," Will told her when they stopped on Mrs. Travers's porch. "I've got obligations, if you know what I mean. I can't do anything about that, but I think we could have a good time together. I hope you'll let me see you again."

"Oh, I will," Nealie said, and in the dark, she blushed, either from the wine or the pretty words.

Will took her hand and kissed her fingers. "Good night, Nealie."

"Good night, Mr. General Grant."

CHAPTER 3

Nealie didn't hear Charlie Dumas until the big man, hat in his hand, called to her from the street. She was sitting on the porch, dreaming about the day nearly two weeks before that she'd spent with Will Spaulding and not paying the least attention to the passersby. Nealie was startled, and Charlie looked crestfallen. "I didn't mean to scare you none, Miss Nealie."

Of course, if she'd had her rathers, Will would be standing there, but Nealie was feeling so happy that she was glad to see even Charlie. "Mr. Dumas, come and sit," she said.

The big man grinned and stomped onto the porch. He towered over her, until Nealie indicated the place beside her on the bench. "Today's a fine day," he said.

Nealie had to agree. In almost the blink of an eye, it had gone from winter to summer. There was no spring in the high country,

Mrs. Travers had explained to her, just mud. The runoff from melted snow still ran high, filling the creeks almost to the tops of their banks, and the streets had their patches of mud yet, but the sun was so bright that it quickly dried the mud into ruts. The yards were greening, and people had begun white-washing their houses and sheds, replacing the paint that the wind and dirt had sanded off during the winter. Houses were going up, and every day, Nealie walked past the place that Will had called the bride's house, stopping to watch the carpenters nail up siding. And each day, she thought of Will walking up the stairs of the house to greet her. It was such a fine house, with a gable in front and a tower with a peaked roof, a porch around two sides, and a bay window that caught the sun all day long.

Smoky-gray bluebirds and the black-and-white birds that Mrs. Travers called camp robbers flitted about, along with red and green hummingbirds that hovered in the air, their wings spinning so quickly that Nealie could scarcely see them. She sat on the front porch, a bit of mending idle in her hands. Before Charlie had called to her, Nealie, eyes closed, had held up her face to the sun, despite Mrs. Travers's warning that the air was thin, and the girl's pale skin would burn before she knew it.

"Why aren't you up at the Bobcat?" Nealie asked. She turned to look Charlie in the face. "You didn't get laid off, did you, Mr. Dumas? Mrs. Travers said there were rumors the vein pinched out last week. She feared you might be out of work."

"Did you fear it?" Charlie asked.

"I fear anybody missing payday," she replied, carefully choosing her words. Of course she didn't want Charlie losing his job. She didn't wish it at all, wouldn't wish it for anybody, because being out of work was a tragedy. Besides, in Charlie's case, if he wasn't working, he'd be hanging around the boardinghouse. She didn't want that, either.

"Well, I've not been laid off. I just took a day to work my claim is all. I've found blossom rock, and I mean to follow it."

"That's fine," Nealie said, holding her tongue, because she did not want to say that every man at the boardinghouse claimed he'd found blossom rock, which was an outcrop of mineral-bearing rock. "I wish you good luck," she said, and surely she did. After all, she liked Charlie Dumas. She just didn't like him that much.

Charlie leaned forward on the bench, his knees apart, his cap between his heavy hands. He cleared his throat a couple of times, as if he was trying to say something but couldn't. Nealie waited, watching Charlie twirl his cap, until he burst out, "There's a play at the opera house on Saturday night. I'd like it awful well if you'd go. With me, that is. Would you?"

Nealie didn't answer right away. She loved the opera house more than anything in Georgetown, was enchanted with the way it took her into another world, and she wanted to go in the worst way. But she'd hoped that Will Spaulding would invite her. He hadn't mentioned going out a second time, however, and that troubled her. She'd turned it over in her mind and wondered if maybe he'd been embarrassed by her table manners. Since that night at the hotel, she'd studied the way he ate his supper at the boardinghouse and was trying to imitate it. She'd read every romantic story in Mrs. Travers's *Peterson's Magazine* to learn how to act, and she'd consulted a book on etiquette that Mrs. Travers kept on a shelf in the kitchen. She'd memorized what to eat with a fork and what with a spoon and how to hold utensils and cut food with a knife. But it was awfully confusing, and she wasn't sure she'd ever get it right.

Or maybe it wasn't her manners but the

fact that Will just plain hadn't liked her and was too mannerly to say so. After all, she was only a hired girl, and he was used to ladies like the ones she'd seen on the streets of Hannibal. There were enough of them in Georgetown to tempt him. Maybe he'd found somebody else and hadn't told her. So if she wanted to go to the opera house, Nealie realized, she'd better accept Charlie's invitation. "Why, I'd like that," she said at last.

Charlie beamed. "I already asked Mrs. Travers if you could have the night off so's I could take you to supper someplace," he said. "I hope you wear that green dress. I never saw anything so bright."

Nealie smiled prettily at him, for after all, she was not immune to compliments.

Of course, it wasn't more than a day later that Will Spaulding, too, asked to squire Nealie to the opera house on Saturday. "I should have told him yes, Mrs. Travers. I wish I had," Nealie said later. "I could have told Mr. Dumas I had a sick headache and couldn't go or that you forgot and needed me here."

"You'd do no such a thing. He'd find out and know right off you put him aside for Mr. Spaulding. You'd shame Charlie, and him being so nice to you."

Nealie was a little ashamed of herself then, although she couldn't help but wish she'd turned the big man down and risked staying at home.

"Besides, it's not such a bad thing to go with Mr. Dumas," Mrs. Travers continued. "You'll make Mr. Spaulding jealous."

Nealie had to think that over, because she'd had no experience with men — with gentlemen, that is. She'd had plenty with the other kind, and she didn't like them — her father and his friends. They were animals. They'd put their hands on her and tried to kiss her and more. Her own pa was the worst of the lot. She'd seen farm animals coupling and figured the same thing went on between her ma and pa. She heard her pa rutting in the bed, her mother crying out in pain, because the old man liked to hurt her. After Nealie came into young womanhood, her pa began to look at her with greedy eyes, staring at her breasts. Sometimes, he came into the barn and touched her there, his eyes hard with longing. Once, he'd put his hand under her skirt, on the inside of her leg and slid it upward. Nealie had run off, but Pa had found her and whipped her, cursing her for being a temptation. Her ma, that sweet, gentle woman worn down from overwork, protected her as much as she could from the beatings, the railings, explaining that Nealie's father had been a good man before hard times turned him sour. Nealie, knowing her mother was fragile, kept her pa's fumblings to herself, although she suspected that dear woman knew and subjected herself to the old man's brutality to keep him from Nealie.

Then her mother died, leaving Nealie alone with her pa, and the girl knew she had to get away. The day came when Pa brought home Hog Davis from two farms over. He raised pigs and leered at her, following her along the fence whenever she passed on the road. Hog had a jug of sillybug, and the men went into the barn and got drunk. Nealie had to milk the cow, but she stayed in the house until she figured the two had passed out. Instead, they were lying in wait for her, and her pa grabbed her as she went into the barn, gripped her in a hand of iron, and said, "The girl's been devilin' me, although I give her a flailin' every time or two. Makes me feel better."

"She's a scoundrel for temptation, all right." Hog ran his tongue over his wet lips. "Red-haired women's as devilish as they can be. I guess I wouldn't mind trying to take it out of her."

"You'd have to pay me something, a dollar maybe."

"I ain't had a dollar in my life. Hell, I don't have two bits. But I got a shoat I could let you have."

"Have at her then, if you can. You'll need sharp luck. She's a vixen." Nealie's father pushed her toward Hog, but Hog was clumsy and didn't get a good hold of Nealie, and she broke and ran for the house.

"Get back here, or you'll get a cowhidin'," her father called. But Nealie barred the door of the house and wouldn't let her father in until he was sober. That night, she made plans to leave, and it wasn't more than three days later that she'd taken the seed money and lit out.

With a pa like that, Nealie had learned to be careful, and instead of schooling herself to flirt and simper like most girls her age, she had taught herself to watch out for men for fear of being disgraced. She was only just now learning there were others — gentlemen like Will Spaulding and even Charlie Dumas.

So the girl had not considered that she could make a man jealous, and the idea confused her. If she liked Will Spaulding, why not let him know it? But Mrs. Travers had had more experience with men, and

Nealie decided the woman might be right. Maybe it was best Will knew there were others anxious to escort her places. Maybe next time, he wouldn't take his time asking her out.

So Nealie went to the performance with Charlie and was so delighted with it that she forgot who sat beside her. The girl could scarcely believe the play wasn't real. For a moment, she hated the villain as much as if he'd been her pa, and although she wasn't a church person, she prayed — prayed that the girl would end up with the handsome man. "Oh, it was wonderful, Mr. Dumas," she said when the gaslights were turned up, careful not to call her escort Charlie.

Charlie beamed. "If you're not too tired, Miss Nealie, we can take supper at the hotel."

"Truly?" Nealie asked. Imagine eating dinner twice at the Hotel de Paris, when Mrs. Travers had never been there even once. She followed Charlie out of the theater, casting about for Will. He was seated in the front row, a woman beside him, but Nealie wasn't sure whether Will had escorted her or she was with the man on the other side of her.

At the hotel, Charlie opened the door, going in ahead of her. Once they were seated, he looked askance at the menu, just as Nealie had the other time she'd eaten there. "You can read, can't you?" Nealie asked.

"Of course I can read. I just never ate anyplace that wrote it down."

Nealie looked at her own menu then, realizing that it was mostly in English with just a few French words. Nonetheless, she had no idea what the dishes were, and when the man came back to take their order, she said, "I want venison and raspberry ice. No oysters. Don't you bring me oysters, for I'm not much of a fool about them."

"Same," Charlie said, and when the waiter was gone, he asked, "I guess you ate here before."

"Well, of course, I have," Nealie replied, then a little ashamed of her pomposity, she giggled, "Once."

"With Will Spaulding?" Charlie asked.

Nealie didn't answer. Instead, she looked around the room, stopping to stare at a woman. "Why, that's the lady in the play. She isn't nearly so pretty up close, is she?" Nealie studied the actress and added, "She's just an ordinary woman and kind of old."

"That's why they call it playacting. It's not real."

"But up there on the stage, it's like magic. I believe I like the magic better. I wonder what it would be like to be a play actress."

"I don't think you ought to be one, Miss Nealie. They're not good women. Some of them are . . . well, you know."

Nealie studied him a minute. Of course she knew, and it surprised her, because Charlie rarely had a bad word to say about anyone. She wondered then if he was hidebound. But before she could consider that further, the waiter set down their plates. Nealie carefully picked up her knife, and pinning down the meat with her fork, she cut a single bite. As she put it into her mouth, she watched Charlie cut the venison into strips, then turn his plate so that he could cut the strips crosswise. He stirred the peas and carrots into the potatoes and gravy, then mixed in the meat, and leaning over his plate, he shoveled in a mouthful. Nealie looked around the room, but no one was watching. She cleared her throat, and Charlie looked up, narrowing his eyes. "Don't you like it?" he asked, looking at her plate, because while he had gobbled a fourth of his food in two bites, Nealie had eaten only a single piece of meat.

"I'm trying to eat slow," she said, but that was not the only reason she had eaten so little. She still had trouble holding her fork the way Will did.

"Well, I don't know why. It'll get cold." Charlie continued pushing food into his mouth, until his plate was almost empty. Then he glanced around the room and saw that the other diners were eating as slowly as Nealie. "These folks all eat as prissy as Will Spaulding," he said.

"I guess it wouldn't hurt a person to learn manners," Nealie replied.

"Don't you think I have manners, Miss Nealie?"

The girl blushed, because she herself had been sensible of table manners for only two weeks. Besides, she was not an unkind person. "I just learned about them myself," she said, adding quickly, so that Charlie would not bring up Will Spaulding again, "I read about them in a book that Mrs. Travers has."

"Maybe she'll give me the borrow of that book sometime."

"Maybe," Nealie said, doubting the man would ever read such a tome.

Charlie speared a piece of meat, then tried to rub off the mashed potato clinging to it, and brought it to his mouth. "How's that?" he asked.

He reminded her of a puppy who wanted a pat on the head, so Nealie smiled and nodded her approval, although she considered Charlie as unmannerable as ever.

The big man finished his meal, then pushed the plate aside. He removed the napkin from his shirtfront and rubbed his mouth, then ran it over his face and set it on the table, as he sat watching Nealie eat. When she was finished, he said, "There's something I'm wanting to ask you."

Nealie stiffened, because she didn't want Charlie claiming another evening before Will had a chance to ask. She wondered how she could turn him down without being rude.

When Nealie didn't encourage him, Charlie fidgeted. "You see . . ." He cleared his throat and moved around. "You see, Miss Nealie . . . that is . . . I've been thinking." He stopped and leaned over the table. "I never liked anybody as much as you. I work hard, and I keep myself clean, and I don't drink or chew. My claim looks good, and I've got a little money put aside. And I own my cabin." He ran his finger around his collar and blurted out, "Would you marry me?" Charlie looked askance then, and his face turned red, as if he'd uttered an obscenity. "I never asked that of anybody before."

"Mr. Dumas —" Nealie replied, her eyes wide. But at that moment, the waiter removed their plates, and took out a small brush to sweep the crumbs around Charlie's place into a silver dustpan. He left, and the two avoided looking at each other. Nealie's face was on fire, and she had a powerful need to dip her napkin into her water glass and rub off the heat. Instead, she stared at the tablecloth, noting a tiny hole that would have to be mended or else the cloth would begin to ravel. With her fingernail, she worried the hole, pulling a thread loose.

"Did you hear what I said, Miss Nealie?" Charlie asked.

Nealie's eyes felt as heavy as flatirons as she raised them to face Charlie. "Mr. Dumas, I . . ."

He leaned farther forward, his forearms on the table, watching her.

Nealie tried to think of something gracious to say and suddenly remembered words from a story in Mrs. Travers's *Peterson's Magazine.* "I am mindful of the honor," she said, not remembering the rest of the sentence, so she thought a moment and continued. "Well, I guess I'm not ready to get married. I haven't been in Georgetown so long, and I don't want to get tied down yet. There's things I want to do before I get married."

"What things?"

Nealie shrugged, wishing her mind worked

faster. "Just things. You know, things."

"You're not saying no, are you?" Charlie held his breath.

She was saying no, the girl thought, but she didn't want to hurt the man's feelings. "I guess I'm not saying yes," she told him.

Charlie let out his breath in a whoosh and grinned at her. "I'll just wait, then. I'm not so good at waiting, but I guess I'll just have to do that." He was so happy that Nealie was glad she hadn't told him outright she wouldn't have him.

The waiter set down their ice, and Charlie watched as Nealie picked up her spoon, not gripping it in her fist but holding it awkwardly in her fingers. Charlie tried to copy her but dropped the spoon.

The sound made Nealie jump, and she looked around the room to see if anyone was staring. But nobody seemed to notice. She ate her dessert with her eyes downcast, not looking to see how Charlie ate. When she was finished, she stood up, saying she needed fresh air, because the room seemed hot and stuffy to her. Charlie paid the bill and followed Nealie to the door. "We could walk around a little, if you want to," he said, as Nealie stood in the doorway, fanning her face.

"I need to cool down," she said.

So they took a roundabout way back to the boardinghouse, going up the hill and circling back down to the bride's house on Taos Street, Nealie's favorite stop.

"I guess that's going to be the prettiest house in Georgetown," she said. "The yard's big enough for an ice-cream social."

"I wonder who's going to live there."

"A bride," Nealie said. "It's a bride's house. Only a bride can live there. She'd plant lilacs all around it, and you could smell them every summer." Nealie turned away so that Charlie wouldn't suspect that she was thinking about Will Spaulding, instead of him, as the bridegroom. It almost made her blush to think she could be so bold as to dream she and Will would live there.

"Her husband'd have to be awful rich."

"And she'd have to be awful lucky."

"If you was to say yes to me, I'd show you my cabin. It's not so big as this, but it's tight, and it's got two rooms." He looked hopefully at Nealie, but she was lost in thought about the house for a bride and didn't reply.

It was not Charlie Dumas's cabin that Nealie visited the next day, however. Will Spaulding called that Sunday, Nealie's day

86

off, and asked her to walk out with him. He waited on the porch while Nealie went inside the house to change into her boots, because a rain had stirred up the mud.

Mrs. Travers followed Nealie into the girl's bedroom, remarking, "You see, going out with Charlie Dumas did make Mr. Spaulding jealous."

"I thought you didn't like him."

"Oh, I like him well enough, but he strikes me as a courting man, a fellow who'll go after all the girls. You wouldn't want to spoil things with Mr. Dumas. He's as good a catch as you'll ever find."

"Charlie asked me to marry him." Nealie had not expected to tell Mrs. Travers. The words just popped out. She stood, the boot half on, looking at the older woman.

Mrs. Travers sat down on Nealie's bed, a cot really, neatly made up with a faded quilt. "He did, did he? I'm not surprised. What did you tell him?"

"I didn't. I don't care to marry him, so I didn't say yes. But I didn't say no, either. I'm not for hurting a person's feelings." Nealie sat down next to Mrs. Travers, tugging at the boot, until it slipped over her foot. She tightened the laces.

"It's you I worry about getting hurt. Will Spaulding is as handsome as a foot racer, but don't waste your time thinking he's the marrying kind. You might lose out on Mr. Dumas."

"I guess I can take care of myself," Nealie said.

"Can you?"

Nealie didn't look at the older woman but, instead, reached for the second boot, annoyed, yanking it on. Then she laughed. "Except for almost getting my purse stole the day I got here. But I'm not taking my purse today."

When Nealie returned to the porch, Will held out his arm to her, and Nealie took it, glancing behind her to see if Mrs. Travers noticed. The woman did. She stood in the doorway and waved, because skeptical as she was, she obviously found the man likable and knew that Nealie cared to be with him. More than that, perhaps, she loved Nealie and wanted the girl to have a little pleasure before the cares of life in a mining town wore her down. The girl had only recently discovered happiness and did not know it would not last forever.

"Where would you have us go?" Will asked. "We'll walk anywhere you like."

"The depot. I like the depot," Nealie said. "It's so busy, and I always wonder where all those folks are going to or where they came from."

"Then that's where we'll go. Everybody there will envy me for being with such a pretty girl." Will put his hand over hers and squeezed.

Nealie was not used to such compliments and, instead of replying, she broke away, embarrassed, and took long steps down the board sidewalk. After a block or so, she turned and saw that Will lagged behind, so she slowed and matched her stride to his. A train whistle split the air just as they reached the station, and Nealie was delighted that they had arrived in time to watch the train stop. "Look at all those people," Nealie said, as the two of them stood outside the depot and watched the passengers climb down from the cars, some standing on the platform looking around. "Why's so many coming here?"

"I'll bet every one of them is here to seek his fortune. How many do you think will be lucky?"

"I was lucky. I met Mrs. Travers right here at this depot. A man tried to steal my money, and she caught him. I'd have been in a pickle if she hadn't. And then she offered me a job. Oh, I was lucky, all right."

Will turned to look at her. "I thought Mrs.

Travers was some sort of relative or a family friend."

"I never met her in my life before I came here. Don't you remember? I told you I ran off. I didn't know until I bought my ticket that I was going to Georgetown."

"I'd supposed you'd meant your folks had let you go adventuring. I've known plenty of fellows who did that, but never a girl. And to do it on your own! I'd say you have your share of pluck."

Nealie didn't know what "pluck" meant — nor "adventuring," for that matter — but she liked the sound of the word. "I do," she said.

They watched as the passengers scurried around the platform, a few hailing hacks or climbing aboard the omnibus, but most of them picking up their bags and boxes and walking down the main street. When only a few remained, Will took Nealie's arm and asked where she wanted to go next.

"Up in the trees," Nealie said. "I've never gone in the mountains, because there's always been snow on the ground. But now it's mostly gone. Let's go up high and see if we can get above the smelter smoke." Because Georgetown was in a valley, the smoke from the smelters hung over the town on days when the wind was still, giving the mountain town a brooding, industrial feeling. Will glanced at Nealie's boots and long skirt, and the girl added, "I'm a good walker."

So they followed a street to the edge of Georgetown and took a path that led them up the mountainside. The trail was littered with pine needles and covered with snow in spots, and they had to climb over rocks that had tumbled onto the path during the winter. But none of that deterred Nealie. "I never saw mountains before I came here. At home, we had hills, and there were bluffs by the Mississippi River. The Mississippi, it's as lazy as a fish worm. But here, the rivers aren't so big — they're not rivers but creeks, I'd call them — but they rush by you like a runaway wagon. I'd hate to get in their way. If you'd fall into Clear Creek, you'd get carried a hundred miles."

"Do you like it here, then?"

"Better than anyplace I've ever been." Nealie thought that over. "I guess I haven't been about much, but I bet Colorado beats anywhere you can name. The air doesn't hold you down, and up here on the mountain, above the smoke, you can see all the way to tomorrow."

"And back to yesterday, too," Will said, taking the girl's hand and helping her over a fallen log.

"I don't care so much about yesterday."

Now that they were almost to the top of the mountain, they encountered old snowdrifts that were crusted over and covered with the footprints of wild animals. "Mountain sheep," Will guessed, then pointed at a different set of footprints. "That might be a cougar."

Nealie glanced over her shoulder to ask what a cougar was, and as she did, she stepped on a rock that was slick with mud and tumbled onto the ground.

"Are you hurt?" Will asked, helping Nealie to sit on a rocky outcropping.

"No, not even a little, but my coat is done for," she said, swiping her hand down the garment, which was covered with mud.

"Let it dry, and it will brush off." Will sat down beside the girl, and the two looked out beyond the mountains. They had climbed farther than Nealie had thought and could see all the way down the valley, dotted with mines that were marked by yellow tailings spills, and smelter stacks sending curlicues of smoke that the wind scattered.

"I hope never to live in another place but this." Nealie raised her face to the sky, because the air was clear and warm. "We're close enough to touch the sun," she said.

"Maybe you'll live in that bride's house someday." Will plucked a wildflower that had pushed its way through the snow and put the stem through the buttonhole of Nealie's coat. "When the snow's gone for good, we'll hunt for mushrooms. They ought to grow around here."

"I never ate a mushroom, but I'd be glad for one right now. We ought to have brought our dinner with us."

"Climbing builds an appetite, all right." Will stood suddenly. "Come with me. I know where we can get a bite to eat." He helped Nealie off the rocks, and she followed him down the trail to a cutoff that led to a short street in Georgetown with no more than two or three houses on it, one of them deserted, an old coat hanging in the doorway in place of a door. The street had no sidewalk, and Will walked carefully through the dirt, slick with rain from the morning, telling Nealie to step in his footprints. He stopped in front of a tiny unpainted house set so far back on the property that she almost failed to see it. "This is my cottage. I have some cheese and crackers and tinned meat. Nothing fancy, but it will do if you're hungry enough," he said. He stood aside and bowed, as Nealie turned in at the gate. "You don't mind, do you? You can trust me. But if you'd rather, I'll take you home."

"I don't mind," Nealie said. She'd read in a *Peterson's Magazine* story about a young girl going to a boy's room and being disgraced and wondered if visiting a man's house was the proper thing to do. She wouldn't have gone to Charlie's cabin unless they'd been engaged — which meant she'd never go there. But Will was different. He was proper and wouldn't ask her to do a thing that was wrong.

The one-room cottage was tidy, but sparsely furnished, with only an iron bed and a table and a wooden stool. Boxes were nailed to the wall to serve as cupboards. There were a trunk and hooks where Will hung his work clothes. A lap writing desk stood on the table, next to a whiskey bottle that held dried grasses. A half-finished letter rested on the desk's slanted surface, and Will put it inside the desk, along with a pen and bottle of ink. "I can make us tea," he said, adding kindling to the banked fire in the stove. He dipped water from a bucket and poured it into the kettle, setting it on the stove. Then he removed food from metal boxes with tight-fitting lids and rummaged through the cupboards, looking at the tins.

"I guess all I've got is oysters. No sardines."

"I don't prefer oysters," Nealie told him. "I surely do not."

"Oh, these aren't fresh ones. They're smoked. They won't come back up on you. I'll open the tin, and you'll try one, won't you? You said you had pluck."

Nealie nodded, although she didn't know that pluck meant eating oysters.

While Will puttered about, Nealie looked around the cabin. She liked the wallpaper, a pattern of red roses on brown vines. It had been glued to cheesecloth that was tacked onto the board walls, and it sagged in the corners, but it was elegant. She admired the leather-bound books stacked on the table and the silver frame containing a picture of a man and woman. "Your folks?" she asked. Will nodded, and she asked again, "Is there any more of you at home?"

"You mean brothers and sisters? I have one sister. She's a little older than you."

"Is that her?" Nealie nodded at another framed photograph, this one of a dark-haired girl dressed in furs, who looked a little like Will.

He nodded.

"Do you like your folks?"

"Of course." Will looked up at Nealie.

"Don't you like yours? Is that why you left home?"

Nealie did not want to talk about her parents, could not stand for Will to know how she'd been shamed by her father, so she said, "Ma's passed, and my pa is disagreeable."

Will didn't pursue the conversation. He poured hot water into a china teapot, then indicated a spread of cheese, crackers, dried apples, and smoked oysters that he'd placed on the table. "It's not the Hotel de Paris or even Mrs. Travers's boardinghouse, but I think we're hungry enough to do it justice."

"Why, it's a fine supper," Nealie said. She placed a handful of crackers and slices of cheese on a tin plate, then looked skeptically at an open tin. "I guess I'll try just one," she said, using her fingernail to snag an oyster. "At least these are little bitty fellows." She watched as Will filled his plate, then used a fork he'd set on the table to pick out a half-dozen oysters.

"What do you think?" he asked, after Nealie swallowed the oyster.

"It's real tasty," she said, surprised. Using the fork, she speared two more. She seated herself on the stool, while Will sat down on the bed. After they had eaten, Will went to the stove and poured tea into tin cups, handing one to Nealie. She held the cup between her hands, for despite the fire Will had built, she was cold. Her coat had been set near the stove so that the heat could dry the mud on it. The house was set back under thick evergreens, and she wondered if the sun ever reached the place, even on the first day of summer. "It's quiet here," she observed, although she didn't care much for quiet. She had been lonely her whole life and liked the bustle of the station and Alpine Street, where the stores and the hotel and the opera house were located.

"I like solitude. I can feel the stillness here. That's why I rented this house, although there were nicer ones available. I guess I like Colorado as much as you do, but it's the quiet I like, the way you can think without having somebody bother you all the time. This house is a good place to work," he said, indicating a wooden box behind the desk that was stuffed with rolled-up maps and diagrams.

"Is that what you do here?"

"Mostly. I want to learn all I can about mining. My grandfather thinks now that I should go back to school to get an advanced degree, but I believe I can learn more here, working in the Sharon. I didn't at first, but I do now. Besides, I like it underground."

"I sure would like to see it," Nealie said.

"You'd like to go underground?"

"Of course I would."

Will looked surprised. "That's a funny thing for a girl to say. Most women would object to the dirt and the muck and the cramped space. Your coat would get awfully dirty there."

"Then I'll just have to brush it again." She paused a minute. "It makes no sense living in a mining town and not knowing what a mine is. Don't you see?"

"A lady who wants to go underground. You're a contradiction," Will said.

"Thank you." Nealie didn't understand the word "contradiction" but thought Will was complimenting her again. She asked boldly, "Will you take me sometime?"

Will was amused. "I might just do that." He got up and refilled their tin cups. Then he went to the desk and opened the lid. "Close your eyes."

"What?" Nealie asked.

"Close your eyes. I have something for you."

"How come I have to close my eyes?"

"You know, you always have to close your eyes for a surprise."

"Oh." Nealie didn't know that. She squinted her eyes shut.

Will stood behind her and tied something around her neck. "You can open them," he said. Nealie touched her neck, confused, and Will told her to look in the mirror hanging by the door.

Nealie stood up and went to the glass. "Oh my. I never saw a thing so fine," she said, admiring herself. "It's a brooch with a lady on it."

"A cameo. I saw you admiring it in a store window after the drilling contest, and I thought you might like to have it."

"You bought it for me?"

"I didn't steal it."

"Oh, I didn't mean . . . it's just, nobody ever bought me anything before. I guess it's the prettiest thing I ever saw. It's something the lady in the bride's house would wear." She looked alarmed. "You didn't rob yourself to do it, did you?"

"Of course not. It's just a trinket."

"It's not. It's real gold."

"Not quite, but it is pretty on you." Will came close to admire the cameo. Then quickly, he leaned down and kissed Nealie on the lips.

"Mr. Spaulding!" Nealie said, stepping back and touching her lips with her fingers. "Aren't you supposed to ask first?" A girl in a story in *Peterson's Magazine* had said that,

99

and Nealie had liked the words.

"I've wanted to do that since the first time I saw you in the mercantile. Forgive me."

"That's all right. I liked it. You can do it again, if you want to."

"I liked it, too." Will grinned at Nealie as he put his hands on her shoulders. "You are an odd girl, all right." He kissed her a second time, and she kissed him back.

CHAPTER 4

Then began the happiest time in Nealie's short life, days so fine she thought she walked on the wind. She spent every Sunday with Will, at least, every Sunday he wasn't working, because despite his grandfather's ownership of the Rose of Sharon, Will took shifts that required him to work nights and Sundays, just like any other engineer. The Sundays that Will was occupied, Nellie went with Charlie, because she was mindful of what Mrs. Travers had said about jealousy. Besides, going around with Charlie was more fun than sitting in the boardinghouse, stitching Mrs. Travers's endless quilt pieces together. Nealie had never been a hand for sewing.

The two men were as different as red and blue. Will brought presents — a packet of peppermints, a box of cheese, a tin of crackers. But Charlie worked around the boardinghouse, chopping kindling, repairing the

101

porch, painting the woodshed and the privy. Once, Nealie and Charlie hung shutters on the house as a surprise for Mrs. Travers. The woman had wished for just such shutters, so Charlie made them, painted them green, and kept them at his cabin until the day when Mrs. Travers took the train to Denver to shop. The shutters were in place when she returned, and Nealie was as excited as Charlie to see the older woman's joy.

"It was Miss Nealie's idea," Charlie said.

It really wasn't. "It was Charlie's," Nealie admitted. "He's the one got the shutters and put them up."

"*We* put them up," Charlie said, smiling at Nealie, but she didn't respond. He had not asked again if Nealie would marry him, but the girl knew he had not given up.

So did Mrs. Travers, who told Nealie, "Charlie's a sticker. I guess you'd have to beat him with piece of cordwood to keep him from coming around."

Nealie didn't mind being with Charlie, although he could be glum at times. He'd stare at her, his eyes dark, and he wouldn't turn away when she caught him at it. He liked to act superior, telling her what to do. Once when the day was hot and she was sitting outside with her skirt up to her knees

102

and her legs stretched out, Charlie came up on the porch and told her it was not right, her sitting with her legs showing, and she'd had to pull down her hot skirts. "You ought not to do it. You ought not at all. You got to be a lady, Miss Nealie."

Will wasn't so critical. He liked everything Nealie did and told her he'd never met a girl who pleased him so much. They ate supper at the Hotel de Paris and took long walks around Georgetown, up one street and down another, always ending up at the bride's house to see its progress. Sometimes, they went up close so that Will could examine the workmanship on the outside, study the framing and the stone foundation or run his hands over the trim, which had been cut by a jigsaw into fanciful shapes, like wooden lace. "It's a sturdy house," he said, looking up at the big gable in front that was decorated with carved trim. They walked around the house and admired the tall windows whose decorative tops seemed like eyebrows. The tower soared into the sky, and Nealie guessed that at night, you could see heaven from it.

Once, as they climbed the stairs to the front porch to see the door, which was made of heavy wood that was painted with circles and swirls to look like bird's-eye maple, they found the house open, and they crept inside. Will called, but no one answered, so they entered. Nealie stopped in the foyer, her mouth open, as she stared at the staircase, its banister a dark streak of polished wood that followed the graceful lines of the steps. "You could follow it to the stars," she said.

They pushed open the pocket doors and entered a parlor that was dominated by a carved wooden fireplace set on a slab of dark granite. "Look it, there's the bedroom next to it. You could lay in bed and see the fire," she told Will.

"I think that's the back parlor. The bedrooms must be upstairs."

"What would anybody do with two parlors?"

Will grinned at her and took her hand, as they went through the parlors into the dining room. Sun came through the bay window onto a chandelier, its dozens of crystal prisms catching the light and turning it into rainbows. "I'd put up wallpaper, yellow wallpaper with gold in it," Nealie said. Then she entered a glass room connected with the dining room, a solarium, Will explained. Nealie didn't know the word and frowned. "For plants," Will added.

"Geraniums?"

"That and bigger ones, too, like palm trees."

"Trees inside the house? Imagine that! I'd plant an oak tree so I could build a tree house in it." There was wonder in Nealie's voice.

"Who's in here?" a man called, and Nealie cringed against Will, wondering if somebody had taken them for robbers. The man came into the room and glared at them, but he recognized Will and said, "Mr. Spaulding, I didn't know 'twas you."

Will apologized, saying they had discovered the door unlatched and were tempted to peer inside. "It's the finest dwelling Miss Nealie's ever seen."

"That it is, built like a rock, as strong as the tipple at the Sharon."

Will nodded approvingly. "I like a well-built structure. Do you think it will stand for a hundred years?"

"And more. Looking for a house, are you?" When Will didn't answer, the man added, "It's for sale. The folks that built it, the wife don't like Georgetown. They're going to live permanent in Denver."

"If I were in the market, this is the house I would buy," Will said, casting a sly look at Nealie. "Miss Nealie says it's a house for a bride."

"It's a house for somebody with money, that's what it is." The man told them they might as well see the rest of it, and he showed them the kitchen, with a fine cookstove and water pipes running to a sink. "You can bucket the water right there in the kitchen," Nealie said, thinking that with such a luxury, she would hardly have to lift a finger to cook. Then they went upstairs to see the bedrooms, rooms as big as the parlors. "This one's where your bride would sleep," the man said. Will looked at Nealie, and she turned away, embarrassed.

They went outside then and looked up at the house, its fine tower outlined against the sky. "What would you say about going there as a bride?" Will asked her. Nealie was too shy to respond, but she kept that remark in a special place in her mind, and each night, she went to sleep with the memory of Will looking up at the sunlight streaming through the clouds, wondering what it would be like to be a bride in that house.

As the summer came on and the ground dried, Nealie and Will went farther and farther from Georgetown. Will rented a hug-me-tight, a small buggy barely big enough for the two of them, and they drove to the towns downvalley, or they climbed the mountains to look at the mines. At times they were caught in storms that sent down chill rain, because rain in that high place came often in the afternoons and was never warm. "It's like standing in ice melt," Nealie observed once when they took shelter under a rocky outcrop to wait out a storm, Will holding his coat over Nealie's head to keep her dry. On occasion, Nealie packed a dinner-on-the-ground, and they took a blanket along with the picnic basket and ate in some high meadow, staying there until the mountains turned blue. Sometimes, Will fixed a dinner of yellow cheese and bread and tins of food that Nealie had never before tasted. He brought wine, too, and she liked how the sweet-tasting stuff made her happy. She liked the way Will kissed her after she was warm with the wine, too, kissed her mouth and her neck and slid his hands over her.

More and more, they ended their days together at Will's cottage, sitting on the bed with their arms around each other, while Will muttered words that made her glow. At night, alone in her room at the boarding-house, Nealie lay on her cot, her arms around herself, and whispered them in the dark.

"You make me come alive. Things are so stuffy back home," Will told her once, calling Nealie his mountain sprite. Then he mused so softly she'd barely heard him, "I wonder what's to become of you."

She saw Will every day, of course, and Charlie, too, because both still boarded with Mrs. Travers. Although each knew she was seeing the other, the two men apparently had agreed to a truce of sorts, for they no longer glared across the supper table. But they rarely had a thing to say to the other, either. The rest of the boarders saw how it was and left off teasing the two men — and Nealie, who would blush furiously if anyone remarked he'd seen her at the opera house or asked what she'd done on her Sunday off.

But at supper one evening, a boarder asked, "Who's taking you out to Independence Day, Miss Nealie?"

Nealie ducked her head, and for a moment, she didn't answer. July Fourth was the most important day in a mining town, bigger than Christmas. The mines shut down for the day, and there were drilling contests, foot races, hook-and-ladder company races, a band concert, and a dance. Neither Will nor Charlie had yet asked Nealie to go, and the two men looked at her expectantly, waiting to see which one of them she'd name. Of course, she wanted to go with Will. She wished he'd spoken up and said so, but maybe he didn't plan on taking her, and she wouldn't embarrass herself by presuming.

"Why, Nealie's going with me," Mrs. Travers said, coming in from the kitchen. "She promised to help me at the cake sale at the church. If any of you men know what's good for you, you'll bid on Nealie's cake — a Gold and Silver Cake."

"I'll bid on it right now — two dollars," Charlie said.

"Charlie's got it bad," one of the boarders said. "I bet President Garfield doesn't pay two dollars for a cake."

"I'll make it five dollars," Will said.

Nealie put her hand to her mouth. She'd never heard of anybody paying five dollars for a cake.

Charlie frowned and was about to go higher, but Mrs. Travers interrupted, "You can't bid here. You have to go to the Presbyterian church. It's the rule." She turned to Nealie and added, "That's the best way I know to get a man in church."

The boarders laughed, and Nealie slipped into the kitchen, grateful that Mrs. Travers had rescued her.

"It's not right, Mrs. Travers not letting me bid on your cake," Charlie said later. "Are you really going to Independence Day with her?"

"I am," Nealie replied.

"I guess there's no law says I can't stand next to you."

"I guess not. I might even dance with you." Nealie was annoyed then that Will hadn't claimed her for the day and liked the idea of making him uneasy.

"I don't know how to dance."

Nealie looked at him in surprise. "Me, neither."

As it turned out, Nealie went to the July Fourth festivities by herself, since that morning, Mrs. Travers was called down to Red Elephant to tend to a friend whose husband had cut off her toes with an axe. The foot was infected, and the doctor told Mrs. Travers he feared the woman would die. It was a certainty she would if her husband nursed her.

"That's the worst thing I ever heard. Even my pa wouldn't do such a thing," Nealie said, although she wasn't sure about that. "Maybe it was an accident."

"Maybe gold jumps out of the ground into a wheelbarrow," Mrs. Travers replied. "The boarders know we're not serving supper tonight on Independence Day. But then there's the next day or two. I'd hire a girl to work in the kitchen with you, but where would I find one on such short notice? Can you do the cooking and serving and the lunches until I get back?"

"I can," Nealie said, proud that Mrs. Travers trusted her.

"Everything's set out for tomorrow's breakfast," Mrs. Travers said. "You go on now, or you'll miss the parade."

But Nealie insisted on waiting on the porch with the older woman until the doctor arrived in his buggy, since Mrs. Travers did not plan to walk to Red Elephant. The girl watched them as they passed the turn in the road and couldn't be seen anymore. Then she went inside and put on the green dress and walked the two blocks to Alpine Street, where a crowd lined the sidewalk in front of stores that were decorated with red, white, and blue bunting. Pictures of President Garfield, who had been wounded in an assassination attempt just two days before, and President Lincoln hung in the shop windows, along with lithographs of the signing of the Declaration of Independence and the burning of the President's House in the War of 1812. The people were decorated, too. Men in white shirts tied red or blue bandanas around their necks, while women trimmed their hats with tiny flags. Nealie was the only one in green.

She stood at the edge of the boardwalk, watching as the foot racers gathered at the starting line at the end of the street. They wore tights that looked like long underwear, and they hopped from foot to foot, slapping each other on the back and bragging about how fast they were. One of them turned and spotted the girl in the green dress and called, "Miss Nealie!" Charlie Dumas grinned and waved at her.

Nealie was too embarrassed to wave back and stared at the dirt street, but that didn't stop Charlie. "I'm going to win you the prize," he yelled.

Nealie slipped back through the thick crowd, until she leaned against the window of the Kaiser Mercantile, beside Mr. Kaiser, who had pinned a flag to his white apron. "That Charlie Dumas is fast," he said. "You want me to get you a chair to stand on so's you can see him?" Before Nealie could reply, there was a gunshot, and the racers took off. Men cheered, and children jumped up and down, but Nealie couldn't watch the racers because all creation seemed to be in front of her. All she saw was a blur as they rushed past. In a minute there was a cheer, and she knew the race was over. Mr.

Kaiser said above the noise, "It looks like Charlie Dumas won, after all."

"He may have won the race, but I've got the prize," Will said, coming up beside Nealie and taking her arm.

The remark made Nealie feel warm, and she knew this would be the best Fourth of July of her life, not that she had celebrated Independence Day so much before. Her pa had taken her to the celebration in Hannibal once when she was small, but only because he'd wanted to go into town to get drunk. She'd had a good time, although her father had passed out, and she'd had to walk all the way back to the farm by herself. She'd missed the fireworks because she hadn't wanted to go home alone in the dark.

Will propelled Nealie through the throng of people and led her to a stand where women sold food. "I bought your cake," he whispered. "I saw Mrs. Travers take it to the church last night, so I paid them ten dollars to let me take it. I left it at my cottage." He smiled at Nealie. "Would you have some lemonade?"

"What's that?" asked Nealie, who had never heard of such a thing.

"It's a drink made from lemon juice. Haven't you ever tasted it?"

Nealie made a wry face. "It sounds sour."

"No, there's plenty of sugar in it." Will handed a dime to the woman behind the stand, and she gave him two glasses. Nealie sipped the drink carefully, then grinned and drank it down. "It tastes as good as wine," she said.

Will took Nealie to see the hose-cart races and the water fights, while they ate sausages and popped corn and white divinity candy that looked as pure as fresh snow. In the afternoon, they sat on the grass in the park and listened to the brass band play in the bandstand above them. The air was hot, and Nealie used a paper fan with MACKENZIE FUNERAL PARLOR written on it to swish the air back and forth in front of her face. She wanted to pull her dress up to her knees, but mindful of what Charlie had said about such a display, she kept her skirt down. She was sure Will wouldn't have minded much if she'd shown her legs, but she didn't want him to think she was a slattern. In the evening, Will escorted her to the town hall where a band played dance music.

"I can't dance," Nealie said.

"You mean you don't approve of dancing?" he asked. "What a pity, for you're as light on your feet as dandelion fluff."

"Oh no. I've nothing against dancing. I just don't know how to do it."

"Then it must be taught, and now. This one is a waltz. The secret is to count." Will led her forward and backward, counting one-two-three, one-two-three, swirling her around, until Nealie understood the rhythm, and Will said, "There, you've got it."

"It's like floating," she said, thinking she could float like that all night.

But the dance ended, and Charlie came up to her. Will bowed a little to him as he relinquished Nealie's hand and retreated to the doorway.

"I guess you didn't have time for me before," Charlie said.

"I didn't see you, Mr. Dumas," she lied. Of course she'd seen him hovering around, the way he always did, but she'd pretended not to. "I looked for you, but I only saw you at the foot race. Mr. Kaiser said you won."

Charlie was gleeful at that. "I got the prize. I'm saving it for you."

"Are we going to dance?" Nealie asked, because she didn't want to carry around whatever it was he'd won. In fact, she didn't want it at all.

"I told you I don't know how, so I guess we'll just sit down."

The two sat on a bench, Nealie looking around the room for Will, but he had disappeared. "Mr. Kaiser said you're fast."

Charlie looked embarrassed. "I guess I do all right." He swallowed, then he took Nealie's hand in his big one. "Miss Nealie, this isn't the right place —"

But Nealie did not want to hear what he had to say, and she interrupted, just as the band stopped playing. "I guess the music's done for."

At that moment, Will appeared beside them. "I will have the next dance with her," he said.

"Just one. Then it's my turn," Charlie replied, glaring at the man.

When the music started, Will danced Nealie across the room, toward the door, whispering, "What do you say we run off? It's too hot in here, and I won't share you with that ox. If you dance with him, he'll crush your feet."

Without a backward glance at Charlie, Nealie nodded and slipped out the door with Will into the darkening street. The happy, patriotic crowd of the day had been replaced by men drinking from bottles or carrying mugs of beer they'd purchased in the saloons. Women from Brownell Street, as drunk as the toughs, hung on to the men's arms. Nealie had never seen a drunken woman before, except perhaps her mother, although she wasn't sure about

116

that. When she thought nobody saw her, her mother drank the silly-bug that Hog Davis made, but she didn't laugh and carry on. She only cried and fell asleep. Nealie stared at one of the whores, wondering if she might have turned out herself if Mrs. Travers hadn't offered her work. The woman, taken with meanness, snarled, "What you looking at, you and that green dress?"

Nealie stepped back, bumping into a man who said, "Let's you and me have a drink, Katy." "Katy" was the name men gave to prostitutes.

He grabbed her arm, but Nealie snatched it away, and Will came up then and said, "Sir, you are insulting a lady. I won't have it."

"Oh," the man said, sizing up Will. "Sorry, miss." He tugged at his hat, which slid off his head into the dirt.

"Maybe we ought to go back inside," Nealie said.

"No such a thing. We'll get away from here. I have it on good authority that the fireworks will be shot off from that mountain." He pointed at a dark hump in front of them. "I have a splendid view of it from my cottage. What do you say we eat your cake and watch the fireworks?"

Nealie thought that a capital idea and followed Will as he pushed through the rough crowd onto a side street. The dusky dark was starting, and the sky, which had been split with streaks of red against the blue when they left the dance, had turned indigo, with a pink glow at the horizon. Will took Nealie's hand as the two walked to his house. He asked if she wanted supper, but Nealie had already eaten enough and told him no. So Will cut slices of the cake and poured wine into tin cups. They took the food and drink outside and sat on a quilt that Will spread on the ground. Nealie shivered a little, so Will fetched a blanket and wrapped it around her. "I shall buy you a proper shawl for these mountain evenings," he said.

"A blanket works as well," replied Nealie, who was mindful that he had already been generous with her, had brought her a handkerchief with an *N* embroidered on it and a pair of gloves, as well as the cameo. She touched her throat, but in her hurry to dress, she had forgotten to put on the necklace that day.

The din from the revelry in town came to them as a dull roar. There was the sound of a brass band playing far away, and gunshots, because that was the way Independence

Day was celebrated in a mining town. A glow radiated over Alpine Street, where the gas lamps were lit. But everything was dark under the dark trees at Will's cottage. Nealie didn't mind. She was glad for the velvet blackness, especially when Will began to kiss her, for she wouldn't have wanted anyone to see them. "We could go inside," he said.

"We'd miss the fireworks."

"We'll stay, then." He slid under the blanket he had wrapped around Nealie and held her tight. "Now we'll both be warm."

The two of them stayed close, their arms around each other, until the fireworks began, bright explosions that lit up the sky. Nealie, who had never seen a show so fine, watched with wonder. The fireworks broke into rings and showers and cascades of light that shone on her astonished face. "You'd think the stars had blown up," she said.

For a time, Will watched the fireworks, but as those things went, it was not much of a display and he had seen better, so he turned to watch Nealie, who broke into cries of delight at each flash. Whenever she glanced at him, he was looking at her, and finally, she asked, "Don't you like watching the fireworks?"

"I like watching you better," he said.

Nealie felt her face get warm. It was hot

under the blanket, and Will's hands were hot as he touched her. She wished for a glass of lemonade or even water from Clear Creek, but she didn't want to move away from Will. His touch pleasured her. The fireworks ended in a grand explosion of gunfire and light, and Nealie gave a great sigh of disappointment. "I won't see them for another year," she said. "Or maybe never." She lay back on the ground and looked up at the sky, which was as dark as Egypt now. "There never was a thing so pretty."

"Except for you," Will said. Nealie sucked in her breath at the words. Will began unfastening the brass buttons of her dress then, murmuring as he did so how soft she was and did she know she drove him to distraction and had ever since the first day he saw her? He said he couldn't stop himself.

Nealie knew she ought not to let him touch her like that, should kick him the way she had her pa the times he'd come into the barn and grabbed at her. But she didn't want to. Will's words and his hands made her feel good, and besides, she trusted him not to do anything wrong. He'd said she could trust him. But in the end, she couldn't. He pushed up her skirt until it was bunched around her waist and gently moved her legs apart. Then he was on top of her, loving her the way married people loved each other, and she was wild with happiness.

When the thing was done, Will held Nealie close. She touched his cheek and felt tears and knew there were tears on her own face. She wanted him to say he loved her. But he did not, and although she'd had little experience with men, she knew from the stories in the magazines that words about love came hard to them, and she decided it was enough that he had *shown* he loved her.

They went to sleep then, lying together under the trees, and the girl slept a long time. When she awoke, she was confused at first, not sure where she was. She thought she heard the sound of water in the creek, but it was only the wind in the trees, and she remembered they had made love and then gone to sleep under the pines. Will lay with his back to her, and Nealie wanted to reach out and touch him, but she didn't care to waken him. She couldn't tell the time but thought it must be very late, because the town was quiet. She remembered that she had to make breakfast for the boarders and pack their lunches, and she slipped from under the blanket and straightened her dress.

She walked quickly down Alpine Street, which was deserted except for a man asleep on the grass, snoring. Under the gaslights, the street looked tawdry, with bottles and broken glasses strewn about. Flags and bunting had been ripped down and lay in the street, crushed and torn by dirty boots, and the walks were littered with bits of food and paper. As she turned the corner onto Rose Street, a man sitting in a doorway called, "Let's you and me have a drink, Katy." He didn't reach for her. In fact, the effort of speaking was too much for him, and he slumped against the door frame. But Nealie jumped off the boardwalk into the dust of the street, catching her dress with her heel and tearing out the hem. She lifted her skirts and fled down the dark street.

Nealie had gone through the gate and come up onto the porch of the boarding-house before she realized someone was sitting on the bench. A drunk, probably, a man who had celebrated too hard and hadn't made it home, she thought, hoping she could slide past him. The house was not locked. They never locked it. So she wouldn't have to fumble with a key, only slip inside and bolt the door, because she didn't want the man stumbling in when morning came, asking for coffee or would she fix him breakfast?

But the man was not a drunk, and he was not asleep. "Miss Nealie?" Charlie Dumas's voice was tired and filled with sadness. Nealie had never heard a voice so sad.

The girl wished for all the world, then, that she were alone, for she was caught up in the night before and wanted a little time yet to recall the words Will had said, the thing they'd done together. She wanted to be glad for it, and now there was Charlie Dumas, looking at her in a strange way. He had no right. Suddenly, she felt shame that he saw her like that, her dress torn and half buttoned, her hair down around her face. He made her happiness seem cheap, and she hated Charlie for making her feel that way. Would he know what she'd done? Nealie wondered, and the wondering made her angry. Charlie had no right to intrude, no right to sit on her porch all night, waiting for her, watching out for her the way he'd done. She'd never asked him to. She mustered her anger and said, "Mr. Dumas, you ought not to be here."

"And you ought not . . ." He couldn't seem to say the rest and gave a great sigh and was silent.

"You bemean me, waiting for me like this."

"You bemean yourself, Miss Nealie."

"I don't know what you say. I've been celebrating Independence Day."

"It's been a long time over."

"Then I best look to breakfast for the boarders."

"Miss Nealie . . ."

But she would not have him talking. The girl wanted him to leave, wanted it in the worst way. She thought about ordering him away from the boardinghouse — and out of her life. She hadn't asked him to come around courting her, hadn't wanted it at all. Why, she'd tried to be easy with him when he'd asked her to marry him, not hurting his feelings. Instead, she should have said no, she'd never be his wife, no more than she'd marry the drunk who had called her Katy and asked her to take a drink. Nealie wanted Charlie to go before he spoiled the thing that had happened between Will and her. "Go home, Mr. Dumas," she said.

"Don't be doing that, Miss Nealie."

She did not ask what. She was afraid he knew. Instead, she said, "What I do's not your business. Go kill your own snakes, Mr. Dumas."

The big man slowly rose from the bench. "I was waiting for you. I brought you the prize." He held out a medal in his hand, but Nealie didn't take it, didn't care to have it. He sighed deeply. "You won't stop me saying it. I wanted to marry you, Miss Nealie, wanted it in the worst way there is. I'd have taken care of you, made you proud to be my wife. I guess you didn't want that, and now I don't want it, either. You've spoiled yourself for a husband. There it is."

"Git, you!" the girl said, stomping her foot. "I wouldn't have you if you were strung with solid gold nuggets."

Charlie stepped heavily off the porch. "Don't be doing that. He'll treat you pretty rotten, and he won't marry you."

Nealie turned her back on the man, rushing inside the house and slamming the door. Everything had been so magical at night, but now morning was coming on, and Nealie wondered if the thing would seem cheap and dirty in the light. She blamed Charlie Dumas.

CHAPTER 5

The summer passed along. To Nealie's surprise, Charlie continued to take his meals at the boardinghouse. She'd thought that after what had happened between them, he would go elsewhere, and she had hoped he would, because seeing him every day was a raw spot in her happiness. Every time Nealie looked at him, she remembered his words and felt her cheeks grow hot with his reproach. But as Mrs. Travers had observed, Charlie was a sticker — a sticker for the boardinghouse, if not for Nealie. He wasn't the same, however. Charlie no longer arrived early for supper, joking with Nealie and offering to help. Instead, he came into the dining room just as the men sat down at the table. He didn't banter with the others the way he used to or hang around after the meal, hoping to catch Nealie alone. In fact, he ignored Nealie, not even asking could he have more gravy or another slice of bread. And he left as soon as dessert was finished. When she did catch Charlie's eye, Nealie turned away quickly, because there was always the look of reproach on his face.

The other boarders, who were there to eat, not to talk, didn't pay much attention at first, and when they did realize that Charlie no longer teased Nealie or watched her with glowing eyes, they did not remark on it. Most were not comfortable with women themselves, and they had marveled at the ease with which Charlie had courted the girl. Besides, Charlie was a favorite, and if the men perceived hurt, they did not want to add to it. Will, too, was quiet when Charlie was at the table. Another man might have gloated, asking Nealie in front of the others would she accompany him to the theater or had she had a good time the night before at the band concert, but Will did not, and Nealie loved him the more for his sensitivity.

Mrs. Travers had returned to the boarding-house after several days of nursing, telling Nealie how the woman whose toes had been severed had died, cursing her husband for a brute. "Those two were so spiteful, they didn't know what to do with theyself," she said. She saw the way things stood between Nealie and Charlie. So as the two women

127

washed dishes that evening, she asked the girl, "Did you fall out with Mr. Dumas?"

"I said I meant not to marry him. I told him it was no use and to give it up, for I don't care a button for him. It discomforts me to have him around." Nealie would not look at the older woman and wiped a plate so long that it was a wonder she didn't wipe off the glaze.

"I worry you exaultify Mr. Spaulding," Mrs. Travers said. "I hope you didn't make a mistake."

Nealie rubbed the plate even harder, because she believed the woman was talking about the thing she'd done with Will — she never put a name to it but always thought of it as "the thing." But then she realized that Mrs. Travers meant turning down Charlie, and the girl said she hadn't made a mistake, that it was only right not to let the man carry on the way he had when she meant never to marry him.

Nealie was even quieter around the boarders now, never looking at Will except to ask, "Would you have another chop?" or "Shall I hotten your coffee?" But when she and Will were together, just the two of them, she grew lively, chattering about the flowers that grew wild in the mountain sun and the birds, as muted as scraps in a faded quilt.

Every new thing delighted her, because she had no reference beyond the farm in Missouri. Will explained to her about ore and how an ordinary rock might have streaks in it that meant it was rich in gold and silver, but that a rock that sparkled might be only fool's gold. He told her how the miners blasted deep in the earth to extract the ore, drawing pictures in the dirt with a stick, and explained how the mills worked, crushing the ore and extracting the precious metal. Nealie said again she wished she could go underground, but Will told her no. He'd inquired about it, he said, and the men refused to allow a woman in the mine. If there were an accident later on, they would blame her. Nealie, taken with superstitions herself, never wondered if Will simply did not want her to go into the mine.

They were seen together in Georgetown less often now. Will still took her to the theater and the Hotel de Paris dining room, but he said he preferred to be alone with her. So they hiked far from Georgetown, sometimes coming together hurriedly in the upper meadows near timberline. More often, they went to Will's cottage, and he laid her on the bed in the dark room where there was no chance someone would come on them unexpectedly.

Will was generous. He gave her the shawl, a bright rose one swirling with pattern like a Persian carpet. Another time, he presented her with a bottle of perfume, a tiny green crescent of a bottle with a stopper of blue enamel and silver. After Nealie doused herself with the rose scent, Will explained she should put only a tiny dab of perfume behind her ears and on her wrists, and Nealie never again made that mistake. He gave her chocolate drops, each one wrapped in a piece of paper, and combs for her hair, and a gold pin with a ruby in it. When fall came, he presented her with another shawl, this one of heavy wool to keep out the winter cold.

Will taught her about manners, because he delighted in instructing her in new things, as if she herself were a piece of ore that needed refining, and she learned more than how to hold a knife and fork. She waited now for Will to open doors for her or help her with her shawl, and she took his arm and walked on the storefront side of the boardwalk so that the wagons wouldn't splash mud on her. Will remarked once that she would look more fashionable in a dove-gray dress instead of the green. The gray would bring out the color in her hair. Ladies wore gray, he said, and Nealie bought the yard goods for a new outfit. She wanted to be a lady, although when the two of them were alone, Will did not care for her to act like one. Sometimes when they had been wild and the thing was over, he would hold her close and tell her he cared for her, calling her "dear" and "sweetheart." Once he even said he loved her, and that was enough. He did not need to say it again, although Nealie wished he would.

The summer was done, and the leaves on the aspen trees were turning scarlet and bright gold when Nealie knew she was pregnant. It came to her when she was pegging the wash on the line, standing in the backyard of the boardinghouse on the platform, built high with steps leading to the top, so that a woman would not have to stand in the snow in winter to hang the laundry. The girl felt a turning in her stomach, and she counted backward, scared a little at first, then foolish with happiness. There was no friend in whom she could confide except for Mrs. Travers, and Nealie did not want to tell the woman, not until things were settled between Will and her, so she remained shut-mouthed.

Nealie did not tell Will, either, not at first. Instead, she teased him along, making sure he cared for her. "I wish this would go on forever," she told him, as she lay beside him on his bed, the branches of a pine swaying in the wind and knocking against the house. She could see through the window into the yard, where a shower of dead leaves floated to the ground.

"I'd like nothing better," he replied.

Another time, she said, "I wonder what we'll be like when we're old."

"I don't believe you'll grow old. You'll always be as pretty as you are now. You'll always be seventeen to me."

"But everybody grows old." Nealie had loosed her hair, and she sat on a stump in a clearing at timberline braiding it. The cold had come on, and they could no longer lie on the long grass in the high mountains.

"Then we'll just have to wait and see." The remark thrilled her, because it meant that Will intended to spend his life with her.

Still, she waited another two weeks, just to be sure, although by then, the waistband of her skirt was tight, and sometimes in the morning, her stomach was upset. When the second of the two weeks had passed, it was time, she thought. She couldn't wait longer.

By then, it was October, and the warmth had gone out of the mountains. Nealie told him on an afternoon when the two had tramped through the trees and stopped at a place where early snow lay on the ground. Nealie had hoped to go higher, because the air hung in the valley, smoky and gray, and she wanted to go above it, to the sun. But Will had called a halt, saying the snow would be deeper higher up. So she sat on a log, forming the words she would say to Will, savoring the moment he would take her in his arms and tell her how happy he was.

Before the girl could speak, Will walked a little away and looked out across the valley, which was in shadow. "I will always remember this, sweetheart. I have been happiest here," he said. He turned and faced her. "My grandfather wants me to go back to school at the first of the year. I don't want to, but I can't tell him no."

Nealie stared at him. She had never considered that Will would leave Georgetown. She loved the place, the mountains and the bright sunlight. In her mind, the two of them would live there forever, in his little cottage or maybe even the bride's house. But it came on her that it might be best if they moved away. They would marry quietly and go back to where Will had come from, and nobody would know the baby had been made before the ceremony.

"There's something to tell you," she said.

She was shy and looked down. Seeing a hole in her stocking, she picked at it with her fingernail.

Will did not hear her. "I will never like a place as well as this," he said. "I told my grandfather I am learning more on the job than I would in a classroom, but he doesn't agree. He's stubborn and won't allow that I might be right. He made plans for me when I was just a boy, and I think he'd cut me off if I didn't follow through with them."

"Will," she said.

"You know I don't want to go. You know it, don't you?"

"There's something needs telling," Nealie said, standing up and going to him, putting her arms around him and laying her head against his back. She opened her mouth, but she did not know how to tell him, and at first the words wouldn't come. Then she said quickly, "I'm going to have a baby."

Will stiffened under her arms, then drew away and turned to look at the girl. "What?"

"A baby."

His eyes were wide. "But you can't."

"Well, I can. It will come in the spring." Nealie waited for Will to hold her then, to tell her he was glad.

"Oh my God," Will said instead, turning his back on the girl. He smashed his right fist into the palm of his left hand. "Didn't you know how to . . . ? No, of course, you didn't. What a mess I've made!" He shook his head back and forth. "Can you get rid of it?"

"What?" Nealie asked, bewildered.

"The baby, do you know how to get rid of it?"

"Why would I do that?"

"Maybe Mrs. Travers knows."

Nealie began to shake and grabbed the bony white trunk of an aspen tree to steady herself. This was not what she'd planned. Then the ghastly thought came to her that Will might think the baby was Charlie's. "It's *our* baby."

"Oh, I know that," Will said softly. Then he grabbed her arms and shook her. "You can't have a baby, Nealie."

When he let loose of her, Nealie put her hand on Will's cheek. "It's all right. I have it figured out. We can go to Denver and get married and say we were married in the summer but kept it a secret. You see, it will be fine. Nobody will know, even your grandfather. You can tell him the wedding was in July. Maybe he'll let you stay on here. We could live in the bride's house." She held her breath, hoping Will wouldn't think she was telling him how to spend his money.

But he loved the house as much as she did.

"We can't get married." Will walked a little ways away, then leaned down and picked up a handful of snow and squeezed, but the snow was too dry to make a ball, and he brushed his wet hands against his pants.

"Why not?" Nealie whispered.

Will's shoulders slumped. His back still to Nealie, he said slowly, "Try to understand. I told you at the start that I had obligations, but I should have said it right out." He paused, and then told her, "I already have a wife."

Nealie's mouth formed the word "what," but the sound didn't come out. She felt as if a nail had been driven through her heart, and she sat down on the log again and put her arms around herself, but the chill she felt was inside her.

Will turned around, angry now, angry at himself. "I should have been clear. I know I should have made you understand, but I was afraid you'd quit me, and I didn't want that. I care about you, honestly I do, Nealie. I never wanted to hurt you."

"You're already married?" Nealie asked, as if he'd made a mistake. Maybe she'd misunderstood.

He nodded and sat down beside her, placing his wet hand on her hand, but the cold made her draw away, so he put his hands between his knees. "Her name is Nancy. We grew up together. Her father and mine had business dealings, and Grandfather thought she would be a suitable wife. He insisted on it, and I've never gone against him. Nancy's a fine person. I've nothing against her. It's just that we don't have much to say to each other, and I've never felt about her the way I do you. I've never loved her."

"Where is she?"

"She didn't want to come to Georgetown, and to tell you the truth, I didn't want her here. She couldn't have coped with a mining town. She's in Europe with her mother and sister. They'll be home at Christmas."

"It was wrong not to tell me, Will. Wrong." The wind caught Nealie's words and seemed to fling them back into her face. Neither of them had noticed that the sky had darkened into twilight, and the wind was strong. "Were you ever going to tell me?"

Will shrugged. "I don't know. Yes, I think I was." He looked across the valley and saw that the dark had come on. "We'd better go down," he said, standing and reaching for Nealie's hand, but the girl sat huddled on the log.

"What will we do?" she asked. "What will

137

I do?"

Will lifted her by her shoulders until she was standing. "I'll think of something. I won't leave you alone. I promise you, Nealie, I'll find a way to take care of you."

Will sent a man to tell Mrs. Travers that he would not be at the boardinghouse for a week or more, because he'd been called away. But he was gone much longer, and Nealie's spirits dropped further each day. On her Sunday off, she told Mrs. Travers that she was going for a walk and went to Will's cottage. The day was cold, and she wrapped her shawl — the warm one that Will had given her — around herself as she stepped on the stones that led to his door. Nealie could tell that Will had not been there, because no footprints marred the snow that lay in the yard. She peered into the window and saw the writing desk on the table and Will's work clothes hanging on pegs. So he was not gone for good. She went back to the street, using a pine branch to erase her steps so that Will would not return and think she had spied on him.

She walked along the streets that were cold and gray from the smelter smoke, past a jack train loaded with rails that would be laid in a mine for the ore carts. One of the burros brayed at her, but she didn't laugh as she usually did at the funny sound. She didn't even hear it. There was no reason to return to the boardinghouse, so she walked along the street behind it, Taos Street, and without thinking, she found herself in front of the bride's house. In the past week, since she had seen it last, the house had been painted as white as a bride's cake, and as she stared at the structure, she saw a beam of sunlight break through the clouds and shine on the tower — an omen, she thought, for she believed in such things. But was it a good or a bad omen? The tower was her favorite part of the house. The staircase was there, and surrounding it on the second floor was a tiny sitting area with windows on two sides that let in the sunlight from the south and the west. If the house were hers, Nealie would hang lace curtains in the windows and put a rocking chair there, above the porch, where she could sit and look out, waiting for Will to come home in the evening. She would run down the stairs and throw open the door before he could turn the knob, and he would grab her up in his arms.

Now she saw herself for a fool and fled to the park, where she sat down on the steps of the empty bandstand, remembering when

Will had taken her to the Independence Day band concert, and they had sat on the grass, eating divinity candy. The sun had been bright that day, but now it was clouded by the smoke, and the air was leaden. Nealie put her head in her arms, wondering what would become of her.

She'd believed Will when he said he would think of something, but what if he never came back? What if he'd run off, leaving his belongings to molder away? Maybe he was with his wife at that very moment, while Nealie sat in the cold, the shawl he had given her over her head to keep out the snow that had begun to fall. Did he have children? She hadn't thought to ask that. Nealie pictured Will and his wife and little ones sitting at supper, a chandelier filled with candles hanging over the table, a maid — someone like Nealie herself — carrying in the food, just like the illustrations in the story magazines. Nobody would have to tell Will's wife how to hold her fork or that she ought to wear a gray dress instead of a green one. Remembering the green dress made Nealie's cheeks grow red. She had been so proud of it, but Will must have laughed at her for wearing such a color.

Nealie leaned her face against the rough wood of the stand. What would she do if

Will never came back? Perhaps someone would take the baby and put it into an orphanage, and she herself would end up on Brownell Street, because Mrs. Travers would never allow a fallen woman to serve the boarders. The anger and unhappiness and the raw wind made Nealie shiver, and she huddled on the steps, her knees drawn up against her chest. But she couldn't stop shaking.

People passed by and saw the girl, but they did not stop, and Nealie did not notice them. She did not see Charlie until he spoke to her. "Are you needing —" he began, then stopped short when he recognized Nealie.

"What do you want, Mr. Dumas?" Nealie asked.

"I didn't know it was you sitting here."

"Well, it is, and I don't want you following me. I told you I quit you."

"I just thought you were a woman needing something."

"I don't need a thing from you. I told you before, and I say again, git! I've got shut of you." All of her anger and unhappiness at Will exploded on Charlie now, as if he was the one who had wronged her.

"Miss Nealie —"

"Go away!"

The big man sighed and took a step

backward. "I won't be bothering you again, Miss Nealie. I don't care about you anymore," he said, and turned and walked off.

Two weeks went by, and Will did not return. Three weeks passed. Then four. And still there was no word from Will.

One night at supper, a boarder asked, "Whatever happened to that Will Spaulding? I thought he's coming back."

Another boarder glanced at Nealie, thinking to silence the man, but Nealie appeared not to hear.

"Maybe he's taking his meals up at the Grubstake with the swells. He's too high-and-mighty for the likes of us."

"Aw, I liked him fine," a third man said.

Nealie looked at Charlie out of the corner of her eye, but he was ignoring the conversation.

"I heard he called it deep enough, just up and quit and went back home," the third man continued, talking with his mouth full.

"He's not coming back," Charlie interrupted. He'd stopped eating and was staring at his food.

"How do you know, Charlie? I don't recollect you were such good friends," a boarder asked. He had his arm around his plate, as if to keep someone from stealing it.

"I just know. That's all." Charlie didn't glance up and looked as if he wished he hadn't spoken.

"Those Eastern swells, they can't take the winter," someone remarked, and everyone laughed, and the conversation changed.

In the kitchen, Nealie put down a platter she was carrying and asked Mrs. Travers, "You reckon that's so about Will?"

The older woman looked the girl in the face and then glanced at Nealie's body, while Nealie made her stomach as flat as she could. "I reckon it is. I got something to tell you, but it'll have to wait till the boarders are gone."

Nealie willed the men to hurry through their supper, but the night was cold, and they were not anxious to leave. After supper, they stayed on and smoked, emptying their spent pipes into the stove in the eating room. At last, one by one, they got up until only Charlie was left, and he seemed dug in. "You better get on home, Mr. Dumas. The snow's shoe-top deep, and it'll be as cold as Missouri out there before you get to your cabin," Nealie told him.

She and Mrs. Travers watched as the big man slowly put on his coat and mittens, then tied the strings of a wool cap under his chin. He nodded at Mrs. Travers but didn't look at Nealie before he went through the door, taking the air out of the place with him so that the room was still and close.

Nealie stood a moment, staring at the closed door, before she asked, "What have you got to say about Will?" She sat down in a chair that one of the boarders had vacated and stared up at the chromo on the wall. It was a picture of a picnic in the Alps, the women in furs and fancy hats, the men looking like dandies. Every time she looked at it, she wondered how anybody could enjoy a picnic dressed like that. Now, she glanced around the room that she had once found cozy and wondered if Will had thought it shabby, with the faded chromo, the mismatched chairs, and sagging wallpaper that was stained from where the roof leaked.

"You're draggy. You want to go on to bed, and I'll finish cleaning up?" Mrs. Travers asked.

Nealie didn't answer, only stared at the woman, and Mrs. Travers sat down across from her, pushing aside a dirty plate. "He wrote me, Will Spaulding did. The letter came two days ago."

"You didn't tell me?"

"I couldn't think how to. I knew you liked him." She stopped and leaned forward.

"Now, you got something you want to tell me? I can keep my mouth shut, you know."

"What did he write?" Nealie's face was white, and her hands were clasped together in a sort of death grip. "Let me read the letter."

"I can't. I was so disgusted with him for not coming back that I burned it up in the stove." She paused a moment, then repeated, "He's not coming back. He asked would I find somebody to box up his things and ship them to him."

Nealie gasped. "Did he send you a letter for me? Did he say anything about me?" Her voice was that of a little girl's.

"He asked me to give you something." Mrs. Travers got up heavily and went into the kitchen and opened a drawer, then came back with a folded piece of paper.

"Is that the letter?"

"I told you I burned up the letter. All he said was to pack up his things and to give you this."

Nealie opened the paper and stared at it, not understanding. "What is it?"

"It's a money order for five hundred dollars."

"Money! He sent me money? Like the girls on Brownell Street? They get paid money," Nealie cried, her voice shrill. "Does

145

he think I'm the same thing as them?" The thought that had always lingered in the back of her mind that something special lay ahead for her, that all the misery she had suffered as a girl would come to an end in some form of happiness, shattered. The girl had never dwelt on that idea, never been fully conscious of it, but some small part of it had propelled her on. Now she felt a blackness where the hope had been. "Is that all the better he thought of me?"

"You know that isn't so."

"Isn't it?" Nealie put her face in her hands, then asked in a muffled voice, "What do I do, Mrs. Travers?"

"There's Charlie Dumas."

"I'd be lower than a snake's belly if I married him now. I couldn't do it. Besides, he's quit of me. He told me so." And he'd never marry her if he found out she was pregnant with Will's off-child. He'd hate her.

"I don't believe it. He's still hanging around, as you can plainly see. But suit yourself." Mrs. Travers went into the kitchen and began to scrape and wash the dishes. Nealie didn't stir from her chair. Mrs. Travers finished the work, set out the breakfast things, then blew out the lamp and went into her own room. When she arose the next morning, she found Nealie asleep in the chair, her head on the table.

After lunches were made and breakfast served, the dishes washed, Nealie went into her room and stayed there through the day, thinking. She'd had such dreams about Will and herself and the baby, all of them living in the bride's house. Maybe he'd come back after all. It would just take a little time for him to leave his wife. But in her heart, Nealie knew that wasn't going to happen. Besides, she couldn't wait. Maybe she wasn't any different from the prostitutes on Brownell Street after all.

Would she put the baby in a home for foundlings and go to work in one of the houses? She couldn't expect Mrs. Travers to keep her on. The woman had her standards, and so did the boarders. They wouldn't want to be fed by a sorry girl. She would have Will's money, but then what? Five hundred dollars was more than Nealie could comprehend, but even she knew it wouldn't last forever. What work was there for her with a baby to take care of? She could go back home to Missouri, but she'd starve first, and let the baby starve, too, before she'd let her father touch it.

Late in the afternoon, Mrs. Travers called Nealie to help prepare supper for the boarders, and the girl roused herself. The two worked silently, Nealie, distracted, dropping the knife on the floor, then scalding her hand when she poured the potato water into a bowl. Mrs. Travers grabbed the hand and plunged it into the water bucket. "I think it will be all right, just a little red is all. It won't blister," Mrs. Travers said. "Does it hurt?"

Nealie shook her head. She'd barely felt the boiling water.

"You look peaked," Mrs. Travers observed. "Do you want to go to bed?"

But Nealie had been alone with her thoughts all day and didn't care to be by herself any longer. She stayed in the kitchen, concentrating on the supper. When the boarders arrived, Mrs. Travers announced that she'd serve them for a change, while Nealie worked over the stove. After the boarders left, as the girl cleared the table, she thought to ask Mrs. Travers's advice. But she wasn't absolutely certain the woman knew her state, and she was afraid that when she did learn, she would throw her out, maybe even that very night. So she was silent as she went about her chores, watching as Mrs. Travers sat at the kitchen table, making out her grocery list. "I thought to make a stew tomorrow. With the weather so cold, I believe it would taste good. What do you think?" Mrs. Travers asked.

"All right," Nealie muttered, wiping off a spill on the cookstove with her apron.

"The larder's as empty as a dead man's eyes. You'll have to go to the mercantile. Potatoes, carrots. I wonder if there are parsnips. I always liked a parsnip. Maybe a red chili to give it flavor, Arkansas chicken." When Nealie didn't understand the term, Mrs. Travers explained she meant salt pork. She continued rattling off the other ingredients until the two heard a knock at the door. "I'll get it. You stay here," Mrs. Travers said quickly.

The thought popped into Nealie's mind that Will might be the caller, and she touched her hair, tucking in loose strands, and bit her lips to make them red. But even as that idea arose in her mind, she knew it wasn't so. He'd quit her as sure as anything.

"Mr. Dumas, did you forget something?" Mrs. Travers asked, opening the door.

"No, I came to see Miss Nealie."

The girl sighed. Soon enough, Charlie Dumas would be gloating, telling others he'd been right about Will, pleasuring himself in her misery. She couldn't stand that. But before she could slip out of the kitchen, Charlie was beside her, saying, "It's

149

such a fine night, so many stars you couldn't count them if you took a year. Would you like to see them, Miss Nealie?"

"Of course she would," said Mrs. Travers, already reaching for Nealie's shawl and holding it out to her. "Go on, you've been inside all day. The air will do you good."

Nealie did not want to go, but she lacked the effort to say no. Besides, the cold might numb her. She wrapped the shawl around herself and put on her mittens and went outside with Charlie, out into the coldest night she had ever experienced in Georgetown. Charlie was right about the stars. They shone as bright as gas lamps, lighting the road. He took the girl's arm, and propelled her to the park, where they made their way across the snow-covered lawn to the bandstand. Charlie brushed off the bench, and Nealie sat down.

"Miss Nealie . . ." Charlie started, and then he was quiet for a long time, looking off toward the mountains. "Miss Nealie, I'd like to ask one more time if you would marry me."

And there it was, Nealie thought with a start, the answer to her problem. Charlie still wanted her to be his wife. She could marry Charlie Dumas, who wasn't such a bad sort and had never been anything but

150

nice to her. Charlie would provide for her, give her a home and the baby a name. He wouldn't know about the baby until it was too late. He might hate her then, blame her for tricking him, but at least she wouldn't have to give up the child. If Will came back later on, he'd be grateful she'd protected his baby, hadn't given it away.

Nealie sat there, silent as snow, for so long that Charlie said, "Miss Nealie?"

The girl looked up at the big man and smiled at him, and Charlie smiled back, sighing with gladness. But the girl couldn't do it. She felt as if someone had handed her a sack of candy, then snatched it away just as she reached for a piece. "You're a good man, Mr. Dumas," she said, thinking she ought to tell him she was sensible of the honor he bestowed on her, but this was no magazine story. "But I can't marry you. I'm what you might call —" She paused to think of the word. "A fallen woman."

"Don't call yourself that, Miss Nealie."

He didn't understand, and so she blurted it out. "I'm going to have a baby, and I can't marry the father because he's already got a wife. I didn't know it before, but he does."

Charlie looked at Nealie a long time, and she did not look away, because she had owned up to what she'd done and would not take a talking-down from him. At last, he told her, "I know."

Nealie stared at him while she considered what he'd said. And then she realized that Mrs. Travers had figured it out and taken things into her own hands. She had gone to Charlie and told him. "You'd marry me anyway?" she asked.

"I'd have married you even if you hadn't told me, but I'm glad you did."

"You don't mind I'm destroyed?"

"Oh, I mind. You can't put spilt water back in the cup. But that's the way of it."

"Will you hate the baby?"

"It's half yours, isn't it?"

The girl laughed for the first time in a long while.

"But I got something to ask of you, Miss Nealie . . . Nealie."

The girl tensed, waiting for him to continue.

"You got to promise me you'll never see him again. I don't blame you for what's happened, but I don't want you to make me out a fool. You got to promise me you won't see him. I don't even want his name spoke. And the baby, it'll have to think I'm its father."

The girl nodded. "He won't ever come back, and if he does, I won't have a thing to

152

do with him." But as she said the words, Nealie knew she didn't mean them. What if Will returned, all sorrowful, saying he'd had an awful time getting out of his marriage, begging her to forgive him? Could she ever say no to him, turn him down and spend the rest of her life with Charlie Dumas?

"And I want you to try to love me," he said.

"I care about you, Charlie."

The big man nodded as if that were good enough. "We'd better talk to the preacher pretty quick. I'm not for waiting. I guess you're not, either."

CHAPTER 6

Charlie needed time to make arrangements, he said, and so the two were not married until late on an afternoon two days later, with only Mrs. Travers standing up with them at the little Presbyterian church. After the ceremony, they went back to the board-inghouse for a special supper with a wedding cake and a bottle of champagne that Charlie had bought at the Hotel de Paris. Then Nealie changed into her green dress. Mrs. Travers had refused to allow Nealie to be married in it and had insisted on loaning her one of her own. "Marry in green, you're ashamed to be seen," she'd explained. "But marry in blue, you'll always be true." Nealie had taken the superstition seriously and had worn the blue dress, but Charlie said he preferred the green one, so Nealie promised to wear it home to Charlie's cabin.

"I guess we better get going," he said, after Mrs. Travers boxed up the remains of the cake and gave it to Nealie. Charlie picked up the dynamite box that contained his wife's things and held open the door for her. Then the two of them bid Mrs. Travers good-bye and went out.

Neither said a word as they walked down the street. Nealie had not been to Charlie's cabin, didn't even know where it was, and she hoped that it had a wood floor, not dirt, and a cookstove instead of an open fireplace. But she would make do with whatever was there, because she was determined to work out things with Charlie. She'd keep the place spotless, cook Charlie's meals, scrub his overalls. She owed him. Even if she didn't love him, she'd be as good a wife as she could.

She glanced at her new husband in his wrinkled clothes and guessed he was not a tidy person. So she would not be surprised to find the place a mess. Well, cleaning it would give her something to do, keep her thoughts away from what might have been. No matter how dirty the cabin was, she would make the best of it. She slid her eyes to Charlie, glancing at him with gratitude, if not love.

A man Nealie didn't know greeted Charlie, and he introduced her as "Mrs. Dumas." The girl grew flustered. She cast her eyes down then, not paying attention to where they walked, because she was embarrassed at the marriage and did not care to see anyone she knew, did not want to be congratulated or wondered about. And then Charlie said, "We're home now," and the girl looked up, surprised, because they had not gone far, maybe only a block or two. Her husband pointed to the big white house on Taos Street, the bride's house — the house she'd dreamed of occupying as Will's bride, not Charlie's. "What's this?" she asked.

"Are you surprised?"

"That's your house?" She thought Charlie had made a poor joke.

"*Our* house," he said. "I bought it yesterday. You called it a bride's house once, and you're a bride, aren't you?" Charlie led her across the walk and up onto the porch. Then he picked her up and carried her inside the house that Nealie could not help thinking was rightly Will's.

Nealie hadn't known Charlie had money. Nobody had. "There's too many people would try to get it away from me," Charlie explained. Besides, he'd had simple needs. There was no reason to spend the money until he married Nealie, he told her.

Charlie had made a good strike in Lead-ville a few years before, had discovered a silver mine and sold out. He'd studied on it later and decided it had been a mistake to sell, he explained to his new wife, but he hadn't had the cash to develop it, so there was nothing else he could have done. He'd gone back to work as a miner, saying he ought to know a mine before he put his money into it. So after working at the Bobcat for a time, he'd bought shares in it. Then he'd found his own promising pros-pect near Georgetown, filed a claim, and contacted a big mining company about forming a partnership to develop it. Even if he'd had the money to build the mine by himself, he wouldn't have, he explained. "I don't want to put all my eggs in one basket, like the fellow says. That's why I invest. I own shares in seven mines. I guess those fellows at the 'Cat would be surprised if they knew they were working for me."

"Well, if you don't hurry, you'll be late, and you'll get laid off there," Nealie told him. They were eating breakfast the morn-ing after the wedding, and Charlie had dawdled, smiling shyly at his new wife. Nealie bit her lip and looked away when he caught her eye, blushing, not because she was embarrassed but because she didn't want him to talk about their wedding night. It was not a thing to be discussed. She'd been willing — after all, she was his wife and grateful to him — and it had gone all right, although Charlie was bumbling and unskilled, not at all like Will. She couldn't help but think about Will when Charlie thrashed around in bed. But Charlie was kind and did not want to hurt her, and it had not gone badly. "I forgot all about your dinner bucket. I hope you put something in the pantry for it," she added, jumping up. Charlie had stocked the kitchen before the wedding, moving everything from his cabin into the Bride's House.

He grabbed her arm. "I quit the mine. You won't ever have to pack a dinner pail again."

"Quit? How'll we live if you don't bring in wages?" She'd never heard of dividends and did not know that Charlie would get a return on his shares.

"Investments. They pay money. I'll be an investment man. I always did have a way of picking a winner." He grinned at Nealie, and she knew he wasn't talking just about mines. "I'm going to turn the front parlor into an office, so I can study more about the mines, have a place besides the saloon to talk to men who want me to invest. And I can be here near you. If you need anything, all you got to do is yell 'Charlie.' "

"Oh my," Nealie said. She hadn't thought about Charlie being around all day and didn't know if she liked the idea. She thought of Will coming to the door and Charlie, not her, opening it. "Oh my."

"Fact is, you need help hanging up a picture or carrying in kindling, you just yell 'Charlie.' " He thought about that a moment. "But you don't need to worry about the kindling, because we'll find us a hired girl."

"But I'm a hired girl."

"Not anymore. You're Mrs. Charlie Dumas. You're a lady now."

And a lady, Charlie told her after she ground more beans for coffee and brewed a second batch, had to decorate her house — the Bride's House; they decided that would be its formal name. It had not come furnished. Mrs. Travers had loaned Charlie some of her dishes and cookware so that they could eat for a few days, while Charlie had moved a cot from his cabin into the upstairs bedroom. The only other furniture was the crate Charlie had set up in the dining room for a table and two stools.

Now as they sat there over breakfast, Nealie looked around the dining room and announced, "I want yellow wallpaper in this room, yellow and gold. Could we do that, Charlie? Could we?"

"Any color you want. We could make every room a different color. What would you say to that?"

Nealie clapped her hands. "Blue for the bedroom. Red for the parlor." Then she added, "Gray for the front parlor," because she remembered Will saying once that he liked a room papered in gray.

But Charlie shook his head. "Green for my office, green like your dress. And we'll have to buy a bed and a table, a desk, everything. What do you say we go to Denver for it?"

"Today? Could we go today?"

Charlie shrugged. " 'Course we could. I'm not on shift anymore."

The train ride to Denver was far different from Nealie's trip to Georgetown in the spring. She was not a runaway girl, but the wife of a mining investor. She said that over and over to herself, "Mining investor, mining investor," so that she could remark on it in an offhand way if someone asked her about Charlie.

She was repeating it in her mind at the depot when Charlie left her to buy tickets

160

and a clerk from the hardware store greeted her. "Hello, Miss Nealie."

"It's not Miss Nealie anymore. I'm Mrs. Charlie Dumas now. My husband's a mining investor," she replied. She liked the way she said it, not bragging but firmly, so that the man knew her husband was important.

"You mean old Charlie that works at the Bobcat?"

"The same, only he doesn't set charges anymore. He's a mining investor."

The man only laughed. "Well, who in Georgetown isn't?"

As she waited for Charlie, Nealie looked around the station. She loved the bustle of the depot — Will had, too, when she'd taken him there — loved wondering about the people, why they had come to Georgetown or were leaving it. Somebody might even be wondering about her, so she stood with her back straight, her head a little too high, not catching anyone's eye, until Charlie claimed her, and they boarded the train. Nealie had ridden a train only once before, on her trip from Missouri to Georgetown, and she had been so frightened someone would come after her and drag her back home that she'd paid no attention to the scenery, but now she stared out the window, asking Charlie a thousand questions about the mines they passed, the towns.

"That's Red Elephant," he told her. "I got a share or two in that mine." The name sounded familiar, and then Nealie remembered that Mrs. Travers had gone to Red Elephant on the Fourth of July, the night that she and Will . . . Nealie wondered if Will would always sneak into her mind like that.

She didn't want to think about him now, however. So she chatted about the freight wagons on the roads up the mountainsides, guessing at what they carried. She tried to see through the windows of the houses and speculated about the people who lived in them, thinking that someday people would stare at the Bride's House and wonder about her. She marveled at how fast the train ran. It seemed she had just settled down for the trip when they arrived in Denver and they climbed down the steps into a huge station.

"I've been here before," she said, trying to sound sure of herself. "I stopped here before I went to Georgetown, after I left Missouri."

"Missouri? I didn't know you came from Missouri."

"And I'm never going back, so don't you think about it."

"Who said I'd send you back? I wouldn't

go back where I came from, but there's no reason. I got no family myself."

Nealie hadn't known that. There was so much they had to learn about each other. It was odd that they were married and they'd never told each other about their families. But then, she'd have married Will, and she'd known even less about him, as it turned out. Nealie had been wed only a day, and already she found marriage a strange thing. There was so much she didn't know.

She'd learned already that Charlie wouldn't put up with certain things. He was sweet and loving, and it seemed that he would give her most anything she wanted, but he expected her to behave herself and to act like a lady. On the train, when she'd pulled her skirt above her ankles so that it wouldn't drag on the floor with the cigar stubs and tobacco spit, he'd pushed it down. And when a man in the depot smiled at her and she'd smiled back, Charlie had told her she oughtn't to be so free with herself now that she was his wife.

Nealie wanted to look around the station in Denver, which was so much bigger than the one in Georgetown, but Charlie hurried her out and found a hack, asking the driver to take them to a store Mrs. Travers had recommended, not that the older woman had ever been to it. She'd heard it was a good place to purchase furniture. A doorman ushered them inside, and Nealie gaped, because the place was as elegant as the Hotel de Paris, with polished furniture upholstered in plush, with tables and chairs, draperies and wall coverings, as far as she could see. She thought that it was the sort of place where Will would shop — and his wife. She glanced at Charlie, wondering if the clerks would recognize them as only a hired girl and a miner and ask what they were doing there.

But in those strike-it-rich times, they were not the first couple with newfound money to enter the store, and there was a certain eagerness about them that made the employees all but rub their hands together. Within seconds, they were taken up and asked about their needs. "We want the very best," Charlie said. "I can pay for it."

And so they were shown the wallpapers and fabrics, the mahogany love seats and chairs, the tables and fern stands, velvet drapes and lace curtains, and a hundred useless baubles. They were not taken in so much as they might have been, however. Nealie had always been frugal, and Charlie saw no need to pay more because a piece of furniture had a manufacturer's name attached to it. At the last minute, Nealie asked if they could get a better price because they had bought so much. When Charlie frowned, she wondered if she'd embarrassed him, but the clerks agreed, and then Charlie seemed pleased at her bargaining.

They ordered yellow wallpaper with a gold Chinese design for the dining room, gold velvet drapes, thin wooden shutters, and a Persian carpet. The mahogany dining table came with twelve chairs upholstered in gold plush. The parlor was all red — red wallpaper, with two horsehair love seats and side chairs trimmed in red velvet, an ingrain carpet in red and orange, a red cloth with gold tassels for the library table. They bought the library table, too, and a stereopticon to go on top of it. Then Nealie selected a pianoforte, a huge square instrument with carved legs, and a matching stool

Since carpets and drapes did not come in the bright green of Nealie's dress, she begged Charlie to use the yellow wallpaper in his study, and they bought matching drapes and lace curtains. Charlie selected a desk the size of a cookstove and cabinets with glass doors and hidden compartments in the bottom. Then they ordered a great brass bed made of pipes that gleamed like sunshine and curved in all directions and walnut dressers and wardrobes.

As they were about to leave, Nealie whispered something to Charlie, and he turned to the clerks. "There's another thing we'll be needing," he said, while Nealie turned away. "A cradle. I expect you could sell us a cradle."

The clerks took them into a side room where cradles and small beds, tiny chairs and high chairs, were displayed. "Which one?" Charlie asked.

Nealie studied the cradles, then pointed to one that was small, made of a light wood that reminded her of the desk in Will's cabin. But Charlie shook his head. "You don't want to bend all the way over to pick up the baby. You'll hurt your back." When Nealie looked at him in surprise, for she hadn't thought about such a thing, he said, "That's what you learn working in a mine."

They left the store pleased with themselves, a little proud of their good taste. "You picked us some pretty things," Charlie told her.

Nealie smiled at him. "I'm glad you like them," she said. But she had been thinking about Will when she chose them.

Once the walls were painted and papered, the floor carpeted, the furniture set in place, the palm trees and ferns and other potted plants arranged in the solarium, Nealie announced she would give a tea. That was what the ladies in Hannibal did. She ordered a silver tea set and two dozen china plates and teacups with pink roses on them and sent out invitations that she ordered from the newspaper office. She'd read about printed invitations in one of Mrs. Travers's magazines and thought that was a swell idea. Then she and Mrs. Travers baked pies and cakes in the new cookstove.

"Do you think they'll come?" Nealie asked Charlie as she waited in the red parlor the afternoon of the tea. "Maybe they think I'm fresh for asking them. Maybe they won't want to come out in the snow." She stood looking into a mirror at herself in the dress that Charlie had bought for her as a surprise. He didn't know maroon was a color that made her skin look pasty or that the style emphasized her pregnancy. Nealie didn't know it, either. "I listened, but I didn't hear a rooster crow three times." She added in case Charlie didn't understand, "That means you'll have company. But I didn't hear a rooster at all." She wrung her hands together with nervousness.

"That's because they've all had their heads chopped off. You can't keep a rooster in Georgetown in the winter," Mrs. Travers said, coming in from the kitchen and standing beside Nealie at the front door. "They'll come, all right. It's just the snow makes them late. Now you run along, Charlie. Husbands aren't supposed to be hanging around for teas."

He clumped out of the house then, looking up and down the street for guests, not knowing it was fashionable to be late. Nor did Nealie, who was frantic until at last the bell on the door clanged, and she answered it, saying, "Well, do come in," in a shrill, nervous voice. "Welcome to the Bride's House."

Within minutes, the house was filled. None of the women invited would have dreamed of staying away, because they had seen the delivery wagons loaded with crates of furniture and were curious about the Bride's House. They were curious about Nealie, too. There had been much talk about the miner and the hired girl who had bought the magnificent place. Some gazed at the rich furnishings in awe and not a little envy, because they had never seen such splendors in a private home. Not only was the house filled with expensive furniture, but every side table was covered with tasseled silk shawls on which were set knickknacks — china figurines and ore samples, nut dishes and marble eggs, the stereopticon, and dried flowers under a glass dome. A few guests rolled their eyes, and Nealie overheard a woman mutter, "Tawdry."

That sounded fine, and she said, "Thank you," not knowing what the word meant, of course. Another remarked that standing in the red parlor, she felt she was inside a love apple. Nealie wasn't aware a love apple was a tomato, and she thought that a fine compliment, too.

If Mrs. Travers overheard any words of scorn, she kept them to herself. Nor did the older woman remark that while the women accepted plates of gingerbread and dried-apple pie, they ate only a bite or two. She had suggested earlier that Nealie might want to order tiny pastries from the Hotel de Paris for the women to nibble on, but Nealie had replied that she didn't want her guests going home as hungry as barn cats.

Not all of the guests were critical, of course. Nealie wasn't the first hired girl who had married well, and for the most part, Georgetown was an accepting place. "You come and call on me," one woman told Nealie as she departed, handing the girl her card. Nealie didn't know about calling cards and thought she should have some made up for herself. Another woman said, "You'd be welcome at the missionary society at the Presbyterian church. We knit for the heathen."

"I got my house to keep up," Nealie replied.

"By yourself?"

"I wouldn't let anybody else touch it."

The woman didn't remark on that, because many of the newly rich were eccentric.

Charlie returned after the guests left, as Nealie and Mrs. Travers were clearing away the dishes. He, too, had wondered why Nealie didn't find a hired girl, but she'd told him it was her house, and she didn't want anybody getting in her way. She took pleasure in the fine cookstove and the icebox that the iceman filled with blocks of ice each week. She said that with the hand pump that was mounted on the sink, there wasn't a thing to washing the dishes, and she loved drying the plates and cups, making them shine.

Nealie's eyes sparkled when she told her husband about the tea. "They said my apple pie was the best they ever tasted, and three ladies asked could they have starts of my ferns. I got so many compliments on my decorating I thought I'd bust," she told him.

"Oh, Charlie, you'd be so proud! One lady said the house was . . . what was that word, Mrs. Travers?"

"Toney. I think it was 'toney.'"

That didn't sound right to Nealie, but she nodded and chattered away to Charlie, describing how the women wore their best silks and velvets, their bonnets trimmed with lace veils and birds' wings, and how they exclaimed over all her pretty things. "It was toney, all right." When she stopped for breath, Charlie hugged her, and she hugged him back, forgetting for a moment that it was Will, not Charlie, she'd thought about when she'd planned the entertainment.

The women began to wash the dishes, chattering over Nealie's triumph, and Charlie left the house, wandering up to Alpine Street to buy tobacco at the Kaiser Mercantile, proud of the way his wife had held her own with Georgetown society. The store was crowded, and he was in no hurry, so he looked at the stock of gold pans and picks, the stacks of yard goods and clothing, and cans of tomatoes and peas and beans lined up on the shelves. He liked the orderliness of the place, because despite his rumpled clothing, Charlie was a tidy man. A stove stood in the center of the room, and Charlie held out his hands to its warmth, because

171

he had left the house without a coat, and it had snowed that morning. He stood there, half hidden by the stovepipe, smiling a little, basking in Nealie's happiness.

And then he heard someone speak his wife's name and mutter, "Hired girl." His smile faded as he listened to the woman continue, "Honestly, Jim, you would laugh if you saw it. One room was all in red — red, for heaven's sake. And the dining room was hopeless. We all know he dabbles in gold mines, but does she have to spread it all over the walls and the windows? There's a piano, and what do you bet she doesn't know a sharp from a flat!" The woman laughed, then said, "Her tongue wags at both ends. She could talk the leg off a chair." She added something in a low voice to the man beside her, and he laughed. "She's been married only three months, but from the looks of her, she's six months along. If we were anyplace else, a person like that wouldn't be accepted in society. It's scandalous. Why, do you know —" The woman stopped suddenly when she spotted Charlie. "Why, Mr. Dumas, I just came from —"

"I heard where you came from." Charlie turned to the man. "Say, Jim, is she your wife?" When the man nodded, Charlie said,

"I want you to step outside with me."

The man started to protest, but when he saw the look on Charlie's face, he exchanged glances with his wife and followed Charlie through the door onto the board sidewalk. Charlie turned to face him, looking down on the man, because Charlie was half a head taller. "You still work at the Bobcat? I haven't been up there in a while," Charlie said.

The man nodded. "Charlie, my wife didn't mean —"

"It's Mr. Dumas. I'm one of the men that owns the Bobcat, so you can call me Mr. Dumas. I guess you could say I'm your boss." Jim would have known that, of course. Few in Georgetown weren't aware that Charlie Dumas had come into money and was now a mining speculator. In fact, already men were seeking him out not just because he was rich but because of his knowledge. Unlike many of the Eastern investors who'd never been underground, Charlie knew all about mining, knew when a claim had been salted or a vein was about to pinch out. He understood a mine was no good if there wasn't a mill or smelter nearby or a railroad to ship out the ore. He could tell when a mine was dangerous from lack of ventilation or shoddy timbering or when it might flood from underground water.

"Mr. Dumas, I'm sorry —"

"Shut up," Charlie said. He stared at Jim a moment, then said slowly, softly, "I never held a thing against a man because of his wife." Jim looked relieved at the words, but then, Charlie continued. "Here's the thing of it. I couldn't hit a woman, wouldn't ever do it, not even if she made me as mad as a yellow jacket, like your wife just did. Mrs. Dumas never did a thing to your missus, but just asked her to have a cup of tea, and your wife insulted her in the worst way. A man can't stand by when that happens. So, I guess this is the only thing I can do." Charlie made a fist and swung, hitting the man in the jaw, punching him as hard as if he'd been hit by an ore cart. Jim's feet went out from under him, and he flew backward off the boardwalk, landing on his back in the muddy street. Charlie stepped down into the street next to him, bent over, hitting the fist of one hand into the palm of the other, but Jim didn't get up. "Now you hear me good. If I ever hear of you or your missus saying a word against Mrs. Dumas, I'll ask you to get your wages and get gone. Do you hear me?" When the man didn't answer right away, Charlie thundered, "Well, do you?"

"I hear you."

Charlie nodded then and put down his hands. He turned to the men who'd gathered outside the store to see what was going on and looked at each one. They'd heard. They knew he wouldn't stand for anyone speaking against Nealie. They knew what he'd do. Charlie waited a moment, perhaps to see if anyone would challenge him. And then one of the men said, "Hello, Charlie," and the others relaxed and shuffled back into the store. The story got about pretty quick, and before long, everybody in Georgetown knew better than to gossip about Nealie Dumas.

Charlie went on home then, waiting on the porch for a few minutes to calm down, reaching into his pocket for his pipe, but he had forgotten to buy the tobacco. Nealie heard him and opened the door and said grandly, "Welcome to the Bride's House, Mr. Dumas." He never said a word to her about what had taken place at the store. And while Nealie found out later on that Charlie had tromped a man the day of her tea, she never knew the cause of it.

That was Nealie's only party in the Bride's House, because she was sensible of her condition and had read in a magazine that

175

women in the latter stages of pregnancy were not to be seen in society. She was content those last months to remain inside the house, building a nest, as Mrs. Travers put it. Each day, she cleaned the Bride's House, waxing the floors, oiling the woodwork, sweeping the carpets. She gloried in the house and kept it as clean as a hymn. The Bride's House was magical, and Nealie could not believe that such a magnificent place was hers. She never tired of wandering through its rooms, examining the house with awe. A dozen times a day, she drew aside the lace curtains to peer at Sunrise Peak or stood in the front hall admiring the staircase that curved up to the bedrooms.

She rarely left the house except to go to the Kaiser Mercantile to buy groceries, and she loved walking home, stopping on the walk beside where she would plant the lilac hedge — Charlie had ordered the bushes — staring at the house and knowing it was hers. Sometimes, as spring came on, she walked a little, stopping to visit Mrs. Travers, and once she stopped for the mail. Charlie always went for it in the afternoons, complaining sometimes that he couldn't walk a block without someone stopping him to swap gossip about the mines, to ask his advice. She thought he'd be pleased she'd saved him a trip to the post office. When she handed him his letters, however, Charlie frowned at her and asked in a harsh voice, "What are you doing with the mail? You got no business picking up my mail."

He never raised his voice to her, and Nealie was taken aback. "I thought you'd be pleased."

"Pleased? The mail's mine. Don't you ever do it again."

Nealie stared at Charlie a moment, confused, and then she understood. Charlie was afraid that Will would write to her. He picked up the mail just in case there was a letter from Will. And maybe there had been. Maybe Will had written to her, and Charlie had torn up the letter. What if Will had sent her a letter saying he was coming for her?

Nealie stared at her husband for a long time, wanting to ask if Will had written. And Charlie stared back at her, perhaps waiting for her to ask. Nealie knew she couldn't, however. She'd promised never to mention his name. So she bowed her head and left the room and never again went for the mail.

As she neared her time, Nealie took to sitting in a little rocker in the upstairs hallway, stitching baby things and staring through the lace curtain at the falling snow, although it was spring. She had never been a needle-woman, but she liked rocking back and forth, thinking, feeling the baby move inside her, dreaming that someday, Will would come back. She would answer the door, dressed in gray silk, and she would say, "How nice to see you, Mr. Spaulding," and hold out her hand. Will would find her elegant and refined, and see how she had come up in the world. He would be impressed with the house, the gardens, and he would ask to see the baby, and it would break his heart. Will would cry because of the way he had treated her. She would forgive him, and he would beg her to go away with him. The dream always turned fuzzy then, and Nealie was never sure how it ended. But the dream never went away. She was thinking about Will when the first labor pain hit her.

Nealie smelled lilacs. But it was too early for lilacs, and besides, the bushes hadn't even been planted. They were her favorite flowers. That was why Charlie had ordered two dozen bushes to be set around the Bride's House. She opened her eyes to the light flooding into the bedroom and looked around. The curtain was open and the window, and through it was the view she'd come to love of Sunrise Peak, its summit dusted with snow. Nealie turned her head a little and saw the lilacs then, a bouquet as big as a sagebush, sitting on the table beyond the baby's cradle. She inhaled the fragrance as she glanced at the sleeping infant, satisfied.

The labor had been a hard one, and long. Charlie had fetched Mrs. Travers when it started, and the woman stayed with Nealie through the night, and the next day. "The boarders will understand, and if they don't, they can eat their shoes," she said. During the second night, Mrs. Travers called in another woman to help, because the delivery was worse than anything she had seen before. They made the girl drink water in which eggshells had been boiled and placed scissors and shoes upside down under the bed to ease the birthing, and the second woman remarked that she didn't understand why Nealie was having so much trouble, because the girl had slender ankles, a sure sign of an easy delivery. But it hadn't been easy, and the two women were afraid Nealie would be torn apart before the baby was born.

The baby came at last, but neither woman had been able to stop the bleeding, so Charlie had gone for the doctor. Nealie remembered the doctor, but when was that —

yesterday or the day before? She had been so tired that she'd slept, and now time was unclear in her mind.

Charlie had stayed with her during her labor, she remembered, holding her hand, telling her it would be over soon. "Now most men, they won't go in a birthing room. They'll pace the floor or go to the saloon and get drunk, but Charlie Dumas, why, we couldn't get rid of him with a stick," Mrs. Travers told Nealie.

And then the baby pushed its way out of her, and she screamed with the pain. She thought of Will and cursed him silently, because she couldn't say his name out loud. Finally, it was over. Mrs. Travers told her the infant was just a little chunk of a baby, too small to give Nealie all that trouble, but Charlie said she was just right, the prettiest thing he'd ever seen. He held her up, still wet, her hair slicked down on her head, so that Nealie could see her.

"Red hair. Fancy hair. She's the spit of you," he said, to Nealie's relief, because she had feared the baby would resemble Will. "We'll call her Little Nealie."

"No," Nealie replied. "I don't want to call her that. Her name is Pearl." She didn't know why she blurted out the name like that. She had been so sure she'd have a boy, one she'd name George for the town, that she hadn't considered a girl's name. She remembered that Will told her once that he fancied the name Pearl, and after all, it was his baby. Charlie didn't need to know about the name, of course.

Now as Nealie looked at the infant, sleeping with her little fist against her mouth, she decided Pearl was just right, because the infant was as smooth and pink as a pearl.

She wanted to hold the baby and tried to sit up, but she was weak, and so she lay there and watched the sun creep into the room, feeling its warmth on her face, which was flushed and fevered. Her hair, which had darkened during her pregnancy, was curly from the damp of perspiration. She felt lethargic, but happy. Charlie came into the room then with Mrs. Travers, telling Nealie he'd engaged the older woman to care for her and the child until Nealie was stronger. And Mrs. Travers had found a wet nurse.

"I told the boarders they could eat at the hotel if they wanted to," Mrs. Travers said, then added, "Not a one of them complained when I said I was taking care of you and your baby."

Nealie hadn't expected happiness with Charlie, and it had come as a surprise. He was a good man. She'd thought that after a time, after they were settled in, he might change, that he'd resent her, might even beat her as her father had her mother, but he'd never once touched her except in tenderness. He brought her presents — perfume, a nightgown with lace on it, a pair of kid slippers. When Nealie's legs cramped in the night, due to some quirk in her pregnancy, Charlie had rubbed them. And as the baby inside her grew so big that she had trouble sleeping, Charlie would go to the kitchen and bring her back a cup of hot chocolate. Then he'd sit beside her in his nightshirt and read to her from a mining book until she was so bored that she fell asleep.

"You've been asleep for two days," Charlie told her.

"Two days? I'm as lazy as a chicken." She pushed the covers aside and moved her legs, and when she looked down, she saw that both her nightgown and the bed were soaked in blood.

Mrs. Travers saw it, too. "Get the doctor. She's still sick from the bornin'," she ordered Charlie, who rushed out. After she staunched the bleeding, the older woman went to the cradle and picked up Pearl, handing her to Nealie. But Nealie was not strong enough to hold the baby, so Mrs. Travers laid the tiny creature beside her mother, and Nealie slipped her finger into Pearl's fist.

"She has a favorance to you, not Charlie," Mrs. Travers said. "Why, you'd think you produced her all by yourself." Nealie barely nodded, and the older woman continued talking. "Did you see the lilacs? Charlie sent all the way to Denver for them. They're blooming down below now, even though they haven't yet budded out up here. They came in on the train. I guess there's not a thing your husband wouldn't do for you. Marrying him was a stroke of luck." Lidie Travers's voice was almost hysterical, the way she carried on, talking to keep both their minds off the hemorrhaging.

"I guess I ought to thank you for that. I never told you I was grateful, you telling him about me," Nealie whispered.

"You're acting druggy," Mrs. Travers told her. "Now don't say another word. Charlie will skin me if I let you get bad-sick."

"Am I bad off?"

Mrs. Travers looked down at the baby, whose mouth was twisting about, and in a minute Pearl opened her eyes.

"Am I?" Nealie persisted.

183

"I don't know about such things, but it looks to me like you're a long way from heaven's gate. Now you rest or you'll be dwindling away."

Nealie heard Charlie downstairs, and in a minute he was in the room, followed by the doctor, who went to Nealie and examined her. The bleeding had started again, and he asked Nealie how long it had gone on. The girl didn't know, so the doctor questioned Mrs. Travers. He poked and prodded and examined Nealie, then turned his back to her and spoke quietly to Charlie.

"Am I going to die?" Nealie asked.

The two men looked at each other. Then Charlie nodded once at the doctor, saying his wife had the right to know. He broke into great, racking sobs then, so the doctor went to the bed and took Nealie's hand and told her she'd be in heaven before the day ended.

Nealie thought about that a long time, and then she told Charlie she wanted to see the preacher. "You fetch him," she said in a weak voice.

"I'll get him," the doctor offered, but Nealie said she wanted Charlie to go. So because dying people often didn't make sense, the doctor nodded at Charlie, who left the room, the doctor behind him. Nealie listened as they went down the stairs and out the front door. Then she turned to Mrs. Travers and said, "I want a paper and an envelope. I got to write something before Charlie comes back."

"If it's a will and testament, I'll witness it," Mrs. Travers said, but Nealie shook her head. Mrs. Travers brought the writing materials and helped Nealie dip the pen into the bottle of ink. Then Nealie began a letter. It wasn't long, just a few sentences, because she was too weak to write any more. When she was finished, she put the paper into the envelope and wrote "Will" on it, handing it to Mrs. Travers. "You make sure he gets it. But don't tell Charlie." Then she lay back on the pillow, exhausted.

Nealie was lying there, weak, her mind a little cloudy, when she heard the front door and whispered, "Will?"

"Hush. It's Charlie. It's your husband," Mrs. Travers said.

Charlie rushed up the stairs and sat down on the bed beside Nealie, taking her hand, not talking, until the preacher arrived a few minutes later. Then Charlie stood and went to the window and stared down into the yard. The big man was not graceful, and his shoulders shook a little as he reached out to the wall to support himself.

The minister studied Nealie, a look of sadness on his face, because he was young and not yet used to ministering to the needs of those dying before their time. He opened his Bible and read a verse that began, "I will lift up mine eyes unto the hills." And then he took Nealie's hands and said a prayer.

"I'm going to die," Nealie murmured.

The preacher looked at Charlie, who turned, his hand still held awkwardly against the wall, and nodded once. "It's God's will," the minister told her, and Nealie felt a great sadness, because she did not want to think God had decided she should go. But then her mind moved on, and in a minute, she was thinking about the lilacs, not the lilacs in the room but the ones that would bloom beside the house.

"I will stay if you like," the minister said.

Charlie told him no. "I'd like to be alone with her," he said, and the preacher nodded and left. Mrs. Travers went, too. Charlie talked to Nealie in a low voice, but the words didn't make sense, and after a time, she stopped listening.

Once, she roused herself and said, "I love you." She wasn't sure who she was talking to.

"I know," Charlie replied, as if he never

doubted that she meant him.

Her hands slowly weakened in his, and she no longer grasped him. Then she took a deep breath and opened her eyes and said, "Take care of my baby."

"*Our* baby," Charlie said, and leaned over and kissed her. He sat quietly, his young wife's hands in his, until Nealie's spirit took leave of her.

■ ■ ■ ■ ■

PART II
PEARL

■ ■ ■ ■ ■

CHAPTER 7

When Pearl Dumas was ten, a man she did not know called at her home. Her father took the stranger into the study and closed the doors, but the girl overheard the conversation. She didn't understand it then. She never understood it, but she remembered it.

The man had come to the door in early summer, because the conversation was entwined in Pearl's memory with the smell of lilacs, and lilacs bloomed in Georgetown at the end of June. Her father had planted the bushes the summer she was born, just after her mother died. That was the first year he'd lived in the Bride's House, which was what people in Georgetown called the place, not the Dumas mansion but the Bride's House. That summer morning when the man came, the long row of lilacs on the side of the house filled the rooms with fragrance.

The front door stood open, so the man knocked on the screen. "I'm looking for

Mrs. Travers," he said, when Pearl answered the door. He was handsome, trimmer than her father and about his age; his hair was streaked with a few threads of gray — silver, really — and he was well dressed. "I called at her little house on Rose Street where she used to take boarders, but a woman there directed me here."

In fact, Lidie Travers had lived in the big white house on Taos Street since Pearl was born and had never again taken in boarders. Charlie had hired her as a housekeeper and nurse for the baby after Nealie died, and she had stayed on and now was as much a part of the household as Pearl and her father. Although she was charged with raising up the child, Mrs. Travers had not played the role of a mother. Instead, she was more of a confidante to the motherless girl.

Whenever Pearl wanted to know a thing about Nealie, she asked Mrs. Travers. Her father, Pearl knew, viewed the dead Nealie through a kind of veil, and his answers to Pearl's questions painted Nealie as more saint than young woman. When the girl asked if Nealie could sew, for instance, Charlie replied that Nealie could have been a dressmaker to the Queen of England. Mrs. Travers, on the other hand, scoffed and said that Nealie liked to choose fabric well enough, and she had good intentions, but she was too impatient to sew a good seam and couldn't have made a buttonhole if you'd given her a pouch of gold dust. "She helped me with a quilt once, and I had to unsew her portion," Mrs. Travers confided to the girl.

Pearl knew a great deal about her mother, because Mrs. Travers insisted on telling her about Nealie. Such talk was unusual in that time, when many thought it was unseemly to mention the dead, that the girl would not miss her mother if the woman's name were never spoken. But Mrs. Travers thought it best that Pearl know her mother as a flesh-and-blood person, not the ethereal presence that lived on in Charlie's mind — *Saint* Nealie, as the housekeeper sometimes referred to her, although not in Charlie's presence. The housekeeper ordered up an oil portrait of Nealie, made from a photograph, to hang in the parlor. A second photograph, framed in silver, had been propped on Pearl's bedside table for as long as the girl could remember. Mrs. Travers chatted about Nealie as if she weren't dead at all but only out on an errand, telling the girl about the green dress her mother had made when she first moved to Georgetown.

"You could see it from here to town," she said. And when Pearl teased for a kitten, Mrs. Travers explained that Nealie feared cats. "She said they'd get in your bed at night and suck the breath out of you. So your father does her honor by not bringing a kitten into the house." Pearl was obedient and did not ask again, although she was not taken with superstition and thought her mother's reasoning silly.

Her father insisted that the house be kept exactly as Nealie had left it, a kind of shrine to his dead wife, and the girl grew up knowing that everything around her had been selected by her mother, was a reminder of her mother. She formed her impression of Nealie through those things. Charlie had left Nealie's clothes hanging in the closet, her hats in boxes on the shelves, her nightclothes and undergarments in the bedroom drawers, her brush and mirror, hatpins, hair receiver, perfume bottle, even her ribbons and gloves neatly arranged on the dresser.

Pearl would go into the bedroom when her father was out and run the brush through her hair, so like Nealie's. She would stare at the clothes, feel the fabrics, the silks like tissue paper, the velvets warm in her hands. She never tried on the clothes. They were Nealie's and precious, and her father

194

would not have liked it.

More than the clothes, the house told her about Nealie. Her mother had loved bright colors, and she had taken delight in bric-a-brac, such as the china figurines that Pearl supposed resembled her mother. When she was anxious, Pearl would pick up Nealie's marble eggs from the table, holding one in each hand, because they were cool and smooth, and soothed her. She liked to study the dead bird mounted under a glass dome, wonder where it had been shot, or maybe someone had strangled it. One glass eye was gone, making the bird appear to be blind in that eye, and feathers had come loose, but she knew that even if the bird molted until it was as bare as a plucked chicken, it would stay under that glass dome on the table.

Nealie had loved red, and the girl wondered about that. Even at a young age, Pearl was aware that red made a red-haired woman look like a wax doll. But maybe Nealie was different. Perhaps the red room had given her fire, something Pearl knew she lacked. Mrs. Travers told her how Nealie had taken pleasure in the kitchen with its icebox and hand pump. Why, she wouldn't let anybody else step inside the room if she could help it, Mrs. Travers said. Even when she was far gone in pregnancy, Nealie refused to have hired help. Pearl knew that that was why she and Mrs. Travers did not have a hired girl to help them keep up the house now.

But it was the lilac hedge that brought Pearl closest to her mother, and that was odd, because Nealie had never smelled those lilacs. As a little girl, Pearl sat under the hedge with her dolls, named Nealie and Charlie, and played that both were alive, and that the three of them lived in the Bride's House. Sometimes, she pretended the house was her own, that the combs and ribbons were hers, the elegant gowns, that she looked like the grown-up woman in the painting. As she lay in her bed at night smelling the lilacs, Pearl knew she lived in the most wonderful house in Georgetown, maybe the world.

They were comfortable there, the three of them, although Mrs. Travers said often enough, "You ought to marry again, Charlie. Pearl should have a real mother instead of a poor old housekeeper." But Charlie always replied that there would never be another woman for him, that no woman was good enough to take Nealie's place. After a time, Mrs. Travers gave it up, because it was clear that Charlie would never get out of heart with Nealie. Besides, it was obvious

196

that the woman liked living in the Bride's House and delighted in her position as the employee of a successful mining entrepreneur, and she must have known a new wife might insist the old woman go. If the truth be told, the girl, too, wondered if Charlie's remarriage would spoil things, because she did not want anything to change. A new mother, she realized, would put away Nealie's possessions, throw out the molting bird and the dried flowers that had turned paper thin and brittle. The memories of Nealie would fade. And if her father married, he might have other children, and the girl relished her place as an only child, her father's favorite companion.

It was clear even to Pearl, who was not an especially perceptive child, that her father was inordinately fond of her. He hired a dressmaker once a year to make clothes for her, including a boy's jumper and work shirts, because he often took her along when he made visits to the mines. He oversaw her education and considered sending her off to finishing school, but he could not bear to be parted from her. If the girl expressed a desire for a toy or a book, Charlie ordered it for her.

Spoon-fed though she was, Pearl was neither greedy nor spoiled, however, and she asked for little. The girl did not place a high value on possessions. She was content with the things her mother had left behind. She reserved her affection for her father and the housekeeper. Her devotion to her father was complete, and she suffered mightily when she offended him. Her greatest wish was to make her father proud of her, and her greatest happiness came when he compared her to Nealie, because Peal knew he grieved yet for her mother. It delighted the girl that she looked like Nealie. She did not know that in making herself agreeable — by being placid, it might be said — she lost that quality that made Nealie intriguing. Pearl overheard Mrs. Travers tell a friend once, "She's good as can be, but she's not a gaily girl like Nealie was."

"Aunt Lidie's not here just now," the girl said as the stranger peered into the foyer, which was dark, and in the darkness, the girl was only a shape.

"Is this a boardinghouse?" he asked.

The girl laughed at such an assumption. "Just for Papa and me. Aunt Lidie takes care of us."

"I was her boarder a long time ago," the man said.

"So was Papa. He's here. Do you want to

see Papa?" The girl opened the screen door so that the light flooded in, and the man stared at her, startled.

"You," he said.

"Yes?" Pearl answered, confused. She touched the cameo that had belonged to her mother. It was Pearl's favorite piece of jewelry. She had replaced its ribbon three times, and fingered the piece so much that the gilt had worn off in places, revealing the pot metal beneath.

The man's eyes widened when he saw the necklace. He stared at it a long time before returning his gaze to the girl's face. "You're Nealie's daughter. You must be. I almost thought you were she."

"Papa says I look like her, excepting I don't have freckles. I'm glad for that," Pearl said. Indeed, Pearl had Nealie's angular face and peculiar red hair and pale blue eyes. She was tall, too, and had Nealie's way of moving.

A strange look came across the man's face when Pearl mentioned her father the second time, and he stood there, confused. "Your mother . . ." he faltered.

Just then, however, having heard Nealie's name, Charlie stepped into the foyer from his study. When he saw who was standing at the door, he stopped, filling the small room with his bulk, and he leveled his gaze at the man. "What do you want?" Charlie asked. Still a big, shambling man, he was dressed in good leather boots and a fine brown suit and vest, a gold watch chain with a fob made from a gold nugget across his stomach. He had improved his appearance and manners since the days he'd been a boarder with Lidie Travers. But the boots were unpolished, the suit rumpled and ill-fitting, and for all his wealth and success, Charlie Dumas seemed more suited to the jumper and brogans of a miner than the smart clothes of a wealthy investor.

"I came to pay my respects to Mrs. Travers. I went to the old place, but they sent me here. I thought this had become a boardinghouse. I did not know you and Nealie lived here. Perhaps I shouldn't have come —"

"She's crossed over. Nealie's dead," Charlie interrupted. "Don't you know that?"

"Dead?" The man put his hand on the door frame to steady himself. "How would I know?"

"Ten years ago. She died when the girl was born."

Will Spaulding removed his hat and held it in front of him. "Is it so, then? I didn't know."

Pearl was touched by the gesture and the idea that the man had known her mother, and she said, "Aren't you going to invite him in, Papa?"

Her father didn't reply but stood aside, and Will came into the house and followed Charlie into his study. Then Charlie turned to his daughter and said, "My dear, this concerns business. You go play in your room." He slid the pocket doors closed behind him.

Pearl stared at the walnut doors with their brass fittings before turning for the stairs. Then remembering she had been setting the table for supper when the man knocked at the door, she went into the dining room and finished putting out the flatware, the glasses, the cups and saucers, arranging them as she always did, the way her mother had. She thought to go outside and play then, but the sun was making such lovely bright slits through the shutters that she sat down at the table in her father's chair and moved her arms back and forth under the stripes of sun and shadow. She was not a child given to secrecy or listening in on conversations that were not her business, but the men talked loudly, and she could not help but hear them, because her father had not closed the study doors to the parlor, which opened into the dining room. And so the girl overheard the conversation, which she did not understand.

"Tell me about her," the man whose name had not been mentioned asked.

"You've no right to know."

"I have every right."

Charlie sighed. "No you don't, but I'll satisfy you. She died three days after Pearl was born."

"Pearl?"

"Nealie named her. Pearl. Her daughter. My daughter."

"*Your* daughter?"

"*My* daughter." Charlie's voice was rigid.

"What is she like?" the man asked.

Pearl knew the man was talking about her, and she leaned forward, her elbows on the table, to hear the answer.

"You saw for yourself."

"She looks like Nealie."

"It's for the best."

"Is she like her, too?"

"Enough." Then Charlie asked, "What are you doing here?"

"I told you. I came to see Mrs. Travers."

"In Georgetown. What are you doing in Georgetown?"

"I'm looking into an investment. My grandfather's failing, and my father's a wastrel, so there was nothing to it but for me to take over the firm. I haven't been back to Colorado since the day . . . the day after you married Nealie. I was at the station in Denver when you arrived, you know. I saw her. I was on my way back East. But I had promised you."

"Nealie didn't see you."

"No. I thought not."

"She believed you never came back."

The two men were silent, and then the visitor said, "I wasn't sure I should return now, but there is a proposition I'm looking into. Since I'm here, I thought to pay my respects to Mrs. Travers for old times' sake."

"And find out about Nealie?"

"No . . . yes, I suppose that was the reason, too."

"Of course it was. You said you didn't know we lived here, but you did. And you were curious about Pearl, too."

There was a silence, and Pearl thought her father might be pouring the man a glass of whiskey or offering him a cigar, the way Charlie usually did with visitors. In fact, his study smelled of bourbon and tobacco and leather. Mrs. Travers complained that as much as she cleaned and aired the room, she never could get rid of the smell. But Pearl liked it. When her father was away, she would sit in the swivel chair at his desk, playing with the pens and ink and pen wipes that she herself made for him, running her fingers over the papery cigars in the box, pretending she was her papa, negotiating mining agreements. Now, she pictured the visitor sitting on one of the chairs in front of the glass cases where her father kept his books and ore specimens and mining memorabilia, while her father twisted around in the chair, leaning back, his feet up on the desk.

"I'll tell Mrs. Travers you called. She works for me now," Charlie said, "here, in my house."

"*Your* house." The man laughed, but it wasn't a happy sound. Then the two were silent, and Pearl wondered what they were doing, perhaps examining one of Charlie's ore samples. Already, Pearl knew her father had a fine collection of specimens.

Then the man said, "I don't suppose you care, but I've paid for what I did. It's not been an easy time for me these last years. My wife and I — she never knew, of course — we get on all right, but we lead separate lives. There aren't any children. I'm sorry for that." He cleared his throat and said, "I never heard from Nealie, so I didn't know the baby was a girl." He was silent for a moment before he said, "I was afraid of my grandfather back then, afraid to anger him. Only later I realized he needed me more than I did him. He would have forgiven me for anything. I made the wrong choice. If I were to do it again —"

"But you can't, and she's dead," Charlie interrupted, his voice hard.

"No, I can't. Please God, I could," the man said, so softly that Pearl wondered if he was talking to himself. After a silence, he asked, "Where is she buried?"

"The Alvarado Cemetery. I put up a stone with an angel on it and her name."

"Nealie Bent."

"Dumas. Mrs. Charles Dumas."

"Do you mind if I visit it?"

Pearl thought her father might have nodded or shook his head, but she had no way of knowing. All he said was, "It's a public place."

There was another long silence in the house, although from outside came the sounds of a mule-drawn wagon making its way down Taos Street, the crack of a whip, a profanity as the driver swore at the animals. In the distance, a stamp mill rumbled as it crushed ore. Then the man said, "You've done well. People in the East know of you. You've got their respect." Pearl heard the creak of leather, and the man asked, "Was she happy with you?"

Charlie's chair squeaked, the way it did when he leaned forward to say something important. "What mine are you looking into?"

There was another pause before the man answered, businesslike, "The Camp Robber. We have a chance to buy it and at a good price."

"I shouldn't wonder." Charlie snorted, and the chair squeaked again. "It's well named, all right. It's a bust."

"We've assayed the ore."

"Salted, most likely. Go back farther in the adit. Take your own samples. There's not much of value in Georgetown any longer, and I advise you to look elsewhere. I'm of the opinion silver's days are done for, so I'm investing in gold mines. You ought to do the same."

"Thank you." The man scraped his boots on the floor as he rose. "Will you let me say good-bye to the girl?"

"No."

At that, Pearl got out of the chair and went into the foyer, sitting down on the stairs, because she was curious about this man who'd known her mother, a man she guessed her father did not like. She concluded that because Charlie had not offered him refreshment and had cut short the interview. Usually her father was genial, even when the guest bored him, because he never knew what he might learn from gossip. The girl was seated on the steps, a book in her hands, when Charlie opened the study doors.

The man did not see Pearl at first, because he was looking up the steep staircase, which clung to the wall, and at the polished banister, which curved gracefully at the top of the stairs. "I remember the house. I was in it once before it was finished," he said. "She loved it. She always wanted to live here, but I guess you know that."

"Everybody calls it the Bride's House. Mama was the bride," Pearl said, rising from the step.

"I know. Was she married in the green dress?" Will looked at Charlie.

"Blue. Mrs. Travers loaned it to her. She told me so." Pearl held out her hand. "Good-bye, sir."

"Good-bye, Miss Pearl," he said, taking the hand and holding it longer than was necessary. "I hope I'll see you again."

"No," Charlie said. "You won't."

Pearl thought that an odd remark, because her father was slow to anger and rarely rude.

At the time, she considered the conversation she'd overheard to be strange, but she wasn't sure just why. She never forgot it, although she forgot pieces of it that didn't mean anything to her or that she didn't understand. She'd missed the nuances, so that in later years, her memory of the visit was somewhat inaccurate. What's more, she forgot what the man looked like, and she never learned his name, so if the two ever met again, she wouldn't have known him. She remembered mostly that it was a meeting between two men who had both known her mother, two men who didn't care much for each other.

That night at supper, the girl told Mrs. Travers, "A man came to see you today, Aunt Lidie." If Pearl had been devious, she might have planned the announcement for its effect, might have looked at her father for his reaction, because she still did not understand what had passed between the two men. But she was not so inclined, and although she knew that her father had not liked the man, she hadn't sensed his agitation. Nor had she thought the visit unusual, because her father discussed mining with many men. Besides, the stranger had explained that his reason for calling was to see

Mrs. Travers.

"Who was he?" Mrs. Travers asked. She had a large circle of friends, although most of them were women.

Pearl shrugged. "He didn't tell me his name. Papa knows him."

"No one of consequence," Charlie said.

Mrs. Travers looked up, curious, because the man had been her caller, not Charlie's.

"He knew my mother," Pearl continued. "He said he boarded with you."

"I would like more water," Charlie said, and Pearl jumped up and took his glass to the kitchen and pumped water into it. When Pearl was out of the other room, Charlie muttered, "Will Spaulding."

Mrs. Travers placed her napkin beside her plate, Nealie's white Haviland with a design of roses on it. Some of the pieces had been broken, and Charlie had ordered replacements. "I haven't thought of him in a long time. He wasn't such a bad egg, but he was . . ." She paused. "I'd forgotten there was hardness between you."

"Was there, Papa? Why didn't you like the man?" Pearl asked. She set Charlie's glass on the table.

When Charlie didn't answer, Mrs. Travers said, "Because both of them sparked your mother. I'm telling you right, your mama made the best choice marrying up with your papa. Oh, he was a nice enough man, but he was just a-spudding. Is that how you'd put it, Charlie? He was just ambling along, looking out for himself?"

"I wouldn't put it."

"You still don't like him, then?" Mrs. Travers chuckled. "What did he want?"

"To pay his respects. You didn't miss much."

"Is he the bull goose of his grandfather's company now? I remember the old man had him under his thumb."

"Says so."

"He didn't know Mama was dead," the girl interrupted, then clamped her mouth shut, because this bit of information was something she'd overheard the man talking about with her father in the study. But Charlie didn't seem to catch that.

"No, how would he?"

"If he comes back, I don't want to see him," Charlie said, rising from the table. "And he's not to see Pearl, either." The two waited until Charlie went out — to a saloon or just tramping about, as he often did for an hour or so after supper. Mrs. Travers had wondered to a friend once — a remark that Pearl had overheard — whether Charlie would have stayed home of an evening if

Nealie had been alive.

"Did Mama like the man?" Pearl asked, as the two cleared the dishes from the table and carried them into the kitchen.

Mrs. Travers picked up the teakettle from the range and poured hot water into a basin. "Yes, she did."

"But she liked Papa better?"

"Wouldn't you?" Mrs. Travers answered, as she began washing the plates. "I was glad for it."

"That man's very handsome."

"And generous. I believe he gave your mother that cameo you're wearing."

The girl looked up in surprise, and Mrs. Travers frowned, as if she should not have disclosed the gift. "You mustn't tell your father about that. You'd hurt his feelings. Most likely, he doesn't know about the cameo, because if he did, he wouldn't like you wearing it." She dipped a plate into the basin of rinse water and handed it to Pearl to dry. "I'd have thought your father was over all his jealousy. After all, Nealie married *him*. But it appears he's not. If I was you, I wouldn't mention the man to your father again."

Pearl considered that as she set the plate in the cupboard. "I thought Papa gave the necklace to Mama or that maybe her own papa did." The girl mulled over something for a minute. "Do you think he's still alive — Mama's father?" Pearl knew that Nealie had been raised on a farm and had left after her mother died, but nothing more, and she'd never asked about her grandfather.

"Oh, I don't suppose so," Mrs. Travers replied quickly, as if she did not want the girl to inquire further. But Pearl had asked only out of momentary curiosity, and by the time she picked up the next plate, she had forgotten about her mother's family.

CHAPTER 8

Pearl Dumas was thirty years old in 1912 when she met Frank Curry, and well on her way to becoming an old maid. The general view in Georgetown was that the girl had a rabbit's chance of marriage. Some people found her attractive in an odd sort of way — distinctive, at any rate, with her strange coloring. But although she looked much like her mother, Pearl did not have those qualities that Nealie had possessed that had made men turn and stare at her. Of course, few compared Pearl with her mother, because except for Charlie and Mrs. Travers, Mr. Kaiser at the store and the minister at the Presbyterian church, nobody remembered Nealie. If they had, they might have been puzzled that this shy, reserved woman with the air of someone twice her age was the daughter of the vivacious young hired girl.

Some wondered that Pearl had ever been

a girl at all. Despite the easy days of her growing-up years, Pearl seemed never to have been young. While Charlie was blustery and outgoing, a man who made his views known to everyone, Pearl was her father's shadow, a quiet, rather simple child who blended into the background. Few remarked that something she said was cunning or even memorable. As she grew into young womanhood, Pearl never blossomed but retained the retiring demeanor of her youth.

Of course, the young woman had friends, many of them, in fact, because Pearl was well liked, kind, and self-effacing and given to charitable acts. She was active in church and might have played the piano there, since she was accomplished in that instrument, having learned on the square grand pianoforte her mother had bought for the parlor, but she was far too shy to perform before anyone but her father.

She took part in quiltings with Mrs. Travers and her friends, sewing quietly and efficiently, never gossiping and only joining in the talk when it turned to serious subjects. And she participated in outdoor exercises such as sleigh rides and ice skating with those her own age, although she was not athletic, and sliding about on blades on the ice frightened her, as did other sporting activities, such as bicycling. She might have turned that fear to her advantage, pleading helplessness, but flirting was foreign to her. In that, she was like her mother, although Nealie's lack of artifice was thought fresh while Pearl's seemed dull.

Pearl dressed tastefully but too plainly to suit. She had come of age in an era when women put aside their bustles and stays and glorified in their uncorseted bodies. Pearl, however, preferred the old-fashioned look favored by Mrs. Travers. In winter, she wore stiff mohair, gabardine, or taffeta, of a severe color, cinched against her bony form. In summer, she dressed in white, which gave her a washed-out appearance. And she eschewed the broad hats then fashionable, preferring bonnets that made her look even taller and thinner.

Charlie had no criticisms of his daughter, perhaps because he preferred that his precious child stay by his side. He wanted her home in the evenings where the two often sat on the horsehair furniture in the parlor and read to each other or discussed the mining business.

Charlie had more than a fatherly devotion to Pearl. He had come to depend on the girl professionally. During Pearl's growing-up time, Mrs. Travers suggested that Pearl go on to one of the universities in Denver or at Boulder. The girl was bright and serious, and Charlie could afford the tuition. Pearl herself hoped to do that, because she wanted to learn more than she had been taught in the Georgetown schools. And since she was not interested in any of the eligible young men in Georgetown, she thought that she might meet her future husband at a university. It had never occurred to Pearl that she would do anything in her life but marry — marry and bring her husband home to live in the Bride's House, because she could not imagine leaving her father.

"I'll ask Papa to send me," Pearl told Mrs. Travers when the two discussed her going on to school. Charlie had never denied her anything, so Pearl believed she had good reason to expect he would agree to her going to a university.

"We'll have to think how to appeal to him," Mrs. Travers said, because she was not so sure Charlie would give up his daughter.

"It might help," Pearl said, "if I told him I would study geology so that I could better understand his mining investments." She would go to a school only fifty miles away and promise to come home every weekend so that he would not miss her.

Mrs. Travers broached the subject of college one evening at the supper table. "It's a shame to end Pearl's education here, smart like she is." Charlie didn't respond, and Mrs. Travers added, "She has her father's blood." When Charlie frowned at that, Mrs. Travers added quickly, "That is to say, she's smart like you, Charlie, clever."

"Clever and smart mean the same thing as hardworking," he replied.

"I never heard of a body hurt by learning."

"I went to school a little, but I didn't learn much," Charlie said. "I've found teachers to be about as wise as rabbits. They don't know good ore from Deuteronomy."

"Oh, now that might have been true in our day, but it's not any longer. The girl could study geology, but who knows what else she might learn."

"Learn to strip her shoulders and bare her legs, that's what."

"Papa!" Pearl interjected.

Charlie reddened a little and cleared his throat. "Now, I'm not saying you'd do that, Pearl, but I don't care to have you associate with that kind of person."

"I believe you can trust me," Pearl said in a rare display of defiance. Then she added,

"Perhaps I would find someone there who would be a suitable husband." She assumed that her father, like her, believed she would marry one day and that he would want her to choose a man as ambitious and hard-working as Charlie.

"I wouldn't have you marry now."

"I'm Mama's age when you married her."

"She's right," Mrs. Travers put in, and Charlie glared at her.

"You're much too foolish to choose a husband," Charlie said, to the two women's distress. Pearl might lack some qualities, but she had never been foolish.

"It's what I want, college, that is," Pearl said at last. "I am asking you to send me, Papa."

Charlie tossed his napkin onto the table. "Lidie, you've forgotten the hereafter. Has your mind gone soft?"

"Oh, I'll get it, Papa," Pearl said, jumping up. "We made a Charlotte pudding."

"Your aunt Lidie can fetch it," Charlie said, and Mrs. Travers rose and went into the kitchen to dish up the dessert. She took her time after the obvious dismissal.

When father and daughter were alone, Charlie asked, "And what about what I want, Pearl? Would you push me aside just to attend classes on subjects of no value to you and to cavort with young men? Have you no feeling for your papa, for how lonely I would be?"

"You would have Aunt Lidie," Pearl replied in a soft voice, a last attempt to convince Charlie of the rightness of her plea. "I will be home every weekend and on vacations. Why, you yourself are gone as much as I would be." Then she added, "Couldn't we try it for two years, even one?"

"Aunt Lidie is not my daughter." Charlie leaned back in his chair and added, "I will allow you to go if you have your heart set on it, but think what it would do to me. It would make me unhappy if you were to go away, and I do not think you would want to disappoint me that way."

So because she had always put her needs second and because disappointing her father was the last thing Pearl had ever wanted to do, she set aside her hopes for a university education.

"Perhaps in a year or two when you are older," Charlie said, but both knew that would never be.

So instead of going away to school, which might have opened up a new world and broken her father's hold on her, Pearl became Charlie's secretary. She handled his correspondence and searched through the volumes in his library when he needed information on ore bodies or geological formations. Although she had grown up in a mining town and was familiar with mining terms, she found much of the work foreign to her, and she set about learning what she could about mining in order to better aid her father. She kept Charlie's accounts for him, and on occasion, she entertained his callers when he was occupied elsewhere. Her father's associates found her knowledgeable if not especially entertaining.

Sometimes, Pearl toured mines with Charlie, who pointed out the way a tiny vein of gold was streaked through the host rock and taught her to differentiate between real gold and fool's gold. Although some of the miners were superstitions about women underground, they did not dare object when the woman in the mine was the daughter of Charles Dumas. Here, Pearl's lack of artifice held her in good stead. She considered gold to be a commodity, not just a metal used for adornment, so she did not remark, as other women did when shown the workings of a mine, that the vein of ore would make a lovely necklace or teased couldn't she have enough for a ring. She understood that gold was measured in ounces per ton, or fractions thereof, not in rings and bracelets. The young woman knew that politics and the economy, not just supply and demand, affected the price of precious metals. So the mining men who escorted her along the adits and into the drifts were comfortable with her.

Moreover, Pearl was not afraid of heights and did not flinch when she climbed into the bucket that lowered the miners and their visitors down the shaft. Nor did she worry about dirtying her skirts in the underground muck. All this made Pearl stand out from other women who were permitted in the mines, although if she had known she was different, Pearl would not have liked it, because she did not care to be noticed.

Several young men thought of Pearl as a special friend, but not many were attracted to her for romantic reasons. She was plain-spoken and direct and far too serious. An older man might find her knowledge of mining to be good conversation, but few men her age cared for moonlight talk about the composition of an ore specimen or how long the ore body at Cripple Creek would last. Those who did court the young woman may have had ulterior motives. They were fortune hunters, or at least that was the impression the girl took from her father. While Charlie did not call them that outright — after all, he loved his daughter and was sensitive of her feelings — he managed to convey to the girl that anyone who came calling was in reality courting an heiress.

Charlie was not wealthy on the scale of the robber barons in the East, but he was one of the richest men in Colorado. Some of his associates wondered why he remained in Georgetown, which by the turn of the century was deep in a decline from which it was clear it would not recover. Never a major metals producer, Georgetown suffered a devastating loss with the silver crash of 1893, because silver was the primary metal in its mines. When the government stopped backing the price of silver, the value of the metal plunged. Charlie knew what was coming, and he had gotten out of silver when the price was still high, investing his money in gold, copper, and other metals.

Charlie's associates thought it odd that he stayed on in the town when he could have bought a mansion in Denver — or in New York, for that matter, because his investments were not confined to Colorado. When asked, Charlie replied that his blood had grown thin in the high country and he'd turn sluggish at a lower altitude. Besides, he said, he was too set in his ways to resettle. Moreover, he told anyone who asked that he had a sentimental attachment to the area where he had made his early fortune. But the truth was that nothing could have lured him away from Nealie's house, the Bride's House. He would leave it only when he was carried out in a box and buried beside his wife under the angel in the Alvarado Cemetery.

Charlie kept the Bride's House in pristine condition, the fanciful trim repaired, the façade painted. He added a fountain in the yard and a fence across the vast expanse of front lawn. A gardener cared for the lilacs and other flowers, kept the grass clipped and the fountain in working order. So it was obvious to anyone who visited Georgetown that the owner of the place was a man of some means. It was also obvious that the big house could accommodate a husband for Pearl, and the young men who did call on her were as aware of that fact as they were of Charlie's money.

Among Pearl's few swains was a young violinist who had opened a music shop in Georgetown. He played duets with Pearl, lavishly praising the young woman's performance at the piano. While Charlie enjoyed his daughter's music, he surely knew she was no virtuoso, and he told Pearl the man was a self-seeker.

"I have come to the same conclusion," Pearl replied, because she had no interest in spending her life with someone who did not know an ore vein from a violin string. In fact, Pearl had discouraged two or three other would-be suitors on similar grounds, before her father could interfere.

She thought better of Tom Glendive, the manager of a gold mine in Cripple Creek, who sought her father's advice on a technical problem. He developed the habit of dropping in on Pearl whenever business brought him to Georgetown, staying for tea and sometimes for supper. Tom was older, somewhere in his thirties, and charming, and he made Pearl laugh.

"Have you heard of Pat Casey, who discovered the Casey Mine in Central City?" Tom asked as he was sitting at the supper table with Pearl, Charlie, and Mrs. Travers.

"The dumbest Irishman who ever lived. He carried a gold watch but couldn't tell the time," replied Charlie.

"You have, then." He turned to Pearl. "He once called into his mine, 'How many of youse are down there?' Five, came the reply. Old Pat scratched his head for a minute, then said, 'Well, half of youse come for a drink.' "

Pearl laughed out loud, for although she herself was not clever in telling stories, she loved to hear them.

Another time, as Tom and Pearl sat in the gazebo, he asked if she knew the story of Silver Heels. When Pearl said she didn't, Tom told her that Silver Hells was a dance-hall girl in Buckskin Joe, a town well to the south of Georgetown. He glanced at Pearl to see if she were offended, for surely she knew that a dance-hall girl was more likely a fallen woman. But Pearl had lived in a mining town all her life, and she accepted prostitutes as a part of Georgetown.

"Go on," she said.

"Silver Heels was named for her shoes, and she was a beauty, a favorite with the miners. Came the smallpox, and all the good women quit the town, leaving only Silver Heels. She stayed to nurse the miners. Her face was the last one many of those poor fellows saw before they left this world. The pox was about done with when Silver Heels caught it, and it destroyed her beautiful face."

"Was she killed?" Pearl asked, caught up in the story.

Tom shrugged. "Who's to say? But every

225

now and then a woman wearing a heavy veil visits the graves of the men who died. I've heard it happens even now."

"Do you think she's Silver Heels?" Pearl asked.

Tom studied her a moment. "What do you think?"

"I would like to believe she is."

Pearl began to look forward to Tom's visits. He took her for carriage rides and hikes in the mountains, and invited her to visit his mine in Cripple Creek, although Pearl quickly demurred, for she thought such a thing improper. Sometimes he brought boxes of pastries that could not be found in Georgetown, cigars for Charlie, and once he gave Pearl a locket made of gold from his mine. He had not been so bold as to put his own likeness inside, so Pearl fitted it with a picture of her father instead. Pearl found herself thinking of the man when she should have been reading mining journals or working on the accounts, and so it was not long before the infatuation came to Charlie's attention.

He said nothing at first, only writing a letter himself and taking it to the post office. Then one night at the supper table, he remarked, "This afternoon at the station I

226

ran into a friend of mine from Butte. He's a friend of Tom Glendive's, too."

Pearl blushed at the name and stared at her plate. At first she thought Charlie would reveal some bit of flattery about Tom, but something in her father's casual way of mentioning her suitor made her wary.

"He's a nice young man," Mrs. Travers interjected, "a sticker." She had once called Charlie that.

"Not so's you'd notice. It seems he's been about a good deal," Charlie replied. "Pearl, did he ever mention to you he'd worked in the copper mines up in Butte?"

"Yes," Pearl replied, playing with her fork as if she knew what was coming.

"He worked in several mines, or so this fellow told me. Tom was fired from one for high-grading and let go at another for fighting. Seems he hit another miner with a shovel, a fight over a girl, the way the fellow tells it."

There was a silence while Pearl stared at her hands. It did not occur to her to speak up for Tom Glendive. She had never contradicted her father for the simple reason that she could not conceive of his being wrong.

When Pearl didn't respond, Charlie said, "The girl was Tom's wife."

Pearl looked up sharply.

Now it was Charlie's turn to look away. "Of course, there could be an explanation, but the fellow said —"

Pearl interrupted him. "No need, Papa," she said.

Mrs. Travers looked at the girl as if she thought Pearl had the backbone of a caterpillar and wished she would defend the young man or demand to know the truth before she dismissed him. "People tell tales. I thought he was a right smart fellow," the older woman said. "Most likely the wife's dead, and he can't bring himself to talk about her."

"No, Papa's right. I was never especially fond of Mr. Glendive, anyway. He was only an amusement." She left the table and went into the study, because her eyes had turned bright. She wiped away a tear or two as she sat in her father's chair, surrounded by the comfortable smell of tobacco and whiskey. She did not wonder that her father had been at home all day and hadn't ventured to the depot. And later, she was not surprised to find among the bills to be paid an invoice from a detective in Butte.

The next time Tom called, Pearl told him, "I believe you are wasting your time, Mr. Glendive."

"I don't understand."

"You don't need to."

"I thought you and I —"

"You have misunderstood," Pearl said, closing the door in his face.

Over time, Pearl finally realized that Charlie found a way to discourage her interest in *any* man who courted her. But she did not question her father, because she was sure that he was only looking out for her. She believed that someday she would find a man who suited both Charlie and herself and did not give the matter a great deal of thought, although she was growing beyond the age when most women married. Mrs. Travers, perhaps, understood that Charlie was unlikely to approve of any man who courted his daughter. "Pearl's almost twice as old as Nealie was when you met her. You ought not to stand in the way of her finding a husband," she told Charlie.

"I'm not," he replied, warning, "It's not your business."

"It is. I raised up that girl from the day she was born."

Charlie gave her a long look and didn't reply. He was not predictable when it came to Nealie and Pearl, and perhaps Mrs. Travers feared a rare explosion of his temper, which could stir up hell with a long spoon. So she said no more.

There was no reason, then, to think that when Frank Curry began to court Pearl, he would be any more successful than her other suitors.

Frank was an exceptionally good-looking man. When Pearl opened the door and found him standing on the porch, she felt her breath stop in her throat, and she reached for the cameo at her neck. It wouldn't do to let the man know she had reacted so, and Pearl swallowed twice and opened the screen, asking if he had come to see her father. Charlie was away but expected back at any moment, she explained.

The man removed his hat and introduced himself, saying he was indeed looking for Charlie, and would she mind if he waited. He could sit on the porch.

"Oh no," Pearl breathed. "Please do come inside." The man entered the house and followed Pearl through Charlie's study into the parlor. They stood for a moment beside the library table, where Mrs. Travers had placed a white pitcher of lilacs. "I smelled them when I came up the walk — Chinese lilacs. They have the sweetest smell," he said.

Pearl nodded and touched one of the purple bunches. She moved the stems around a little in the jar. She had seen other women arranging flowers, standing as if in a tableau, but she herself was not any good at either placing the boughs or posing. Still, she played with the flowers, because she did not know what else to do with her hands. In a moment, she realized the man was still standing and asked him to be seated. "Would you like a cup of tea?" He said he would if it wasn't any trouble.

"No trouble," Pearl breathed, and fled into the kitchen to calm herself. She added kindling to the banked fire in the cookstove, then poured water into the kettle, setting it on the stove to boil. She took out the tea things, the cups and saucers and the silver teapot, set them on a tray, then took down the tin of tea and measured out the leaves. When the water boiled, she filled the teapot and carried the tray into the parlor and set it on the table next to the lilacs.

"It makes a very pretty picture, the silver against the purple and the white," Frank told her. Another man might have flattered Pearl by adding that she was a part of the pretty picture, but that would have embarrassed the girl, knowing it was not true. So the young man was wise not to say too much. Pearl sat on one of the horsehair love seats and gestured to Frank to take the other. He set down his hat and walking stick and seated himself.

Pearl hated times like this, when she was expected to be clever and charming, engage in superficial talk, and usually, she was mute. At that moment she felt acutely her inability to make small talk. She sat stiffly, clasping and unclasping her hands, pondering and discarding possible subjects for conversation.

"You may be wondering why I called," the man said at last, and Pearl nodded, although she hadn't. She was used to men requesting her father's advice. "I've come to ask Mr. Dumas's opinion about molybdenite. Do you know of it?"

"Oh," Pearl said, forgetting her shyness. "I *have* just learned about the ore molybdenite — I believe the metal is called molybdenum, is it not? — and I've wondered what possible good it is."

"Oh." The man seemed surprised that she should have heard of the mineral. "And you can pronounce it correctly, too."

"Why shouldn't I pronounce it correctly?" Pearl asked, surprised.

"Most women can't."

"I never saw the sense of being ignorant about a thing."

"Other women wouldn't agree."

Pearl blushed, wishing she weren't always

so frank, but that was the way she was. "What's the good of it?"

"Of not agreeing?"

"Of molybdenite."

"Ah, that's the question, isn't it? That's why I've come to see your father."

Pearl wondered if the remark meant the man didn't want to talk about molybdenite with her, so she stood abruptly. "I've forgotten the tea. It should be ready." She poured the tea into cups and set them on saucers, handing one to Frank, then held out the spooner and sugar bowl.

He shook his head and waited until Pearl returned to her seat before he sipped his tea. Pearl held hers in her lap. She did not especially care for tea, although she found sitting in the parlor in the late afternoon with her father, over the teacups, to be a pleasant habit. It was something they did often, a time she cherished, because she liked nothing more than being with him. "You know about mining, then?" he asked.

"A little."

"I should say more than a little."

Pearl shrugged, and the two were silent, Pearl embarrassed at her lack of social grace. Frank finished his tea, then stood and began to examine the objects in the room. At the same time, Pearl studied him. That he was handsome, she had already observed, but now she saw that he was well formed, slim in the hips with broad shoulders. He wore his clothes casually, like her father, but his suit was well fitted and pressed, not wrinkled like Charlie's clothing. Pearl liked the man's manner; he was sure of himself although not cocky. She thought it odd that while she was ill at ease in the room she had known all her life, he was comfortable.

Frank went to the ore case and picked up a chunk of rock and held it out to Pearl, a question on his face.

"Cripple Creek. The Gold Coin," she identified it.

He selected another specimen, and she said, "A mine in Russia. Someone sent it to Papa. The quartz in it is odd, don't you think?"

"Unusual. I saw one like it at school. Did you go to college?"

Pearl shook her head, knowing now that not continuing her education had been a mistake.

"Oh, I thought maybe you'd attended the Colorado School of Mines in Golden." It was a little joke, since women were not allowed to enroll in Mines. Pearl was not used to being the subject of a joke, however, and she thought Frank might be making fun of her. She frowned, so as if to reassure her, Frank said, "You could have gone. I'd bet you know more about mining than any girl I ever met."

Pearl was not sure that was a compliment, and she went to the tea table. To occupy herself, she emptied the dregs of her teacup into the waste bowl before holding up the teapot and asking Frank if he would like another cup.

"To tell you the truth, I don't like tea much. I prefer coffee."

"Oh, I do, too," Pearl breathed. "Tea tastes like straw."

"I've never tasted straw."

Pearl thought that an odd remark, and it took her a moment to realize Frank had made another joke. Unsure how to respond, she said, "I could make us some — coffee, that is, not straw."

Frank laughed, although Pearl had not intended to be funny but had only clarified her statement. "Your mother surely would not approve of your wasting both tea and coffee on me."

"I don't have a mother," Pearl said, adding quickly, "Of course, I *had* a mother, but she's among the unloving." The young woman thought she should not have used that old-fashioned term for the dead, but in her mind it had always fit Nealie. The girl knew her mother and father had loved each other, because married people did; that was why they married. But she had always wondered how Nealie felt about her. After all, Pearl had cost her mother her life, so why would she love her daughter? But Nealie might have loved her at least a little. Besides, her father and Mrs. Travers did, and that was enough.

"I'm sorry. You must miss her."

"She died when I was born," Pearl said matter-of-factly.

"And your father never remarried?"

The man was inquisitive, and Pearl said flatly, "No."

"I've offended you," he said. "Let's talk about something else. Have you always lived in Georgetown?"

Pearl sat down again, wishing she had not set aside her teacup, because her hands were restless. She clasped them together to calm them. "I was born here."

"Well, I find it a very quiet place. I suppose when you know it, the town is much more exciting."

"No," Pearl said, searching her mind for something amusing to say about Georgetown, but failing.

"I think much better of it since I've met

you," Frank said. Then he laughed. "You must think me a flatterer. I daresay I've been bold, and I don't even know your name."

"It's Miss Dumas — Pearl Dumas."

"Pearl," he repeated. "What an oddly fitting name."

"I've never thought so." It did not occur to Pearl to ask why he thought the name fit her.

Frank, perhaps sensing she was uncomfortable with flattery, did not continue. "Do you play tennis? I've just taken up the game and say it is splendid."

"I'm not much good at sports," Pearl answered miserably.

"Oh, that doesn't matter. Would you like to watch me play sometime?"

Pearl hesitated, but before she could reply, she heard her father at the door. She was both disappointed and relieved as she stood up and announced, "Here's Papa now. I will introduce you — Mr. Curry, didn't you say?" she asked.

"I did. Frank Curry." He stood and picked up his hat and walking stick.

Pearl repeated the name, not to commit it to memory, because she knew she would not forget it, but because she liked the sound of it. After Charlie went into his study, she led the visitor through the parlor doors and announced, "Papa, you have a visitor. Mr. Frank Curry. He is here about molybdenite."

"Ah," Charlie said. "Has anybody found a use for it yet?"

"That's why I've come to see you, sir."

Charlie shook hands with the young man. As he sat down, he nodded at the chair in front of his desk. Pearl stood quietly to one side, hoping her father would not notice and she could stay, but Charlie dismissed her with, "Would you close the parlor doors when you leave, my dear?"

Frank bowed a little to Pearl and said he was glad to have met her, but by the time Pearl had closed the pocket doors, Frank was sitting on the chair, talking with her father. She had been piecing when Frank knocked on the door, so she picked up the sewing and took it upstairs, seating herself in the little rocker in the hallway, the chair where Nealie once sat with her own sewing, looking out the long window at the mountains. Pearl did not quilt then but held the scraps of fabric in her lap until she heard the screen door close an hour later and glanced out to see Frank Curry walking away. He paused by the lilac hedge, but he did not look up at the window, and Pearl was glad. What if he had seen her sitting there, hoping to catch a glimpse of him?

Pearl did not mention Frank Curry at dinner. Had she done so, Charlie might have wondered at her interest and stopped the young man from returning. She yearned to know what Charlie thought of him, of course, and even considered asking her father about molybdenite in hopes the conversation would turn to the man who had brought the mineral to their attention. But she held her tongue.

Just as Pearl was sure her father had forgotten their afternoon visitor, Charlie himself brought up the subject of Frank Curry. Mrs. Travers had served him a bowl of pudding, and as he picked up his spoon, Charlie said, "You were right about that fellow who was here, Pearl. He came to see me about molybdenite."

Pearl toyed with her spoon, then dipped it into the chocolaty custard, while she carefully considered her words. "So he said."

"What's molybdenite?" Mrs. Travers struggled with the word, tried it several times, before giving it up.

"A mineral with no use as far as I can see," Charlie replied. Some of the pudding slid off his spoon onto the tablecloth, and

239

he wiped it with his napkin.

"Leave be," Mrs. Travers told him. "I'll spot it out."

"Darn spoon." Charlie grabbed the utensil again and held it the way he had in the boardinghouse days, like a pickaxe. "Whoever invented these dabs of spoons? Remember those big ones you used to have, Lidie? A fellow could get half his meal on one."

"Many did. They were all I had, and not much smaller than a gold pan."

The conversation veered off into a direction Pearl did not want, and she feared her father had forgotten his remark about molybdenite, so she said, "Didn't the man who was here tell you what it was used for? Molybdenite, that is. He seemed awfully interested in it. I have to say I'm curious about the metal."

Charlie scraped out the dish and said, "I'm sorry I wasted your pudding, Lidie." Then he turned to Pearl. "Oh, he is. Frank Curry claims he has the market all sewed up, that is, if there is a market." Charlie laughed. "He's a likely fellow. I told him to stop by anytime he was in Georgetown, and I'd be happy to talk about mining with him. But I said I'd as soon invest in a pile of dirt as a molybdenite claim. That was why he was here, of course. He's looking for investors. I'd get a better return from a sandbox." He looked a little smug. "Folks around Leadville call the stuff molybedamnite." Charlie chuckled as he pushed back his chair. "Now, if you'll excuse me. I want to see a fellow . . ." That was what he always said when he left to visit the saloons. The two women watched as he went into the hall and took down his hat, then left the house. After he was gone, Pearl and Mrs. Travers sat at the table, finishing their dessert.

"You didn't have much to say about Mr. Curry. Did I get his name right?" Mrs. Travers asked.

"I believe so," Pearl said.

Mrs. Travers studied the girl. "It seems to me if I were Charlie Dumas's daughter, I wouldn't say much about a man I fancied, either."

"Oh, Aunt Lidie, you do go on."

"And you blush just like your mother did. It was Nealie's burden — and yours, too. I saw you color when your father said the young man's name. Lucky for you he didn't notice."

Pearl looked down at her pudding, hoping she wasn't blushing at that moment. "I don't know what you mean."

"Oh, I think you do. Your father puts a stop to any likely man who comes calling.

He believes none of them is good enough for you." That reason would do for both of the women, because neither was the sort who delved into the complexities of the human psyche.

"I only met the man today. I don't know him."

"I didn't say you were frenzied over him, but I've known you since ever, and I guess I can tell when something strikes you. I can't say's I blame you. I caught a glimpse of him as I was coming down the street. He's as slick as a peeled onion."

"He is, isn't he?" Trying not to smile too broadly, Pearl looked at the older woman.

"He is that, but I advise you not to let your father know you think that way."

The girl nodded. Then her eyes grew wide and she asked, "You don't suppose he's married, do you?"

Mrs. Travers frowned. "I believe he'd have said so."

"Yes," Pearl agreed, although she was not so sure.

Mrs. Travers rose from the table and began clearing the dishes. Then she turned to Pearl, who was staring out the window at the lilac bushes. "I'm glad you met a man you fancy. I'm glad for it." Then she muttered to herself, "But I don't believe old Charlie Dumas would be."

CHAPTER 9

Pearl did not forget Frank Curry, but as the weeks passed, she came to believe he had forgotten her and that she would not see him again. And, indeed, it was nearly six weeks before he stopped the second time at the Bride's House, knocking on the screen door and asking for Charlie.

"He's away," Pearl said, and went on to explain that it was Wednesday, and her father always took the train to Denver first thing on Wednesday mornings to go to the Mining Exchange. He would not be back until late in the evening, perhaps not even until the next morning.

"Well, I am sorry," Frank said. "He asked me some questions, and I should like to give him some answers."

"Papa doesn't think much of molybdenite, you know," Pearl told him.

"I'm hoping he will after I talk to him. I have just formed the Colorado Molybdenite

Company and want to tell him about it. I suppose I'll just have to come by another time."

"Oh, but you'll come in now, won't you?" Pearl asked, surprised at her boldness.

Frank smiled, as if he'd been waiting for the invitation. "If you're busy —" he said, but he stepped inside before she could answer.

"Oh no," Pearl interrupted. "I mean, it would be a pleasure to stop dusting."

"You do the dusting?"

Pearl was flustered. In truth, she enjoyed cleaning the big house as much as her mother had, and it pleased her that the two had that in common. It made Pearl feel that the house was hers, not just Charlie and Nealie's. She was forever polishing the woodwork, making the floors shine, blackening the kitchen stove until it looked new. She liked cleaning her father's office best, creating orderliness out of the papers and reports Charlie left scattered about. But she was aware that housework did not fit her position as the daughter of a wealthy man, and she didn't want Frank to think her father was either poorer than thought or too parsimonious to hire the work done.

"We can afford servants, of course, but Papa doesn't like them running about, you see. They make him nervous. So Mrs. Travers and I keep up the place and do the cooking. It's little enough we can do for Papa, who is so kind to us. Of course, someone comes in to do the laundry and wash the windows and varnish the floors, but we just keep things up ourselves, and it's not hard work. . . ." Pearl's voice trailed off, and she thought Frank must consider her a dullard. What man would want to engage in a conversation about housekeeping? No wonder she was thought to be poorly spoken.

"Why, I say that's splendid," Frank said. "It never hurts a person to do a little work. Folks spend too much money on frivolity when they might put it to better use."

"On molybdenite?"

Pearl did not realize she had been witty and was startled when Frank laughed. "You're a very clever girl," he said.

No one had ever said such a thing to her, and Pearl turned aside to hide her bright cheeks. "Would you like lemonade? Mrs. Travers has just been about making it. I was going to sit on the veranda. It's so much nicer than being indoors."

Frank agreed that was a fine idea and offered to help, saying, "You see, you're not the only one who is handy about the house."

He followed Pearl into the kitchen, where Mrs. Travers was putting the lemonade pitcher into the icebox. Pearl introduced them, and Frank said smoothly, "I've been offered a glass of lemonade on the porch. Would you do us the pleasure of joining us?"

The older woman smiled at the fine words but shook her head. "I've got slathers of sewing needs doing on the machine in my room. You young folks go ahead." She seemed ready to say, "However . . . ," but Frank did not press her.

So the two took the pitcher and their glasses out onto the veranda and sat down, Pearl making a pretty picture in her white dress, sitting on the white iron bench on the porch of the white house. She sat quietly for a moment, searching her mind for some topic of conversation. Then she asked, "Have you been playing tennis?"

"You remember," Frank said, and Pearl was pleased with herself for mentioning the game.

"Yes," she said.

"If I had my racket with me, I would show you how it's done," he said. He looked across the expanse of yard. "There's enough land here for a court."

"Sometimes we play croquet on the lawn," Pearl said. "I'm not especially good at it."

"What a fine idea! What do you say we play a game right now? I believe you're dressed for it, if you'll take off your apron."

Pearl looked down at her skirt in embarrassment. "Oh, I didn't know," she said, reaching behind her, untying the offending garment and thrusting it aside.

Frank stood and reached for Pearl's hand to help her rise. "You tell me where the set is, and I'll put it up."

"We'll do it together." Pearl led him to a shed where the equipment was stored, and the two carried it onto the lawn. When the wickets were in place, Frank stood back to allow Pearl to go first. She picked up the mallet with the brown stripes on it and gently nudged her ball through the wire. Then she hit it a second time, the ball landing short of the next wire. Frank selected the mallet with the red stripes and whacked his ball through the wire, then on the second stroke, the ball landed next to Pearl's. "Ah, I've got you," he said. He placed his foot on the ball and struck it with the mallet, sending Pearl's ball into the lilac hedge. When the young woman looked at him in surprise, Frank grinned. "I'm not a man to let someone win just because she's a girl. I give no quarter," he said.

They continued the game, and by the time

Pearl caught up with Frank, they were almost to the end of the course. She hit the ball through a hoop, and when it bumped into Frank's, she said in a sort of apology, "I was lucky."

"Luck or not, you've got me," he replied.

It was Pearl's turn to send Frank's ball across the yard, but she hit it gently, and it rolled a few feet away.

"We'll have none of that," Frank said, picking up the ball and returning it to its spot next to Pearl's. "I may be a guest, but I'm willing to take my punishment."

Pearl stared at him a moment. Then she placed her foot on top of her ball and hit it with all of her might, shooting Frank's ball straight across the lawn and under the veranda. "There," she said, with a little thrill of excitement. "I give no quarter, either."

"Why, you are heartless." Frank grinned. "I should have kept my mouth shut."

Pearl won the game, which pleased her immensely, because she was not much of a competitor and generally finished last in any sport. Nor was she aware that most men didn't like to be bested by a woman, although Frank did not seem to mind. "Shall we play again?" she asked.

"What? Haven't you shamed me enough? I think I'd rather celebrate your championship with a glass of lemonade." The two returned to the porch, and when they were seated and Pearl had refreshed their glasses, Frank asked, "Do you think your father would be agreeable to talking about molybdenite again?"

"He thinks it's worth no more than . . ." She was about to say dirt, but instead, she finished, "He doesn't know what good it is. But he told you that."

"I would like to change his mind. How can I do so?"

The question caught Pearl by surprise, and she felt conflicted. Of course, she wanted to encourage the man, but she was loyal to her father. It would not be right to tell Frank about Charlie's weaknesses. But then, she thought, her father hadn't any. "I believe he can be convinced by facts, not pretty words," she said.

"Of course." He reached for the pitcher and, without asking, poured himself more lemonade, which Pearl thought was the least bit presumptuous, although she did not mind. She liked the idea that he felt at ease with her. "And what about you? How do I convince you?"

Pearl stiffened. She thought he was playing with her. "Of what?"

"That is the question, isn't it? Do I want

250

to convince you of the value of molybdenite, or do I want to convince you of something else?" When Pearl didn't respond, he added, "I hope to convince you to let me call on you again."

Pearl straightened her skirt across her lap, afraid to look up. "I would like that," she said at last. "I am always grateful for a discussion about metals."

"And I should hope about other things, as well."

"Yes."

Frank rose. "Then I should call on Wednesdays, when I know I will have you to myself."

Pearl felt faint, so she remained seated. "And you are welcome to call on Papa at any time, of course. He told me he likes you."

"I'm glad for that. I hope you feel the same way."

Pearl was uncomfortable flirting and replied, "I would be glad for a reason to put down my dust rag."

"Then I am happy to be of some use."

Frank went out then, and after he disappeared down the street, Mrs. Travers came from upstairs, because she had not been sewing at her machine but, instead, been sitting by the very window where Pearl had sat weeks before, watching Frank Curry depart. "He's a seemly young man. Do you care for him?" When Pearl didn't answer, she added, "I guess you want to tell me to mind my own taters."

Pearl was afraid she had been rude and answered quickly, "I like him. I like him fine." She turned to Mrs. Travers and took her hands. "He said he would call again, on Wednesdays, when Papa's away. Do you think that's right?"

"I don't see it's wrong."

"Must I tell Papa?" Pearl wasn't sure why she'd asked that, but she feared that Charlie would spoil things if he knew about Frank.

The older woman paused, looking past Pearl to the street, where a man in an old-fashioned buggy was passing by. The buggy was similar to the one she had ridden in with the doctor on that Independence Day some thirty years before, when she'd gone to tend the sick woman in Red Elephant. "No, not unless he asks."

So Frank began calling at the Bride's House on Wednesdays, not every Wednesday, of course, because he lived in Leadville and was busy with his molybdenite claim there. But he had a connection with a mine in Silver Plume, just above Georgetown, so there was reason for him to visit the area on a regular basis. On occasion, Frank called on Charlie during the week, and Charlie usually asked him to stay to supper. "I like the fellow," he told Pearl and Mrs. Travers.

"That's because he reminds you of yourself when you were younger. I never saw a man as bound to succeed as you were, Charlie," Mrs. Travers said, while Pearl did not comment.

When Frank was a guest, the conversations at the supper table were mostly about mining. While Pearl had never told Frank to keep their Wednesdays quiet, the young man seemed to sense that what happened between the two of them was private and not to be shared with Charlie. So Pearl's father had no idea what went on in his own home when he was away.

It was not as though the two young people did a thing that was improper. In fact, their companionship was quite innocent. Sometimes, Pearl played the piano while Frank sang. They sat on the porch or in the parlor and talked about mining and books. Some days, when the weather was nice, Pearl packed a basket, and the two ate dinner-on-the-ground high up in the mountains. Although she was a poor participant in sports, Pearl was surefooted and liked to

hike and could outpace anyone in Georgetown when it came to mountain climbing.
Sometimes, Frank brought along a pair of
rackets and tried to teach Pearl to play tennis in the side yard, screened by the lilac
bushes, but she was never very good at it.
Frank had another effect on Pearl, one of
which the young woman was not fully
conscious. That summer, she put aside the
stiff, somber dresses she had long favored
and began wearing simpler, more flowing
styles, some with touches of color. And she
gave up high-button shoes for soft slippers.
She did not cut her hair, which was so much
like Nealie's, because she knew that would
displease Charlie. But she wore it looser, so
that the curls escaped the knot at the nape
of her neck and softened her face.

Charlie did know, of course, that Frank
came to the house at times when he was
not there. Pearl and Mrs. Travers would
never lie to him. But the two women gave
him the impression that the man asked for
Charlie and they had only been polite in
entertaining him. Since Pearl was courteous
to all of Charlie's business associates, Charlie seemed to accept the explanation. Pearl
complained to him once that "I am getting
rather tired of molybdenite."

■ ■ ■ ■

Every year, Charlie left Georgetown for two or three weeks to visit the mines in which he invested. In past years, he'd invited Pearl to accompany him, and although the girl had dutifully gone with her father in her younger years, she now preferred to stay at home. In fact, the young woman actually looked forward to her father's trips away, because at those times, she and Mrs. Travers tore apart the house for spring or fall cleaning. They put on their oldest clothes and covered them with big aprons and wore dust caps on their heads, and scrubbed the Bride's House until it looked as new as the day that Nealie had moved in. It was also a time when they did not have to prepare the big meals Charlie preferred and instead dined on ham salad or lettuce and cream with a bit of sugar bread.

When Charlie announced he would go to New Mexico for two weeks to look into the copper mines there, he did not even ask Pearl if she wanted to go with him, knowing that unless he insisted, she would decline. The two women helped him prepare for the journey. They brushed his clothes and starched his shirts and collars and packed them in his valise, and on the day Charlie left, Pearl drove him to the station in the buggy. Charlie had only two horses, one for the buggy, the other for riding. Pearl did not like horses much, so she did not have one of her own. A boy came in daily to feed and water the animals, brush them and clean out the stalls, and Charlie asked him to remain in the stable until Pearl returned that day so that the young woman would not have to unhitch the buggy herself.

"What will you do while I'm away?" Charlie asked as the two sat in the conveyance at the depot, waiting for the train.

"There are the accounts to be gone over and letters to answer. Then Aunt Lidie and I will commence cleaning. I believe we will begin with the clothes presses, since I discovered when I packed your bag that a moth had been at your coat, and I had to mend it. I've already got out the turpentine to sprinkle in the presses to keep away those pesky things. The stable boy has promised to hang the carpets on the line outside so we can beat them."

"You'll work yourself into a frenzy," Charlie interrupted, and Pearl believed he did not care to hear any more about house cleaning. Then he patted Pearl's hand and said, "Perhaps when you're finished, you should surprise your aunt Lidie with a trip to Denver as a reward. You could shop and take in a moving picture show and whatever else young ladies do. Stay at the Brown Palace, and put the charge on my bill. What would you think of that?"

"Oh, Papa!" Pearl exclaimed. "If we stayed the night, we wouldn't have to take the late train home." The girl had never cared to go on such an outing before, but she had changed in the past few months, something of which she was only vaguely aware and he not at all.

"Would you like it?" he asked, surprise in his voice, because he knew his daughter did not care to go about. "Stay two nights then, as many as you wish."

"I should love it, although I would much prefer you were along."

"You'll have a better time with another woman, because I can't abide shopping. Spare no expense. Take enough money to enjoy yourself."

Pearl took her father's hand and squeezed it, and Charlie might have wondered then at the reason for so much excitement at an adventure that Pearl in the past would have refused, but they heard the train whistle, and Charlie stepped down from the buggy.

He kissed her cheek and said he would miss her.

Pearl sat in the buggy until her father boarded the cars and the train started up, and then she went home at a fast clip and turned the buggy over to the stable boy, hurrying into the house. "Aunt Lidie, what do you think?" she called as she went inside. "Papa wants us to go to Denver and see a picture show. We'll spend the night at the Brown Palace Hotel, maybe two. Oh, won't that be splendid?" She did not realize that she had picked up the word "splendid" from Frank.

"What's that?" Mrs. Travers called, because she had her head inside the pie safe, the one she had brought from the Rose Street cottage. She had already removed the dishes and washed the shelves, and now she was rinsing out the cupboard with water that held a few sprigs of dried lavender to make the wood smell sweet.

"As soon as we've finished cleaning, Papa wants us to take the cars to Denver and stay in the Brown Palace Hotel."

"Whatever for?"

"For our hard work. Papa says it's our reward. We're to shop and see the sights and have a good time." Pearl all but danced around the kitchen, while Mrs. Travers put down her rag and looked at the young woman in wonder. Pearl had never shown the least interest in the two of them going off anywhere. The old woman smiled then. The changes in Pearl since Frank Curry had begun calling on her seemed to be obvious to the housekeeper, if not to her employer or the girl herself. "If we hurry with our work, we can leave on Friday morning. We'll have Saturday to amuse ourselves and on Sunday, we can attend services at one of the great churches."

If Mrs. Travers did not care about the church services, she said nothing, because she was delighted at the break in her routine and would have gone anywhere with Pearl. "We must shuckle if we want to finish so soon," the old woman said.

That was Monday, and the two women spent all day at their work, barely stopping to eat a bite of dinner, and that evening they were too exhausted for a supper of anything but tea and toast. By Wednesday, the carpets had been rolled up, the floors scrubbed and waxed, the cupboards and windows cleaned, the brass chandeliers polished and the crystal drops washed with vinegar water, the banister rubbed down with buttermilk. When Pearl heard a knock on the door, she thought it was the stable boy come to carry out the carpets, and she called, "Go around to the back, please, and come inside," because she and Mrs. Travers had carried the carpets to the back of the house.

"So, I've been relegated to the servants' entrance," Frank Curry said, as he walked into the kitchen and spotted Pearl kneeling on the dining room floor, hammer in hand, prying out a loose nail in a floorboard that had caught her cleaning rag.

"Oh!" Pearl nearly fell over, caught herself, and sat down on the floor. "Mr. Curry, I didn't expect you." She looked down at her dirty apron, then felt for her hair, which had escaped from the dust cap. "I am a fright."

He reached for Pearl's hand and helped her up, the young woman snatching the cap off her head and attempting to smooth her unruly hair. "Mrs. Travers and I are 'shuckling,' as she says, so that we can go to Denver on Friday."

"On business?"

"For pleasure."

"I'm sure your father will show you a fine time."

"Oh, he isn't going. Didn't I say it?" Pearl asked, flustered. "Papa's gone to New Mexico and won't be back for, let's see, twelve days. Mrs. Travers and I have been abandoned."

"Well, not by me," Frank said. He paused a moment, then added. "I shall be in Denver myself this weekend, and if you don't think me too forward, you might consider letting me escort you and Mrs. Travers wherever you want to go. I do know something of the city, and I'd be honored to be seen with you."

"Oh!" Pearl squeezed her hands together. Frank's presence would make the outing more than pleasurable. "Aunt Lidie," Pearl said as the older woman came through the room, her arms filled with cleaning rags. "Mr. Curry has asked to show us about Denver."

Mrs. Travers started to reply but bit her lip instead. "Have you?" was her only response.

"I hope I'm not intruding. Miss Dumas seems so excited about the trip."

"You'd as soon keep a squirrel on the ground as calm that one," the woman said.

"Then you don't mind?"

"I'm not the one you're asking." The woman frowned. Frank Curry calling on Wednesdays was one thing, but it was quite another that he would meet Pearl on an overnight trip to Denver. It was clear from the look on her face that the old woman was not sure about the propriety of such a thing. But Pearl ignored Mrs. Travers's displeasure and accepted Frank's offer.

Pearl grew so flustered after Frank's visit, putting the hammer into the cutlery drawer and rinsing the clean woodwork with dirty wash water, that Mrs. Travers told her to go to her room and commence packing for the trip. The older woman would finish the housecleaning for the day, she said. Not one to shirk her duties, Pearl would have protested at any other time, but she did want a moment to herself to think about Mr. Curry. So she did as Mrs. Travers ordered.

Once in her room, Pearl went to the clothes press and removed her fall dresses, laying them out on her bed. It did not take long, since Pearl was not a spendthrift, and with little interest in clothes, she had a paltry wardrobe, especially for the daughter of a wealthy man. But she was sensitive enough to know that her dresses were all wrong. The black taffeta had rust spots and the brown bombazine was of a style that had gone out five years earlier. She inspected each dress, then discarded it, wishing for the first time in her life that she had cared a little more about fashion. "I haven't a thing to wear," she complained aloud.

Mrs. Travers, coming up the steps, only grunted.

"Papa said I might go shopping in Denver, but whatever I buy will need to be altered, so I'll be forced to wear what I have already, and nothing is up to the mark."

Mrs. Travers watched the girl with a smile of amusement. "What about that gray one you had made in the spring, the one that's the color of a mouse bush? You've never even worn it. You've got it hid away somewheres."

Pearl stopped, remembering it. "I put it away, because after it arrived, Papa told me he disliked gray dresses." But she took it out, along with a brown frock for sightseeing, then selected hats and gloves and got out the pair of diamond earrings her father had given her. She'd thought them flashy and never worn them, but now they seemed just the right thing.

A dozen times in the next day, as she worked frantically to finish the housecleaning, the young woman returned to her room and removed another frock from the clothes press and examined it or took down a hat from the shelf and considered it. Once, she dropped the carpet beater on the grass and exclaimed, "I'd forgotten. I must take a dress to wear when we go out in the evening."

"You go ahead. I'll finish," Mrs. Travers said, and indeed, if the old woman had not worked herself as hard as she had in her boardinghouse days, the cleaning would not have been finished by Thursday night.

But it was, and in the morning, the stable boy drove the two women and their baggage to the station, drove them there, at Pearl's insistence, a full hour before the train was to leave. Pearl wore a black mohair dress that was severe but not unflattering, although she seemed to think it was, and she convinced herself that Frank Curry would be displeased at being seen with such a dowdy creature.

But Frank seemed not to pay attention to her outfit. He was waiting beside the tracks and grinned at the two women when he spotted them peering out of the window, rushing to help them step from the train. He engaged a porter to carry the baggage outside, where he hailed a taxicab, a motorized one.

"Have you ridden in an automobile before?" he asked, after he directed the driver to the Brown Palace Hotel.

"Not in Georgetown," Mrs. Travers replied for the two of them. "There aren't many, and they have to be put up on blocks most of the year. I don't see the sense in them myself. I believe they'll disappear when folks get tired of the novelty." Then she added, "Of course, Pearl's seen them here with her father."

"I forgot you've been to Denver," Frank said, sounding disappointed. "You've probably seen as much of the city as I have."

"Not so much," Pearl said quickly. "We meet with people at the Mining Exchange all day and don't often spend the night. Papa doesn't have time to see the sights."

"Have you been to City Park? Or the zoo? Or the top of the capitol?" Each time Frank asked a question, Pearl shook her head, until the young man beamed at her again and said that in that case, he had plenty to show her.

So after the women left their luggage at the hotel, Frank ordered the driver to take them to the zoo. "A camel," Frank told Pearl, pointing to an animal.

"Just like the pictures," Pearl exclaimed. "I wonder what it would be like to ride such an animal. Oh, Aunt Lidie, wouldn't it be wonderful to go to Greece and ride a camel?"

"Egypt. They ride camels in Egypt. The Greeks ride donkeys."

Instead of simpering at her mistake and

pleading feminine stupidity, Pearl said, "I'm glad you told me, Mr. Curry. I won't make that mistake again."

"Perhaps they have camels in Greece after all. You should go there and find out and write me a postal to let me know."

"To Greece?"

"And Egypt."

"But how would I go?" Pearl thought the idea as preposterous as traveling to the moon.

"Wouldn't your father escort you? If I were your father, I should do so."

Pearl clasped and unclasped her hands in confusion. "I've never wanted to travel. I've always been perfectly happy to stay in Georgetown."

"There's a world beyond Georgetown, an exciting one, and you ought to see it. I wish I could show it to you." They had drawn a little away from Mrs. Travers, who had spotted a trio of monkeys and was absorbed in watching their antics. "You've already taken the first step, coming to Denver by yourself."

"Oh," Pearl said, turning away and staring at the camels. She was not sure how to respond to such a remark.

Frank put his hand on her arm. "There are tours. You could go with Mrs. Travers."

He added slyly, "Or with a husband, if you had one."

Pearl reddened and turned away. "You are making fun of me, Mr. Curry."

"Nonsense. Any man would be proud to accompany you. I know of no woman more suitable as a traveling companion — or a wife."

"Mr. Curry . . ." Pearl said, and stopped, thinking she should reprimand him but not sure why.

"I apologize for my boldness. But surely you know how much I admire you. You're not silly like other women. You are anxious to learn about a subject, and you possess calmness and fearlessness."

"Surely not fearlessness." Pearl had to smile.

"Few other women have the pluck to ride to the bottom of a mine shaft in a bucket and walk through the tunnels."

He started to say more — or at least, Pearl thought he did — but Mrs. Travers came up to them and remarked, "Have you been watching the monkeys? The little one looks just like a boarder I once had on Rose Street." She laughed, but when the other two did not respond, she looked at them curiously.

"Oh yes, the monkeys," Frank said at last,

267

taking his eyes away from Pearl and looking at the older woman. "They're very clever, aren't they? Now, how would you like to take a drive about the city?"

As they passed the capitol building, he pointed to the dome and said they could go to the top the next day. "I remember you are a better climber than I am," he told Pearl.

"Well, you won't catch me gadding about up there in the air," Mrs. Travers said. Pearl thought she saw Frank smile, and she hoped they could climb the steps together, just the two of them.

When they returned to the hotel, Mrs. Travers announced she was tired and that it would be a good idea to order supper sent to their room, "for you will want a soon start in the morning." Pearl was disappointed. She wanted to spend the evening with Frank, but being agreeable, she nodded.

"Tomorrow night, I'll take you to dinner and a movie," Frank told them, "unless you prefer a play. There is the Broadway Theater just across the street."

"I can see a play in Georgetown. I want to go to a picture show. Besides, Papa suggested it," Pearl told him, a little surprised at herself, since she'd never cared to see a movie before. But then, she'd never been asked to attend a movie by Frank Curry.

CHAPTER 10

In the morning, the two women took the omnibus down Sixteenth Street to Daniels & Fisher, the fashionable store that Frank had recommended, where Pearl chose a delicate pink wool frock that was cut in a severe style. The pink was an odd choice for a woman with Pearl's red hair and pale skin, but it looked so stunning on her that Mrs. Travers sucked in her breath when Pearl modeled the gown for her. Made without trimmings, the dress gave the girl a sophisticated air. "You look pretty as thundersnow," the older woman said, referring to that rare combination of lightning, thunder, and snow, a phenomenon that turns the sky a strange shade of pink. "It's the color of your name," Mrs. Travers added, a look of self-satisfaction on her face at her bit of poetry, because she was a plainspoken woman.

After the dress had been fitted, Pearl gave the clerk the Georgetown address, then asked suddenly, "Could you alter it today, so that I might wear it tonight?" The clerk consulted with the seamstress, and they agreed that it might be done and delivered that afternoon. "I can wear the dress to the picture show, Aunt Lidie," Pearl said, her eyes glowing. "Now we must find something for you."

Mrs. Travers protested that she had enough dresses to last her till the noon of doomsday, but Pearl insisted. "Papa said we were both to go shopping, and I mean to buy you something fine to wear." So they found a tweed suit that Mrs. Travers pronounced finer than anything she had ever seen at the Presbyterian church in Georgetown, and the two hurried off to O. P. Baur's to meet Frank for luncheon.

Inside the restaurant was a pink and white marble soda fountain the likes of which Pearl had seen only in photographs. The fountain stretched the length of the room, and a mirror behind the back bar made it appear even larger. Silver knobs and handles gleamed against the marble, and young men hurried back and forth with dishes of ice cream and tall glasses and spoons — "ice cream and soda water. It's called a soda and was invented in this very restaurant," Frank told them.

"Then we must have one," Pearl exclaimed.

"I thought you didn't care for ice cream," Mrs. Travers whispered.

"Oh, but I do," Pearl replied, adding softly, "Now."

After they were seated at a table and had ordered their luncheon, Mrs. Travers announced, "We followed your advice and went to Daniels & Fisher, where we spent enough money to ransom the Queen of Sheba."

"I did not know the Queen of Sheba had been kidnapped," Frank said, and they all laughed. Then he added, "I'm glad for it. I'm sure the money was well spent."

"I suppose you'll see this evening," Mrs. Travers said. "Pearl insisted that her dress be finished in time for the outing."

Pearl colored, embarrassed that Mrs. Travers had told on her. "Where do we go next?" she asked quickly, looking aside to hide the flush on her face.

"I'm sorry it's late in the year, or I'd take you to see a baseball game. But I think you would like the capitol building. We'll climb all the way to the top. You can see Mount Evans from there."

"I can see Mount Evans from home and up close. I'm too beat out to climb all those stairs just to look at a mountain," Mrs. Travers told them.

And so, after they had finished eating — and Pearl had pronounced the ice-cream soda as good a thing as she had ever tasted — the couple delivered Mrs. Travers to the hotel, and then they walked the two blocks down Broadway to the capitol building. Pearl delighted in the structure, the dome that was covered with gold from the Colorado mines, the halls lined with marble, the grand golden staircase. They made their way to the top floor and found the wooden stairs leading to the dome. There were not so many steps, and they were not very high, and Pearl wondered if Frank had exaggerated the climb to Mrs. Travers to discourage her from accompanying them. The idea that Frank might have fibbed in order to be alone with her sent a thrill through the girl, until she decided that the more practical reason was Frank thought Mrs. Travers too old to manage the stairs and was only saving her from discomfort or embarrassment. As she ascended the stairs, Pearl felt Frank's hand on her back, the warmth of his skin through her dress, and she moved slowly, savoring his touch.

As they climbed to the dome, they passed a party of four men coming down from the top. The men stepped aside on the landing to allow Pearl to pass and doffed their hats, exchanging pleasantries with Frank. Then as three of the men started down the steps, the fourth looked closely at Pearl and said, "Why, it's Miss Dumas, isn't it? We have met in Georgetown when I've called upon your father."

Pearl did not know if she cared to be recognized, but there was nothing to be done about it, and she introduced Frank to the man. "May I present Mr. Frank Curry," she said to him. "Mr. Curry, I have the honor of introducing you to Governor Shafroth." The two men shook hands, and Pearl added, "Mr. Curry is an associate of my father's. He's in the molybdenite business. In fact, he is president of the Colorado Molybdenite Company."

"Ah yes," the governor said. "I wish you well, young man. I must catch up with my party. Germans they are, come to look at our mines. Give my kindest regards to your father, Miss Dumas."

Pearl and Frank watched as the governor hurried down the steps and disappeared, and Frank said. "You are full of surprises. You never told me you knew the governor."

Pearl shrugged. She was not so impressed with rank and office. "He wasn't governor when I met him. He was plain Mr. John Shafroth, come to ask Papa about a legal matter. In another year — or three, if he's not reelected — he'll be *Mr.* Shafroth again."

They reached the top of the steps and walked out onto a little balcony that circled the dome, Pearl glad that no one else was there. "Look," Frank said, making a wide gesture with his arm. "Isn't it fine? Straight ahead is Georgetown. We could see your house if the mountains weren't in the way. I bet you can see for a thousand miles." He turned to look at Pearl.

Pearl considered that. Then, since she was not one to exaggerate, she replied, "A hundred miles anyway."

"A thousand miles straight up into the air," Frank said.

Pearl stretched her neck, raising her head to stare at the clouds. After she looked down, she suddenly felt dizzy and reached out for the railing but clutched Frank instead. When she saw what she'd done, she drew back, but Frank would not let go of her. He took both of her arms and asked, "Are you light-headed?"

"Oh no," Pearl answered quickly, because she did not want him to think her one of those women who fainted at the least thing. "I'm all right." After a pause, she said, "You can let go of me now." She wished he would not, however.

"I don't want to," Frank said.

Pearl drew in her breath at the words. Then thinking she had misunderstood, she repeated. "I am perfectly all right, Mr. Curry."

But Frank did not let go. "Of course you are. Everything about you is all right."

Pearl only stared at him, confused, looking for an explanation, telling herself Frank surely was talking about her health, but she hoped he meant more. After all, he had said such lovely things at the zoo the day before.

The young man gripped her arms tighter. "Miss Dumas — Pearl. May I call you Pearl?"

"Yes," she answered tentatively.

"You are the finest young woman I know. I've never met anyone like you. I knew that first day, when you opened the door and let me into your home, that you were someone I could care about. And I do care about you. In fact, I believe I love you." He paused a second. "I mean I do love you."

Pearl stood so still that it was as if she no longer breathed.

"Might I hope you could feel the same way about me?" Frank continued.

He looked into Pearl's eyes, waiting for

her to reply. But all Pearl could say was, "I . . ." and she grew mute. Her heart and tongue did not seem able to work together, and she felt all-overish. She turned away from Frank and began wringing her hands. "I . . ." she said, and was mum again.

"I hadn't planned to declare myself just yet. After all, we've known each other only a few months. But something made me say it. Besides, what's the reason to wait? I don't want someone else to claim you. Surely you have other suitors."

"But I haven't," Pearl told him.

Her lack of guile seemed to embolden Frank. He took a deep breath and said, "I believe you've known all along how I feel."

"Oh no. I haven't. No," Pearl said, her face crimson. Nothing in her life had prepared her for such a pronouncement.

"Tell me to stop, and I will."

"No. I don't want you to stop," Pearl said, finding her voice at last. "You have judged me rightly, Mr. Curry. I have never cared for another man as much as I do you. In fact, I have never cared for another man at all."

"Then I will ask if you would consider joining our lives together, for it would give me so much happiness if you would agree to be my wife."

"Oh," Pearl replied, barely able to speak, so overcome was she with happiness. "Oh yes, I would consider it. I mean, I don't need to consider it. I can answer now. Yes."

"Splendid!" Frank replied, gripping Pearl's arms so tightly that the young woman was afraid he would cut off the circulation. "But I must be square with you. I haven't much to offer, although I believe if you'll be patient for a while yet, my molybdenum mine will be worth a fortune as large as your father's. If we marry now, we won't be able to entertain lavishly or live in a grand style, but I think you do not care for such things."

"No," Pearl breathed, and emboldened, she added, "I care only for you."

"We'll find a modest house — in George-town or Leadville or Denver, wherever you prefer."

"But you could live with us," Pearl said, because she had never considered living anyplace but the Georgetown house. "After all, it's called the Bride's House. My mother went there as a bride, and now I will. There is no better house in the world." Pearl closed her eyes as a thrill of emotion went through her. She thought of herself dressed in an ivory gown standing beside Frank in the red parlor as they took their vows.

"Besides, Papa would want us to live with him. Would you do that?"

"If it would make you happy," he said. "I wouldn't want to tear you away from your father." He stopped talking then and drew Pearl to him and kissed her on the lips.

The girl stared at him in surprise. She had never been kissed before and did not know how to respond. But in a second, she closed her eyes and kissed him back. "Are we engaged, then?" she asked.

"We are that," Frank told her. "I consider us promised, and I shall hold you to that promise for the rest of your life."

"Then I have never been so happy."

"Nor I. You decide the day, but I would like it to be soon."

"First, you must speak to Papa. He will expect you to, you know. We don't want to get off on the wrong foot with him."

"I will at the first opportunity. You don't suppose he will object, do you?"

"Papa? He thinks only of my happiness. He's never said no to me. And he won't this time, not when he knows how much I care about you."

Frank put his arm about Pearl's waist and held her a moment longer, and the two of them looked out over the city to the mountains toward Georgetown, where they would make their home. They went back inside the dome, with Frank descending the stairs first in case Pearl should trip. The young woman, who was sure-footed and did not need such protection — indeed, she was so overjoyed that she might have floated down the steps — nonetheless reveled in that solicitous gesture from her future husband.

Pearl did not return until half past six, just thirty minutes before they were to meet Frank in the lobby of the hotel. If Mrs. Travers noticed Pearl's mussed hair, her high color and dreamy demeanor, she would have chalked it up to the girl's excitement over the climb to the top of the capitol building, her new dress, and the upcoming outing to Curtis Street. The old woman herself was greatly agitated at seeing her first picture show. "Shuckle now. You're as slow as sorghum," she chided. But in fact, the two were dressed and waiting downstairs when Frank arrived. They planned to take in the motion picture, then return to the hotel for a late supper.

Pearl was ecstatic when she saw Frank walk into the lobby, his clothes perfectly pressed, a gray felt hat in one hand, an ebony walking stick with a gold knob in the other. She could scarcely believe that this handsome man had just declared himself to her and asked for her hand. Frank looked over the new pink dress and motioned for Pearl to turn about so that he could see it from all sides. Then he declared it to be perfection — the most striking gown he had ever seen and a perfect complement to Pearl's complexion. "Every man in the theater will envy me escorting two such lovely ladies," he said.

Mrs. Travers ran her tongue over her teeth in what might have been a gesture of humbug, but the other two failed to notice.

Frank procured a taxicab that whisked them to Curtis Street, which was aglitter with electric lights. The streets and the picture palaces were covered with thousands of them, "more than all the stars in the heavens," Pearl exclaimed, and even Mrs. Travers was made speechless at the sight of them. Frank purchased the tickets and handed them to an usher, who showed them to their seats. Pearl sat between the other two.

In a few minutes, the theater grew dark, and the velvet curtains opened, revealing a large screen. The movie began, and so did a piano player, whose music heightened the action. The picture was about a train robbery, and Pearl was so taken by the reality

281

of the movie that she sat on the edge of her seat and cried, "Oh no, look behind you," when the villain pointed his gun at the hero's back. After the picture was over, she put her hand to her throat to finger the cameo, her gesture of nervousness, but she had not worn it. So she clasped the neckline of her dress and told Frank, "I was so caught up . . . I mean, for a moment I thought it was real."

"And so did everyone else. You weren't the only one who warned him, was she, Mrs. Travers?" Frank asked.

The older woman raised her chin and said, "It's perfectly understandable," because she herself had cried out louder than Pearl.

They stayed for the second picture, a comedy with two silly men caught up in foolishness. Pearl did not care much for slapstick and watched silently, not paying so much attention this time, because halfway through the picture, Frank put his hand over hers and let it rest there, under her purse, where Mrs. Travers couldn't see it. The old woman, however, was so caught up in the picture — her laugh could be heard all over the movie palace — that the young couple could have stolen out of the theater without her paying the least attention.

Pearl had hoped Mrs. Travers would plead tiredness as she had the night before, and thus leave the couple alone. But she was in high spirits and accompanied them to supper and even for an evening stroll past Frank's hotel, just a block from the Brown Palace, to the capitol, which shone with electric lights. "This is the best day that ever came down over my head," she declared, as she took Pearl's arm and all but dragged the young woman to the elevator, after they returned from the walk.

"Yes," Pearl replied, looking at Frank. "Yes, I believe it is."

So Pearl and Frank were denied the pleasure of being alone that evening. Nor did the two manage a moment to themselves the next day, because Mrs. Travers was with them every moment, from the time Frank met them for church until he escorted them to Union Station.

Pearl longed to ask Frank when he would come to Georgetown, but she did not want to seem anxious. She was delighted when Mrs. Travers asked, "Will we see you again this week, Mr. Curry?"

Frank shook his head. "I am going east on business and won't return for a month."

When Pearl uttered a disappointed, "Oh," he said, "Perhaps two weeks if things go

283

well. I will come as soon as I can, for I have something important to discuss with Mr. Dumas."

"Where will you go?" Pearl asked.

"New York, Washington, perhaps New Orleans." He smiled at her, as if the words had a secret meaning, and Pearl smiled back, because now she knew that Frank, not her father, would take her to those places, perhaps on their wedding trip.

"Not Egypt?" she asked.

"Not this trip."

Mrs. Travers did not pay attention to the silly words or see the long look the two gave each other; instead she watched the train back into the station. When the conductor put down the stool, and the passengers began to board, Mrs. Travers told Pearl, "Get aboard, or we shouldn't have a decent seat." The young woman reluctantly followed the older woman to the train.

Mrs. Travers immediately climbed aboard and went inside the car to claim a seat, but Pearl stood on the observation platform, looking down at Frank. "Are you all right?" he asked. "I shouldn't —"

"Hush. Never have I felt better. Or been happier."

"I'll come as soon as I can, dear, for it's very important business, indeed," Frank said. He touched his fingers to his lips.

"Shuckle," Pearl told him.

Charlie Dumas cut short his trip to New Mexico, because one of the mines he had expected to visit had experienced a cave-in, shutting off the main adit, and he had decided to put off his investment decision until he could inspect it. So, to his daughter's delight, he returned to Georgetown only days after the women. Pearl longed to tell him about Frank's proposal. Charlie was the only person in whom she ever confided, although those confidences usually involved business or were observations about people. She did not discuss personal matters with her father for the reason that she didn't have many. But she would have to tell him Frank's intentions before the young man sought an interview, because she believed her father would be disappointed if he learned of her future plans from anyone except herself. She had not yet decided when or how to inform him, however.

Charlie arrived in late morning and immediately went into his study to take care of business that had come up in his absence. Pearl and Mrs. Travers unpacked his bags and put away his things. Then Pearl went into the study to take dictation and write her father's letters for him. There was no time to discuss anything else, and indeed, the girl wanted to wait until Charlie was rested and not overwrought with work before she surprised him with her announcement.

As if to make up for the days she had spent away from her work, Mrs. Travers prepared Charlie's favorite dishes for supper. She went to the market for a hen, which she stewed with dumplings, boiled and mashed potatoes, opened a bottle of green beans and cooked them to a pulp, with bacon. She baked bread and a Snow Cake, which Pearl iced and set on a glass stand on the sideboard in the dining room.

When Charlie went into the room, he surveyed the feast set out and sighed that if he could help it, he would never leave home again. Between bites of supper, he told the women about his trip, pointing his fork at Pearl from time to time (when Charlie was excited, his table manners reverted to his early days in Georgetown) to emphasize his point about a mine or a smelter he had toured. "You should have seen the amalgamation process, Pearl. The equipment was so clean, you could put it into your kitchen and eat off it."

"And have you decided to invest in any of

the mines?" she asked.

Charlie thought that over. "I wish you'd been with me, since you have a good head. I don't know. Only the King Mine seems like a good prospect, but there's something about it. . . ." He paused with his fork in the air. "I can't put my finger on it. Perhaps I'm getting old and overly cautious. Besides, since I couldn't inspect it thoroughly, I've put off a decision."

"You are not old, and your instincts are always good, Papa. Perhaps you should listen to them."

"I would not want to miss an opportunity as I did with Utah Copper. I thought the ore there was too low-grade to be economic, and that was a mistake. If I'd invested in it, the two of you would be wearing furs and diamonds."

"We could wear furs and diamonds now, if we chose to," Pearl told him.

Charlie chuckled. "Yes, I suppose. But you don't want them."

"You forget that I have a pair of diamond earrings —"

"Which you never wear."

"And a little fur."

"That belonged to your mother."

"She spent a pretty penny on a dress in Denver," Mrs. Travers interjected. "I believe you'll like it. It is the color of apple blossoms."

Charlie nodded his approval. "So you went to the city, then?"

"Oh, Papa. We had a wonderful time. We stayed two nights," Pearl said. "We visited the zoo and the park and the state capitol, and I had an ice-cream soda. I believe we should get some ice cream and soda, and I'll make one for you — chocolate, vanilla, or strawberry. It is mighty good. Perhaps we should have an ice-cream social on the lawn next summer and serve sodas."

Charlie looked at his daughter curiously. She had always disliked entertaining. "And did you see a picture show?"

"Oh yes," Mrs. Travers told him. "It's a good thing I didn't have a gun, or I'd have shot the robber myself. It was that real. Do you remember when you took Nealie to the Opera House and she thought the story was taking place in front of her eyes?" The old woman chuckled. "Well, that's just the way we felt at the picture show."

The two continued talking about the trip, and when dinner was over and Charlie had taken himself uptown to the saloons, Pearl realized that neither one of the women had mentioned seeing Frank Curry. Pearl had not asked Mrs. Travers to refrain from saying his name, but the old woman, like Pearl, seemed to sense that Frank Curry should be kept out of their conversations with Charlie Dumas.

Several days later, Pearl came into the house just as Mrs. Travers was setting supper on the table. The young woman had gone out for a short walk, but instead, she'd started up the mountain, and lost in her thoughts of Frank Curry, she had gone farther than she'd expected. But the hike had been fruitful, because along the way, she had decided how to tell her father about the engagement. She would ask him to accompany her on that same walk on Sunday, after church, when he generally put aside business cares and was in a jovial mood. He would have a week or more to accustom himself to the idea of Pearl's marriage, before Frank arrived in Georgetown.

"I'm sorry, Aunt Lidie. I walked too far and left you with all the work," Pearl said, hanging up her shawl, an old one that had belonged to her mother, and hurrying into the dining room.

"You'd have done a better job of it," the older woman said. "The chops are dry, and I burned the Arkansas wedding cake. It's a poor supper."

"I'm sure the meat is edible, and as for the cornbread, Papa doesn't care much about it anyway. Besides, your poorest is better than most women's best," Pearl said, because she was in high humor. "Shall I fetch Papa?"

Mrs. Travers nodded, and Pearl knocked on the doors of the study, then slid them open. Charlie sat reading his mail and did not glance at her until Pearl said, "Papa?" He looked up in acknowledgment, and she added, "Supper is on the table."

"I'll be there." He waved his hand in dismissal, and Pearl went into the dining room, where she and Mrs. Travers sat down. They waited, Mrs. Travers frowning at the food that was cooling, until Pearl got up and went back to the study and asked, "Papa, are you coming to the table, or should we go ahead without you? I can bring you a plate in here if you like."

Charlie sat with his back to the girl, staring out the window. "I'm coming," he said. But it was several more minutes before he sat down at the head of the table.

"Are you very busy, Papa?" Pearl asked.

"I have had a setback."

"Oh," Pearl exclaimed, because Charlie rarely had business downturns. "I hope it's not bad." She buttered a piece of cornbread and took a bite, frowning at the burned taste. She did not feel much like eating and set it down.

"It is a disappointment." He chewed on a piece of meat and said, "Mrs. Travers, this chop is as dry as granite."

Both women stared at him, since Charlie never complained about the food. "I'm sorry, Charlie," the older woman said. "I told Pearl —"

Charlie waved his hand. "Supper doesn't matter. I've had a great shock." The women set down their forks, and Charlie continued. "It seems my daughter, whom I believed to be a woman of virtue, sneaked off to Denver with a man while I was away." He looked at Mrs. Travers while he spoke, but when he was finished, he turned to stare at Pearl.

"Papa!" the young woman cried.

"Charlie Dumas!" Mrs. Travers exclaimed at the same time. "There was no carryings-on. You yourself suggested the trip, and I was with Pearl every minute."

"Were you?" He gave her a look that would have scorched the cornbread, if it had not already been burned. "Then it's an odd thing that the letter I received from the governor doesn't mention you. John Shafroth wrote to say he was delighted to meet Pearl in the capitol building — and her

291

companion, Frank Curry. But he did not remark on a Mrs. Travers."

"There was only that one afternoon." Mrs. Travers paused, stiffening her back. "But they were hardly alone, unless you think the capitol dome, which is in plain sight for half of Denver to see, is a place for talking moonshine. You've no right to accuse your own daughter —"

Charlie interrupted her. "Is there some reason you didn't tell me you went to Denver to meet a man?" he asked Pearl. "I believe your mother would be ashamed of you."

Pearl gasped. Charlie had never evoked Nealie in that way.

"No such a thing, Charlie," Mrs. Travers broke in, remembering, perhaps, that Nealie had had a daring streak and that Pearl had been born less than nine months after Nealie married Charlie. "You know Pearl is an honorable girl. I won't let you say that."

Charlie ignored the older woman, and his eyes bored into Pearl. "Are you struck dumb?"

For the first time in her life, Pearl feared her father's anger. "I can explain that, Papa. Mr. Curry called here a day or two after you went to New Mexico. When he discovered we were going to Denver, he offered to show us the sights. We would never have seen so much if he hadn't taken us about. We did nothing behind your back."

"Then why did I learn from the governor that you were in Denver with this man? Why didn't you tell me yourself?"

"Hold your taters, Charlie," Mrs. Travers broke in. "It's no wonder Pearl doesn't confide in you, because you find something wrong with any young man who catches her eye. I believe it goes back to the day when you were jealous over —"

Charlie gave the old woman a hard look. "Do you value your job, Lydia?"

Mrs. Travers was taken aback and didn't reply. In all the years she had worked for Charlie Dumas, he had never suggested she leave. She was as much a part of the household as Pearl.

"If you do, I suggest you hold your tongue," Charlie continued.

"You'd fire me, then? Well, fire away, Charlie. You won't shut me up." Still, the old woman kept silent after that.

"You don't know what you're saying to Aunt Lidie," Pearl told her father.

"I know exactly what I'm saying. But don't let's change the subject. We were talking about you and Frank Curry. What am I to think of you, Pearl, if the governor of the state knows more about my daughter than I? Frank Curry is no longer welcome in this house. I forbid you seeing him again. Am I clear?"

"You can't mean that, Papa."

"Do I usually say things I don't mean?"

Pearl gripped her hands together so tightly that her knuckles were pale. Her forehead was damp, and her heart beat so hard that she thought her father must hear it. "I . . ." she said. She dropped her eyes to her lap, while both Charlie and Mrs. Travers stared at her. Without looking up, she said, "Frank Curry and I are going to be married, Papa. He is coming to the house in a few days to ask you for my hand."

"He has my answer now!" Charlie thundered.

Pearl raised her eyes to study her father for a moment. She was not angry exactly, but she was greatly disappointed. She did not shout as he had but instead said quietly, "I believe that is my decision, not yours."

"Just as it will be your decision to live in poverty, then. Your Mr. Curry won't get money out of me."

"We'll do without your fortune. Mr. Curry does not expect a cent from me."

"Oh no, but he expects it from me. Where do you plan to live?"

"Why, here in the Bride's House, of course. I thought you'd want us to."

"Without paying a penny for upkeep, I imagine. And how will Mr. Curry support you?"

"He has an income."

"Has he?" Charlie's voice was lower now, less angry. "If he has money, why does he ask me for funds?"

"To invest in his molybdenum mine."

"Oh yes, since no one else will back him. Child, don't you see that Mr. Curry is only after our money? Do you think he would care for you if I were a fireman on the railroad?"

"That's not fair, Papa. Mr. Curry loves me. He told me so."

Charlie pushed aside his plate and leaned across the table toward Pearl. "Why does he love you, Pearl? Is it your beauty? Your charm? Perhaps you are a clever conversationalist or a fine horsewoman. Is that it? It couldn't possibly be that Mr. Curry has fallen in love with your fortune, can it?"

Although she knew she had none of those qualities her father mentioned, Pearl was hurt more than she would have believed by Charlie's words, for she had always thought she was perfect in her father's eyes. She slumped in her chair, one hand to her cheek. "That's not so," she said. "Frank loves me, not your money."

"You've no right, Charlie," Mrs. Travers snapped. "Toss me aside like fool's gold, but I'll speak my mind. Any man would be lucky to marry Pearl. She is a fine young woman, and if you don't know it, then shame on you."

"I do know it. Of course I do," Charlie said, not unkindly. "I wouldn't wish for any other daughter. But you must look at it plainly. There is a reason she is a spinster."

"How can you say that, Papa?" Pearl cried.

"Because it's the truth. And because I'd rather hurt your feelings now than see you live a lifetime with a man who cares only for your money. Do you want that?"

"It's not so. You don't know Frank. I believe you don't want me to marry anyone at all. You've ruled me all my life, and if you have your way, I'll stay here and pay your bills and write your letters and be your companion as long as I live." The thought had only then occurred to Pearl that her father wished to keep her by his side always, and it flickered through her mind that he had foiled every attempt on her part to leave him. Charlie had prevented her from going to college, and he had spoiled things between Pearl and any man he thought she liked, even going so far as to hire detectives to turn up the suitor's vices.

Charlie ignored the outburst, and said, "Your Mr. Curry is a sharper, a fortune hunter."

"He's not," Pearl said. "He loves me."

"We'll see," Charlie told her. "I'll get my supper elsewhere." He stood and left the house.

CHAPTER 11

The next days were a time of great strain in the Bride's House. Pearl and Mrs. Travers talked about superficial things — how many bushels of tomatoes they should order from the Western Slope to bottle, whether they should take the chance of planting tulip bulbs in hopes the deer wouldn't eat the flowers in the spring, who to hire to bring firewood. The boy who normally did chores for them had quit, so Pearl took over the job of chopping kindling herself. The hard, rough work appealed to her, quieted her nerves. Since the confrontation with her father, she had been listless and had lost her appetite.

Worried, Mrs. Travers suggested that the young woman unburden herself, saying, "Nealie used to talk to me. She thought me a good friend."

"I'm glad for it," Pearl said, making it clear that what had been fine for her mother was not for her.

Pearl continued to assist her father, looking up research, filing company reports, writing the endless letters, but the two talked only when necessary now. Frank Curry's name was never mentioned. Nor was there the casual banter that had made the working arrangement so pleasurable for each of them. In fact, nothing was said that did not pertain to business.

At dinner, Mrs. Travers chatted about the weather or passed along the gossip she had picked up in town, but when neither Charlie nor Pearl joined the conversation, the older woman fell silent. The three ate their meals quickly, then went their separate ways.

More than a week passed, and Frank Curry had not appeared, when Charlie asked Pearl to step into his study and close the sliding doors to the hall. "Sit down," he said.

"I prefer to stand," Pearl told him.

"Please." The word seemed to cost him a great deal of effort, and Pearl sat stiffly on the edge of the chair, her hands folded in her lap.

"Do you still expect to marry Mr. Curry?"

"Yes."

"Have you heard from him?"

"I have had a letter, two, in fact. He's been

delayed in New York. He'll be here before the week is out."

"Have you told him I forbid the marriage?"

"No." Pearl did not add that the reason was she had no address for Frank.

Charlie, who had been standing, sat down behind his desk and picked up an envelope. "You have got the wrong pig by the ear. I have had a private detective look into Mr. Curry's background."

"I expected it. You have done it before."

Charlie looked surprised but didn't respond. Instead, he said, "Your Mr. Curry is not what I expected."

"No one is."

Charlie stared at his daughter, who had never spoken so frankly to him before. Then he opened the envelope and removed several sheets of paper. "Frank Curry was expelled from Dartmouth for fighting. The details are here if you care to read them." He handed a sheet of paper to Pearl, and when she did not take it, Charlie said, "Very well. I will go on. He did not graduate from the Colorado School of Mines, either, but dropped out, contrary to what he has led us to believe. He has worked for three mining companies and was let go from each one for a variety of reasons — insubordination, mostly, and then there was the question of missing funds in one case, although no charges were filed. He lives beyond his means and has debts. And he does not come from a prominent family."

"Neither did you."

"No, but I never pretended I did. Did you know his father served time in a penitentiary — for theft, I believe?"

"Papa, you would investigate Jesus Christ and find him a charlatan if He wanted to marry me."

"Pearl! Don't blaspheme."

The young woman looked abashed at what she had said, but she stood her ground and did not apologize. Instead, she asked, "Did you hire a detective agency to look into my mother's background before you married her?"

"How dare you!" Charlie lunged forward over the desk with his hand raised, and only at the last second did he control himself and not strike his daughter. He stood there a moment, then looked at his hand, shame on his face, and slowly sat down. "Frank Curry has turned you into a shrew."

"No, Papa," Pearl said, leaning forward and looking at her father intently. "He has awakened me. He has made me aware I have abilities I did not know about, and he has taught me not to be afraid. He's opened up the world to me. Why, he's promised to take me to New York and New Orleans, perhaps on our bridal tour, and maybe one day we'll go to Egypt." Pearl gripped her hands together, because confronting her father was difficult. She had never done it before.

"And haven't I offered to do the same, but you turned me down?" Charlie sighed. "Was your life so bad before you met him? Is there anything I did not give you, any request I refused? I thought you were happy."

Pearl was conflicted. "I was happy. I thought I was. But now I am so much happier. You're making a muddle of things."

"No, Pearl, Frank Curry has done that. He's driven a wedge between us."

Pearl turned away from her father, looking over her shoulder through the partially open doors of the parlor at the stiff furniture, worn with age, the red wallpaper, the walnut table with its now-faded shawl, the formal portrait of her mother above the mantel, the dried flowers that had crumbled into dust under their dome. She knew every object in the room, had known each since she could first remember. Nothing had ever changed, and suddenly, she felt as if the room was as dead as the stuffed bird caught in its glass prison. Her eye caught a movement, and she realized that Mrs. Travers was sitting there. Pearl rose and said, "Papa, I intend to marry him. There is nothing you can say to dissuade me."

"Then I have a proposal. Tell Mr. Curry that if he marries you, I will disown you. You will be penniless. Then see what how much he wants you to be his wife."

"I won't!" Pearl said.

"Are you afraid of what he'll say?"

Pearl did not answer, but swept out of the study into the parlor, closing the doors behind her.

Mrs. Travers stood, and said, "I know it isn't something of my business what went on in there, and I'll keep quiet." Before Pearl could respond, the older woman added, "Your father didn't know any more about Nealie Bent when he asked her to marry him than a pig knows about Sunday."

The wait for Frank Curry to arrive in Georgetown now seemed interminable to Pearl, who divided her days between heavy household chores and needlework, although none of that improved her state of mind. She would have liked to hike in the mountains, but the weather had turned cold, and snow covered the ground higher up. Besides, she was afraid that if she left the house, Frank would arrive and thus would have to face her father without knowing that Charlie despised him. Since she had no address for Frank in the East, she could not send him a warning letter. Frank wrote her again, saying he had been delayed another day or two. It was a missive that seemed to her more like a business communication than a love letter. But she prized it and read and reread it a dozen times a day, lingering over the closing, "My tenderest love to you, dearest Pearl."

So more than three weeks passed following Pearl's return from Denver before Frank Curry appeared in Georgetown, on a blustery day when snow threatened the town. He came on a Wednesday, the day that Charlie Dumas usually went to Denver, perhaps expecting only Pearl and Mrs. Travers to be at home. But Charlie had not left Georgetown since he'd confronted his daughter, so the young couple was not to have time to themselves, and Pearl would have no way to prepare Frank.

Pearl answered the door, gasping in surprise when she saw Frank standing on the porch, although she had expected him every time the bell had rung. They stared at each other a moment. Then Frank said softly, "My dearest. I've missed you." He stepped inside and took her hand, raising it to his lips.

Pearl glanced toward the study doors, which were not quite closed, and snatched back her hand.

Frank frowned and asked, "Is something wrong?"

"Everything is wrong," Pearl whispered. "Papa is opposed to the marriage."

"I'll talk to him."

Pearl clutched the cameo at her neck. "You must be careful or you'll put him in a rage. He is already very angry."

"Have *you* changed your mind?"

"Oh no," Pearl breathed.

"Then that's what matters. I don't mind facing your father."

At that moment, Charlie called from the study, "Who is there, Pearl?"

The young woman stiffened her back and slid back one of the study doors, replying as evenly as she could. "It is Mr. Frank Curry, Papa."

"Is that so? Very well. Ask him to come in."

Frank and Pearl looked at each other for a long time, until Frank said, "Well, I must give it a go. There is a great deal at stake."

He gave her a reassuring smile and whispered, "My very life is at stake."

Pearl pushed open the other door then and entered the room, Frank behind her. As she glanced back at him, she noted how dashing he was, dressed in a stylish overcoat and felt hat, leather gloves, and his walking stick. And despite herself, she wondered where the money had come from to purchase such clothing. Charlie's investigation had affected her more than she wanted to admit. Frank removed the glove on his right hand and held the hand out to Charlie, smiling as if he was as welcome as he had been in the past.

Charlie shook it cordially, saying, "Won't you take a seat. My daughter tells me you have been traveling. I hope you had a pleasant journey." Pearl realized then that one of the reasons her father was such a good negotiator in his dealings with mine owners was his amiable manner, his ability to hide his true feelings. Others found him pleasant and agreeable, not understanding until it was too late that his manner covered up a crafty and sometimes devious nature when it came to investing his money.

"Quite pleasant, but I have been anxious to return."

Pearl started to sit beside Frank on one of

the two chairs, but Charlie said, "My dear, would you excuse us? I believe Mr. Curry and I should speak alone."

Pearl started to object, but she feared she would anger her father, making things even harder for Frank. So she left the room, closing the doors behind her and tiptoeing out onto the front porch, where she sat as close to the window of the study as she could. But the walls of the house were thick, and she overheard little of the conversation.

The two men talked for a long time, while Pearl shivered in the cold, but she would not leave her post to fetch her shawl. At times, she heard the men's voices rise and made out the words. Once Frank said, "I guess I have a higher opinion of your daughter than you do," and Charlie replied, "You believe you know her better in a few months than I who've lived with her for thirty years?" Later, she heard Charlie boom, "Fool with me, young man, and there'll be a new face in hell tomorrow."

After a while, Mrs. Travers, who had gone to the market, came home and went up onto the porch and sat down beside Pearl, who cautioned her to be quiet, telling her that Frank Curry was inside.

"Listen to that carryings-on. The two of them would wake snakes," Mrs. Travers whispered when they heard an outburst from the study. "Has your father softened?"

"It appears he has not."

Mrs. Travers, who was not a demonstrative person, suddenly took the young woman's hand. "I never knew Charlie Dumas to be so hard. Once with Nealie —" Pearl looked up, and the older woman shut her mouth. "It has to do with that other man. That's as true as gospel. I believe Mr. Curry brings him to mind."

Pearl could not think what the older woman meant by "that other man" and said, "No. I believe Papa doesn't want me to marry anyone, and I have told him as much. He says he is looking out for me, but he wants me for himself." She thought that over and nodded. "It doesn't matter, because I intend to marry Mr. Curry, even without Papa's blessing."

"You'd be poor as Job's turkey."

"I don't care about money."

"That's because you've never been without it."

Pearl stared at Mrs. Travers.

"It's not a thing you'd want, being poor. Nealie was."

"But she married Papa, when she thought Papa had no money." Pearl had been told a hundred times the story of Charlie letting

Nealie think they were going home to his cabin the day they were married, when instead, he took her to the Bride's House, how shocked and delighted the new wife had been to learn the house was hers.

"Yes. None of us knew he had money. I don't know to this day where it came from. Still, it's one thing to pretend you don't have money when you do. It's quite another when you pretend to have it and you don't," the older woman said, and Pearl wondered if Mrs. Travers had read the detective's report when she was dusting Charlie's desk. Or perhaps Charlie had attempted to gain her support.

More than an hour after Frank went into the study with Charlie, the two women heard the sound of the heavy doors sliding open. Mrs. Travers scurried around to the back of the house, because she did not care to have her employer know she'd been snooping. But Pearl went into the front hall and watched as Frank emerged from the study, his hands shaky, his face splotched red. His hair was mussed, his brow damp. Charlie followed him out of the study, look- ing gray and tired. "Mr. Curry has some- thing to say to you, Pearl," Charlie told her, and turned and went back into his study. She heard the chair squeak as her father sat down heavily. He stared at his desk.

The house seemed too small for all of them. Besides, Pearl did not want her father listening to Frank's words, perhaps bringing them up later and twisting their meaning. So she snatched her shawl and said, "I would like to go for a walk."

Frank nodded and held the door for her. He did not take her arm until they were on the street, and neither of them spoke until they were out of sight of the Bride's House. Then Pearl stated instead of asked, "It did not go well, then."

"No."

"You did not change Papa's mind?"

Frank shook his head. "He believes I am the devil incarnate."

"Well, I do not. And it is my opinion that matters."

They did not talk again until they reached the little park and stood on the steps of the bandstand, the very bandstand where Nealie and Charlie had sat so many years before. And although Pearl would not have known it, Nealie had worn the same rose shawl with the picklelike designs. "What did he say?" Pearl asked at last.

"Not only does your father oppose the marriage, but he said he would disinherit you if you married me."

"He threatened me with as much."

"Will he carry through with it?"

"Oh yes. Papa never says a thing he doesn't mean." They stood quietly a minute, then Pearl boldly took Frank's hand. "But I don't care. Money doesn't mean a thing to me. I am thoroughly practical. We can go only to New York on our bridal tour instead of taking in Chicago and New Orleans, and I can have a seamstress make my clothes instead of buying them at Daniels & Fisher. Why, look at this shawl." She indicated the faded rose wrap. "I have had it all my life and believe it is as good as the day my mother bought it. I think you will be surprised at how frugal I am."

"You don't know what it means to be poor," Frank said.

"I wish people wouldn't keep telling me that," Pearl told him, a little annoyed.

"But it's true. Being poor doesn't mean having a sewing woman make your clothes. It means buying no dresses at all, and as for a wedding tour, we would be lucky to stay in a shabby hotel in Denver. I'll grant you know about housekeeping, but you don't scrub laundry on a board until your hands are raw or carry buckets of water from a town pump. Have you ever slept in a house so poorly built it has rats? Or lived on onions because you didn't have money for anything else?"

Pearl was taken aback. "But surely you don't live that way."

"Don't I? Your father was right when he told you about my debts. I have spent a great deal of money keeping up appearances with mining investors. He's right about the rest of it, too. My father was a thief. I was thrown out of school for fistfights with fellows who mocked me about it. My brother was no better. He stole money from a mine where we both worked and let others believe I did it." Frank removed his hand from Pearl's and sat down on the steps of the bandstand, looking out at the mountains. "I can deal with all that, Pearl, but you can't. I won't let you."

"I can live with it, and I will. Besides, that's my decision to make, not yours."

"No, it's mine." Frank said. "It would kill me to see you live in poverty, and I believe in time, you would grow to hate me."

Pearl didn't protest. Her knees felt weak, and she sat down beside Frank. "Then Papa has talked you out of it."

"No. He has made me realize how selfish I am to expect you to endure such hardship."

"Couldn't you get a job?"

312

"And abandon the molybdenum company?" He thought a minute. "Yes, I suppose I could find employment in one of the mines. We wouldn't live well, and there would not be the chance to make a strike, because I couldn't work the molybdenum claim. We would have to accept that we would never rise in the world."

Pearl considered the words for a long time, and then she knew that while she might be able to live the life Frank had described, she could not ask him to make such a sacrifice. And perhaps she realized that if she did, she would cause *him* to hate *her*. "Then we must wait," she said.

"No. That won't do. That would give your father time to turn you against me. Besides, I would not ask you to do that. What if the molybdenum prospect never pays off? You could wait your whole life." He sighed deeply and looked out at the mountains, which were blue in the dusk, the trees standing black against them, the clouds beginning to let go of their snow. "I must ask you to release me from our engagement."

There it was, then. Her father had convinced Frank to abandon her. Pearl shivered under the worn shawl. Perhaps if she had been wiser in the ways of young lovers, she would have cried and begged, and Frank would have changed his mind. But she was not that kind of woman, and with great effort — for she did not approve of emotional demonstrations — she held back the tears and said, "Very well." She would have said more, but she did not trust her voice.

"Will you remember I love you? No matter what your father says, I love you."

Pearl nodded, not able to speak.

"And I will love you for the rest of my life." When Pearl did not respond, Frank said, "You are like no other woman I know. You —"

Pearl touched his arm, and he stopped. "Go," she said.

Frank stood and reached for Pearl's hand, but she shook her head. "It's starting to snow. I'll walk you home."

"No." Without looking up at Frank, she dismissed him with a wave of her hand.

"Pearl, I love you."

"No, Frank," she said, then added formally, "You are released."

The young man looked at her for a long time, the snow falling on his bare head. Then he put on his hat and strode away. Pearl did not look up. Instead, she sat alone on the steps of the bandstand, much as her mother had once sat in a savage wind and

314

wondered what would become of her. She stayed there for a long time, until her clothes were soaked through. Then she wrapped her wet shawl around herself and made her way back to the Bride's House.

Mrs. Travers, who had been watching from the upstairs window, opened the door and said, "It's pouring the snow down. You'll catch pneumonia. I'll get some ooze for you."

But Pearl did not want medicine and shook her head.

"Hot tea, then?"

"No. I'm going to my room. I won't be down for supper." Pearl started for the stairs, but stopped then and added, "I am no longer engaged."

"Oh," Mrs. Travers said, her face wrinkled in sadness.

"Oh, Aunt Lidie," Pearl said, longing to throw herself into the older woman's arms as she had as a girl. But she was a grown woman who was responsible for her own poor decisions.

"Give it time," Mrs. Travers advised. "The future will not be so dim when the sun comes out."

"But I have no future," the young woman said. "I have only the past." She went upstairs to her bedroom in the house that

315

from that moment on seemed to her a prison.

Pearl was ill for several days. Her head hurt, and her stomach churned, and she stayed in her room, drinking beef tea and eating nothing more than a little toast and boiled egg. There was no sign of pneumonia, and she was never in any great danger, but Charlie insisted that the doctor visit her twice a day. Once, when she was alone in the house, she got up and wrapped the pink dress from Daniels & Fisher in tissue, placing it in a box and putting it away on a high shelf in the storeroom.

When she finally emerged after several days, she was more haggard than ever. By then, Charlie Dumas had left for Denver, and so father and daughter did not see each other for some time. When he returned, Charlie did not remark on Pearl's demeanor. Nor did she comment on his aged appearance. She hadn't noticed before that he was growing older and wondered if he had aged since he had found out about Frank Curry. Charlie said nothing about the engagement, although Pearl was sure that Mrs. Travers had told him it had been called off. In fact, Charlie never again brought up the subject of Frank Curry. Instead, he told Pearl that he and Mrs. Travers had been worried about her health, and he hoped she was feeling better. He was glad to see her at the table again.

"I am quite well now, thank you," the young woman replied.

The next day, Pearl went into Charlie's study and resumed her duties as his secretary. There was much that had been left undone during her time in bed, and she set about writing the letters and filing the papers, making entries in the ledger, and over the next days, father and daughter fell into their old pattern of working together, although they said nothing to each other that did not concern business. And they no longer had tea together in the afternoons.

Charlie's desk was cluttered with ore samples that he had collected, and one afternoon when he was out, Pearl labeled them in her neat handwriting and set them in the cabinet on the far side of Charlie's desk. As she closed the glass door, she glanced down and saw that the wallpaper beside the cabinet had been cut away and something inserted in the wall, something she might not have seen if she had not been on her father's side of the desk. She knelt and examined the wall, discovering that the lath had been cut away to accommodate a strongbox. There were hidden drawers in the cabinet, Pearl knew. Charlie kept stock certificates and negotiable securities and sometimes large amounts of cash in them, because they were so cleverly concealed that nobody but Charlie and Pearl knew they were there. Why, then, would Charlie need a hidden strongbox? And why had he gone to the trouble to take it out just then? The wall would have to be repapered with one of the rolls left in the storeroom.

So Pearl was more than curious, and she lifted the heavy container out of its hiding place and placed it on her father's desk. The box was not locked, and she lifted the lid. Inside were a letter, certificates, what appeared to be a deed, rolled up and tied with a ribbon, and odds and ends of paper. It was a paper on top that caught her attention, a receipt. She picked it up, turning it around to read it, but then her hands shook so that she dropped it and slumped down in her father's chair, her head in her hands.

She calmed herself a little, thinking it could not be so, that her eyes had betrayed her, and when her hands were still, she picked up the paper again, smoothing it with her hand, and slowly focused on it. The paper was a receipt, written in her father's hand, a receipt dated the day she had broken her engagement. The amount was $50,000, and it was signed "Frank Curry." Pearl slowly placed it back into the box, too stunned to wonder about the papers under it, and swiveled around in Charlie's chair to stare out at the mountains. They had always given her solace, just like the Bride's House, but no longer. Nothing in that brooding house could comfort her. If there had been a tiny bit of hope that she and Frank would be together one day, it was gone.

The house was as quiet as death. Her father and Mrs. Travers were not at home. Outside the air was as chill as Pearl's heart, and she listened as the wind rattled the windows, blowing so hard that the front door slammed open. At first, Pearl thought her father had returned, and she didn't care. He could come in and discover her there with the strongbox, know she had looked into it, that she now understood Frank had been a fortune seeker and that her father had saved her by buying him off. Then she wondered if her father had left the strongbox displayed on purpose, thinking she would find it and read the receipt, discovering for herself Frank's perfidy. But she could not bear to admit to Charlie that he had been right. After a time, she returned the box to its hiding place and picked up the bits of plaster that had fallen onto the floor when she'd removed it.

She went to her room then and later told Mrs. Travers that she was unwell and would not be down for supper. The bedroom that had once been her refuge seemed now like a cell. The next day, when she went into the office, she found the wall had been patched so cleverly that no one would ever suspect that something was hidden behind the paper.

The knowledge of Frank's faithlessness gnawed at Pearl, but as much as she blamed him, she blamed her father even more. She loved Frank, and she believed that he cared for her a little. Would it have been so wrong if Charlie had given the couple the money, underwritten the marriage? Frank would have made her happy. Did her father care at all about her happiness? Perhaps Frank was only a little weak and would have married her anyway, and that was why Charlie had given him the money, to buy him off. The questions ate at her until Pearl could not stand it, and one day when she and her father were in the office, she remarked, "You are not what you seem."

Charlie looked up from the report he was reading and frowned. "What's that, Pearl?"

"I believe you are a different man than I had supposed." She kept her hands in her lap so that her father would not see that they were shaking.

"And why do you say that?"

"I have learned a great deal about you." Pearl stood and went into the parlor, where she picked up a marble egg and held it in both hands to calm herself. Perhaps she should have kept quiet. But she couldn't. The thing hurt her so.

Charlie said, "Come back. Have you something to say?"

"I believe it is you who should say something, Papa. To me." Pearl went as far as the doors separating the two rooms.

"I keep nothing from you, Pearl, except what is for your own good."

"And was it for my own good that you gave Mr. Curry a great sum of money?"

Charlie raised his hands dismissively. "Not so much."

"It was fifty thousand dollars, was it not? That was the amount on the receipt. I consider that a very great deal of money." She did not wait for him to respond but went on. "Did you leave off a zero? I should feel ever so much better if you bought me

321

for five hundred thousand. Or perhaps you added an extra zero by mistake, and my price is only five thousand dollars. Surely that is cheap."

"Pearl, you should not have looked in there. Did you read the other —"

Pearl cut him off. "I suppose I ought to enter the amount in the ledger, but do I put it under 'household expenses' or 'bad debts'? Perhaps I should start a column for poor investments."

"Don't," Charlie said, his voice sad. He picked up a chunk of ore that he used as a paperweight and turned it over and over.

"You bought him off for fifty thousand dollars?" Pearl could not look at her father. Instead she gazed through the lace curtain at the snow that was falling again, falling sideways, because the wind was strong. She heard the wintry blasts and tightened the shawl that was over her shoulders.

"I invested in his molybdenum company."

"Then I would call that a very poor investment. You yourself have told me the metal is worthless." She took a deep breath. "Forgive me, Papa, but I don't believe you. I think you paid Frank Curry the money to break off the engagement."

"And what if I did? It's a small amount to show you he was only after your money, a bargain to me. But as I told you, the money went for stock in the company. If you like, I'll tear up the stock certificate."

"No, you mustn't do that. I would like you to sign it over to me." The young woman felt the chill as the wind came through a crack beside the window. "After all, you don't pay me wages for my work. You have made it plain to Mr. Curry if not to me that all the money in this house belongs to you, so I should like to get a little something for my labor. The worthless stock will do."

Charlie stared at his daughter, who slowly lifted her face and stared back at him. "I don't pay you, because you know I will give you anything you want. But if you care to have the stock, I'll sign it over to you." He studied a vein of color in the ore sample and did not look up as he asked, "Are you very sure?"

"I am sure. Thank you, Papa," Pearl said in a businesslike manner. And then her voice broke, and she cried, "Would it have been so wrong to let us marry? Did it matter so much if he loved my money more than me?" She broke off and fled, flinging over her shoulder, "Oh, Papa, you should not keep secrets." She did not see how Charlie blanched at her words.

CHAPTER 12

A few weeks after that, as Pearl, Charlie, and Mrs. Travers sat at the supper table, Pearl announced, "I am going to take a trip."

Charlie seemed pleased, probably because of the coldness that had developed between them over the Frank Curry affair. "Go anywhere you like — Chicago, New York. California is nice this time of year."

"I am thinking of going to Europe, on what is called the grand tour."

"I couldn't accompany you just yet, not until the summer," Charlie told her.

"I am thinking of going by myself."

"Alone?" Charlie asked. "Surely you wouldn't go abroad by yourself."

"Of course not alone. I'll take Mrs. Travers."

The old woman looked pleased, although not surprised, and if Charlie had not been so taken aback at the announcement, he might have wondered if the two women had already discussed the idea. But the look on his face told that he was not thinking about them. In fact, he appeared hurt. "You have never wanted to travel before, certainly not alone."

"I am a different woman now."

"Very well."

"Oh, Papa," Pearl said quickly. "You mustn't think we don't want you. But we'll be attending plays and visiting art galleries, taking in the opera and the museums, and I know that would bore you. You would hate it." She seemed almost frantic that Charlie stay home.

"Perhaps you could join us at the end of the trip, Mr. Dumas," Mrs. Travers said.

Charlie nodded, and his face softened a little. "Yes. That would do. I don't care much for looking at pictures. Perhaps we could visit some of the European mines. I could make arrangements."

"Of course," Pearl said, but only because she knew that would please her father. She did not care much about seeing mines. She only wanted to get away.

The two women left in late winter so that they could spend the spring and summer in Europe. "I don't fancy looking at snow over there," Mrs. Travers said. "If I'm going to see snow, I might as well stay at home." And if the trip were more spontaneous, with less planning than normally might be given for two ladies embarking on a grand tour, Pearl and Mrs. Travers enjoyed it all the more. When they tired of one place, they simply packed up and headed for another. "We're gypsies," Pearl wrote her father, not realizing that in the past, that was the last thing anyone would have called her. Pearl admitted to being a little bewildered, but she was enchanted, nonetheless, for she had never realized that the world was filled with so much richness. She might have thanked Frank Curry for opening her eyes to the wonders beyond the Bride's House. But Pearl did not want to think about Frank, not any more than she had to.

She wrote to her father each week, describing what they had seen and done, remarking about the beauty of old Europe, the elegance of the stores, the collections of ancient artifacts displayed in the museums. She told him about the books she had purchased, the antiques for the Bride's House, and a cameo for herself, to replace the one she had worn as a girl. "Mrs. Travers says to tell you her feet have been in every museum in five countries," she wrote.

Charlie wrote, too, telling them he had engaged a Mr. Randal, a bookkeeper from one of his mines, as a secretary, and he would keep track of business affairs so that Charlie could join them later. "He is not so engaging as you, Pearl, but I have complete trust in him."

The women went to France, where, Pearl wrote, she had contracted the influenza and been ordered to bed. "You must not worry. I shall be perfectly fine and think the doctor overstates the case when he says I am fragile and must rest for several weeks. Aunt Lidie agrees with him, however. So I humor them by staying abed in the mornings like the laziest of creatures. Still, I do want to be fit when you join us, so I do not protest too much."

Charlie met them in Paris at the end of the summer, and the three retraced the journey the two women had taken a few months earlier, detouring on occasion so that they could visit mines. In Florence, Pearl admired a diamond bracelet in a shop window, and the next day, Charlie presented it to her. Only a year or two earlier, Pearl would have been uncomfortable wearing such an expensive bauble, but she had become a different woman. The events of the past year along with the worldliness that she acquired on the tour had made her both more sophisticated and more fashionable.

Back at home in Georgetown, Pearl settled into the Bride's House, although she no longer thought of it as the refuge it had been for so many years. She roamed the rooms that had once delighted her — and her mother — and found them dreary, oppressive. So she threw out the heavy velvet drapes and reupholstered the horsehair furniture with damask — red damask, for Charlie insisted the room be kept the shade that Nealie had chosen for it. She got rid of the old plants in the solarium and added exotic ones, including orchids. She added to Nealie's knickknacks with antiques that she acquired in Europe. If Charlie noticed, he didn't comment, perhaps feeling he owed something to his daughter.

Influenced by the fashionable shops in Europe, Pearl changed her own style, as well. She put aside the matronly dresses she had worn all of her life for simpler, more youthful fashions that could be worn without confining foundations. She never again wore pink, but she experimented with colors that complemented her pale complexion and red hair. One day in Denver, Pearl went into a salon and had her hair cut off — not short by any means, but shoulder length.

Like Pearl's body, her hair seemed un-corseted now. It flared and curled around her face, giving her a girlish look. When she returned to Georgetown after the haircut, dressed in a green frock that had caught her eye, and walked into the Bride's House, Charlie stared at her as if he'd seen a ghost. "You look like Nealie," he said, his voice choking. And Mrs. Travers put her hands over her face and cried.

Pearl had not intended to cause them distress, especially not Mrs. Travers. The two had grown even closer after Frank broke the engagement. Sometimes when they worked together in the kitchen, Mrs. Travers, her eyes wet with tears, would put her arm around Pearl's waist and hold her, wordlessly. Pearl herself was distracted and listless at times, melancholy, often retiring to her room in the middle of the day. Char-lie blamed lingering effects of the influenza, but Mrs. Travers frowned at him as if to say that Pearl still mourned Frank Curry.

No one other than her father and Mrs. Travers knew about her brief engagement, so people attributed the changes in Pearl to her exposure to the outside world, and to the fact she was no longer her father's secretary. They thought that Mr. Randal's replacing Pearl was a healthy thing. It was not natural that Pearl was cooped up in the foul-smelling study with her father all day. That particular change was not Pearl's doing, however. She had intended to resume her duties at Charlie's side once they returned from Europe, but Mr. Randal, a small, unctuous man with a great sense of his own importance, made it clear she was a usurper, remarking more than once that as a woman, she did not understand mining matters.

When her father failed to contradict the man, Pearl withdrew, believing Mr. Randal's ill temper came from a fear of losing his job, and she did not want to be responsible for putting a man out of work. She still kept up on mining, reading reports and prospectuses, but when father and daughter talked about investments now, Pearl did not voice an opinion. Once, the young woman had been full of questions about the mines whose shares her father bought, and her observations influenced Charlie's decisions. He had valued her insights. But now when Charlie spoke of investments, Pearl listened politely and did not comment. Charlie, for his part, appeared to approve his daughter's changing position at the Bride's House. She was less secretary and more hostess.

To outsiders, it seemed that Pearl, who

was in her early thirties, had blossomed. She joined a literary society that met monthly and whose members gave papers on a variety of subjects — flower arrangements, table settings, glove etiquette. When Pearl's turn came to make a presentation, she read papers she had written on ore extraction methods and on increased mechanization underground. She even gave a talk on labor issues in Colorado's mining towns. If the other women were surprised at her choice of topics, they did not show it. In fact, they were impressed, because despite the fact that mining had waned, Georgetown still considered itself a mining town.

Pearl was one of the founders of a hiking club and was much admired for her tireless climbing and sure-footedness in the mountains. In winter, she determined to improve her skating and did, and although she was never proficient at it, she at least was good enough to stay on her feet. She learned to play tennis, too, and one summer, she asked Charlie if he would permit the side yard to be turned into a court. Charlie said he was happy to oblige and even suggested that he hire a man to string electric lights so that she and her friends — single men and women as well as married couples of her

age, many from the Presbyterian church —
could play at night.

For the first time since Pearl was born,
her life no longer centered on her father.
She had become a person in her own right.
Charlie did not remark on any of the
changes in his daughter, and perhaps he was
not much aware of them. Pearl was, however, and knew they had to do with Frank
Curry. She wasn't sure just how. Maybe
Frank had given her a sense of herself. More
likely, she wanted to show him that her life
was complete without him, but if that were
the reason, it was of no consequence,
because she never saw Frank. Or perhaps it
was that in some part of herself, she expected that one day Frank would admit his
mistake, would come back for her, and he
would love her more than ever.

There was another change, one of which
no one but Pearl seemed to be aware. A
friend had given her a journal for her
European trip, in which Pearl had recorded
the sights she had seen. Now, back home in
the Bride's House, she continued to write,
sitting at the dressing table in her room,
recording her thoughts in pen and ink in
notebooks. At first, she made grand and, it
must be said, trite observations — "everything in London is so old," for instance —

but as time went on, she developed a keen eye and a wry assessment of the people around her. She wrote about her friends and the ordinary people she met, the grocer, the stable boy, the miners, about their foibles and their virtues, drawing trenchant and often witty conclusions from simple events. Sometimes, she wrote about emotions close to her — loss, unrequited love, betrayal. On occasion, she recorded her thoughts about the Bride's House, wondering if houses, like people, grew old and died. In her writing, the house was no longer a place of warmth and comfort but a house of secrets, a boarded-up building where life stood still.

Charlie was not aware of his daughter's writing, and even Mrs. Travers thought the woman was doing no more than recording her days in a journal. Pearl never showed the essays to anyone, although at times, she would have liked to discuss them with Frank. In many ways, she wrote the stories for Frank.

To all appearances, Pearl put the serious, introspective woman she had once been behind her. Now well into her thirties, Pearl found that men began calling on her at the Bride's House — and not just because she was Charlie Dumas's daughter. Albert Sabra, who managed the Golden Fleece Mine, met Pearl at a summer frolic. He escorted her about town in his new autocar. They drove down the valley at awesome speeds, and Pearl returned home greatly excited and covered with dust. The roads were poor, filled with sharp rocks that punctured tires. When a tire had to be changed, Pearl helped Albert with the patching, instead of sitting helplessly by the side of the road. On one such occasion, Albert impulsively said they made such a good team that they ought to marry. He took her in his arms and tried to kiss her, but Pearl stepped away from him and told him as politely as she could that his affection was not returned. And after a few attempts to change her mind, Albert found someone else to help with punctured inner tubes.

Otto Hemp, who owned dry-goods stores in both Georgetown and Idaho Springs, a few miles away, was another suitor. He was a widower with two young girls, and all three of them adored Pearl. They ate dinners-on-the-ground in the park or hiked in the mountains, picking wildflowers that the little girls carefully divided into bouquets for friends. When Pearl remarked that his daughters were the sweetest little girls she had ever known, Otto said she might be

their mother if she would only say yes to
him. But Pearl said no, and Otto looked
elsewhere to complete his family.

If Charlie were aware of these romances,
he said nothing. Occasionally, he brought
young men to the house. Pearl did not know
if they were business associates or if her
father had softened and was suggesting they
were suitable candidates for her hand.
Charlie's reasons were not important to her,
however, because none of the men interested her. She would not have her father
pick a husband for her. But then, she
thought, perhaps her father had introduced
them to Pearl for the very reason that he
knew she would not care for them. She
wondered if Charlie would still oppose any
man who wanted to marry her. But it did
not matter since no one entered her heart
as Frank had, and she did not intend to
marry.

And so the next years passed. If they were
not joyously happy ones, they at least were
not unpleasant. Although Pearl found gray
hairs and she developed wrinkles about her
eyes and mouth, she seemed to others not
to change at all. Charlie, on the other hand,
began to look old. He was as white headed
as cotton now, and his step was not so sure.
He had lost some of his vigor, and when he

went out at night to make the rounds of the saloons, he stumbled home or was carried there by friends. Pearl wondered how his investments fared. After the world war, Charlie began putting his money into factories and land development. Pearl suspected he had invested a great deal in the King Mine, a copper property, but she did not know the details, because she had distanced herself from her father's business interests and did not pay them much attention. When Pearl asked Mr. Randal about an investment that struck her as odd, the bookkeeper patted her hand and said he was keeping an eye on things.

Mrs. Travers was growing old, too, of course, and Pearl took over management of the household. With her outside interests, the young woman no longer cared about cleaning and preparing meals, and so she employed a cook and a hired girl. Mrs. Travers fussed that the house was not as clean as it should be and the food was undercooked and never properly seasoned, although in fact, the Bride's House was as spotless as ever and the food tasted better than that prepared by the former boarding-house proprietor, who had a tendency to use too much salt and to keep things on the stove until they turned to mush.

After the one trip to Europe, Pearl forgot
about travel, except for short visits to
Denver or occasionally accompanying her
father on business trips, although she went
shopping or visited museums instead of attending meetings with Charlie. The two
were never again as close as they had been,
but over the years, both worked to repair
the breach created by her engagement.

On one such trip to New York, Pearl
returned to the hotel room to find her father
agitated. "By damn," he said, balling up a
telegram and tossing it onto the floor. He
went out in a rush to send a reply, and Pearl
picked up the crumbled paper and read it:
"YOU RIGHT ON ORE ASSAY. ADVISE." No
name was included, so Pearl didn't know
what mine the wire referred to. Nor could
she judge how serious the problem was,
because she no longer was involved in her
father's business transactions. But she knew
from Charlie's reaction that something had
gone wrong, so she was not surprised that
when he returned from the telegraph office,
he announced they were going home.

Back in the Bride's House, Charlie clos-
eted himself in his study with a string of

mining men who called on him day after day. He pored over the books late into the night with Mr. Randal, and when Pearl asked if the two wanted dinner at the desk, Charlie waved her off, saying they were too busy to eat. One afternoon, the bookkeeper stormed out of the study, slamming the front door of the house as he left. When Pearl, sitting on the porch with a book, wished him a good evening, he only frowned at her and did not reply.

"I shall see you tomorrow, then," Pearl said.

"No you won't!"

A few minutes later, Charlie stepped onto the porch and told Pearl that he had fired the bookkeeper. "He is incompetent," was his only explanation.

Charlie did not ask Pearl to resume her former duties, but since her father didn't hire anyone else, she appeared in the study the next morning and each morning after that to take dictation or rush to the depot with telegrams to post. At night, Charlie picked at his supper, then went off and got drunker than usual. He was more upset than Pearl had ever seen him, but he was closemouthed, and the letters she wrote did not explain the dilemma, so she could only guess at what had gone wrong. She felt sorry for her father but was not unduly concerned, because he had suffered down-turns in the past, as did any investor with the slightest bit of daring. Although he was never a plunger, Charlie hadn't believed in playing it safe, either. He'd told his daughter often enough that if a man didn't lose from time to time, he was too cautious. Picking bonanzas, he'd said, meant picking borras-cas, too.

But as the days went on, Pearl grew concerned that this latest loss was greater than usual, and she sought to have her father unburden himself. So one afternoon, she persuaded Charlie to join her in their old ritual of afternoon tea. She carried the silver tea service into the parlor and set it down on a table, then poured a cup for her father and handed him a slice of cake — Gold and Silver Cake, Charlie's favorite, made from a recipe of Nealie's. But Charlie only picked at the cake, and finally, Pearl asked, "Papa, I am worried. What is it that troubles you?"

She expected her father to take her hand and reassure her that everything was all right or perhaps tell her that the copper recovery method used in the King Mine was more costly than he'd thought. He might even say that a mine in which he held a stake had suffered a cave-in or that labor agitators were threatening to shut it down.

Instead, Charlie removed the spectacles that he had begun wearing and massaged the bridge of his nose. He set down his teacup, staring at the bits of tea leaf in the brew. "I had hoped to keep this from you, but you will find out in time," he said. Then he looked directly at Pearl. "Daughter, I am ruined."

"Ruined?" Pearl asked, stopping with her cup halfway to her lips. She slowly set it down, her hand shaking. "What do you mean, Papa? Surely not ruined."

"Do I say things I don't mean?" Charlie asked harshly. Then his voice softened. "Yes, Pearl, I am ruined. I have made a series of bad investments, and there is nothing to it but to admit it."

"The King Mine?" Pearl asked.

"The ore has run out, and the management was incompetent. I sold my gold holdings to finance it. It has been good money after bad for years. Now all of it is gone."

"The land you bought?"

"A swamp and a swindle."

"The factories?"

"One made corsets. You know yourself what has happened to that market. The shoe factory in Europe — I had thought there would be a good market for shoes after the war, but it seems that nobody has the money to buy them. And the company that makes mining equipment was run by fools and profligates. It is closed. I have lost my touch."

"What about your stocks, Papa?"

"I sold shares so that I could put the money into copper."

"But why, Papa? You always diversified. You told me yourself that only a fool puts all of his eggs into one basket."

"Then I am a fool." Charlie slumped in his chair. "I did it because I wanted to be another Spencer Penrose," he explained, naming the Colorado Springs millionaire who had backed the Utah Copper Company and its process for treating low-grade ore. "I'd thought the New Mexico prospect was another Bingham Canyon. But there wasn't enough copper in the ore for even a low-grade treatment. I didn't want to admit the mine was a bust, so I threw good money after bad. Just like I made it, I let it get away from me."

Pearl stared at her father, confused. "I don't understand why you wanted to be Mr. Penrose. You never cared about being as rich as Croesus, and you are hardly a spend-thrift."

Indeed, Charlie owned only one automobile and preferred horses to motorcars, and Pearl and Mrs. Travers had to coax him to purchase clothes. "When it comes to spending money on himself, your father is so tight, he squeaks," Mrs. Travers once complained.

"I have my reasons. I hoped to leave something to you. I didn't want you to be poor like your mother was."

"But there is plenty of money for me."

"Is there?" Charlie picked up his fork and cut a bit of cake, but he set the fork down with the uneaten confection. "Perhaps if I'd been more cautious, I might have saved something. But I gave Mr. Randal too much power to buy and sell stocks. I put trust in his judgment, the way I used to put it in yours. But he was not as knowledgeable as you. And he was flattered by stock promoters. Perhaps if you had been by my side instead of Mr. Randal, the outcome might have been different."

"Did Mr. Randal profit?"

Charlie shook his head. "I don't know. If he did, I can't prove it, and I expect he was enriched only a little. He was arrogant and overestimated his ability. He wasted hundreds of thousands by selling my shares and speculating in others that are worthless. If we had even that money . . ." Charlie wrung his hands.

"What does it mean, 'ruined,' Papa? Are you a bankrupt?"

"No. It's not quite that bad. We have enough to allow us to stay on in the house, but we must live simply. That means you must let the cook and hired girl go, and I'll sell the horses. That will eliminate the need for a stable boy. There won't be money for travel, and I must ask you to keep your own expenses to a minimum."

"Mrs. Travers? Surely you won't ask her to leave."

"She'll stay. She has always been with us." Charlie looked so discouraged then that Pearl wanted to put her arms around her father and tell him that she did not mind. But they had never been a demonstrative pair, so she only patted his hand. "We will manage," she said.

They sat quietly, Charlie opening his mouth to say something, then closing it again. In a minute, Pearl asked, "Is there a little left to be invested?"

"A little," he said. "But I don't dare risk it in speculation. If it's lost, so are we. We'll invest it safely so that you will have something to live on when I'm gone." He leaned forward, his hands clasped between his

343

knees. Pearl had never seen her father look so old or so beaten. "I could go back to work. I was considered a good man with the dynamite, you know. But that was long ago, and I do not believe anyone would hire me now."

"You'll do no such thing, Papa," Pearl told him. She had grown up on stories of once-wealthy mining men who lost everything and were forced to return to the mines as day laborers, and she would not have her father subject himself to such humiliation. She vowed that if it came to it, she herself would find employment. After all, she was a good typist and took dictation reasonably well. Surely there was a demand for such a person. The idea even excited her a little, because she had missed being a part of the business world in those last years. But that decision would come later, and only if it were absolutely necessary, since she knew Charlie would oppose it. She would have to present the idea to her father in such a way that it didn't shame him. Now, she could only console him and tell him that things surely were not as dark as he pictured. Pearl wondered then what their situation would have been if she'd been allowed to marry Frank Curry. But that was needless speculation. She had not married him; she had no idea where he was. He had never come back.

Although the months and years of the 1920s were ones of retrenchment, Pearl was not forced to seek employment, because the situation was not as perilous as it might have been. There was a little money left, and the woman — because it was now Pearl who managed the accounts — invested it prudently, saving out only a small amount for speculation, at which she was successful. Mrs. Travers resumed the cooking, and if she was at times forgetful and the chicken was burned and the biscuit-bread scorched, the other two did not complain. Pearl undertook the heavier work of housecleaning and discovered that she'd missed the pride she'd once felt in making the house sparkle, although if the truth be told, she hadn't missed it *that* much.

Charlie, who had never been afraid of hard work, sold the auto and kept the old horse to pull the buggy, but he eliminated the stable boy and did the work himself. Mucking out a stall wasn't that much different from mucking out a mine, he told Pearl, and the shovel loads were lighter. He let the groundskeeper go, and he and Pearl remade the garden so that the upkeep was simpler. Charlie hauled stones to construct the flower beds, while Pearl tended the plants. He cut the grass, Pearl weeded, and together, they planted apple trees where the tennis court once stood. Pearl figured the trees would pay for themselves when they produced, because she and Mrs. Travers would use the fruit for pies and fritters and sauce. They also planted a vegetable garden, although at Georgetown's high altitude, they couldn't grow much more than lettuce and root vegetables. Still, the labor reduced the food bill a little. Charlie made benches from timbers scavenged from deserted mines and placed them along the lilac hedge.

Working with her father in the garden was comfortable for Pearl. She would never forget that he had forced Frank Curry out of her life, but over the years, she had forgiven him. And she had come to understand him a little better. She understood that his love had been so consuming that he was jealous of any man who entered her life. Perhaps it had something to do with Nealie dying so young. Pearl thought that Charlie must have wanted his daughter close to protect her. Whether he had changed and would now allow his daughter to marry, Pearl did not know, but it didn't matter, because no suitors called on her, had not for a long time.

The family let it be known that Charlie had retired, so no one was surprised to see the man working in his garden. Mining men were eccentric, and if Charlie wanted to toil in the earth or wander about town without a collar or even drive a buggy with a horse so old it couldn't go faster than a walk, people simply said, "That's Charlie Dumas." At first, no one suspected that the Dumas fortune was gone, but later, when the Bride's House went unpainted and the porch sagged, when the rugs and upholstery frayed, the plants in the solarium died and were not replaced, people understood that Charlie had fallen on hard times. But that was not news in Georgetown, where so many mines had been shut down and most people faced financial difficulties. Eventually, it became common knowledge that Pearl, not Charlie, invested the money that kept them going.

Some of the treasures that Pearl had acquired when she was in Europe disappeared from the house. The diamond bracelet went first and then the antiques. Pearl even inquired about selling the shares of stock she held in the Colorado Molybdenite Company, the shares that Frank had given to her father in return for breaking the engagement. Pearl knew that there had been a demand for molybdenum during the war — it was used to strengthen steel — but she no longer followed stocks, especially that one, and Charlie told her that Colorado Molybdenite had not done well, whether due to a poor ore body or inept management, Pearl did not know. The company had shut down after the Armistice. So Pearl was not surprised that the stock had no value, and she was even a little glad, because if she were honest with herself, she knew she did not really want to dispose of that last tenuous connection to Frank Curry.

Once, Pearl suggested to her father that they find a smaller house where the upkeep would be easier and cheaper, but Charlie only looked at her with a stunned expression on his face. "Sell?" he asked. "Sell Nealie's house?" And because she realized it would kill her father to leave the Bride's House, she dropped the subject. He would live out his days there, in the frayed rooms with their shabby furniture. And so would she. Just as Mrs. Travers did.

In the late 1920s, the old woman's heart gave out. She gasped for breath and complained of pain, and the doctor who examined her ordered her to a hospital. But Mrs. Travers refused. She would spend her final days, her final hours, in the Bride's House, with Pearl and Charlie, just as Nealie had. They moved her into Charlie's room then, into the old-fashioned bed with its brass tubes and flutings and the view of the mountains, and they nursed her themselves. Pearl made beef tea and puddings, but the old woman could not eat. She was troubled. Her mind wandered. "I'll be with Nealie before long. I expect I'll have to answer to her."

"For what?" Pearl asked.

"For one thing and another. For her and you."

"You've led an exemplary life. You've been a mother to me since the day I was born."

"There's things I could have done, wished I'd done. It might have eased your life. I could have told Frank Curry —"

Pearl put her hand over the old woman's mouth. "You could have told him nothing. He didn't love me."

"I've been thinking about what Nealie would have wanted. She'd have told me different. I made bad decisions. I promised to take care of you, and I let you down."

Pearl shushed her, troubled that at the end, Aunt Lidie's mind was no longer clear. She took a washcloth and wiped the old woman's forehead, and Mrs. Travers began to mutter. Charlie came into the room and stood at the foot of the bed. "Your mother died here, in this bed." His voice trailed off, and he turned and went to the window.

Then he paced the room, until Pearl said, "Papa, please sit down." But he didn't. He left the house and did not come back for a long time. When he did, Pearl was sitting on a straight chair beside the bed, her hands over her face, tears seeping out from between her fingers. Mrs. Travers lay still, the sheet drawn up to her chin.

"She's gone," Charlie said heavily.

Pearl nodded, wiping her eyes with the backs of her hands. "She asked me to forgive her, asked me over and over again, but I didn't know what she meant."

"Was there a final word?"

Pearl nodded. "It was 'Nealie.' "

Mrs. Travers had been dead for more than a year that morning in June 1929 when a man in a fine automobile called.

Pearl saw him from the upstairs window as he alighted from the car, but she did not recognize him. Not so many men called on her father now, although the visitors had not stopped altogether. Men still sought out Charlie for his knowledge of ore bodies or simply to talk about old times. Charlie's

350

greatest pleasure was sitting down with longtime friends and business associates who remembered the past, so Pearl was glad to see one of them coming up the walk.

She did not pay much attention to the man as she peered out of the window, since she was more interested in his car. She had not seen one that large in Georgetown, although there were many autos in the county now. The road to Denver had been improved, and one could make the drive in a couple of hours, although a few drivers returning to Denver could not manage the steep grade on Floyd Hill and had to either put their cars into reverse and climb up the mountain backward or place their vehicles on flatcars and ride home on the train. And the road was passable only in decent weather, so only a fool would drive it in a snowstorm. But this was June, and it was a common sight to see sightseers, a few in old-fashioned dusters and goggles, roaring about Georgetown in their flashy convertibles. The visitor's auto was obviously expensive, and Pearl wondered if it was a Pierce Arrow or a Cadillac, but she was not up on such things, so she could not tell.

The man rang the bell, and because she supposed that Charlie was downstairs, Pearl did not answer. When there was a second ring, Pearl remembered that her father had gone out, so she went down the steps, a little curious now to find out who was driving such a splendid vehicle and why he was calling. She hoped he would stay until Charlie returned.

She opened the massive wooden door and pushed at the screen, then stopped with her hand on the frame, unable to move. The smell of lilacs overwhelmed her, and she thought, they were blooming the first time he called. The scent always reminded her of him, and sometimes the connection was so strong that she closed herself in her room to keep from melancholy, for even after all those years, memories of him still did that to her. She could not speak then but only stared. It was a meeting she had supposed in her mind a thousand times, but one for which she was not prepared. So she said nothing, only stood mute.

"Hello, Pearl," Frank Curry said.

"Mr. Curry," she replied, her voice working a little.

"Frank. You used to call me Frank."

Pearl wanted to say there were a great many things that used to be, but she swallowed the retort. She would not greet him in anger. She had forgiven her father, but had she forgiven Frank Curry? She did not think so.

"Will you invite me in?"

"Yes," Pearl said, opening the screen. She did not hold out her hand but stood aside to let him enter. "Papa is not at home."

"It's not your father I've come to see. It's you."

Pearl didn't know what to say, so she turned and led the way into the parlor, conscious as she went into the room that it was as worn and as dated as the outside of the house. She hoped that Frank hadn't noticed. She did not want his pity. When Pearl turned, he appeared not to be looking at the house but at her, and that disoriented her. She could not think what to say, so she pointed to one of the love seats, the damask threadbare, while she seated herself in a small, hard chair, as far from Frank as possible.

He sat down and placed his hat on the sofa beside him. Pearl noticed that he did not carry a walking stick and wondered if he had given it up or simply left it in the automobile. They sat awkwardly a moment, before Pearl found her voice and said, "You are looking well."

"A little fleshier, and my hair has its share of gray, but I am healthy, thank you." He laughed easily, and Pearl remembered how he had always been more at ease with her in that room than she had been with him. This meeting would not make his heart flutter as it did hers. "And you," he added. "You wear the years well yourself. Before, you were merely pretty. Now you are beautiful."

Pearl felt the color rise in her face, and she touched her cameo — not the old one that had belonged to her mother but the cameo she had purchased in Italy. She had not sold it with her other possessions. It was her one extravagance, and she was glad she'd worn it. Perhaps Frank would notice it instead of the dismal appearance of the house. "It has been a long time since I saw you last. Now I am nearly fifty." She wondered why she had said such a thing.

"I've embarrassed you," Frank said. "I didn't mean to. I remember you do not like compliments, but I am only speaking the truth."

Pearl blushed even more and turned aside for a moment. Then she said in a business-like tone, because she could not bear for Frank to say another thing to her that was personal, "You said you are here to see me. Is it because you want to talk to me about mining?" She wondered if he heard the sarcasm in her voice.

"It's that very subject I've come about."

He reached into the inside pocket of his jacket and removed an envelope, which he held out to her. "Your good judgment about mining brought me here."

Pearl looked at the envelope, but she did not take it until Frank stood and dropped it into her lap. Then she picked it up and opened it and removed a check. She stared at it in disbelief before looking up and saying, "I don't understand."

"It's the return of your father's loan to me. The shares are in your name, so I believe the money is to be repaid to you. I did not include interest, because you still have the shares."

"But the stock is worthless."

Frank grinned. "*Was* worthless, but now automobile makers are demanding molybdenum steel, and so are other manufacturers. My partner and I bought up all the claims in the area and have a monopoly, and we are about to announce that the mine will reopen — at far greater capacity than anyone could imagine." His face lit up the way Charlie's once had when he talked about mining. "So your *worthless* stock is going to be worth a great deal."

"How much?" Pearl could not help blurting out the question.

Frank leaned forward as if they were

conspirators. "I can't say, but I would guess that in six months, it will be worth the fifty thousand dollars that it cost when it was issued. And beyond that, who knows? It can only go higher. You are, by the way, a major shareholder, so there will be significant dividends."

Pearl was stunned. The $50,000 check was more money than she had ever expected to see again. She and her father could live very well on that for the rest of their lives. But another $50,000 worth of stock, as well, with dividends coming in! They would be rich again. "Are you quite sure?" she asked.

Frank laughed. "No, of course I'm not. You have been around mining all your life, so you know that nothing about it is sure. But I believe my figure is a good guess. Molybdenum will be in demand for a great many years, and we have the finest prospect in the country."

"We?"

Frank smiled at Pearl, and she remembered how white and even his teeth were. "As you know, I had the devil's own time raising money. The dogs in Georgetown were friendlier than the bankers in New York. But in time, I found a partner. He doesn't want to be identified, but I'll give you his name if you promise not to tell your father."

"Not tell Papa? Why shouldn't I tell Papa?"

Frank shrugged. "He said he knew your father years ago, and they did not get along."

"Who is he?" Pearl couldn't imagine anyone who didn't like Charlie.

"My partner is Minerals Investment Company. The principal is Will Spaulding. He and Mr. Dumas had a falling-out over something."

Pearl said nothing.

"Will didn't know I was acquainted with your father until recently, when Mr. Dumas's name was mentioned quite by accident. I'd worked with Will for four or five years before the subject of Georgetown came up, and that led to your father's name — and yours."

"Mine?" Pearl asked sharply. She did not care to have Frank discuss her. She wondered if Frank had told the man how he had shamed her by breaking their engagement.

"Not long after that, Will became interested in the molybdenum venture. But of course, we had done other investments together. I made sure he knew everything I had done, and not done. I had learned my lesson about pretending to be someone I wasn't. He said he admired my honesty. We get on famously."

"Then you have done well?"

"Very well. But of course, I couldn't come back to Georgetown until the molybdenite claim had proven itself. Even at that, I am premature, but I think your father will have to agree that it will be successful."

Pearl did not understand. "Papa cares nothing about molybdenum."

"He cares fifty thousand dollars' worth."

The woman rose and turned her back on Frank, fussing with the objects on the piano. Without looking at him, she said, "I believe that was the price he paid you to break off our engagement."

Frank took a few steps toward her until his hand was on her shoulder. "You may think of it that way, but it's not the truth."

"Did you believe I wouldn't know what the money was for? Papa paid you fifty thousand dollars to stay away from me." Pearl squared her shoulders and held her head high, hoping Frank would not guess how humiliated she had been — and was still.

"And he never told you?"

"Told me what?"

Frank took a step backward and braced

himself against the back of the sofa. "He said he would never allow you to marry me, would stop the wedding at all costs. After he made me see that I could not provide for you, I agreed. Then he loaned me the fifty thousand for the molybdenum project and said if I paid it off and made as much again off molybdenum, I could come back, and he would not stand in the way of our marriage. I had to promise him I wouldn't tell you. Nor would I ask you to wait. It has taken me almost twenty years, but I have made the money on molybdenum. I thought that over the years, he might have told you."

Pearl turned around and stared at Frank. "I have never heard such a preposterous story. You were after my money. Papa gave you the fifty thousand dollars. Later, I found the receipt. I have often wondered if Papa arranged for me to find it."

"How awful for you." Frank bowed his head. "That's not true, but I admit that without your father's money, I could not have provided for you in the beginning, and I would not ask you to live in poverty. Over the years, I've wondered if that mattered, wondered if we should have married anyway even though we'd have had to live on a miner's pay. Will Spaulding said I was a fool, that he himself had given up a woman he loved and regretted it the rest of his life."

When Pearl did not respond, Frank said, "I could have come back with the money I made with Will in other ventures, but your father was quite insistent that the money had to be repaid from molybdenum, and I'd agreed."

Confused, Pearl slowly pressed one key of the piano and then another. "Why would you take his money?"

"Why wouldn't I take it? What was there to lose? I needed it to develop the claim. And I believed at the time that without it, there was no chance of our ever being together."

Pearl felt weak and gripped the back of the love seat, clutching at it to steady herself as she made her way back to her chair and sat down. "It has been nearly twenty years."

"Eighteen."

"Seventeen years and seven months," Pearl corrected.

Frank laughed. Then Pearl laughed, and of a sudden, her heart felt as light as the blossoms on the lilac bushes. The room seemed filled with sunshine. She heard the birds outside and again smelled the scent of lilacs carried by the breeze.

"Do you still care for me?" Frank asked.

Pearl looked down at her hands and did

not reply, would not reply.

"This is not so easy," he said. "We are middle-aged, and we both have changed a good deal over the years." Pearl started to say something, but Frank held up his hand. "Oh, I know how you have changed. Mrs. Travers kept me informed. She wrote to me every year."

"She's gone," Pearl said, and Frank nodded as if he already knew. Then Pearl asked, "Have *you* changed?"

"I'd like to believe I'm a better man." He thought a moment before adding, "And I have more money."

"Yes, there is that." She played with a tack that had come loose on the chair, jabbing the edge of it into her finger. "Perhaps you will wonder then if *I* would be after *your* fortune? You must know that Papa's wealth is gone, and we live like imposters in this house."

"I know that, and if you choose to marry me for my money, then I am well satisfied." He paused. "One thing for certain has not changed. We still love each other."

Pearl pushed the tip of her finger so hard against the tack that it popped out and fell onto the carpet. "How do you know?"

"I know my own feelings, and I know that you are constant."

"What are you saying, Frank?"

"That I hope to marry you."

Pearl wanted to stand, to go to the window and look out across the town at the mountains, which had always steadied her, but she could not get up. She looked at her finger and rubbed the tiny indentation of the tack with the forefinger of her other hand. "Didn't you ever marry? I would have thought you would."

"I told you I'd always love you. Those were my last words to you. There was never anyone else. And I am bold enough to think there was never anyone else for you. After all, you promised you would marry me, and you never told me you took back that promise."

Pearl stared at him.

Frank went to her then and slowly raised her from the chair, until she was standing in front of him. "Now, I'll ask you a second time. Will you marry me, Pearl?"

"Yes."

"Now?"

"Yes."

"Today?"

"Today?" Pearl repeated.

"My automobile is outside. We can drive to Denver this minute and be married."

"But I'm not ready. I have no wedding

dress, no trousseau. You must ask Papa first."

"No. I will not ask your father. I am asking only you. And you had a pink dress once. Do you still have it?"

"I never wore it again."

"No, you wouldn't have." Frank kissed her and held her a long time. "I have already reserved the bridal suite at the Brown Palace Hotel."

"But what if I had said no? You'd have lost your money."

"The risk was worth it."

When he released her, Frank told Pearl, "Shuckle," and she went upstairs into the storage room and took down the box with the pink dress. She packed a bag and wrote a note to her father, telling him that she had gone to Denver on an important matter and would be back the next day. Then Frank helped her into the automobile — a Packard, as it turned out — and they sped away.

The two were wed that afternoon in Denver in the Presbyterian church in sight of the capitol building. Pearl wore the pink dress, which was a little old-fashioned now, but what did that matter? And then the two retired to the Brown Palace Hotel.

Frank suggested they send Charlie a telegram, telling him that Pearl was now

Mrs. Frank Curry. But Pearl thought that would be cruel. Besides, the shock might affect her father's health. So the next afternoon, they motored back to Georgetown, drove slowly to enjoy each other's company. At the Bride's House, Frank helped Pearl from the car, then holding hands, the two climbed the steps and went inside. Although she was used to entering the study without knocking, Pearl tapped on the door nonetheless, and Charlie looked up. "You're home. I was concerned —" He stopped when he saw Frank standing behind Pearl. Charlie did not rise but sat there, staring at Frank for a long time. "What does this mean?" he asked, although it was clear that he knew.

"Mr. Curry has repaid the loan you made him so long ago, and we were married yesterday."

"Against my wishes?"

"It was my wish."

"Mr. Dumas," Frank started, but Charlie waved him away.

"You did not get my permission," he told Pearl.

"No, Frank asked only me, as he should have done eighteen years ago."

"You are leaving, then?"

"That's up to you," Pearl told him. Frank

and Pearl exchanged a glance, and she continued, "We can live in Chicago where Frank's business is located, or we can live here with you. But if we do, you must accept that I am married now and that my husband comes first. If I must choose between the two of you in any matter, I will choose my husband."

Charlie glanced down at the papers strewn across his desk, then looked around the room, his gaze stopping on the portrait of Nealie. He looked at her a long time. He did not speak, but at last he turned to Pearl and nodded.

Pearl went into the kitchen then and returned carrying a tray with three of Nealie's crystal goblets and a bottle of champagne that Frank had purchased in Denver. Frank opened the champagne, poured it into the glasses, then handed them around.

"Mr. Dumas," he said, waiting for Charlie to make a toast.

Charlie raised his glass slowly. "To the Bride's House." The three of them sipped the champagne.

Then Frank turned to Pearl and lifted his goblet. "To the bride."

"And the groom," Pearl added.

Charlie stared at Frank and then at Pearl. And then he drank.

■ ■ ■ ■

PART III
SUSAN

■ ■ ■ ■

CHAPTER 13

Susan loved the mountains best at their blue time, when twilight touched the valley that lay between the steep peaks, that soft gloom between daylight and the indigo black of a starlit night. In the dusk, the evening was comforting, like one of the Bride's House's worn quilts whose fibers had broken down from many washings, and it seemed to welcome her after all the months she had been away.

Bert Joy turned off the highway onto the dirt street in his old Ford truck with the stick shift in the floor. Susan had had to ride all the way from Denver with her legs pushed over to the side to accommodate it, but she was too excited to be aware of the way her back ached from that unnatural position. They drove along the rutted street, Susan listening to the shouts of mothers calling their children home from play: "Jimmm-may! Come and get your supper or I'll throw it out." And "Betty 'n' Billl-eee." Then there was the shrill sound of a whistle, one mother's signal for her children to hurry to the table. Mothers in Chicago didn't summon their little ones that way, at least not in the Curry neighborhood of aging mansions, where Susan lived the rest of the year. A nursemaid collected the younger children for dinner in the nursery or the older ones to dress for dinner with the adults.

The sounds of Georgetown came back to Susan, not just the mothers calling but the trucks gearing down as they climbed toward Silver Plume, the wind in the jackpines, and she thought she could even hear the crashing of Clear Creek. The sounds had been dormant for her since fall, and they, too, seemed to welcome her back. As a child, she had heard those noises as she arrived in Georgetown and knew they meant she had the whole summer ahead of her, a summer to run free, to stay out until dinnertime, exploring the mines and the creeks, the mountains, to collect ore samples and gather wild raspberries and currants, to roam the barn and the secret places of the Bride's House. She could forget about dancing school and music lessons, about deportment and all the other things she must learn as a young heiress, and be just another Georgetown kid. She loved that more than anything in the world and hoped that although she was eighteen now, she could still run barefoot in the Georgetown streets, still climb to the high meadows and lie in the sun.

"Jo-eee." The sound came from behind, and without thinking, Susan turned to the truck's back window, although she knew the woman was not calling *that* Joe. After all, Joe Bullock was twenty, too old for his mother to yell for him at suppertime. Still, Susan looked out the window, stretching her neck so that she could see across lots to Rose Street where Joe lived. Just hearing the name made her glad. Joe Bullock was another of the reasons she loved the summers in Georgetown, maybe the main one. She thought about Joe and squeezed her arms against her sides. It wouldn't be long until she'd see him.

Bert Joy geared down with a scraping noise and stopped his truck in front of the Bride's House, honking the horn in a series of taps. Susan's mother, Pearl, opened the passenger door and stepped out onto the running board, Susan behind her, squirming a little to get out the kinks from being crammed behind the gearshift. She stared at the big white house for a moment, at the two pine trees that rose nearly a hundred feet in front of it, and the lilacs. Even from the truck, she could smell the lilacs.

Although she spent only her summers in Georgetown, Susan loved the house as fiercely as her mother did. When she was a girl, she had dreamed of living there, of being the first bride married in the parlor, of walking down the staircase in a white silk dress, holding on to her father's arm, a veil covering her face, a white orchid bouquet in her hand. There would be candlelight and the smell of lilacs, a harp playing in the study. And Joe Bullock would be standing in front of the fireplace waiting for her. It had been a little girl's silly fantasy, inspired no doubt because the place was called the Bride's House, but now as she stood on the running board of the old truck, Susan thought of it again and knew she had never stopped dreaming of marrying Joe Bullock there.

As she stepped onto the sidewalk, Susan glanced down at her wrinkled skirt, her scuffed saddle shoes, and nearly laughed to think she looked as much like a bride as Bert Joy did in his overalls and motoring cap. She was tall and thin like her mother, but she had failed to inherit her mother's and grandmother's red hair and pale blue eyes. Her eyes and hair were a nondescript brown, and she had as many curves as one of the porch posts. Still, although she was not aware of it, Susan had a certain vibrancy, a joy in living, a purpose that was reminiscent of her grandmother Nealie — although except for her grandfather Charlie Dumas, there were few in Georgetown who remembered the hired girl. Those qualities that Susan had inherited from her grandmother were not ones the girl appreciated, however. She would have preferred blond hair and curves. After all, this was 1950, and those were the attributes young women prized.

The door of the house opened, and Charlie Dumas came out onto the porch, walked slowly, because he was very old now and needed a cane. "Papa," Pearl called, and rushed to him, and the old man put his arms around her, patting her back.

Susan waited, and in a moment, her grandfather gestured to her, and she went up onto the porch and let him hug her. He smelled of cigar smoke and wool, but like the lilacs, those were summer smells, too, and gave Susan a feeling of welcome. "Our miracle baby," he called her, because it was rare that a woman Pearl's age could have a child. The pregnancy had both stunned and delighted Pearl and Frank — Charlie, too. It had helped alleviate Charlie's bitterness over his daughter's marriage and her move to Chicago.

"It's about time the two of you got here." His voice was still firm, and there was a trace of excitement in it. He called to Bert, "That worthless machine of yours break down, did it, Joy? My auto goes faster, even if it is up on blocks."

"The train was late," Pearl explained. "You're looking well, Papa."

"At my age, it's a surprise I'm looking like anything at all." He added, "I'm in my ninety-seventh year, Bert. Did you know that?"

"Who doesn't? If you hadn't told everybody in town, we'd have thought you were a hundred, being so cranky like you are."

The two men laughed, and Charlie said, "How's your day going?"

"There is nothing wrong with it at all."

"Well, I'm glad to hear it. I guess you could say it's always a good day for me when my daughter and granddaughter come to see me."

"Okay, then," Bert replied.

Charlie escorted the two women into the house, into the parlor, which had always been red, faded now to the soft shade of dying roses. The room contained Susan's grandmother's two love seats and her bric-a-brac, and of course, Nealie's portrait still hung in a prominent spot. Susan's mother had made only one change. The year before, she had thrown out the dead bird under glass that Nealie had purchased when the Bride's House was new. Nearly all of its feathers were gone by then, and Joe had told Susan it looked like a baked Cornish hen. Charlie had noticed at once that the bird was gone and raised his voice in protest. After all, Nealie had bought it. "She bought a plucked bird?" Susan had asked her mother, who smiled but told her to hush.

Like her grandfather, Susan did not want the rooms to change, and she looked at them with satisfaction, glad that he had not replaced the Victorian furniture or repapered the walls. When the house was hers — for of course, she expected it to pass down through her mother to her one day — she would reupholster the frayed furniture and store some of Nealie's knickknacks, update the kitchen and bathrooms. But she would keep the feeling the house gave her, the sense of family, the warmth that the Chicago mansion with its formal rooms kept up by servants never seemed to convey.

The Bride's House was home to Susan, just as it had been to her mother and her grandmother. As a little girl, she had promised herself she would live there someday. For Susan, the Bride's House represented not just the past, but the future — a future with Joe Bullock.

"We expected you earlier, daughter. Mrs. Warren left supper on the table, where it's cold, and she's gone out. Now if it had been your aunt Lidie, she'd have had a hot supper waiting for you," Charlie Dumas told his daughter, Pearl.

After Pearl moved to Chicago, Charlie had had a succession of housekeepers, who lived in Aunt Lidie's old room off the kitchen. Mrs. Warren was the latest. Pearl had thought to engage a nurse, but Charlie "bore easy maintenance," as Mrs. Warren put it, saying she could meet the old man's needs. "It doesn't seem right, Aunt Lidie not being here," Pearl said.

"I'll be the next to go," Charlie told her. Then he turned to Susan. "I'm not the only one who expected you to be here earlier. You already had a caller — called twice, in fact."

"Joe Bullock?" Susan couldn't help but blurt out. She hadn't seen him since the fall, and she could hardly wait.

"Not unless he wears a dress. It was Billy Purcell's daughter. Billy, you remember him, Pearl. He never was no-account anyhow, and now he says he's disabled to work. His money goes easy."

"I thought he'd found God."

"Oh, he confessed religion, all right. He sings and shouts on Sunday, but then he raises the devil with his neighbor on Monday. Nothing much good ever hatched out of that family. It's a wonder young Peggy turned out as well as she did."

The two older people continued talking, unaware of Susan's disappointment that Peggy Purcell and not Joe Bullock had inquired about her. Susan had hoped that Joe was as anxious to see her as she was him. She'd even allowed herself to dream he would be waiting on the porch, talking to her grandfather. He'd rush to Bert's truck and tell her, "I've been counting the minutes." And then sometime during the summer, he would tell her how much he cared about her, maybe even propose. After all, she was eighteen. Several of her friends were already engaged.

Of course, that was only a dream, although it was one she'd had since she was eleven, when she'd decided she was going to marry Joe. He'd been in college for two years now, however, and maybe he'd forgotten about her. How awful to think she had cared about him what seemed like her whole life, and he never even knew it. What if he'd already found somebody else, and she'd never get a chance with him? Maybe it was Peggy Purcell — Peggy with her long blond hair and her smashing figure. She didn't need a padded bra, hadn't even when she was fourteen.

Susan would find out about Joe soon enough, of course, because Peggy would come by the Bride's House at breakfasttime the next day. Peggy had done that since she was a little girl, when she'd discovered that the housekeeper served hotcakes and bacon, waffles, eggs, cornbread, and cinnamon buns and she was welcome. "Peggy's mother doesn't make anything but mush. Those Purcells never have had plenty to eat," Charlie had said after Susan complained once that Peggy was mooching. And Susan had been ashamed of herself.

Susan was right about Peggy showing up. As she started down the stairs the next morning, she heard the harsh sound of the bell, the rasping of metal on metal, and heard her mother open the door and say, "Why, Peggy, don't you look pretty. Susan will be so happy to see you. Come in and have breakfast with her." And Peggy, dressed in short shorts and a plaid blouse whose tails were tied at her waist, her blond hair held with barrettes and turned under in a pageboy that made a V down her back, flounced into the house, more grown-up than she had been in the fall. Perky, Susan thought, sexy, resigned that nobody would ever apply either of those words to her.

The girls said hello, looking each other over, and Susan was reminded of the way dogs sniffed each other before committing themselves. Although she'd often borne the brunt of Peggy's ill humor, Susan was fond of her friend, and said, "I was just about to have breakfast. Want some?"

"All right, I guess."

The two went into the dining room where Charlie was getting up from the table. "Pearl, I could use your help with a few letters," he said, and Susan exchanged glances with her mother. This happened every summer, her mother holed up in the study with her grandfather. Susan knew the letters were of no consequence, that her grandfather simply liked to keep her mother with him — and away from her own work. Pearl Dumas Curry wrote a newspaper column about patriotism and sacrifice, American drive and ingenuity, all values that were

379

prized during the war and were still popular in 1950. Susan found the columns a little cloying, but out of loyalty, she read them. Besides, she never knew when her mother might mention someone from Georgetown.

To everyone's surprise, most of all her own, Pearl had become a newspaper columnist. She'd begun writing on a trip to Europe with Mrs. Travers and had never stopped. At a dinner party when Susan was still a child, her father, Frank, had bragged to the editor of a Chicago newspaper that his wife was "quite a writer. You ought to read her work."

"Indeed," the editor replied, for he had heard that remark often enough and didn't care to read another dilettante author.

But Frank was persistent, and Susan in tow, he had showed up at the editor's office with a sheaf of Pearl's work. The man liked what he read and printed an essay about a Georgetown prospector who'd donated the two dollars he'd set aside for winter shoes to buy war bond stamps. The essay had resonated with readers, and Pearl was offered space in the paper for a weekly column. Within months, the column was syndicated, and now, a little more than five years after she was first published, Pearl had a book of her columns. Once Pearl had mentioned Joe, and Susan, thrilled to see his name in print, had mailed him half a dozen clippings. Susan's friends were a little in awe of her having a famous mother, but to Susan, Pearl was simply her mother.

The two girls chatted through breakfast, telling each other what they had done in the past months. Susan hoped Peggy would mention Joe Bullock, but she did not, and Susan would not bring up his name for fear Peggy would figure out she cared. Then Peggy would prod and tease and maybe even tell Joe, and that would be so embarrassing. After a time, Susan said, "Oh, I forgot. I brought you something."

"Not another doll," Peggy said. When the two were small, Susan had brought her friend Storybook Dolls, tiny china dolls dressed to illustrate stories.

"Of course not," Susan replied, a little embarrassed that Peggy would think she would consider such a childish gift.

They went to Susan's room, which seemed almost as big as the Purcell house, and Peggy flopped down on the carved walnut bed, the one Susan's grandmother had chosen when she had furnished the house. A spot of mud the size of a half dollar dropped from Peggy's sandal onto the white lace spread, and Peggy flicked it off, spreading the dirt across the lace. "So what did you bring?" she asked.

Susan had not yet unpacked, and went to her suitcase, taking out something wrapped in tissue, handing it to her friend. Peggy removed a wide piece of black elastic with fasteners on each end. "It's called a cinch belt," Susan explained.

Peggy held it up. "Too small."

"You put it around your waist and pull it tight — *cinch,* get it?"

Peggy stretched the belt until she could fasten it, then looked at herself in the big mirror over Susan's marble-top dresser, preening a little. "Wow!" she said, admiring the way the elastic made her waist smaller, her bust and hips larger. Susan couldn't help but be jealous. A cinch belt on her was like putting a sash on a yardstick, but the belt made Peggy even curvier. Joe would compare the two of them, and Susan would come out second best.

Peggy studied herself in Susan's mirror, then looked down at the tiny drawers on either side of the long mirror, where Susan kept gloves and scarves, jewelry. Peggy removed a charm bracelet, looking at the charms one by one. Susan had bought them on trips to California and New York, and even to Europe. "I have a charm bracelet,"

Peggy said, holding Susan's bracelet shoulder high, then dropping it onto the marble beside a Bible that had belonged to Nealie. She picked up a silver hand mirror that had been Nealie's, too, and glanced at herself in it, then banged it on the top of the dressing table as she put it down. Susan was used to Peggy's carelessness, knowing it was done from jealousy, but still, she resented the hostility. It wasn't her fault that she was rich. She didn't flaunt it. Peggy didn't have to put her down for it.

Peggy removed the stopper from a crystal bottle and smelled it, then returned it, but not before a drop had spilled on the dresser scarf. "Too sweet. It smells like Evening in Paris," she said disdainfully, although the perfume was an expensive one.

Susan gave a tiny shake of her head, thinking it was odd that they were such good friends. There were other girls her age in Georgetown. But Peggy was the smartest and funniest and the most fun. Besides, Peggy and Joe were close, so Susan couldn't be friends with him without being Peggy's friend, as well. Pearl had explained once that coming from the family she did, Peggy couldn't help but be envious. The girl would never have the money or the opportunities Susan did, so Susan should be understanding, kind even, when Peggy made cruel remarks. So Susan overlooked Peggy's rudeness and concentrated on her friend's good qualities — her liveliness and sense of adventure. Besides, she knew, as the summer progressed, Peggy would lighten up.

Peggy rummaged around Susan's dresser and picked up the bracelet again, flipping through the charms. "Joe gave me a charm. Did I tell you that? It's a little piece of gold ore. He told me I was as good as gold, if you know what I mean." She raised her chin a little, running her tongue over her teeth.

Susan didn't know what that meant. Had Joe kissed her? Maybe they'd necked. Or petted. Susan was dying to know, but she didn't dare ask, because she didn't trust Peggy to tell the truth. Besides, Peggy would be coy, would string Susan along and make her feel stupid. She'd probably said that just to get Susan's goat. So instead, Susan asked, "How's he anyway?" She said it slowly, with what she hoped sounded like a lack of interest. Then she went to her suitcase and straightened the things Peggy had rumpled, not because she was neat but because, like her mother and grandmother, she blushed easily, and she was afraid the red face would give her away.

"Who?"

"Joe Bullock." Just saying the name out loud pleased her, and she wished she could say it over and over again.

"I heard he got, what-do-you-call-it, pinned."

Susan turned around quickly and found Peggy staring at her. "Oh really?" She tried to sound casual, although her heart was beating wildly.

"But he said he didn't. I think stuff like that, you know, like going steady, is dumb, don't you? I told him I'd never go steady."

"He asked you?" Peggy smirked and looked away, and Susan gave a tiny sigh, almost certain that Peggy had lied. "So is he here this summer?"

"Sure. I saw him last night."

"What's he doing?"

"Who?" Peggy asked again.

"Joe." Susan cringed at the way she couldn't shut up, but she *had* to know about him. Peggy was sure to figure out how she felt.

"He's working at the Texaco station. He always was crazy about cars. He's going to buy Mr. Joy's rattletrap." Peggy paused and glanced over at Susan. "We're going to the movies tonight. You can come if you want to."

Susan tried to sound nonchalant.

"Maybe," she said, "if I haven't seen the movie. What's on?" She didn't care if she'd seen the motion picture a dozen times.

Peggy shrugged. "I don't know. Some detective thing. If we're not there, go on in." Susan thought that over, trying to figure out if she had just been caught up in one of Peggy's devilish tricks. It happened every summer.

For as long as she could remember, Susan had had to prove herself each June after she arrived in Georgetown, perform some sort of initiation, before she was accepted as one of the gang of children who roamed the town and the mountains around it. Only when she was older did she realize that was because she was wealthy. The others wanted to make sure she did not put on airs or consider herself superior. Once, she had had to float down Clear Creek in an inner tube. The creek was at flood stage, and Susan's body was numb with the snowmelt that carried her, swirling her along the creek banks. If she'd fallen through the inner tube, she'd have drowned, but she held on, and Joe fished her out after she got caught in some branches.

Another time, Peggy dared her to climb one of the pine trees in front of the Bride's

House. Susan was afraid of heights, and she shivered at the thought of going eighty or ninety feet up into the air, but she was more fearful of the disdain if she didn't take the dare, and started up the tree.

At first, it wasn't so bad. She went from limb to limb, more than halfway to the top, worrying more about scratching her legs than about falling. But then she looked down and realized she was fifty feet above the others. Her hands began to perspire, and she started to shake, grasping the branches of the tree so hard that the needles made her hands bleed.

"Go on. You have to go to the top," Peggy called.

Susan looked down, saw Joe watching her, and she reached for a higher branch to pull herself up, but her hand slipped, and she threw herself against the trunk of the tree. She wasn't in any real danger of falling. After all, she was holding on with one hand, and her feet were firm. But the idea of going higher made her almost ill. Her breath came fast, and she could feel her heart beat so hard that she thought it would knock her out of the tree. "I can't," she called.

"Scaredy-cat," Peggy yelled.

"I am not!" Shaking with fear, Susan reached again for the branch above her.

"Oh, forget it. Nobody else ever got that far," Joe said. "Come on down, Susan," he called. But Susan was petrified, and she could go neither up nor down.

Peggy scoffed at her. "You'll starve up there if you don't come down. We'll have to go up there and get your bones."

But at last, Joe climbed up the tree, until he was beside Susan. "It's okay. You can do it. I'll be right below to catch you if you fall, but you won't. You're as game as anybody," he told her. Then quietly, branch by branch, he talked her down.

"Well, you didn't make it to the top," Peggy said when Susan jumped from the lowest branch onto the ground.

"Neither did you. Remember?" Joe defended Susan, and nothing more was said. The others gathered around Susan, and she was one of them for the summer.

The worst time, however, was the tire. Susan had been eleven that summer, and Peggy had announced she'd come up with a new game. She told Susan to meet her and Joe and the other kids at the top of Taos Street, and Susan had agreed, apprehensive about what challenge Peggy had in store for her this time.

She walked slowly up the hill, conscious that her feet were still tender and she was wearing sandals, while the others were barefoot, except for one boy with scuffed high-top shoes.

"Where's Joe?" Susan asked.

"He went to get the tire," Peggy replied, giving Susan a strange smile. "I told him to. He'll be here after a bit." She walked a little ways away so that she could see over to Rose Street. "I think that's him coming." The others turned and watched Joe roll a large tire up the hill.

When he reached them, Joe grinned at Susan. "Hi, ya," he said. "You grew some."

"Everybody grows in a year," Peggy told him.

"Did Peggy tell you about our new game?"

Susan shrugged. "Not really."

Peggy grinned at her. "Here's what you do. You climb inside the tire, and we roll you down the hill. It's pretty simple." A boy snickered, and Peggy told him, "Shut up."

Susan stared at her. "You want me to go down the hill inside a tire?"

"You bet."

"That's crazy! What if I get hit by a car?"

"Oh, don't worry. Somebody will stand down on Sixth Street to let us know when the coast is clear."

"Swell," Susan said. This sounded like the worst game she had ever heard of. If the tire didn't get hit by a car, it might roll into Clear Creek, and she'd drown. Or it could run into a house or a rock pile, and she'd get knocked out. The rolling would make her dizzy, and she'd throw up, and the kids would laugh at her. What if the tire landed in the yard of the Bride's House and her mother saw her? "That's the dumbest game in the world. Who'd do that?" she asked.

"Joe did it," Peggy said. "So did I. So did all of us."

"From all the way up here?" The street went straight down the mountain for three blocks. In fact, in the winter, it was the sledding hill.

Peggy shrugged, and then she turned to Joe and said in a loud whisper, "I think she's chicken." Joe turned and looked at Susan as if thinking Peggy was right.

Susan swallowed hard then. There was no worse insult. If the kids thought she were chicken, they'd never let her live it down. It would be a disastrous summer. She couldn't bear it if Joe looked down on her. Maybe he wouldn't want anything to do with her. "Okay," she said at last.

"Don't worry. The tire always falls over before it gets very far." Joe grinned. He held the tire, while Peggy helped Susan curl up inside it. She felt claustrophobic, and her

390

back hurt from being bent over. The edges rubbed against her skin, and the rubber smell made her nauseous.

"I'll shove it off," Peggy volunteered, elbowing Joe aside. She held the tire stationary at the top of the hill, then gave it a hard push.

Susan held her breath as the tire began to roll down the mountain street, gathering speed. The kids had forgotten to station someone on Sixth Street, and Susan thought she'd get hit by a car. She tried to recognize Sixth, but she couldn't because everything was a blur as she turned over and over. Maybe she'd passed it already. The tire sped up, she knew that. There was a flash of green, and Susan feared she might be veering over to the creek. The tire would sink to the bottom, and she'd drown before she could get out. But she kept rolling, her heart wild, the taste of her breakfast in her mouth. Her back hurt so much from being curled up that she thought she'd never stand up straight again — that is, if she lived. The tire kicked up dirt, all but smothering her, making her cough, her eyes water. A dog barked as she rolled past, and someone yelled, "Stop that fool thing!" Another voice called, "Those darn kids. Somebody's liable to get killed." She was the somebody, Susan thought. Maybe the tire would knock down an old man or a little kid, and she'd be arrested.

Then suddenly, the tire slowed. The feel of the ground beneath the tire changed, and she knew it had left the dirt road and was on grass. The tire bumped against something, wobbled a little, then circled, and finally, it fell over and was still. Susan heaved a deep sigh, relieved and a little surprised that she was still alive. This was the worst trick Peggy had ever pulled, worse even than climbing the tree.

That was not the end of it, however. Susan gripped the tire to pull herself out, but she was stuck. The edges of the tire held her inside, and now she had a new fear. What if the kids didn't help her out? Maybe they were scared that she was hurt and they would get into trouble. What if they scattered? She'd have to stay there until somebody discovered her. There might be rats or snakes in the grass. A mosquito bit her, and with her arms pinned to her sides, she couldn't slap it. Susan shivered. Then she saw a broom and heard a voice. "Don't you worthless kids run that tire into my fence!"

"Get me out of here," Susan called.

The woman screamed. "The devil's inside that tire."

Then Susan heard laughter, and someone said, "Oh, it's just Susan Curry."

"Well, you could have knocked her dead, running that tire right smack-a-dab in the middle of the road. And wouldn't that be something? Now get her out of there."

"Nobody ever rolled that far before. It's a record." That sounded like Joe.

The kids were around the tire then, gripping Susan, pulling her out. She wobbled and would have fallen if Joe hadn't caught her. Her stomach churned. She felt like vomiting, but she couldn't, not in front of everybody.

"You okay?" Joe put his arm around her waist to hold her up.

"She's probably sick," Peggy said. "I bet she throws up."

"Leave her alone," Joe said. "I wouldn't feel so good, either, if I'd gone that far. Are you all right, Susan?"

Susan nodded, although her back ached and her head hurt. She was dizzy, too. But she stood up straight and looked at the bunch of kids around her. "That was fun," she said. And then she turned to Peggy. "Who's next?"

Peggy studied her a moment, scowled, but then she smiled a little and said only, "You don't have to be so biggity acting."

Joe grinned. "Good going, Susan," he said. It was the highest praise he could give her, and Susan basked in the words. That was the moment she decided she was going to marry Joe Bullock.

Peggy worked at a clothing store called the Miner's Daughter, and she left shortly after breakfast. Susan unpacked, then sat down at the dressing table and picked up the hand mirror. It was silver with an *ND* monogram on the back and was part of a set that included a hairbrush, comb, and shoehorn that her grandfather had bought for her grandmother. She liked using it, liked the sense of connection it gave her with the women who had lived in the Bride's House before her.

She ran her finger over the engraving, the flowers and vines that swirled around the monogram. She loved Nealie's bric-a-brac as much as the fusty old house. The Bride's House was warm and safe with its sense of permanence, and it was the place she went in her head when she was lonely or unhappy. She dreamed of living there with Joe. Susan never pictured the boys who had courted her in Chicago — and there had been several, since seventeen was not too young to be engaged — in the Bride's House. Only Joe.

Susan placed the mirror on the dressing table, got up, and went downstairs, waving to her mother, who was taking dictation in the study. "I'm going to walk down to the park," she called, knowing as she said it that her goal was the Texaco station. She should wait until she ran into Joe or he stopped by the house, but it had been nine months! She couldn't wait any longer. Joe didn't have to know she was there. She'd stand across the street and get just a glimpse of him.

So Susan went to the highway and stared at the white station with its two gasoline pumps, and then she saw him filling the tank of a prewar Plymouth. Happy just to see him, she watched as he replaced the pump, took a rag, and cleaned the windows. His shirt sleeves were rolled up, his arms golden in the sunlight, and Susan wished she could run her hand over his skin.

The driver held out some bills, and Joe went into the station and returned with change, handing it through the window to the driver. He watched the car pull out onto the highway, and then he glanced across the street and pushed back the hat with the red star on it. He recognized Susan and grinned, and his smile made her glow.

She crossed the road, aware that her hands were sweaty from the sun and that the wind had whipped her hair. She had on a pair of old shorts from last summer and a blouse that hadn't been ironed. Why hadn't she put on something decent, something like what Peggy had worn? Joe would think she looked just like another grubby tourist.

"Hey," Joe said. "When did you get in?"

"Last night." She looked down at where the toe of her sandal dug into the asphalt so that he wouldn't see how she blushed just from the pleasure of being with him. "Mr. Joy drove us up from Denver."

"That's some truck he's got."

"It has a shift in the floor."

"I know. I'm going to buy it from him — two hundred bucks. Cool, huh?"

The boys Susan dated in Chicago drove new cars — convertibles with leather seats and automatic transmissions, radios and whitewall tires. They'd have looked down on a 1927 Ford truck with a cracked windshield and a blanket covering the ripped seats, but at that moment, she'd rather ride in Bert Joy's truck than any other vehicle in the world. "A steal," she said.

"I can work on it here at the station when we're not busy."

"Are you ever not busy?"

"Not yet."

The conversation was easy. There was no fencing as there had been at first with Peggy. It was as if the two had seen each other only yesterday. "What's with the bow tie?" Susan asked.

Joe touched the tie. "Texaco makes us wear them. It's leather."

"Oh, I thought you just had good taste."

"I do. I hang around with you, don't I?"

A man inside the garage called Joe, and he said, "I have to go." Then he asked, "Hey, do you want to go to a movie tonight?"

"I already have a date."

"Oh."

"With you and Peggy."

"Hey, you've got good taste, too."

Susan watched Joe disappear into the garage and knew it would be a good summer.

That night, Joe, Peggy, and Susan walked home from the movie. Joe turned into Peggy's street, and she asked, annoyed, "You're taking me home first?"

"You're closer. Besides, I haven't said hello to Mrs. Curry."

Peggy pouted. "See you around."

After they left Peggy, the two walked down the street in the soft dusk, not talking. The silence wasn't awkward. Being with Joe was easy. Susan matched her stride to his, wishing she could take his hand, hoping he would take hers, but he didn't.

Her mother was on the porch of the Bride's House when they reached it, and Susan sat down beside her on the bench. Joe leaned against a post, exchanging pleasantries with Pearl, welcoming her home. As Joe talked, Susan stared at his face in the dark, making out only his profile — the straight nose, the firm chin. Joe Bullock was a handsome young man with brown curly hair and brown eyes, not so tall, only five feet ten inches or so, an inch or two taller than Susan, but he was sturdy, strong. He was good-natured, with a smile that made everyone like him, including Charlie and all three Currys. In fact, Frank had offered him a job after college, with the molybdenum company. And Pearl had told her daughter once or twice that Joe Bullock would go places, no matter what line of work he went into.

"How do you like college?" Pearl asked.

"It's good. I'm thinking of going on to law school."

"What about the draft?"

"As long as I stay in school, I'm okay."

"Did you know Susan's going to attend

the University of Denver, too?"

"You're kidding. You're going there?" he asked Susan. "How come?"

"I love Colorado more than anyplace, and if I go to DU, I can spend time here with Grandfather. And you talked it up so much last summer. *You* said I ought to go there." She added quickly so that Joe wouldn't get the idea he was the reason for her decision, "Mother says she would have gone to DU." Susan hadn't known her mother had even considered attending college, until Susan brought up the University of Denver and Pearl told her she would have gone there if her father hadn't needed her at home.

"Maybe we'll have classes together," Susan told Joe.

She could not make out the look he gave her in the dark. "I'll be an upperclassman."

"You mean you won't have anything to do with a freshman?"

"I might if you show the proper respect."

Susan leaned over, bowed her head, and stretched out her arms so that they touched her feet. "Will that do?"

"For a start."

"It's good Susan will know at least one person when she begins school," Pearl said.

"DU has a lot of kids from Illinois," Joe replied, to Susan's disappointment. She'd hoped Joe would promise to show her around, to look out for her.

Susan was sitting with Joe and Peggy and several others from the group she'd played with as a kid, when Peggy invited her to go on a snipe hunt. "Do you know what that is?"

"A what?" Susan asked.

"A snipe hunt. I bet you never heard of it. Maybe they don't have snipes in Chicago? Maybe they're just in Colorado."

"What's a snipe?" Susan asked

"Oh, it's a sweet little animal, like a kitten sort of. It's real friendly. You never see them in the day. They come out just at night. There are a bunch of them at the cemetery."

"Are they dangerous?"

"No, of course not."

"Do you shoot them?" Susan's eyes were big.

Peggy glanced at Joe, who had been watching her, and asked, "Why don't you tell her?"

Joe thought a moment and said, "You sure you want to do this, Peggy?"

"Of course. It's so much fun."

Joe thought that over, and to Susan's disappointment, he said, "Okay, then." He turned to her. "We don't kill them. It's not like you eat them or anything. We just play with them, like cats, just capture them, then let them go."

"How do you do that, capture them, I mean?"

Joe glanced at Peggy, who told him to go on. "Like Peggy said, we go to the cemetery. You walk very quietly and touch the gravestones. That brings them out."

"That doesn't sound like much fun to me." Susan stared at Joe, wishing he'd wink at her or give some sign he wasn't going along with Peggy.

"You won't have to do that. You can hold the bag, since you've never been on a snipe hunt before," Peggy told her. "You can be the first to catch them."

"Do they bite?"

"They don't have teeth," someone interjected. "They don't have much of anything." The others laughed.

"We'll go tonight, after dark," Peggy said.

"I don't know," Susan told them.

"You aren't afraid of ghosts, are you?" Peggy turned to the others. "Maybe she's chicken."

Susan shook her head, then said, "I guess it's all right." She'd show them, show Peggy and Joe, too. She was disappointed that Joe was being as big a jerk as Peggy, had hoped he would look out for her.

"Okay, then," Peggy told her, and she nudged Joe with her elbow.

That night, just as the sky was turning an ominous dark gray, Susan met Peggy and Joe and four others on the road to the cemetery. "I don't know about this," Susan remarked. "It looks like it's going to rain."

"Snipes love rain," Peggy said.

Susan turned to Joe, but he was silent.

"Don't worry. We'll be with you," Peggy said, and the group set off along the long road lit only by stars and a sliver of moon. They could hear the rushing water in the creek and the sound of the wind as it bent the aspen trees, making the leaves quiver. The air was damp on Susan's skin, with the feeling of rain — not a soft summer drizzle as in Chicago but a cold mountain rain.

"It's sort of spooky," Peggy said. "Did you ever read that story in school about the headless horseman?"

Susan nodded. Then because Peggy couldn't see her, she said in a small voice, "Yes."

"Don't worry. Nobody here's ever seen a headless horseman," Joe said.

"Or lived to tell about it," Peggy added.

When they reached the cemetery, Peggy stationed Susan at the entrance and gave her a gunnysack, telling her the others would scare up the snipes. All she had to do was catch them. "Sometimes it takes time — a long time — so don't worry. You're not scared, are you? You don't believe in ghosts?"

Susan hunched her shoulders. "Is this some sort of joke?"

"No, of course not," Peggy said. She sounded indignant.

Susan sat down on a headstone with the bag and watched the others scatter in the dark. She waited until they had disappeared into the mountains beyond the cemetery and she couldn't hear them anymore. Then she dropped the bag and hurried back up the road to Georgetown, smiling a little, hoping she got home before the rain. But she was angry, too, not at Peggy but at Joe, because he shouldn't have done this to her.

She sat on the front porch in the dark, watching the rain come down, then stop, waiting, until finally Peggy and Joe walked by. They looked up at her bedroom window, which was dark, and she thought they laughed, and that hurt her feelings, hurt her that Joe would help Peggy play a trick on her like that. After all, they weren't kids anymore. Susan wished Joe had told Peggy to forget it or that he'd whispered to Susan it was all a trick. She thought to let them pass, but instead when she heard Peggy giggle, Susan called out to them. "Did you get caught in the rain?"

The two stopped and turned to each other, then stared at the porch. "When did you get home?" Peggy demanded.

"Oh, a long time ago, just before the rain started." She came down off the porch and walked to the gate and looked at Peggy, whose wet hair was plastered to her head. Joe looked sheepish. "It didn't take me as long as you because I just went back up the road. You had to take the long way so I wouldn't see you." Then she added, "A snipe hunt! How dumb do you think I am?" She hoped she didn't sound as hurt as she was.

Joe grinned, and that made Susan feel a little better. But Peggy turned away and walked quickly up the street, shivering in her wet clothes.

Susan called after her, "How many snipes did you catch?"

Joe let Peggy go, then he laughed. "I guess you showed us. Good going, Susan!" he said.

CHAPTER 14

Because they did not have a car in Georgetown, Susan and her mother walked everywhere, and if they needed to go to Denver, Pearl hired Bert Joy to drive them. Every week or two, they walked down to the Alvarado Cemetery to tend to the Dumas plot where Nealie as well as Lydia Travers was buried under the wings of a stone angel. They took along implements to dig dandelions and trim the grass that grew under the iron fence that surrounded the plot. And they either brought lilacs or peonies or daisies in a jar or stopped along the way to pick wildflowers. Susan would spot them in the weeds along the road, shining in the sun like bits of bright fabric — the red paintbrush, the blue columbine, the magenta flowers the women called summer's-half-over.

Susan loved roaming through the cemetery with its elaborate tombstones carved to look like stumps or angels or lambs. There were a few marble slabs marking the graves of soldiers from the Civil War, World War I, and the last war. But she liked the wooden markers best. The wood was silvery with age, weathered and splintery, and the names once painted or carved into the wood had been sanded off by the wind and snow. Susan speculated about the men and women buried there, believing they were young people like Joe who'd come west to strike it rich, not elderly men like her grandfather. The old people lay under the stolid stone and marble markers.

One afternoon, as Susan and her mother passed the filling station on their way out of town, they spotted Joe pumping gas into a Studebaker, a silver and green one, and stopped to admire it. "Isn't this a honey?" Joe said.

"It's too low for mountain roads," Pearl observed. "I wish we had an old car, one higher off the ground, for the summer."

"Why don't you take that old car of Mr. Dumas's off its blocks?" Joe asked. "Is it still in your barn?"

"That's a great idea, Mother," Susan said, then turned to Joe. "Do you think it can be made to run?"

Joe shrugged. "It's a heck of a car."

Susan's father had bought Charlie a black touring car twenty years before, a high one, and her grandfather had driven Susan over the rough mountain roads in it when she was a small child. But the old man's eyesight had grown poor, and the automobile had sat on blocks in the barn since before the war, its whitewall tires stored in a horse stall. When she was younger and by herself, Susan had played in the car, polishing the hood ornament or sitting in the front passenger seat, imaging Joe sitting beside her, one hand on the wheel, the other around her. She went through the glove compartment and took out the packages of matches and maps that Charlie had acquired in his travels, dreaming of places she and Joe would go. She picked sprigs of lilac and put them into the crystal vases in the holders between the front and back seats. Sometimes, she even rolled down the shades and lay down in the back seat with the plaid lap robe over her.

Now, she turned to her mother and said, "Maybe Joe could fix it up."

"Maybe," Joe said. "At least I could take a look."

"We'd appreciate that," Pearl told him. She shifted the shears she was carrying from one hand to the other. "We're off to the cemetery."

The two started on, but Joe called, "Hey, Susan, you want to go explore the old Poor Boy Mine on Saturday? Maybe you can find a miner's candlestick." Susan collected the twisted bits of metal that the miners had shoved into walls underground to hold their candles.

"Great! I'd love to go." She stopped herself from adding, "with you," but that was what she meant.

"I'll take a look at your grandfather's car when I pick you up."

Susan hummed a little as they walked on. Pearl looked at her but was silent. After a time, however, she remarked, "You like that boy, don't you?"

"I guess," Susan said, turning aside so her mother wouldn't see her blush, embarrassed that Pearl might know how much she cared about Joe. "But I think he likes Peggy."

"I'm not so sure. A boy with the ambition Joe has is too smart to tie himself to a girl like Peggy Purcell."

They walked along quickly then, since Pearl had never been one to stroll, and when they reached the cemetery, they passed the Bullock plot. Joe's grandparents were buried there along with his aunts and his older brother, who had died in the war. There was room for other graves, for Joe's parents and sister, for Joe and maybe Joe's wife. If *she* were Joe's wife, would she prefer to be buried there or with her own family? Susan wondered.

She and Pearl stopped at the Dumas plot, a large one with a stone monument the size of a double-bed headboard, with "Nealie, Mrs. Charles Dumas, 1865–1882" on one side and "Charles Dumas, 1853–19 —" on the other. Mrs. Travers's grave was to one side with just "Lydia Travers." "She never told us when she was born," Pearl remarked.

Susan's mother took out her shears and began to clip the grass around Nealie's grave. "They were married less than a year, and my father's grieved another seventy for her. Maybe he'd have been better off if he'd never met her."

Susan looked up, waiting for her mother to explain, but Pearl was watching a hearse pull out, driving slowly — respectfully — over the rocky road to the cemetery gate. The mourners, some of the men in Masonic regalia, the women in black dresses with high heels and nylons that would be ripped by the weeds and brambles before the women reached the cars, turned away from the open grave and went to their vehicles.

A few of the mourners stopped at graves

to throw out bunches of dead flowers stuffed into rusted tin cans or to discard Decoration Day flags, their red and blue already bleached by the sun. Pearl waved to a couple placing a tin can of daisies beside a tombstone. "How do?" she called, and the two came over to chat, the woman tipping from side to side because her legs were angled from rickets.

"We brought flowers to decorate Mother's grave," the woman explained. "She was a multiplying woman. The old man wanted babies, and she just had them. She asked him once not to have them too close, but he cuffed her. He wasn't the one having the babies, and she had to obey. Then he took off with her money — took her lucky dime and spent it on tobacco — and all she got was babies. My whole life, I raised them, raised her come-after child all by myself. That's why I never had any of my own."

"What's a come-after child?" Susan asked.

"One that's born after its father's gone."

"Its father?"

"Well, it wouldn't be born after its mother died, now would it?" The woman chuckled.

"Oh," Susan said. "Is your father buried here, too?"

"He is," the man answered and shook his head. "We was letting the coffin down in the grave when he knocked on the inside of it. Knock. Knock. We buried him anyway."

Susan's mouth dropped open, and the woman said quickly, "Oh, you know that's not true." She thought a moment. "But it could have been. Yes, it could. You think twice about who you marry, young lady."

The man cleared his throat, and his wife put her lips together in a straight line. After a moment, she said to Susan, "It won't be long before your grandfather joins Nealie now. He's waited a long time. I guess she has, too. Funny how it was him that lived in the Bride's House all those years, when she was the bride, and she didn't live there hardly at all."

Susan studied the woman, not sure what to say, while Pearl only nodded.

"That woman's too sentimental," the man put in, meaning his wife. Then he turned to her and said, "Sounds like you're trying to put the old man in his grave. You don't know if he'll go on up to heaven."

"Oh, for goodness' sake! How can you say such a thing? And in front of Pearl and Susan, too."

"He's in his ninety-seventh year, so I imagine it won't be long," Pearl said. "My mother was only seventeen when she died, just Susan's age."

The realization her grandmother had died so young shocked Susan. Of course, she'd *known* that, but it had never registered that Nealie had married, had a baby, and died when she was younger than Susan was now.

On Saturday morning, Susan dressed in blue jeans and shoes with hard soles, because mine sites were graveyards of rusty iron and old nails sharp enough to penetrate tennis shoes. She put on a plaid blouse and tied the tails together the way Peggy had, but it looked stupid. Then she tried on a blue blouse, but it was dowdy. Finally she put on a white shirt, which showed up the tan she had acquired sunbathing with Peggy. She hoped Joe would notice.

She packed a picnic — making deviled eggs and ham-salad sandwiches, and she'd talked her mother into making cinnamon buns for breakfast, because Joe had told her once that he loved the smell of cinnamon and dabbing the spice behind her ears didn't seem like a good idea.

Joe showed up at ten, saying the sky looked like rain, so he'd take a look at Charlie's car in the afternoon, after they returned. They rode in Bert Joy's old Ford truck, Joe's now. It wasn't as good as an army-surplus Jeep, but it was high off the ground and was better on a rocky trail than a car.

"I brought along lunch," Susan said, as Joe helped her up onto the running board.

"And I brought some beer," he replied. He pulled onto the highway, and the truck being noisy, they were silent as they drove down the asphalt, then turned off near the old town of Red Elephant, starting up a road that was no more than a dirt trail winding through evergreens and aspen. Joe drove slowly, bouncing over the ruts made by trickles of snowmelt, dodging rocks and stumps that could have punctured a tire or high-centered the truck, gearing down to go up the steep grades. At last, he stopped where there was a place wide enough to pull off and said the truck could go no farther. They got out, Joe carrying two bottles of beer, Susan with the picnic basket over her arm.

She didn't mind leaving the truck, because she loved to hike, especially with Joe, and she followed him up the trail, staring at his broad back, picturing what he looked like without his shirt, imagining how it would feel if he put his arms around her and held her against his bare chest.

Aspen trees had grown up in the middle of the trail, and wildflowers bloomed in the faint ruts. "Look, there's a lady's slipper. I bet I haven't seen a dozen of them in my whole life," Joe said, pointing to a pale green plant in a spot where rain collected in a protected area under an aspen tree. They stopped to admire the flower, and Joe said he'd pick it for Susan, but it was so rare that it ought to be left alone.

They saw the tracks of a Jeep that had come up through the timber. "I hate those damn things," Joe told her. "Why can't people leave the mountains alone? And the trash!" He leaned down and picked up a discarded Chesterfield cigarette package, shoving it into his pocket. "Someday they'll ruin this land. I wish we could do something about them."

"They shop in Georgetown. Peggy says the tourists are the best customers she has. Her store couldn't make it if it had to rely on local people."

"That's the problem. It's damned if you do and damned if you don't. The only way these old mining towns can survive is tourism, but the tourists destroy the mountains."

"So what do you do?"

"Conservation's the best answer. You have to teach people to be careful, people like the idiot driving that Jeep. See those tracks he made? Other people will drive there, so before long, it'll turn it into a road. That's how erosion starts. There ought to be laws."

"To keep people from going into the mountains? Lots of luck. Who'd introduce laws like that?"

"I would."

Susan switched the picnic basket from one arm to the other, as she thought Joe could do that. He could protect the mountains or make people pick up trash or do just about anything he set his mind to.

They reached the mine and set the picnic basket and beer on a round wooden structure that had once been a cable spool. The area was littered with the detritus of mining days — piles of machinery, discarded dynamite boxes, shacks that had fallen in and were no more than boards containing rusty nails, an ore bucket. The mine tipple sagged, its boards weathered to a rich brown, but it had not caved in.

"You're not going inside?" Susan asked, alarmed.

"Too dangerous. You could fall down a hundred feet and never be found."

Susan was relieved. If Joe had gone inside, she'd have had to follow to show she wasn't chicken. She looked around then and found a cache of old bottles, some of them purple from the sun. She picked through the glass and pulled out two that weren't broken. "Aren't these pretty?" She felt a little foolish asking that because men — she thought of Joe as a man now — didn't care about pretty things.

But Joe held up a bottle and nodded. "I always look for old bottles. My mom likes to keep them in the window."

"She can have these," Susan said, pleased that she had found something to give Joe. Maybe he'd be reminded of her each time he saw the sun shining through the purple glass.

He held up a glass jar that had a label on which something had been written in pencil. "I bet this was a still. There were plenty of them up here during Prohibition, dozens. Peggy's grandfather had one, although she won't admit it."

"No lie?" Susan wished he hadn't mentioned Peggy. She thought there ought to be a moratorium on mentioning Peggy that day.

Joe nodded. "Ask her, and see what she says."

"No, thanks. I've seen her get mad before."

"Who hasn't? For all I know, her dad still makes moon. He sure drinks enough of it. What a jerk."

Susan wanted to reply that Peggy probably drank it, too, but she held her tongue for fear Joe would think she was catty.

He lifted a pine branch that had fallen onto the ground and picked off the needles, while Susan turned her face to the dappled sunlight coming through the aspen trees, her eyes closed. There was just enough of a breeze to keep the sun from being too hot. She'd like to take off her shirt so that she could get a tan. She and Peggy did that sometimes when they were hiking in the back country, but of course, she couldn't do it now, because Joe would think she was a tramp. Besides, Susan thought, she was so flat-chested that he'd be disappointed.

"So, you're really going to DU?" Joe asked.

Thinking of the two of them together at school in Denver brought back her good mood. "My father wanted me to go east to a women's college, but what fun would that be?" Susan asked, a little sleepy from the sun now. She wished she could put her head in Joe's lap instead of on a log, and he'd run his hands through her hair. She opened her eyes, thinking if he were beside her, she could lean against him, but he sat some distance away, his legs crossed.

"I'll tell you the best sororities. Heck, I

could even tell you what guys to date."

Susan shaded her eyes so that she could look at him. "I don't think I need your help there."

"No, you wouldn't. You'd probably have so many guys on your string, you wouldn't even look at me."

"I'd consider it. You might be a Big Man on Campus."

"BMOCs always have pretty girls hanging around."

Did he mean she was pretty? Susan couldn't think how to respond, and Joe didn't say any more, so she stood and said, "Let's go look inside the mine shack."

They walked over to a small building whose door was ajar. The steps had rotted through, and inside, the floor was buckled. Weeds grew up through the floorboards. Wires hung down from the ceiling, and an old shirt and a pair of overalls were pegged to the wall. A boot, its sole half off, lay on the floor under rusted springs that had fallen through a makeshift bed. A tiny cook-stove that had been used for cooking as well as heating was still standing, although its stovepipe had crumpled and lay on the floor.

On impulse, Susan opened the oven door, which shrieked from disuse, and they discovered a pot inside filled with mummified beans. "Somebody expected to be home for supper, but he never came back."

"He could have died in a cave-in or just walked off the job."

"Or maybe a woman left it here. She might have been the one who died." She might have died in childbirth. Susan suddenly remembered her grandmother. She thought how awful it would be, dying when your life had barely begun, leaving behind a husband like Joe and a baby for him to raise. "I feel like an intruder, like we walked in on ghosts." She went outside and sat on a log in the sun, its warmth taking away the chill of the shack.

Joe brought the picnic basket and the beer and sat down beside her, and they ate the lunch, throwing bits of sandwich and cinnamon bun to a striped chipmunk that perched on a boulder across from them. A black-and-white camp robber flew down from the branch of a pine tree and pecked at a crumb, then flew off.

"I'd miss this if I ever left Colorado," Joe said, picking up a rock and tossing it at a bucket whose bottom had rusted out.

"You'd leave?" Susan felt a sort of panic. She'd never thought about Joe living anyplace but Georgetown.

"I'm not planning to. I wouldn't want to

live anywhere else. It's my home. But who knows? Would you live here?"

Susan nodded. "It's my home, too, even though I live in Chicago most of the year. I love Georgetown. There's a foreverness to this place, to the Bride's House."

"I know what you mean." Susan waited for Joe to say more, but he stood and reached out his hand. "Come on. Let's see if we can find any candlesticks." He helped Susan rise and led her through the piles of machinery and waste rock. Joe looked into an ore cart that lay on its side, poking the rubble with a stick. A mouse ran out, and he shouted, "Careful. There are living things in here."

"Yuck," Susan said, thinking she should have shrieked and grasped onto Joe, as Peggy would have done, but it was too late now. She walked a little away and spotted something in a boulder field. "I found one of those old leather hardhats," she called, and reached for it. Then she stopped. A rattlesnake that had been sunning itself on the rocks began to slither toward her. In a moment it would curl, and shaking the rattles on its tail, it would lunge at her, sinking its fangs into her leg or arm, even her chest or neck. She knew she should jump back, should run, but instead, looking into the snake's eyes, she froze, unable to take even a step. "Joe," she called in a high voice.

Joe turned and frowned at Susan for a second. Then he saw the snake, and in an instant, he was beside her. He grabbed the rattler by the tail. Then he pulled back his arm and popped the snake like a whip. The snake's head snapped off, landing in the dirt not far from Susan, and Joe yelled, "Don't touch it. There's venom in the fangs."

He put his arms around her, holding her up, making Susan feel safe. She looked over his shoulder at the head of the snake. Its eye stared unblinking at her like a living thing, and she gulped air. Joe patted her back and said, "It's okay. You're all right. The snake's dead." Susan began to shiver, holding on to Joe, afraid he would let her go, but he led her to a rock and made her sit down. He glanced around, searching for other snakes.

"You saved my life," Susan said. She balled up the tail of her shirt with her hand.

Joe frowned and looked at his hands. "You'd have been okay."

"No, really. You popped off its head," she whispered in awe. "How did you know to do that?"

"I don't know. I just did it."

"That'll teach him."

Joe laughed. "You want to see the rest of him? You know, a little like getting back on a horse after it's thrown you?"

Susan didn't, but she forced herself to stand up, and holding on to Joe's arm, she went to where the snake's body lay and peered down at it. The snake was stretched out and looked alive, because at first, she couldn't see that the head was gone. She stared for a long time at the body, which looked like a tree branch, then turned and put her face against Joe's chest, closing her eyes, as he held her again. She wanted to stay there all day.

"It's an old snake. You can tell from all the rattles," Joe said. Then he asked, "Do you want them?"

"The rattles? You mean cut them off?"

"Why not? *He* doesn't need them." Joe took out his pocket knife and leaned over the snake, but Susan stopped him. "Let me," she said. She was not sure just why she should cut the rattles, but it seemed to her that she, not Joe, should do it. Whatever the reason, she squatted down beside the snake, taking the rattles in one hand and lopping them off with the knife she held in the other. She shook the rattles, and they gave off a dead sound. They felt dead, too, no longer menacing, and she wrapped them in waxed paper from the lunch and placed them in the picnic basket. "I'll have to remember to take them out before I get home. Mrs. Warren would have a fit if she found them there."

Joe raised an eyebrow.

"Of course, I could always leave them." And they both laughed, Joe because of the joke, Susan because she was relieved. She hoped that when she thought of this day with Joe, she'd recall the sun and the scent of wild roses instead of the snake. But she wouldn't. She had wanted it to be a day to remember, and it was, but in a horrible way.

"I can't believe that I couldn't even move," Susan said, as they started back down the trail toward the truck, Joe staying close behind her. "I was transfixed."

"I thought you were brave."

"Yeah, like the time I went halfway up that pine tree in front of the Bride's House and couldn't get down." She shouldn't have brought that up. It was one more thing that would make Joe think she was stupid.

"You went halfway up. That's farther than I'd gone, and Peggy never made it more than four or five branches. I really do think you're brave. What other girl would touch a dead snake? You actually cut off its rattles. That's pretty impressive."

Susan turned around, gripping a branch of an aspen tree, because the slope was steep. "I really was scared."

"Yeah, but you faced it." He paused and said, "I don't know what I'd have done if it'd bitten you. I couldn't stand it if something happened to you." He stared at her for a long time, and Susan shivered again, this time at Joe's words, not the snake.

He opened the passenger door of the truck, and took her arm to help her on to the running board. But then he stopped. "Hey," he said. When Susan turned around, he kissed her. She'd waited almost half of her life for that moment, had dreamed of being in the moonlight with Joe when he took her in his arms. This was not what she had imagined; it was better. She loved that Joe had kissed her there in the mountains with the sun shimmering off the aspen leaves. She closed her eyes and kissed him back. Then Joe pulled away a little and smiled at her, running his finger down the bridge of her nose. He kissed her again, then let her go, put the picnic basket into the back of the truck, and climbed into the driver's side. "You okay?" he asked, waiting for her answer before he turned on the engine. Susan nodded, too happy to say anything.

They drove back down the trail and turned onto the highway, not talking. Joe hummed a little. Susan couldn't look at him, because she felt giddy. She thought about the kisses, but her mind kept going back to the snake. She envisioned it again, not only stretched out on the rocky ground but coiled, striking, and by the time they reached Georgetown, she'd begun shaking again and couldn't stop. "You're in shock," Joe said. "Come on. I'll help you." He half dragged, half lifted Susan out of the truck, and picking her up, he carried her to the porch, then banged on the screen with his elbow and called, "Mrs. Curry." Pearl rushed into the foyer from the office, Charlie behind her. "She almost got snake bit, biggest rattler I ever saw," Joe said, although Susan knew it wasn't. "She's in shock."

"The rattles are in the picnic basket, in waxed paper," Susan told her mother, her voice high and out of control.

Joe carried Susan upstairs to her bedroom and set her on the bed. Then he returned to the foyer, where Charlie stood, the picnic basket at his feet and a wad of waxed paper in his hand. The old man held up the rattles. "That was some snake. We'll put these in the cabinet with the ore specimens. Some of them came from snakes, too." He chuckled.

Upstairs, Pearl sat down in a chair beside Susan as the girl stared at the shadows on the wall made by the sun coming through the blinds. She stared at them a long time before she closed her eyes. She shivered under the quilts her mother had piled on the bed, and at last, she went to sleep. When Susan awoke, her mother was still sitting beside her. On the dressing table was a vase of wildflowers. "Joe brought them," Pearl told the girl. "He said to tell you he wanted you to have something better than snake rattles to remember your day."

But she already did. She had the memory of Joe's kisses.

CHAPTER 15

In the fall, Susan registered at the University of Denver. But Joe Bullock wasn't there. He had transferred to a school in California. In late August, he'd come by the Bride's House to tell her. Susan had fixed iced tea, and they sat in the gazebo, across from each other on stone benches, Joe with his hands between his knees, looking at the floor. "I got a scholarship, and I want to go to law school there later on. I'm really sorry. I was going to show you around. But you'll like DU anyway. I can still fix you up with one or two of my fraternity brothers."

"Why would I want second best?" Susan asked, trying to sound lighthearted, although the truth was that she was crushed. She'd had such great plans. The two of them would go to football games and dances together, to fraternity and sorority exchanges. They'd get pinned and then engaged. Maybe they'd marry after Joe graduated. She'd had no business dreaming such dreams, of course, because there'd been nothing more between them than a few kisses. But that hadn't stopped her. And now she was faced with how foolish she'd been in basing her future on Joe. She smiled at him, said she was disappointed but wished him well, all the time digging her nails into the palms of her hands, making little half-moon indentations in her flesh. Then she asked, "Did you just find out?"

Joe hung his head. "I've known since June. I couldn't bring myself to tell you."

Susan looked at him sharply. "You should have. You should have told me." She couldn't say more for fear Joe would know she'd picked a college just because of him.

"You mad?" he asked, and she shook her head, although she was. After he left, she went upstairs to her room in the Bride's House, angry at Joe for going to California, sure that she was only a summer diversion and he didn't care about her, and stared at herself in the mirror, muttering, "Stupid, stupid, stupid."

The next month, back in Chicago, Susan packed her clothes and college gear, and she and Frank drove to Denver in a new cream-colored Mercury convertible that he had purchased for her. She registered for classes, wore the stupid little freshman beanie for a week, and pledged Pi Beta Phi. And to her surprise, she loved the university. Still, she was disappointed and very much annoyed that Joe was not there.

Just a few weeks after school started, Susan met Peter Fanshaw, met him on the Colfax streetcar, of all places, since it had stormed that morning and she wasn't used to driving her car on ice. So she'd taken the streetcar to her friend's house where they were planning to study for an exam.

Susan glanced sideways at Peter, because he was that handsome in his air force blues — honey-colored hair and eyes as velvety brown as a fawn's, tall, well-built, stocky, a little like Joe Bullock. Susan thought later on that it might have been his resemblance to Joe that attracted her. She watched him again out of the corner of her eye as she stood up at her stop, wishing she could ride a little farther. Susan didn't notice that her billfold had slipped out of the pocket of her polo coat onto the seat, and only after she was gone did Peter, who was seated across the aisle, discover it. He called to the driver to stop, then jumped off the trolley, running after her, splashing the slush of the snow-storm onto his uniform, calling, "Miss, wait!" and holding the billfold high in the air.

"Oh my gosh! It's got all my money. I'd have had to walk home," Susan said. She wanted to offer the airman a reward, but she was conscious that she might offend him, might depreciate his act of gallantry, so instead, she said, "The least I can do is give you carfare back to the base, since you're going to have to pay to get back onto the streetcar."

When Peter refused, Susan astonished herself by saying she would buy him a Coke, and they went into a drugstore whose front was a sleek mix of glass and black and green tile. They sat on stools at a soda fountain and looked into the mirror in front of them, looked through the places where the day's special was written in black crayon ("tuna salad sandwich with pickle chips 25 cents,") just below the six flavors of ice cream ("cones 5 cents, double-decker cones 10 cents,") and a list of ice cream concoctions ("try our Black-and-White Sundae 15 cents"). Susan sneaked glances at Peter through the word "sandwich," and he stared frankly at her, grinning every time he caught her eye. She noticed then that his teeth were even and white but that a front tooth was chipped.

It wasn't a date. Girls knew better than to be picked up, especially by military men. Her Pi Phi sisters would have been appalled at Susan's audacity. But he'd returned her billfold with all her money in it, so she could trust him, couldn't she? And they were right there in public where anybody could see them. Besides, she wasn't dating anyone, certainly not Joe Bullock, who'd made it clear that he cared so little about her that he had gone off to California.

So there was nothing wrong with sitting at the fountain with Peter. In fact, it was kind of nice with people nodding at him, one or two saying, "Luck to you," because the war in Korea was serious and folks admired a young fellow who was fighting for his country. Who knew but whether the police action over there would lead to World War III?

They ordered coffee instead of soft drinks, since with the sun setting, it had grown cold outside. A blue glow had settled over the street, and the slush was turning to ice. Susan drank two cups of thick black coffee that had been sitting on the burner so long that it had boiled down and tasted bitter. Although she tried diffusing it with cream, the coffee was still foul. She finished the second cup, and then not wanting to end the conversation, she ordered a dish of

431

chocolate chip ice cream, which came in a paper cone inserted into a nickel holder. She ate slowly, while Peter talked, hoping he didn't realize she was dragging out the conversation, hoping he wasn't bored, because he was older and he'd probably been around.

At first they talked about the storm, whether the snow would melt the next day or there would be another blizzard, then about the trolley, how drafty it was, the wicker seats too hard.

"I wish I had my car. I sold it when I joined the Air Force. If I'd been driving it, though, I wouldn't have met you," Peter said.

Susan cocked her head. "Do you pick up a lot of girls with that line?"

"I don't know. You're the first I've tried it on."

Peter offered Susan a cigarette, but she shook her head. She wished she smoked, because she'd seem more sophisticated, but she was afraid to start just then, afraid she'd appear like the girls in sorority rush who thought the cigarettes would light if they held them out at arm's length over a match flame.

"I really don't approve of women smoking," he said.

"That's a double standard," Susan told him.

"You sound like a suffragette."

"What if I were?"

"I could handle it."

Conscious that they were flirting, Susan switched to a safer subject and asked if Peter had joined the Air Force instead of waiting to be drafted into the Army.

"Sort of. I joined five years ago, at the end of the war," he told her. "I never knew my folks — I grew up in an orphanage — so after high school, I went to Alaska and worked on a road crew. Talk about cold. That's spring outside compared to Alaska." Peter shook his head, then looked about for the waitress. She had gone off, so Peter went around the counter and poured the dregs of the pot into his cup. The coffee didn't seem to bother him. "Things shut down in the winter in Alaska, and there's nothing to do but drink. I did enough of that the first winter, so when fall came around the second time, I signed up for the Air Force. I'd had enough of the cold. Besides, I figured I wouldn't get anywhere working construction six months of the year. I'm stationed at Lowry Air Force Base."

"Do you like it?" Several of Susan's sorority sisters dated military men, but the men

433

were college graduates. Most had been drafted. None were career military.

"The Air Force isn't so bad, but it's not what I want to do the rest of my life. I'm planning to go to college on the GI Bill after I get discharged. Maybe I'll study engineering."

Susan added up the years in her head, figuring out that Peter was twenty-five, maybe older. "There are some boys in college now on the GI Bill, men, I mean."

"You go to school."

She nodded, remembering then that she had been on her way to her friend's house to study for an exam. She didn't care now. "The University of Denver."

"Family? You got family?"

"Just my parents. They live in Chicago."

"How come you came all the way out here for school?"

"My mother was born here. We spend the summers in Colorado, in a house . . ." She glanced at Peter in the mirror. His head was turned toward her. "Well, it's more like a cabin. My grandfather was a prospector."

"One of those guys who struck it rich?"

Susan had dated more than one boy who was interested in her fortune, and she was cautious about others knowing the extent of her wealth, especially somebody she'd just met, so she replied, "Don't I wish."

"I like the mountains. Maybe you'll take me to your place sometime." When Susan didn't reply, he added, "I guess that was out of line. You don't know me. You might think I'm a masher. But I would like to see you again, maybe go to the movies."

"You're right, I don't really know you."

"Well, I tried."

When he didn't pursue the movie idea, Susan added, "Maybe I could meet you sometime, like for a matinee. I think that would be all right."

He grinned at her, as if he'd known all along that she'd go out with him. "By the way, I'm twenty-six."

"Twenty-two," Susan lied.

"Yeah, right," and Susan knew he didn't believe her.

"Almost," she said. In fact, she was eighteen.

They met downtown the next Saturday afternoon and saw *Samson and Delilah* with Hedy Lamarr and Victor Mature, sitting in the balcony of the Denham Theater so that Peter could smoke. Susan had put on a black dress with a full skirt and crinoline petticoat, hose and high heels, instead of the pleated skirt, sweater set, and penny loafers that she usually wore at college. She had on a hat, too, a black one with a tiny veil pulled back, and black leather gloves. The outfit made her look older, more sophisticated, less like a student. That mattered to her because Peter seemed worldly — and certainly sexier than anybody she'd ever gone out with. She didn't feel altogether comfortable around him, she thought as she put on her good coat with the fur collar. And that intrigued her.

As it turned out, Peter didn't notice what she wore. Susan learned later that trappings didn't mean much to him. She could have worn diamonds, and he wouldn't have noticed them. They sat through the movie, the cartoon, the previews, the Movie-tone News, and Peter didn't so much as touch her hand. So it surprised her later when Peter kissed her hard on the mouth.

They were walking down Sixteenth Street, looking into the department store windows, at the back-to-school displays still up in the Denver Dry, the toys in the May Company, the elegant mannequins in formals and furs in Neusteter's. The wind blew newspapers and dead leaves down the street, and it was cold, although it was not yet Halloween. They stopped in front of Neusteter's, Susan studying her reflection in the glass, thinking how unsophisticated she looked compared to Hedy Lamarr, how wrinkled, how un-glamorous, with her hair hanging limply under the stupid little hat.

"That might have been the worst movie I ever saw," Peter said.

Susan agreed, but she was too polite to say so. "It wasn't so bad."

"Oh, come on. Admit it."

"Well."

Peter stared at Susan's reflection, too, then he put his hands on the glass window, one on either side of her, and when she turned around, he kissed her. A woman coming out of the store already wearing a Christmas corsage of tiny ornaments clutched her brown paper shopping bag and gave them a look of disdain.

"Oh." Susan stared at Peter, surprised. She couldn't make up her mind whether she was shocked at his presumption, kissing her like that and in public, or pleased by his boldness. Whatever it was, she liked it. And she didn't think about Joe Bullock when it happened.

Peter smiled and said, "I thought we should get that over with."

Peter was different from the boys Susan had dated both in college and at home. They

437

were polished, tentative when they kissed her, except when they were drunk, and then they were sloppy. Peter had rough edges, and he was self-assured. He scared her a little, too, because he was hard to second-guess. He didn't kiss her again until their third date, and then he did it as if he had the right to, French-kissed her, and no boy had ever done that. She was sure he had been around, and it gave her pause. What did a man like that want from her? And what did she expect? She'd never marry Peter, of course. He was so different from anyone she knew — so different from Joe, was what she really thought. But Joe was a long way away, and by changing schools, he'd made it clear he didn't care about her. There was no reason to feel guilty about Peter Fanshaw, Susan told herself. And there were plenty of reasons to like him.

In early December, Charles Dumas died. He was ninety-seven years old. Bert Joy called Pearl in Chicago and told her gently, "Your father went to sleep last night. It looks like he's not going to wake up."

Susan's grandfather had always been a part of the Bride's House, and Susan couldn't imagine the place without his presence, the smell of his cigars that mixed with the scents of lilacs, cinnamon, and fresh bread, jam boiling on the stove. He doted on her, walking along the streets with her as he pointed out deserted mine workings on the hillsides and told her about the old days. He even took her into Curley's, the coffee shop in Georgetown, to show her off.

Charlie liked to go to the post office at mail time, talking with the other old men who gathered there, discussing politics, speculating on metals prices, recalling old times. Sometimes he sat on a bench in the sun as he read through his letters, warming himself, greeting people as they went inside.

On that particular day, Susan tagged along to mail a postcard to a friend in Chicago. The postcard showed a pumpkin the size of a car, with the caption "Third Place Winner," and Susan thought it was very funny. As they left the post office, Charlie said he wanted to stop for a cup of coffee. "Curley makes coffee as thick as spring runoff, the way it ought to be," he explained. "You coming, or you going back home?"

"I'm coming," Susan said, because the café had doughnuts. They went inside Curley's, where old men sat at the counter with heavy white mugs of coffee held in their rough hands. They dunked glazed and powdered-sugar doughnuts into their coffee, leaving a sugar slick that looked like oil on top of the dark liquid. One man had a white sugar trail running down his beard onto his shirt. Charlie sat down next to him, and Susan climbed onto a stool beside her grandfather, turning around and around on the revolving seat until Charlie put out a hand to stop her. The morning was cold and rainy, and the café was steamy with the smell of wet wool of the men's jackets.

"Aren't you working today?" Charlie asked an old man next to him. The man's long underwear covered his forearms below his rolled-up shirtsleeves.

"I can't work in this rain."

"Any excuse will do. He hates work like God hates sin," a man whose fingers were crippled with arthritis interjected. Susan knew him. He was Joe Bullock's grandfather.

"I disremember you were in any hurry to pick up a shovel yourself."

"Come day, go day. God bring Sunday."

The men laughed, and Susan wrapped her arms around herself. The girl was observant and she liked being in the café with the old men, listening to them tease each other, smelling the burned coffee and the greasy doughnuts. They reminded her a little of the gardeners and caretakers her father employed in Chicago. At noon, those men gathered in the gardening shed in bad weather, or on nice days, they sat outside in the sun, their backs to the stone wall surrounding the property, pouring coffee from thermoses and eating huge sandwiches and meat pies wrapped in waxed paper that they took from their lunch buckets. They laughed with each other and talked in a language that Susan didn't understand. Once, she brought her little sandwich, the crusts neatly cut off, and sat down with them. They wiped crumbs from their huge mustaches and stood up respectfully, embarrassed, shifting from one foot to the other, saying, "Can we help you, missy?" and, "You got something you want doing?" She realized that they thought it wasn't proper for her to sit with them and, more important, that they didn't want her there, and she never again joined them.

Georgetown was different. She wouldn't have gone into Curley's by herself, but the old men there didn't fidget when she sat down, wouldn't treat her as if she didn't belong. They accepted her. Mr. Bullock leaned in front of Charlie and touched his cap in a gesture of politeness. Another gummed his doughnut and lisped, "You got a mighty nice young girl with you, Charlie."

441

Charlie ordered a cup of coffee and two doughnuts, one for each of them, then glanced up at the man behind the counter who hadn't moved. "What, you want your money now? You don't trust me to pay you when I'm done?" Charlie asked and guffawed.

"I'm wondering who this is." He nodded at Susan. "I don't very often see a pretty young lady with an old geezer like you."

"That's my granddaughter. The Bride's House is going to be hers someday."

"Granddaughter? You mean Pearl's girl?"

"Who else would it be?"

"Well, I was just thinking she don't look a bit like you. She looks a little like her mother, but then Pearl don't favor you, either. You sure this one's yours?" He laughed at his joke, but Charlie didn't.

"What's that you say?" Charlie's face grew black, and he pounded his fist on the counter so hard that he rattled the coffee mugs. The others stopped talking to stare at him. Before the man could respond, Charlie told him, "I said she's my granddaughter, and don't you ever question it. You just forget my business."

The man went to the coffeepot, shaking his head. "Forgetting is what I do best, Charlie."

■ ■ ■ ■

"Bert Joy asked me if you were going to sell the house," Susan's father said after Charlie Dumas's funeral was over, and he and her mother were sitting on a love seat in the parlor, Susan across from them.

Pearl, who had been leaning against her husband, his arm around her, sat up. "Sell the Bride's House? I'd as soon sell my childhood."

"You want to keep it, then, even though nobody'll be living here?"

"I can't imagine not having it."

"What will you do with it?"

Pearl shifted, trying to get comfortable in the love seat. "Do you remember when this was covered with horsehair? Those hairs used to come loose and scratch the backs of my legs." Susan's parents smiled fondly at each other, as if enjoying some memory. Then Pearl added, "I'll do what I've always done — live here in the summer. With Susan." She looked at Susan across from her. "Do you want to do that?"

Susan gave a sigh of relief although it had not occurred to her that they would ever let the Bride's House go. "Of course I do. I'd hate it if you sold this place." "This place,"

443

Susan thought, was her connection to Joe. Without it, there was no reason to return to Georgetown, and she might not ever see him again.

"There, you see?" Pearl told Frank.

The three of them sat silently for a time, Susan staring into the fire that was mostly ashes now. Her mother stood and went to the window, pushing aside the lace curtain and looking out at the street, cold in the moonlight. "I never thought he'd die," she said, and she began to cry softly. Susan had never seen her mother cry. "He was a hard old man, but I loved him. I hated him, too, but mostly, I loved him."

When her father didn't reply, Susan studied him, thinking there had been something between the two men. She remembered overhearing her mother tell a friend that she had married against her father's wishes, but Susan couldn't imagine why Charlie would have objected to Frank. Then Frank said, "It's over."

"Yes," Pearl said, dropping the curtain and turning around. "It's over." And then she added, "At last."

Something had gone on between her parents and her grandfather that she didn't understand, Susan realized. The old house had its secrets. And then she had the curious thought that maybe she would add to them one day.

As they were leaving the next morning, Susan suddenly said, "Why don't we come back and spend Christmas in the Bride's House?"

"But we've always spent it in Chicago. We've already ordered the invitations for the New Year's party," her father said.

Pearl thought for a moment. "I suppose we could change our plans. Why couldn't we have a party here instead? Christmas is magical in Georgetown. You've never seen it in winter, Frank."

"I saw it this week. It's cold."

"It's cold in Chicago, too. And damp." Pearl turned to Susan. "That's a wonderful idea."

"Really?" Susan was pleased. After all, Joe Bullock would be home for Christmas, and maybe he'd tell her it was a mistake he'd changed schools.

"Mrs. Warren won't be here," Frank pointed out. The housekeeper had already found another job and Pearl had hired Bert Joy and his wife, Ruth, as caretakers.

"That doesn't matter. Susan and I can do the cooking. You remember how Aunt Lidie and I kept up that house all by ourselves, and we had Papa to contend with."

"If that's what you want, we'll do it," Frank said. "I always did like this old house when your father wasn't here."

Just two weeks later, in the third week of December, after Susan had finished the fall quarter, she met Pearl at the airport, and the two of them drove up to Georgetown. Frank planned to fly out a few days before Christmas and rent a car.

The house was different in the winter — cold, drafty, with the wind blowing through the cracks. But then, the Chicago mansion was drafty in winter, too, so Susan didn't mind. She loved waking up in the morning, warm from the flannel sheets and the three quilts that Pearl had put on the bed, only the tip of her nose icy.

The two decorated a tree that Bert Joy had cut down and hauled inside the Bride's House, put evergreens and red poinsettias in the solarium and around the doors, on the fireplace mantel. They bought evergreen garlands and red bows for the outside of the house and were stringing up white lights when Joe Bullock stopped by. "I'll get up on that ladder, Mrs. Curry," he said. "Hi, Susan." He grinned at her as if they were still the best of friends. "I'm really sorry about your grandfather," he added.

Susan stared at him. She knew she'd see him at Christmas, but she hadn't expected him just then and couldn't think what to say.

"Thank you for your condolence note," Pearl said, and Susan was surprised because she hadn't known he'd written, and she smiled at Joe. The two looked at each other, not talking. Pearl glanced from one to the other and said, "If you two will finish hanging these lights, I'll make cocoa." Neither Joe nor Susan replied, and Pearl went inside, leaving them alone.

"Hey," Joe said quietly, and Susan's heart warmed.

"Hey yourself."

Joe lifted his hand as if to touch her cheek, but then he turned and went to the ladder and picked up a string of lights. He climbed to the eaves of the house and began attaching the lights to hooks. After a bit he called down, "Are you still mad at me?"

Susan wanted to say yes, because she was, but she didn't want Joe to know how much she cared. "For what?" She flushed, but her face was already red from the cold so she hoped he wouldn't notice she had blushed.

"For switching schools and not telling you until the last minute."

"Why would I care?"

Joe didn't answer as he concentrated on securing the lights to the hooks along the eaves. When he was finished he stepped off the ladder. "Because I do."

"Well, you wouldn't know it," Susan said. She wasn't ready to let it go just yet.

"I should have written you, but I'm not very good at that." He went up to her. "Come on, Susan. Give a guy a break. I know I should have told you as soon as I found out." He leaned over and kissed her cheek. "Your nose is red."

"Who couldn't forgive somebody after a compliment like that?" she told him and laughed. She couldn't help herself. She was glad that was behind them. Joe was too precious to let his changing schools spoil the years of friendship.

As they went inside, Joe asked, "Do you want to go sledding Saturday?"

"Down the hill on Taos Street?"

"I almost forgot. You have good memories of that place." He laughed, and Susan was warmed by the sound. "No, up on Loveland Pass. We've got a toboggan, two in fact. It's great up there in those bowls. Besides, we have a lot of catching up to do."

"I'd like that."

She took off her coat and threw it over a

love seat, and Joe saw the tiny arrow pinned to her sweater. "So, you're a Pi Phi?" When Susan nodded, he said, "I guess you didn't need my help, then. You must be having a good time at DU."

"Of course," Susan said, but she knew that now that Joe was back in Georgetown, she was going to have a better time at Christmas.

They drove up Loveland Pass, above timberline, in Joe's truck, Susan sitting next to him in the unheated cab, huddled against him and feeling his warmth. A Georgetown girl whom Susan had known for years sat beside her, and four young men rode in the back of the truck. They got out when Joe stopped at the top of Loveland Pass. "I'll drive down and meet you, then drive you back up. Somebody else can drive the next trip," Joe told them, backing the truck around and starting down the mountain. Susan wanted to say she'd go with him, but that might make her feelings obvious.

The others pulled the sleds to a snowfield, then plotted how they would descend. "That's an avalanche area over there." One of the young men pointed to a cornice of snow. "Stay away from it." He sat down on the sled, two others behind him, and they took off down the open slope to a chute between the trees. Susan and the others followed on the second sled, flying down the snowfield. But their sled hit a mound of snow and rose into the air, flipped over, throwing the sledders into the soft snow. Susan rolled over twice, then landed on her back, staring up at the sun, whose rays almost blinded her. She turned over on her hands and knees and looked around for the other two, who were sitting in the snow, looking sheepish.

"Not our best effort," Susan said. The three waded through the snow after the toboggan, which had lodged in a pine tree, then pulled it to the road, where the others stood, waiting for Joe to drive them back up to the top of the pass.

"Are you hurt?" Joe asked Susan.

"I did better with a tire." Joe laughed, and so did several others, because they had been among the children who had watched Susan roll down Taos Street inside the tire. This time, however, she didn't have to prove herself, and it seemed that she and Joe were on the same side.

They got into the truck and rode up the mountain for a second run, which was more successful. Both sleds made it that time. They finished half a dozen runs, and on the last one, Susan sat behind Joe on the toboggan, while one of the young men drove his truck. There were just the two of them, and they took off, the sled aimed perfectly toward the chute, Susan exhilarated by the speed and the feeling of her arms around Joe's back. She leaned forward, tightening her arms around him, feeling his hard body through his wool jacket. She laid her face against the rough fabric and closed her eyes, and then she heard a crack, and Joe pulled away from her as he shouted, "Avalanche!"

Susan glanced over his shoulder at the cornice that had broken off and fallen into the snow below it, setting off a slide that was rushing toward them. It would reach them in seconds if they continued straight down the slope. "We can't outrun it. We're going to the side," Joe yelled, as he jerked the sled to the right, nearly toppling it, in an attempt to get out of the way of the avalanche. But the motion slowed the sled, and the edge of the slide caught them, throwing the two into the air.

Susan was enveloped in a swirling mist and tumbled into the snow, landing facedown, as the white rushed onward, covering her, not stopping until it reached the trees. She tried to turn over, but she was pinned down in the snow, which held her tight, and she thought she would suffocate. She would lie there until her air was used up, and she would die, and at first, the thought did not scare her, because she was warm and comfortable under the blanket of snow. But then she realized that Joe was buried, and she had to get him out. He would run out of air, or maybe he'd been crushed by a boulder or a tree. He could die, she thought, as she struggled to free her arms and legs. Joe could die! The others might not know they'd been caught in the snowslide. It was up to her to tell them where Joe was buried, although she herself didn't know. She panicked as she shoved at the snow, which held her like wet clay.

At that moment, someone touched her leg. Then hands were on her head and back, scooping up the snow. In a minute, she lifted her head and saw the others around her, pushing the snow off her. "Joe?" She looked around, frantic. They had to find Joe.

"I'm here."

She sighed deeply, coughing as she let out the air. "Are you all right?" She mumbled because her mouth was stiff from the cold.

"I'm fine. I rolled out of the avalanche. You were the one who was buried. How about you?"

She nodded. "I thought maybe you were dead."

The others had gone to dig out the toboggan and the two were by themselves now. "No such luck. It takes more than a dinky avalanche to get me."

"Oh, Joe, I was scared," she blurted out.

He squatted down in the snow next to her.

"Not for me. For *you!*" Susan began to cry, the tears warm on her cold face.

"Hey, kiddo, it's okay." He put his arms around Susan and held her until she got control of herself. Then he helped her stand.

Susan felt foolish for the outburst and said, "First the snake, and now an avalanche. This is the second time you saved my life."

"It's an honor. You're worth saving." Joe put his arms around her and held her upright. "We'll take it slow," he said, but he didn't move. "I'm glad you weren't hurt." He took a deep breath. "I was afraid you were buried. It was like that time when you were in the tire and I thought you were dead. I was never so relieved in my life when I heard you yell." He leaned down and kissed her, and Susan didn't care that the others were watching.

Susan and her parents attended the Christmas Eve candlelight service at the Presbyterian church, and as they tramped through the snow on their way home, Pearl remarked that she'd always planned to be married in that church.

"Your father would have stopped us," Frank said, but Pearl told him fondly that nothing would have prevented her from marrying him. "Maybe you'll be married there," her father told Susan.

"I'm going to be married in the Bride's House," she replied. "I've always wanted to be married in the Bride's House."

"Do you have somebody in mind?" her father teased, and Susan blushed and turned away.

On Christmas Day, the three of them ate dinner in the dining room, watching the snow that fell in big flakes outside, and then they went into the parlor and lit the candles. Pearl sat down at the big pianoforte and began playing "Silent Night," just as the doorbell rasped, and Susan answered it.

Joe Bullock stood on the porch, bundled up against the storm. "Merry Christmas," he said. He stamped his feet and brushed off his coat, then stepped inside, dripping snow onto the worn Persian rug in the foyer. He went into the parlor and greeted Pearl and Frank.

"We haven't had coffee yet. I'll go fix it. Come and help me, Frank." Pearl took her husband's hand and led him into the kitchen, leaving the two young people alone.

"I have a present for you," Susan said, going to the tree and picking up a package. She handed it to Joe, then sat down on the piano stool, while he unwrapped a red wool scarf. "I knitted it. You can probably tell," Susan said. "It's a little crooked."

"It's perfect. I'll take it to school."

"You mean you'll wear it on the beach?"

"It's just the thing for the desert." He reached into his pocket. "I got you something, too. I'm pretty lame at wrapping." He handed her a white box.

Susan turned over the box in her hands, rubbing her finger over the white string that he had tied around it. Joe had never given her a present and she savored the moment.

"Aren't you going to open it?"

"Sure." She slowly untied the string, then took off the lid and removed the white cotton and caught her breath as she lifted out a sterling silver snowflake with a pearl in the center. "It's beautiful," she told him, holding up the brooch so that it glimmered in the candlelight. "Oh, Joe, it's beautiful."

He seemed relieved. "I had Gusterman, the silversmith, make it for you. He had all these Christmas orders to finish, but I told him this was more important. Here, I'll pin it on." Joe unfastened the clasp and pinned the snowflake to Susan's sweater, then stood back to admire it. "I thought you'd like it better than a toboggan. Or a snake."

"Lots better," Susan said. In fact, it was the best present she'd ever received, and she kissed him on the cheek. Before Joe could return the kiss, Susan's parents came into the room with cups and a silver coffeepot.

On New Year's Eve, the house shone in the light of white candles set in the evergreens and red poinsettias. Pearl and Susan had baked a ham and a turkey, prepared side dishes and canapés, and Frank had driven to Denver for champagne and liquor, caviar and petits fours. The invitations suggested formal Victorian dress, and Susan rummaged through trunks in the storeroom until she came across a dove-gray gown that made a perfect background for the silver snowflake Joe had given her. Joe arrived in a black suit of his grandfather's, a beaver top hat on his head. Others came smelling like mothballs, and some who had misunderstood the invitations were clad as prospectors. Peggy was dressed as a dance-hall girl, with fishnet stockings and plunging neck-line. A few of the younger guests drank too much, Peggy among them. Joe had to take her home, and to Susan's disappointment, he missed the stroke of midnight and the toasts to 1951. He came back as the guests were leaving, and offered to help clean up, but Pearl said they'd worry about that in the morning. She and Frank were ex-hausted, and they were going to bed.

Joe and Susan were not tired, however. So because the house was stale from the ciga-rette smoke and the candles that had gut-tered in their holders, they went out. The temperature was near zero, and Susan put on her mother's Persian lamb coat and a wool scarf, while Joe donned the top hat, and the two walked up Sixth Street, past shop windows still decorated for Christmas. They passed the Red Ram, the town bar, where a pair of drunken soldiers came out of the door, glasses in their hands. One of them stumbled and sloshed his drink onto Susan's fur.

"Watch it, fellow," Joe told him. The soldier, offended, put up his fists, but Joe only laughed at him. "Happy New Year to you," he said, and he and Susan went on, leaving the revelers covered with confetti and blowing tin horns. They walked through the dark streets of the old residential district, where the Victorian houses were decorated with evergreen wreaths and garlands, just as they had been the only Christmas that Susan's grandparents had spent together. Susan found the scene enchanting and thought spending Christmas in Georgetown had been a brilliant idea.

The two reached the park and sat on the steps of the bandstand, talking about their studies and the upcoming election, about politics and President Truman and the Korean War. "It's wrong. Our boys are going to die there. Think about it. Guys we know won't come back," Joe said. Susan remembered Peter then and shivered. She hadn't told Joe about Peter; in fact, she hadn't thought much about Peter since she'd left school, hadn't exchanged Christmas presents or even cards with him. But why should she? It wasn't as if there was anything but a good time between them. Peter wasn't Joe Bullock.

She had ruined her satin slippers in the slush, and her feet were cold, so they didn't stay long in the park. Joe put out his hand to help her up, and then he kissed her and said, "Happy New Year." It wasn't much of a kiss, not like last summer. It was the sort of kiss you'd give anybody on New Year's

Eve, and she was disappointed.

Still, Joe held her hand as they hurried back to the Bride's House, and once inside, he agreed to have another glass of champagne. She opened a fresh bottle, and while Joe built up the fire Susan poured the champagne into stemmed glasses, and they toasted the New Year.

They sat across from each other on the love seats, Joe with his tie tossed aside, Susan rubbing her stocking feet because they were red with cold. In a moment, Joe sat beside her, saying, "Let me do that," and he began to warm her feet in his hands. "What changes do you think we'll see a year from now?" he asked after a time.

"A new President for sure."

"Not that. I'm talking about you and me, us."

Susan didn't know what "us" meant, because Joe had never said anything about the two of them, so she replied, "I guess I'll be a sophomore, and you'll be getting ready for law school. Or maybe you'll be drafted." She turned and faced him. "I'd hate that, Joe, if you got drafted and sent to Korea."

He shrugged, and Susan leaned back against the love seat. "I mean us. Do you think we'll be together to celebrate next New Year's?" he asked. Susan had barely

touched her champagne, but Joe had finished his and refilled his glass — twice. He'd
been drinking during the evening, too.

"That would be nice," she replied, hoping
"us" meant the two of them as a couple.
She didn't want Joe to know she assumed
that, however, so she said, "Maybe Mother
and Father will want to spend Christmas
here again next year."

"I'm not talking about that. I'm asking
whether you think we have a future together,
you and me?"

Susan studied his face in the firelight, his
head down a little, his curly hair falling over
his forehead. His brown eyes seemed to
bore into her, seeing all the way to her
heart. She wanted to tell him yes, but she
was too unsure of herself. "You saved my
life," she said instead.

"I guess that means I have a claim on
you."

"I don't understand what you're getting
at."

Joe brought his head close to hers, and
she could feel his breath on her cheek. "I'm
not sure. You're pretty special, you know.
You always have been. I've been thinking . . ." He didn't finish.

"Thinking what?"

"I don't know. It's a long time out. I've

got to finish college and law school before I can even think about getting married." He poured more champagne and drank it down.

"Married?" she said in a tiny voice, not able to look at him for fear she hadn't heard him right. Instead, she stared across the room at the Christmas tree, the branches thin, set far apart. If Bert hadn't cut it down, the tree might have grown as tall as the jackpines in front of the Bride's House. The tinsel glittered in the light from the fire. "What are you saying?" she asked.

Joe didn't answer for a while. "I'm saying I think you're the greatest girl I know, and I think I might be in love with you." He gave a self-conscious laugh. "How's that for a way to start the New Year?"

The firelight seemed to glow inside Susan now, as she heard the words she had longed for, heard Joe say he loved her . . . well, maybe he loved her, but that was good enough. "You're what?" she asked when Joe was silent.

"You heard me. I never said that to any-body before." He took Susan's champagne glass out of her hand and set it on the table beside the love seat, but it rolled off and fell onto the floor. Joe ignored it as he pushed Susan down on the sofa and began kissing her — her face, her neck, her shoulders. He stopped and put his mouth against hers, and she kissed him back, kissed him long and hard and pushed her tongue into his mouth the way Peter kissed her.

Joe sat up and held her tight, and she could feel him grope at the stays and lacings and bands of her Victorian dress. "Who designed this, your mother?" he asked, his voice low.

"I think it was my grandmother. It has hooks and eyes." She sat up so that Joe could unfasten the dress, and then his hands were all over her, warm against her skin, touching her, making her radiate happiness. Peter had tried that with her, but she hadn't let him. But Joe was different. She loved him.

Then suddenly, Joe pulled away. "This isn't right."

"Why?" Susan asked with a little cry. Her heart dropped. Had she done something wrong? She wanted to tell him, "Don't stop."

"I'm sorry. I never should have started this. It's the champagne. I'm not used to it." He stood up and picked up his tie. "I've been a real jerk. I'm sorry."

"You're not a jerk," she cried.

He stared at Susan, her crushed dress shining like wrinkled silver paper in the

462

candlelight. "I should have kept my mouth shut. I didn't mean to say . . . you know," he finished lamely. Then suddenly, he grabbed his coat and the hat, and without another word, he opened the front door and left.

"Joe," Susan called. But he had shut the door, and she was alone.

She stayed there a long time, gray dawn seeping through the windows, the fire dying, the candles burning down and then going out. Just a few minutes before, she had been glowing with happiness, knowing that Joe loved her and was thinking of their future together. But then he left — walked out on her — leaving her miserable, thinking that she had experienced both the beginning and the end of a love affair in one night.

CHAPTER 16

Joe didn't write to Susan after she returned to school. Nor did he phone. She thought how great it would have been if he really had proposed and she'd returned to school with an engagement ring, had announced it by blowing out the candle at dinner in the sorority house. But he hadn't, and Susan was bewildered, at times angry and at others sad. She didn't understand what had happened between them, but she knew that Joe's silence meant he didn't care. She picked up her life as it had been before the Christmas vacation, dating boys she met in classes or at fraternity exchanges, attending parties and basketball and hockey games with them.

And she continued to go out with Peter Fanshaw when he could get away from the base, because he was the most interesting man she'd met in Denver. She took him to sorority dances, but Peter was a poor dancer and had little in common with the girls in the sorority house. Once or twice, they went bowling with Peter's friends, fellows with their hair in ducktails, packs of cigarettes in the rolled-up sleeves of their T-shirts, girls with poodle cuts and pierced ears. Susan was no more at ease with them than Peter was with her college friends, however, so usually the two of them spent their time alone.

Peter took her to the Crimson and Gold or the Stadium Inn, two bars near DU where they drank beer, Susan using a fake ID borrowed from a sorority sister. On occasion, they went to jazz clubs in Five Points, the Negro section of Denver, or on Colfax, where Peter sat in with the musicians, playing drums. Sometimes they just met in City Park and walked around the big lake, finding an isolated bench where they could neck. Peter was nice and funny and incredibly good-looking, and he liked to kiss her, to run his hands over her. He was more experienced than Joe, Susan thought, feeling a twinge of regret that Joe wasn't the one kissing her. She felt a little guilty, too, because it was Joe she loved. But he had treated her shabbily. He'd said he loved her, and then he'd run off and never even written. Maybe he'd lied and didn't care about her at all. He wasn't part of her life now, so why shouldn't she enjoy herself with Peter Fanshaw?

In February, Peter invited her to go skiing. He'd learned to ski with his Air Force buddies and promised Susan that she would love it. They drove up into the mountains with another couple, Alan and Cynthia, an Air Force man and his wife, went to Berthoud Pass, which wasn't far from Georgetown. Alan strapped on skis and took off, while Cynthia stayed at the bottom of the hill, watching. "You couldn't pay me to do that. They're crazy," she told Susan.

Peter rented skis for both of them and put on his own while Susan stared at the steep runs, thinking she could never maneuver them in the long skis, shivering when she remembered the avalanche at Christmas. She saw a woman fall on the slope, sliding into a tree. "I don't know. Maybe I should just watch this time. That way, I can get the hang of it without breaking my leg," she told Peter.

"Oh, come on. It's not hard."

Susan made a face. "I'm not very athletic."

Peter stood and stabbed his pole into the snow. "I didn't think you'd be afraid."

Susan stared at him for a moment, thinking she would not have said no if Joe had

466

asked her. She liked Peter and was unnerved by the disappointment in his eyes. He'd told her she was different from other college girls, more serious, less frivolous. "Oh, it's not that," Susan replied. She wanted to tell him about the avalanche, but then she'd have to mention Joe, and she didn't want to do that. So she took a deep breath and said, "I guess I'll try it since you paid for the ski rental."

"Good girl," Peter said, and helped her with her skis.

They grabbed onto the rope tow that pulled them up the mountain, then Peter showed Susan how to maneuver her skis, how to turn, and more important, how to stop. They started down slowly, Peter coaching Susan, and when after a long time, they reached the bottom, Susan hadn't fallen once. She was not so lucky the second time. One ski crossed over the other, and she tumbled, then slid to the edge of the run. As Peter helped her up, he asked, "Are you hurt?"

"Only my pride," Susan said, although for a moment, she had panicked, feeling that she was being carried along in a snowslide.

"You can spare a little of that."

Susan made a snowball and threw it at Peter, hitting him in the chest. Peter grabbed a handful of snow and put it down Susan's neck. "Don't mess with me," he said, and she knew he wasn't joking.

They skied for nearly three hours, until Cynthia said she was bored and wanted to go home. So Alan and Peter and Susan returned their skis, and the three of them headed for a warming hut that sold hot dogs and candy bars. Susan lagged behind the others as she zipped her jacket, and at that moment an out-of-control skier careened down the slope, people jumping out of his way. But Susan didn't see him, and he knocked her down.

Peter lifted her to her feet, and when she said she was only a little bruised, he turned to the man who had run into her. "You hurt the lady."

The man ignored Peter as he looked around for a ski that had come off.

"Hey, I'm talking to you." Peter grabbed the skier's arm.

The man tried to shake it off. "Watch it. Who do you think you're talking to?"

"I'm talking to you. You apologize to the lady."

"It's okay," Susan told Peter.

"It's not my fault if she's too dumb to get out of the way." The skier looked down at the hand on his arm.

Susan recognized the man then, a student at DU. She'd sat next to him once at a fraternity exchange. "I'm all right, Peter." People had turned to stare, and she was embarrassed. She wished he'd brushed it off the way Joe had at New Year's when the drunk had spilled his drink on her.

"It's not okay. This punk owes you an apology, and I'm going to make sure you get it."

"Easy now," someone said, while Susan whispered that she wanted to leave.

"Who are you calling a punk?" the man asked. Suddenly he pulled away from Peter and swung at him, connecting with the side of Peter's head. Peter was stunned for a moment. Then he made a fist and smashed it into the skier's nose. The man dropped to his knees, both hands over his face. Susan wanted to tell Peter to stop, because he had scared her by the way he'd exploded.

"Get up," Peter said. "Apologize to the lady."

"You broke my damn nose, you son of a bitch. You'll be sorry."

"No he won't. That's the end of the fighting." A man in a jacket with a ski-patrol badge yanked the skier to his feet.

"I'll sue him. He broke my nose."

"Forget it. You swung first. I saw it." He

turned to Peter. "You! Back off."

"I will after he apologizes. Not to me, to the lady."

People were staring, and Susan's face was crimson. She touched Peter's arm.

The ski patroller looked at Peter, then back at the man, who was standing up now. "Well?"

"It's all right," Susan interjected, but Peter held up his hand to stop her.

"Sorry," the man said at last. He glared at Susan, and she hoped he didn't recognize her.

"That's not much of an apology," Peter said, but Susan took his hand and said she was satisfied.

Later, as they walked to the car, Cynthia whispered, "That was so romantic. I've never had anybody fight over me."

Susan reddened, thinking that maybe it *was* a little thrilling that Peter had defended her honor. Still, it had been embarrassing, and she told Peter, "Please don't ever do that again."

Peter looked at her, surprised. "Why not? I wouldn't let anybody insult you. I wouldn't think much of myself if I didn't look after my girl."

Susan smiled wanly, thinking she didn't like him calling her "my girl."

■ ■ ■ ■

In the spring, Peter borrowed Alan's car and drove Susan to Central City. Except for the time when Susan was in Georgetown during Christmas break, she and Peter had gone out once or twice a week for five months. Susan liked him more than the college boys she dated, although he frightened her a little. He was too serious, and sometimes when he kissed her, she had to push him away, especially when he'd been drinking. There were times she thought he went too far, and she had to be on her guard.

The tulips and flowering crabapple trees were blooming in the parks in Denver, but the mountains were still cold and wet, still gray with winter. They motored up along the Clear Creek, whose banks were brown with the detritus of long-ago mining operations, the creek itself polluted from mine tailings. Peter said he was disappointed. He'd thought that when the snow melted, the mountains would be pretty, like pictures he'd seen of the Alps, all green with snow-capped peaks beyond and wildflowers — not brown with patches of dirty snow, the hillsides covered with scraggly jackpines. "There is no springtime in the Rockies,"

Susan told him, snuggling up against him, because the car's heater didn't work. Peter put his arm around her.

Alan's car was a prewar Chevrolet, and just as they reached Central, its radiator began to boil over. So they parked the car and wandered around town, looking at the buildings, peering into shop windows. They prowled through a junk shop that was filled with ore specimens and carbide lamps, lampshades and broken figurines and books misshapen from being soaked by water. Susan picked up a leather-bound *A History of Colorado* and flipped through the biographical section until she came across a biography of Charles Dumas. "My grandfather," she said, pointing to the steel engraving of Charlie.

Peter took the book from her and read the text. "My God, you're an heiress."

He had already figured out that Susan's family had money, enough to send her away to college anyway, but he had no idea of the extent of the wealth, and she hadn't cared to tell him. "Oh, my grandfather lost it all. My father had to support him."

Peter smiled, as if he was relieved. "You want me to buy you that book?"

"Mother has three of them already."

"Then I'll buy you a cup of coffee." They

left the store and found a restaurant, sat down at a table by the window where they could look out at the crooked street, ordered cocoa instead of coffee because the coffee looked thick, black as ink. "That your blue star in the window?" Peter asked the waitress, a portly woman in a white uniform with a flowered handkerchief spilling out of the pocket and splayed across her chest.

"My youngest boy, Art. He's over there in Korea."

"Well, I hope he makes it back okay."

"You, too, son."

"He's lucky to have somebody at home who cares about him."

The remark saddened Susan, who said, "You'll have someone, too."

"You a flyboy, are you?" A man at the next table leaned over and looked at Peter.

"You're a smart one. What do you think he's doing in that uniform?" his companion asked him. Both were old men with a one or two days' growth of beard, and between them, they had a mouthful of teeth.

"Yes, sir. I'm at Lowry Field," Peter said.

"Well, good luck to you then, you and your missus." He nodded at Susan who dipped her head at him.

When the two men went back to their conversation, Susan, embarrassed, whispered to Peter, "Some assumption."

"I don't mind." Peter grinned at her.

The waitress brought their cocoa, two green glass cups in one hand and the coffeepot in the other. She turned to the men to warm their coffee, but at that moment, the door was flung open and a man as ancient as the two seated in the restaurant rushed in, a wild look on his face.

"Well, Billy . . ." the waitress said and stopped. "What is it?"

"It's Luke Bascomb's boy, he's went and got hisself killed in Korea."

"No!" the three said together.

Susan and Peter looked at each other, and she said softly, "I'm glad that's not you."

"He hasn't been over there a month," the waitress said, sitting down, the pot of coffee in her hand.

"He get shot?" Peter asked, putting his hand over Susan's.

"I don't know. I just heard the news. All's I know is the boy's dead."

"You want coffee?" The waitress wiped her eyes on her sleeve as she lifted the coffeepot.

The man shook his head. "I got to go call on Luke and them."

"Okay, then. We'll go with you." The two men stood, and one reached into his pocket for change, but the waitress waved them away. "You tell them I'm real sorry. I'll be over later with a pie. I got a lemon meringue that hasn't got but one piece cut out of it."

She returned to the kitchen, while the men went out the door, one of them touching his cap to Susan and telling Peter, "You be careful if you get sent over, you hear, son? You come back to that pretty wife of yours." Peter nodded and touched his forehead in a sort of salute, and the man closed the door. The restaurant was quiet, except for a radio in the kitchen that was playing "Shrimp Boats."

Susan squeezed Peter's hand. "You better keep safe," she whispered.

Peter smiled, then fiddled with the air force cap that he'd set on the table, straightening it, brushing off a piece of lint.

"Are you afraid?" Susan asked, her eyes searching his.

"Sure I am. You hear something like that, and you know it could be you. Guys don't get killed because somebody decided there's a bullet with their name on it. They die because they're in the wrong place, a foot to the left or an inch to the right of where they ought to be. It just happens."

Susan shivered when she thought of Peter being hurt, maybe lying dead on some battlefield as barren as the banks of the Clear Creek they had just driven along. She liked him — liked him a lot — and wanted him safe.

"That boy getting killed kind of spoils things."

It was an odd remark, and Susan didn't understand it. "He's dead," she said a little indignantly. "That does more than spoil things for him."

"I mean for us. I brought you up here to ask you to marry me. Now it doesn't exactly seem like the right thing to do." He let go of the cap and looked at Susan. "But maybe it is. Life's uncertain, and I guess that means we ought to take what we can get of it before it's too late." He added, "That wasn't what I was going to say. I had this nice little speech thought up, but it seems lame now. So I'll just ask you. Will you marry me, Susan, now, before I go to Korea?"

Susan felt the blood drain from her face as she looked at Peter, dumbfounded. She hadn't expected this. She cared about him, of course, cared more than she'd thought she would, but she'd never considered him for a husband. They were just having a good time. Susan couldn't believe he was serious about her. Maybe she should have seen the signs, but what signs? She tried to think of something Peter had said that she'd ignored, but there wasn't anything.

She looked into her cup, at the bits of chocolate that clung to the sides, rubbing her fingers across the glass. Of course, he excited her. Peter was so handsome, and when they sat in the car and he kissed her and touched her, she felt a longing so great that she wanted to lose herself. She liked the way his eyes searched for her in a crowd and crinkled with pleasure when he saw her. He was different from Joe — demanding, sexual, and he certainly wouldn't say no to her the way Joe had.

It would be exciting to be engaged. Sometimes, she thought that half the Pi Phis had engagement rings, some from men who expected to be drafted and sent to Korea. She and Peter could be married in the Bride's House. Susan stopped. He'd never even seen the Bride's House, and it wasn't Peter Fanshaw she'd dreamed of marrying there. It was Joe. And that was the crux of it. She cared for Peter Fanshaw, but she loved Joe Bullock.

Susan realized Peter was watching her, waiting, but she didn't know how to answer. She stirred the dregs of her cocoa with one of the mismatched spoons, the silver plate worn off at the edges, that the waitress had set down. "I don't know what to say," she told him at last, looking up.

"You could say yes."

"I can't Peter. I don't even know you."

"How long do you have to know somebody before you know she's the right one?" He said softly, "I know you're the right one for me."

"But I'm not even nineteen."

"You told me your grandmother died when she was seventeen." He reached across the table and touched the silver snowflake pinned to her sweater.

Susan took in a deep breath, as she thought, Marriage, childbirth, and death, all in a year. That was hardly what she wanted. "I've got three more years of college."

"You don't have to drop out of school. I'd want you to keep on. I'll pay your tuition, and when I get back and you graduate, you can work while I go to school. I've got it all figured out." He grinned as he added, "Children can wait."

Children! Susan's eyes widened. They'd never talked about children. For all she knew, he wanted a dozen.

"We can elope and keep everything secret until you're ready to tell."

She shook her head. "It's too sudden. We

shouldn't think about getting married until you're back. You might change your mind or meet somebody else. What's the hurry?" She thought she should just tell him no. But what if he did find someone else? What if, later on, Joe found somebody else, too, and she really did fall in love with Peter?

He reached across the table and took away Susan's spoon so that he could hold her hands. "If I get killed, I want something of me to live on, a wife, maybe a kid. All my life, there's been just me, no family, nothing. I want more than that, even if I don't come back."

They sat at the table for a long time, looking at each other. The waitress came over and asked if they wanted something to eat — chili, hamburg steak, ham and eggs, pie. She had apple and cherry. And there were cinnamon rolls, baked that morning. But they said no. Susan was glad for the interruption, because she'd grown uncomfortable. It was as if they'd used up the air in the café. So she put her arms into the sleeves of her coat, which had been resting on her shoulders, and the two of them stood up. As they reached the door, Peter stopped and pulled Susan to him, holding her tight. "You'll think about it anyway?"

Susan nodded, and she would.

"There's not anybody else, is there?" Peter knew she dated others. He'd said he was too old to go steady, so he'd never asked her to date him exclusively.

"No. There's nobody," she told him. But there was, of course. And that was the reason she wouldn't marry Peter Fanshaw.

Susan didn't go home to Chicago that summer of 1951. Instead, at the end of the school year, she met her mother at the airport, and the two drove to Georgetown earlier than usual. Ruth Joy had opened the house and put a vase of daffodils on the parlor table, since it was too soon for the lilacs to bloom. The women were still unloading the car when Joe stopped by. Susan hadn't seen him coming, and she caught her breath when he was suddenly beside her. She clasped and unclasped her hands, then wiped them on her skirt because they felt wet. They hadn't been together since he'd rushed out of the house at New Year's, and she couldn't think what to say, so she stood there awkwardly, her hands wrapped in her skirt, wishing that first moment was past them. She'd thought about their meeting that summer, of course. She'd say something sophisticated, maybe condescending, so Joe would know that what had happened on New Year's was of no importance to her. But she hadn't come up with the words yet, and all she could mumble was, "Hi." She sounded tentative.

Joe was at ease, as if he'd forgotten all about New Year's. His smile was warm when he looked at her, leaned toward her and said he was glad to see her, that it would be a good summer now that she was there. "You want to hike up Guanella Pass in the morning?" he asked.

Just like that, Susan thought. New Year's had meant nothing to him. He wasn't even embarrassed. And then she thought, Of course, he would say something the next day when he wasn't standing in front of the Bride's House where her mother could hear. He would wait until they were alone, explain himself, maybe apologize, ask her to forgive him. Or maybe tell her he'd found someone else. The thoughts collided in her head.

"I'll get that luggage, Mrs. Curry," Joe said, although he was looking at Susan, waiting for her to answer.

The girl still didn't speak, but Pearl thanked him and said she and Susan appreciated it. He reached for the suitcase that Susan had taken out of the trunk of the car, and their hands touched, but Joe didn't seem to notice it. She had hoped this might be the best summer ever, but maybe it would be the worst.

"What about Guanella?" he asked, as he picked up the last suitcase.

"Sure."

Joe and Susan walked quietly up Guanella Pass the next day. The first of the wildflowers lined the road, and the sun was in her face, and Susan felt content. Joe helped her climb over a rock embankment, his hand warm against her back, and when she slipped on damp leaf mold, he caught her, steadying her with his arms, which were tan and a little freckled. They came to a grove of aspen trees, their leaves a pale green, and sat down on a granite outcrop.

"I've got something to tell you," he said.

Susan pushed her elbows into her sides and closed her eyes, thinking, At last. He was going to explain himself. Maybe more.

"I've been waiting for you to get here."

She searched his eyes, her anger gone now.

"I've decided I'm going into politics," Joe said.

Susan stiffened. Politics! He'd brought her up there to talk about politics! Peter proposed when she didn't want him to, while Joe talked politics instead of asking her to marry him. The irony of it actually made her laugh.

Joe thought she was laughing at him. "I know. I know. You think I'm crazy."

"No I don't," Susan said, thrusting aside her disappointment. "You'd be terrific at it."

"Really? Do you think so?"

"Of course. You care about people. And the mountains." Susan's voice was a little high, and she tried to control it so that Joe wouldn't get the idea that she had expected a different conversation. "You'd be very effective. My father thinks so, too."

"He does?" Susan had her back to the sun, and Joe shaded his eyes so that he could see her face.

"He'd rather you'd go to work for the molybdenum company, of course, but he did say once that there was something about you that reminded him of Governor Stevenson when he was younger."

"Adlai Stevenson?"

Susan nodded.

"You know Adlai Stevenson?"

"Sure, we live in Chicago."

"He's going to be the next President."

Susan picked up a rock and examined it, then threw it into the trees. She shook her head to think how far this conversation was from what she'd wanted. "You believe he can beat Ike?"

"I hope so. I want to be just like him." Joe grinned and added, "But with hair." He selected his own rock and sent it skimming down the mountainside.

"Would you stay here?"

Joe leaned back, his hands behind his head, his T-shirt tight over his chest. "Yeah. That's the real reason I went to school in California. I think it's important to have experience outside Colorado. I'm too narrow. I ought to learn somebody else's point of view. But I'm coming back here."

"It sounds like you've got it all figured out." Susan smashed a mosquito that had bitten her arm, then wet the tip of her finger and placed it on the bite.

Joe nodded. He picked a blue columbine and threaded the stem through the top buttonhole of Susan's shirt.

"How does Peggy feel about it?" Susan looked off across the mountain range, at once sorry she had asked that. She really didn't want to know how Peggy felt.

"Peggy?" Joe frowned. "We don't talk much about politics."

"Oh," was all Susan could say, although she wanted to ask if he was dating Peggy. She'd worried all spring that Peggy was the reason Joe had left her so abruptly at New Year's.

They were quiet as they descended the mountain, and when they reached the Bride's House, Joe said, "I promised I'd take a basket of stuff to a family down by where Red Elephant used to be. The man was hurt in a logging accident, and of course, he doesn't have any insurance. They've got kids. Do you have any old clothes you could donate?"

"Sure." Susan led him inside the house, where she explained to her mother that Joe was collecting things for a needy family. Pearl offered canned goods, some jars of rhubarb jam she'd made the summer before, while Susan went upstairs to sort through her clothes. She returned with half a dozen garments that she hadn't worn since the previous year, and handed them to Joe.

"Do you want to go along?" he asked.

Susan didn't want to play Lady Bountiful, but she wouldn't turn down a chance to be with Joe. "I can drive," she said, but Joe shook his head, telling her they'd take the old pickup that he'd bought the summer before from Bert Joy. "I've named her Asthma," he said.

The two of them turned off the highway onto a dirt road that led up the mountain to a log cabin. The roof was covered with tarpaper, held in place by battens, but the roofing had come loose in places and was flapping in the wind. An outhouse stood in back of the cabin. Joe knocked at the door and told the woman who opened it, "We've brought a few things from the church. We hope you can make room for them."

The woman invited them inside. Susan did not want to go, but she followed Joe into a room that smelled stale, although it was neat, the linoleum floor mopped. Two children sat on a daybed, and Susan spotted a girl she knew from town half hidden in a doorway to the second of the cabin's two rooms. Susan thought she must be mortified at being given a charity basket by someone she knew.

The two stayed for only a few moments, Joe talking easily, inquiring about the man's health, when he'd return to the job, asking if there was work around the place that needed doing. Susan was silent, admiring Joe's easy way with the woman. He fit into that ugly shack as effortlessly as if it had been the Bride's House. But Susan was awkward. She didn't know whether to say hello to the girl or pretend she didn't recognize her. She couldn't help frowning at the mean cabin, at the sagging shelf over the cookstove that held only half a dozen cans of food, at the water bucket perched on the sink, the slop jar just visible in the next room. She shivered at the idea of living in such a foul place, without running water.

Back in the truck, Susan said, "That was awful. I've seen that girl in Georgetown. She must be humiliated, accepting charity from someone she knows. Why doesn't she get a job?"

"She has one. She tends kids for twenty-five cents an hour."

"If that's all she makes, couldn't she take care of the kids at home and let her mother work?"

"Doing what?"

Susan shrugged with embarrassment. She had no idea.

"The mines and the construction companies don't hire women. The kind of work she could do, I doubt she could make any more than her daughter."

"There has to be a better way."

They had reached the highway, and Joe stopped the truck and turned to Susan. "There is. The government has to take care of people like that. It's why I want to run for office. You understand, don't you?"

Susan nodded. She thought of the poor family she had just left and did understand.

"I do," she told him.

"I know," he said. "Peggy wouldn't."

Susan spent time alone with Peggy, too, that summer. They hiked in the mountains, exploring the deserted mine shacks, looking for miners' candlesticks, but most of the structures had been picked over by generations of children before them or by tourists, who were exploring the ghost towns in their army-surplus Jeeps. They played badminton and croquet in the side yard of the Bride's House, shielded by the lilac hedge. Or the girls sunbathed, drinking Coca-Cola from the small green bottles that Pearl ordered by the case from the grocery.

"How long are you staying this time?" Peggy asked, as the two lay on beach towels on the lawn of the Bride's House. Peggy raised herself up on one elbow to look at Susan, who was stretched out on her stomach.

"Probably till sometime in September, since Father has to go to Europe to look at some mines. Then he'll drive out. He just bought a Chrysler Town and Country." Susan was sorry she'd let that slip out, because Peggy's father didn't even own a car. Joe wouldn't have made such a gaffe, she thought.

"Can you drive it?"

"I guess."

"Will you let me drive it?"

"You'll have to ask my father."

"Yeah, right." Miffed, Peggy reached for Susan's suntan oil and knocked it over, letting some of the liquid run into the grass before she righted the bottle. "Joe's still got Bert Joy's old truck. He calls it Asthma. Did you know that?"

"That's what he told me."

"Well, aren't you Miss Know-it-all?" Peggy smiled to take the sting out of her words. "I bet you haven't ridden in it."

Susan knew better than to answer.

"He took me down to Idaho Springs in it right after he got back from California. We got swacked. He couldn't even . . . well, you know."

"He couldn't what?"

"Don't be naïve."

"What?"

Peggy studied Susan a moment. "You really don't know, do you?" She laughed. "You've probably never even done it."

Susan stared at her friend as she realized exactly what Peggy meant. Joe and Peggy, she thought. That was why Joe had left her that night. He could go all the way with Peggy but not with her. He'd softened her up with talk of marriage, but then he'd decided she wasn't worth it. Peggy was, however. Devastated, Susan put her head on her arms.

"Am I right?" Peggy asked. "Oh, come on. You can tell me."

But Susan didn't want to talk about it, and she wouldn't answer.

The week after Pearl and Susan returned to Georgetown, they invited Joe to dinner at the Bride's House. Susan hadn't seen him since Peggy's confession, and she was uneasy. But he was the same as always, friendly, good-natured. Of course, he wasn't aware that Susan knew what had gone on between the two of them.

"Susan says you know Governor Stevenson," Joe told Pearl, who nodded. "I know he'll be elected."

Pearl wasn't so sure. "Don't get your hopes up. You're too young to remember how people looked up to General Eisenhower during the war. Now, they're hoping he'll fight the communists the way he did the Nazis."

"Your mom's really up on things," Joe told Susan later. "You wouldn't know it from what she writes, but she's shrewd about politics."

"You read my mother?"

"Sure, don't you?"

"Of course," she replied, although she didn't know anyone else her age who did.

Pearl had gone into the study and turned on the radio, and Joe and Susan went outside to sit on the porch in the dark. Suddenly, he took her hand and said, "That's what I really want to do."

Susan rubbed her thumb over the back of Joe's hand, feeling its warmth. "Write inspirational columns for a newspaper?"

"No, be the President of the United States. I don't just want to be in politics. I want to go all the way to the top."

Susan was quiet, looking at the lilac bushes because she knew Joe was staring at her, waiting for her to respond. It had been an odd thing for him to admit, for heaven's sake. Of course, most boys wanted to be President at some time in their lives, but they outgrew it. Joe was serious. He could be President, she thought. He was smart and compassionate and good to people. She tried to think of something meaningful to reply, something that would show she believed in him.

"What are you thinking?" Joe asked after a time.

Susan shook her head in the darkness.

Then because Joe couldn't see her, she said, "I think you could do it, Joe. I think you can do anything."

"Do you mean it?"

"Of course I mean it," she replied, and she caught a glimmer of light in his eyes when he looked up at her.

"Thank you." Joe let go of her hand and stood up, leaning against the porch pillar and looking out at Sunrise Peak in the moonlight. "I told Peggy once that I wanted to run for the U.S. Senate — I couldn't bring myself to admit that I actually wanted to go higher than that — and she said it would be great to be rich and famous. But that's not it. I want to do things, like, you know, help those people down by Red Elephant. There's such a gulf between rich and poor. Around here, there were always the wealthy mine owners and the poor miners."

"You mean mine owners like my father and grandfather?"

He thought a moment. "Yeah, I guess so." Then Joe asked, a little defensively, "Do *you* think it's fair that they had so much money when their workers made so little?"

She'd never thought about it, but because Joe asked, she pondered the question. "If you talk like that, people will call you a communist."

"People like Joe McCarthy, I suppose. You know, there are some good things about communism." Susan didn't reply, and Joe said, "I've offended you."

"No, I'm still thinking about what you said."

"That's the nicest compliment I've ever had." Joe sat down again and took Susan's hand, interlacing his fingers through hers. Then he leaned over and kissed her. It was a light kiss, more a kiss of friendship than of passion, not like the kisses at New Year's, and she longed for more.

He started to kiss her again, but they heard Pearl switch off the radio in the middle of the *Dragnet* theme, and they pulled apart, Joe whispering, "Damn!"

In a moment Pearl joined them on the porch. Joe stood so that she could take his place, but Pearl seated herself on the porch steps, and Joe leaned on the post beside her. Pearl didn't seem to feel the awkward silence caused by her interruption, because she looked up at the stars and said, "You ought to go into politics yourself, Joe. The country could use smart boys like you."

"Gee, that's nice of you, Mrs. Curry."

"Joe and I were talking about his doing just that," Susan said. "I think he'd be

493

wonderful, don't you, Mother?"

"It's only a thought." Joe sounded embarrassed. So Susan said no more, and in a
minute, Joe took his leave, and Susan
watched him walk down Taos Street,
watched the way he held his head up and
his shoulders moved under the tight shirt.

"That young man will make his mark one
day," Pearl said in the darkness. Then she
added as an afterthought, "You could do
worse than Joe Bullock."

Susan hugged herself and thought that she
could do no better. But fat chance.

CHAPTER 17

If Joe didn't seem to pursue Susan that June, Peter Fanshaw did. Before the lilacs bloomed, he wrote, asking if he could spend the weekend in Georgetown. He'd take the bus and get a motel room, since he didn't want to impose.

"You remember I told you about Peter Fanshaw? He's stationed at Lowry," Susan said to Pearl the afternoon she received the letter. Susan rarely interrupted her mother when Pearl was writing, but she would have to answer Peter's letter right away.

"Um, what?" Pearl asked, distracted. "By the way, what was that superstition Bert Joy told us, the one about a dog lying in a doorway?"

"If a dog lies outside the door with his head inside, you'll get a new family member before the year ends. If the dog lies inside the door with his head out, someone will die. That one?"

"Is that it, or is it the other way around?"
Pearl thought a moment. "I'll have to ask
Bert."

"We don't have a dog."

"I saw one down the street. I'm writing
about superstitions. I was told my mother
believed in them." She turned back to her
typewriter, then looked up at Susan. "That's
not why you came in here, is it, to talk about
superstitions?"

Susan shook her head.

Pearl smiled. "You were talking about a
young man, I believe, the enlisted man."

"His name is Peter. I told you. I just got a
letter from him." She held it out. "He has
the weekend off, and he wants to come to
Georgetown."

"Do you want him to?" Pearl's hands had
been poised over the typewriter, but now
she put them into her lap.

"I guess so." Peter didn't know anything
about her family, and she wasn't sure she
wanted him to.

"Is this serious?"

"Not for me."

"But for him it is." That was a statement,
not a question.

Susan shrugged.

"I see. He's probably bound for Korea,
isn't he? I should think any young man in

that situation would be serious. Should I write and invite him to stay in the Bride's House?"

"Would you?" Suddenly, Susan liked the idea of Peter visiting in Georgetown, Joe knowing that he was staying with her and her mother.

Pearl nodded.

So the following Friday afternoon, Susan met Peter as he got off the Greyhound. He looked handsome in his uniform, and she couldn't help speculating what Joe would think when he saw him, whether Joe would be jealous. She hoped so. Peter put his arms around her and tried to kiss her, but Susan broke away, embarrassed, saying, "There are too many gossips in Georgetown."

"Later then," he told her, swinging his flight bag into the back seat of the Mercury, then getting in beside Susan. "Nice town," he said, as she drove down Rose Street, then over to Taos. When she stopped the car in front of the Bride's House, Peter looked up at it, a little intimidated, and said, "You told me you had a cabin."

"Did I?" Susan remembered then that when she'd met him, she had not wanted Peter to know she had money. "The Bride's House is a little better than a cabin, but it's not any big deal. Nobody wants these old houses. You can't give them away."

"It's huge. It's bigger than the orphanage I grew up in."

Susan found the remark unsettling. She loved the Bride's House with its history and its sense of family. How awful to have none of that, to have your childhood memories centered on an institution. Without realizing it, she took Peter's hand and led him up the front walk, telling him that her grandfather had built the house for his wife, repeating the story about Nealie dying after giving birth to Susan's mother. "She's inside, Mother, that is. She's anxious to meet you." In fact, Pearl hadn't appeared anxious at all. She'd said little about Peter.

They went into the foyer, Peter whistling when he saw the polished walnut staircase that clung to the wall, circling as it reached the second floor. He dropped his bag onto the floor and stepped into the parlor, where Pearl came to meet him, her hand extended. "We're delighted to have you here, Peter," she said.

"Thanks, Pearl." Pearl's face tightened a little at the familiarity. She was nearly seventy. None of Susan's friends had ever called her by her first name. "This is nice for such an old place," he said, and Pearl replied somewhat stiffly that she hoped he would find it comfortable.

"Would you like something to drink? We have lemonade and iced tea in the refrigerator."

"Got a bottle of beer? No glass. I'll just hold the bottle by the neck in case I have to hit some ghost over the head. I bet a house as old as this has ghosts, doesn't it?"

"None that we've encountered." Pearl raised her chin a little. "I'll see about the beer."

Susan bit her lip, thinking this weekend might not have been such a great idea. She'd been excited for Peter to visit, but now she wasn't so sure. She took Peter to his room, then went into the kitchen. "Mother, for heaven's sake, lighten up. He didn't go to prep school. He grew up in an orphanage."

Pearl was silent for a moment, then said, "I'm sorry for that, Susan, but I don't know what you're talking about."

"He's nervous. He's nicer than you think."

"I'm sure he is." Pearl took out a bottle of beer, rubbing her hand up and down the neck.

"He's old enough to drink. He's twenty-six. Do you want his ID?"

Pearl didn't respond. Instead, she asked, "Are the two of you getting together with

Peggy and Joe? You could invite them here for dinner tomorrow."

Susan thought that over. Peter would be at a disadvantage at the Bride's House, where he would realize how much Pearl liked Joe. He might say or do the wrong thing, and Susan wanted him to look good. "Maybe we'll just meet them at the Red Ram," she said. Peter would fit in at the Ram. Maybe there'd be a band, and he would sit in on drums, which would impress everybody. Peter came into the kitchen then and opened the beer, grinning at Susan. When Pearl left, he put his arm around Susan and leaned down and kissed her on the ear.

The next day, Susan and Peter stopped at the Miner's Daughter to ask Peggy to join them at the Ram that evening. Peggy didn't notice Susan enter the shop, but she saw Peter and gave him a sly smile. Peter grinned back, looking so sexy that Susan preened at being with him.

"What are *you* doing in Georgetown? Did the Air Force invade?" Peggy asked Peter.

"He came to see me," Susan answered for him.

"Oh, hi, Susan," Peggy said, looking back and forth from one to the other, a little disappointed.

Susan introduced the two, then said, "Peter came to spend the weekend with *me*. We stopped to ask if you wanted to go to the Ram tonight, you and Joe."

"You bet. We were going to the movies, but this sounds better." Susan felt a pang of jealousy that Joe had invited Peggy out. Maybe he'd know how *she* felt when he saw Peter. The three made small talk, until Peggy said, "I put aside a scarf I thought you would like. It's in the storeroom." She turned, and Susan followed her. "He's a hunk. How come you never told me about him?"

"Didn't I? He's one of the guys I dated in Denver."

"Is he serious?"

"Oh, Peggy."

"Well?"

Susan gave Peggy a knowing look. "I don't want to talk about it. Where's the scarf?"

"There isn't any scarf, dummy. I wanted to know what was going on. How long have you known him?"

"Since before Christmas. What's with the third degree?" Susan really didn't mind, because she knew that Peggy would repeat whatever she said to Joe.

"It's because you've been so secretive.

Where did you meet him?"

Susan took her time answering. Then she said slyly, "He picked me up on the streetcar."

"So, are you career Air Force?" Joe asked Peter, after they had ordered a round of beer.

"No, I'm thinking of going to school when I get out."

"Where?"

"That depends." He sent a knowing glance at Susan, who looked away. She wanted Joe to think she was interested in Peter but not *that* interested.

"Are you getting shipped out to Korea?" Peggy asked.

Peter nodded. "The end of the month, it looks like."

Susan jerked her head around and stared at him. He had not told her that. Of course, she'd known he would go sometime, but she hadn't thought it would be so soon. That was why he'd come to Georgetown — to tell her.

"I admire you for joining the service," Joe said.

"Then why don't you join up, too?" Peter snapped. "I get sick of guys who admire the rest of us for putting our lives on the line for our country."

"Hey, that's not fair," Susan said, unable to keep from defending Joe. "He's going on to law school."

"It's called draft dodging."

"I'm not even sure why we're fighting over there," Joe said. "I'd like to think there's a purpose to it."

"I don't think about that. I signed up to defend my country."

"From who?" Peggy asked.

"Anybody you've got."

Susan didn't like the way the conversation was going. She'd wanted the four of them to have a good time, not a confrontation over Korea, and she patted Peter's hand under the table. He took a deep breath and leaned back in his chair, balancing it on two legs.

But Joe was not ready to let up. "It's not even a war," he said. "It's a police action. You'll be part of a police action."

"Tell that to the men who've died there." Peter sat up suddenly and the chair almost fell over. The waitress set down four bottles of beer, no glasses, and Peter paid her before Joe could get out his wallet. "I don't want to talk about it anymore."

"Fine with me, but I can't imagine anybody joining the Air Force to fight for something you don't even understand," Joe replied. They were silent a moment, then he asked, "So who are you backing for President, Peter?"

"I haven't thought much about it. General Eisenhower, I suppose."

Joe scoffed, made a face. "I'm for Adlai Stevenson. Susan, too, of course, since he's a friend of her parents."

Peter turned to Susan. "Your folks know Stevenson?"

"Well, yes."

"Anybody that rich is bound to know him," Peggy said. "Frankly, I like Ike." She giggled.

"Yeah, Peggy, you and me both," Peter agreed. "He's a military man."

"The worst President we ever had was General Grant. Generals make lousy Presidents," Joe said.

Peter leaned back in his chair again, his hands behind his head, his chest out. "You mean like *General* Washington?"

Susan had to laugh. "Good one," she said, while Peter grinned at her.

"He's the exception," Joe said, not wanting to concede. "In general, they're not very good."

"In *general*," Susan punned, and Peter

toasted her with his beer bottle, while Joe glared.

The evening wasn't going well. It certainly was not going the way Susan had planned it. Instead of being jealous, Joe was annoyed, with her as well as Peter. He probably had decided Peter was an idiot, might even think Susan was one, too, for dating him. Perhaps he thought she couldn't do any better. That idea angered Susan, because Peter was perfectly nice, a man who had done all right for himself. So what if he planned to vote for General Eisenhower instead of Governor Stevenson? "Why don't we have another round?" she said, hoping they would find another topic of conversation along with it.

"We're going to the movies," Joe said, as if meeting Susan and Peter hadn't been important. "You coming, Peggy?" And Peggy said she was. Susan felt a wave of disappointment watching the two stand up together, Joe with his arm around Peggy, as if she was his property.

Then as Peggy reached for her glass to finish off the beer, a young man bumped into her, making her spill the drink. "Watch it, twerp," she told him, and the boy laughed as he headed for the door.

"Hey." Peter started to grab the man, but

Susan put her hand on his arm. "That's her brother," she told him.

"Some luck, huh?" Peggy said. "I've got two more at home just like him. I wish I'd been born an orphan. Yeah, I should have been Little Orphan Annie. Orphans are lucky."

Joe laughed as if Peggy had said something witty, while Susan tried to think of a retort — for Peter's sake — but he took her hand and squeezed it and she was still.

"Well, see you around," Joe said, when the four of them stood outside. He turned to Susan with a look she didn't understand, and she thought maybe it was disdain. To hell with you, she thought.

The two couples parted, Susan and Peter watching Joe open the door of Asthma for Peggy, then pulling away without waving or looking back. Susan shrugged, thinking she should apologize to Peter for Joe, but she didn't want to talk about him.

"Hey, why don't we drive up into the mountains?" Peter said. "I'd like to see them at night." They went back to the Bride's House for Susan's convertible, and she drove west on the highway, through Silver Plume, toward Loveland Pass.

"Pull off here," Peter said, when they came to a side road, a trail that led through the pine trees.

Susan stopped the car. She'd been mulling Peggy's words as she drove along, embarrassed by what her friend had said. "Peggy didn't mean anything by that orphan business. She doesn't know about you. What she said was insensitive and crude, but she didn't do it on purpose."

"Most people don't understand what it's like — growing up in a dormitory without a single thing to call your own. Even your name. I was dumped at a fire station, and some nurse named me after her boyfriend. That girl doesn't know how lucky she is with a bunch of brothers, even if they are jerks. If I die in Korea, nobody's going to be sorry, no father or mother or grandparents. Nobody."

"I would."

"Would you?"

"Of course I would."

"Then let's get married, before I leave. Let's not wait. We'll have a couple of weeks together, and then if something happens to me, you'll get the survivor benefits." He removed a strand of hair that the wind had blown into her eye. "But maybe you don't need them. You're not who I think you are. This car, that house. You're rich, aren't you?"

"Sort of."

"So why did you pretend you weren't?"

"I didn't really. I just didn't want you to know about the money. People treat you differently when they find out you have it. When I was a kid up here, Peggy acted like I was an outcast because we're rich. So I keep my family to myself. But if you want to know, my father's head of a molybdenum company, and my mother is a famous newspaper columnist."

"Pearl Curry." Peter thought that over. "Pearl Something Curry. Oh yeah, that's why her name sounded familiar. I've heard of her. They sell a book she wrote in the PX. That's your mother?" Susan nodded, and then Peter said something that surprised her. "I wish you were just ordinary. If you were, you might need me. Like I need you." He put his arms around her and kissed her, and when she kissed him back he began pulling at her clothing.

"Don't," Susan said, straightening up. "We can't do this."

"Why not?" When Susan didn't answer, Peter tugged at the buttons on her blouse. Then he unfastened her bra and gently pushed her back against the soft leather seats of the car and kissed her.

"No, don't. We can't." Susan put her

508

hands against his chest.

When he turned to her, Peter's face in the moonlight was a series of soft gray planes. The starlight reflected in his eyes. He took her hands and kissed them. "It's exactly right. Come on, Susan. We both want this." He pushed at her clothes and then at his own. "I'll stop if you really want to," he murmured.

Susan closed her eyes and felt a shiver that went all the way through her, and then a longing so great it brought tears to her eyes. Why shouldn't she do it? After all, Joe and Peggy did, and Joe had made it plain he didn't care about her. She felt Peter's hands move over her, and for an instant, she confused him with Joe. But then she knew he wasn't Joe, and she didn't want to do this thing with him. "Peter, don't. I don't want this," she said, trying to push him off her. But it was too late, and Peter didn't stop. And when it was over, Susan blamed herself.

Susan offered to take Peter to Denver on Sunday, but he told her no, that he didn't like the idea of her driving back on the highway by herself. "I've done it a dozen times," she said.

"If we say good-bye here, I can remember

you in the mountains, remember the way you were last night." His eyes were soft and warm. "Are you okay?" Susan glanced at the ground, embarrassed, but Peter told her, "Look at me. There's nothing wrong with what happened. It's what people do when they love each other."

Did she love him? Maybe a little, or she would have tried sooner to stop him. But enough to marry him? Not yet, she thought as the two walked from the Bride's House to the bus stop beside the Red Ram, carrying Peter's flight bag between them.

"If anything happens . . ." Peter said, but she shushed him, and he didn't finish. Instead, he took her hand, and they stood in the summer sun until the bus arrived.

He sat on the far side of the Greyhound, where Susan couldn't see him, but she stood there until the bus pulled away, watching until it disappeared down the highway. She felt regret as well as an overwhelming sadness that she didn't understand. She was confused, too, and she didn't want to go home, didn't want to face Pearl. That morning, before the two had gone downstairs, they'd had a disagreement. She'd asked her mother, "How come you don't like Peter?"

"I like him perfectly well," Pearl insisted.

510

"No you don't. You're different with him, stiff, not like you are around Joe."

"That's because I've known Joe for twenty years, and I just met Peter."

"Is it because he hasn't gone to college?"

"Your father never finished college. Your grandfather had only four or five years of schooling."

"He didn't even know about our money, so you don't have to worry that he's a fortune hunter."

Her mother turned to Susan with a fierce look. "How can you say that? Such a remark is beneath you, Susan. I would never accuse a young man of that. It's a horrid thing to say! Despicable!" Susan had never seen her mother so agitated, and she stared as Pearl got control of herself and added, "It's just that I think you can do better."

So instead of going back to the Bride's House and her mother, Susan walked up Rose Street and circled around, finally going into Kniesel & Anderson to buy a bottle of Pepsi, because she was hot from the sun. Susan liked the old store with the bins of tomatoes and heads of lettuce, the displays of washing powders and canned goods, jars of licorice and jawbreakers and Double Bubble gum that were lined up on the counter. She didn't see Peggy until the girl spoke. "So are you going to marry that guy?"

"Peter?"

"Well, duh. Who else do you think I'm talking about?"

Joe, Susan thought, but she knew that wouldn't happen. "Peter's going to Korea."

"That's not what I asked."

Susan rubbed the toe of her sandal over the worn wooden floor. "Why do you care?"

Peggy grabbed Susan's arms with her hands and dug in her nails. "I care because I have this sneaking little suspicion you're after Joe Bullock. He's mine. You try to take him away from me, and you don't know what I'll do. Don't you dare ruin it for me. Do you hear?"

Susan stepped back, as Peggy dropped her hands. "I'm not marrying Peter Fanshaw so that you can have Joe," Susan said. "All my life, you've told me what to do. I'll date anybody I like, and there's nothing you can do about it."

"Don't cross me," Peggy said.

"I think I just did."

Susan found the note on her car the afternoon her mother left for Denver. Pearl had a doctor's visit, a hair appointment, and errands to run, and since Bert Joy was going down to Denver to see his sister, Pearl decided to ride along and spend two nights at the Brown Palace. Susan stayed in Georgetown.

She didn't know when the note had been left. She'd gone out to put the top up on the Merc because she was afraid it would rain and had found the piece of paper tucked under her windshield wiper.

Meet me at the cemetery at 8. Walk down. I'll drive you back. Don't tell anyone. I have something to tell you.

Joe

She had never received a note from Joe, and she read it three times, confused, worrying at first that this was some joke, another snipe hunt maybe. But they were too old for such things now. Perhaps she should ignore the note. If Joe asked, she'd tell him she hadn't found it, that it must have blown away. But what if Joe did have something important to tell her, some surprise? Maybe this was another New Year's, but this time, he wouldn't back off. Not likely, however, not after the disastrous evening with Peter at the Red Ram. Still, if she didn't show up, she'd always wonder. Susan shoved the note into her pocket and looked about to see if Joe was watching, but no one was around.

She went upstairs, thinking she might clean her room, but she was nervous, fidgety, and couldn't help pondering what Joe wanted. She ate lunch, taking it into the yard by the lilac bushes, which were blooming now. The smell of lilacs, no matter where she was, made her think of the Bride's House. The scent comforted her, just as the old house did.

Susan thought of Peter then, thought what a shame that he had no sense of home, no place to remember, to bring him comfort when he was in Korea. He had told her that she was what he would remember, she was what he would come back to, and he wanted to think of her in the mountains — in the mountains and the Bride's House. He'd said it almost as if he'd wanted to be a part of those places, too. It bothered her that she hadn't told him yes or no, but she couldn't. She brooded over what had happened between them. It was her fault. She should have known what Peter wanted when he suggested the drive in the mountains, and she should have stopped him when he first began fumbling with her clothes. She should have known he wouldn't stop. But she'd been angry at Joe. What had happened had been as much about Joe as Peter.

Susan sat near the lilacs for a long time, stretched out in a lounge chair, thinking about how she wished Joe had been in the car that night instead of Peter.

"I could have robbed your house, and you wouldn't even have known."

Susan shook herself from her reverie and shaded her eyes. "Joe?" She hadn't encountered him since that night at the Red Ram two weeks before and was surprised to see him.

"You're lucky I didn't come to rape and pillage."

Susan swung her legs to the ground, excited that he had stopped by. "My poor luck."

"No lie." He grinned and sat down on the lounge beside her. "Your friend isn't such a bad guy. I wasn't very nice to him. Maybe I feel a little guilty that he's going to Korea and I'm not."

Susan liked that. "I don't think he minded."

"Or maybe I was just jealous that he was with you."

Susan mulled over the remark, wondering if Joe really meant it, and didn't reply

"So what are you doing out here?"

"I was thinking about you."

"That's good."

"I was trying to figure out why you wanted to meet me." When Joe frowned, she said, "You know, your note." She reached into her pocket and handed it to him.

Joe glanced at the note and thought a moment. "Some things are easier to put in writing. Are you going?"

"Do you really want me to walk down there by myself?"

"I guess I wasn't thinking. Asthma's at the filling station. I'll pick you up, eight o'clock. Is that okay?"

"I guess so," Susan said, wishing Joe weren't so mysterious. She was still thinking this might be a trick. Maybe he was being a jerk, and he and Peggy had cooked up something.

Susan dressed carefully. She put on a sweater set and her best shorts, a little makeup, and at eight, she climbed into Joe's truck for the drive to the cemetery. To her relief, there were no signs of other vehicles, so it didn't seem as if this was a game. The gate was locked, and they parked Asthma and walked up the road, Joe carrying a six-pack of Coors. The two sat down on the grass, and he took out a church key and opened two beers, handing one to Susan.

"Here's to us," he said, tapping his beer against hers. He leaned back against a tombstone and looked up at the sky.

"So what are we doing here?" Susan asked.

Joe gave an embarrassed laugh. "I don't know. It doesn't make sense, I suppose, but it seemed like a good place to talk. Nobody's ever around at night — except snipes." He grinned. "I stood up Peggy tonight. She'll be furious, but I don't care. You're the one I care about."

Susan put her arms around her knees and looked up at the sky. She didn't understand why they couldn't talk at her house on the front porch or in the gazebo, but the idea of meeting out there in the starlight seemed romantic. She was happy that Joe wanted to be with her instead of Peggy, and he'd just said he cared about her — whatever that meant. After all, he cared about Pearl and Frank and baby snipes.

"I come out here sometimes when I want to get away from everything. It's a good place to think. There's so much I want to do, and what if I'm just some dumb lug with no talent."

"Don't say that." Susan dropped her knees to one side and twisted around to face Joe. "You're smart and you've got compassion

517

and ambition. Mother says so, too. I shouldn't tell you this, but she wrote Governor Stevenson, recommending you for a job if he gets elected."

"She really did that?" Joe drained his can of beer and opened another, offering it to Susan, but she shook her head. She'd barely tasted the first one.

She looked away, embarrassed. "I told her to."

"You did that for me?" Joe was still a moment, then set down the beer can on the gravestone. "You're really something, you know that?" She leaned against him and tilted her head toward the sky. There was no moon now, only the darkness and the pinpoints of starlight. "Do you know how I feel about you?" Joe asked.

Susan shivered. "No."

"You're cold." She'd left her cardigan in the truck, so Joe leaned forward and took off his jacket, putting it around her shoulders. Susan hoped he'd continue what he'd started to say, and in a moment, he did. "I can talk to you better than anyone. You understand. You'd make a great politician's wife."

The words thrilled her, although they were vague, just like at Christmas, and Susan was wary. "I don't understand what you're saying."

"Last winter, I started to tell you, but I was tight as a dollar bill then, and I just sort of let it slip out. I shouldn't have clammed up afterward like I did, and I'm sorry. I was too embarrassed to even write you, because of the mess I'd made of things. But now, well, I have only a year left of college, and . . . oh hell, you know what I'm saying."

Susan was confused. She didn't dare assume anything. Don't lead me on again; please ask me to marry you, please, she prayed. "I guess I don't," she said.

"I didn't put it very well." He stood and swiped at a grass stem, pulling it up by the roots, then breaking off the stem and shredding it. He lifted Susan to her feet. "I really want you, Susan. That day I pulled you out of the tire, I thought we'd killed you, and I was scared to death. When I heard your voice, I decided I was going to marry you. Do you remember that? You didn't even know who I was."

"Oh, I knew. I've always known who you are, Joe."

He held her against his chest. "I guess I ought to just say it outright. Will you marry me?" He looked almost as surprised at the words as she did.

Susan felt the wind on the back of her neck, blowing her hair into her face, and she brushed it away as she stared at Joe. She shivered, but not from the cold. She couldn't feel anything but a warmth like pinpricks of flame under her skin. She was so happy she couldn't speak.

Joe searched her face in the moonlight and said, "I'd get down on my knees, but it's sort of rocky here."

Susan smiled, her face glowing. "Of course I'll marry you. I've been in love with you my whole life." She looked at him with such tenderness in her heart.

Joe grinned at her and gave a sigh of relief. "That was easier than I thought." He kissed her again, and holding hands, they sat down in the grass.

"I didn't know this was why you wanted to meet me here," Susan said.

"Neither did I." Joe made a pillow out of his jacket, then gently pushed Susan down until her head was resting on it. "But I think it was a pretty good idea." He kissed her, and then his hands began to roam over her body. She could feel his mouth on her neck, on her breast. A grass stem poked her back, scratching her. She squirmed a little, thinking there were red ants at the cemetery but not wanting to take her arms from around Joe's neck. Suddenly, he stopped and sat up. "This isn't a good idea. We should wait."

"Wait?" Susan asked.

"Until we're married. I don't want to spoil things."

"But Joe," Susan protested, thinking he had done this with Peggy. And after all, she had had that night with Peter. "It's not wrong."

"You're not a tramp, and I'm not going to treat you like one. You're worth waiting for." He put his arms around her and held her tight and they sat in the moonlight for a long time, Susan thinking she, too, could wait.

Joe came by the next night, but not until late. He'd said he would, and Susan had sat in the front parlor in the dark waiting for him, sat on a Victorian love seat, tossing a marble egg from hand to hand, asking herself if Joe really would show up. What if this was another New Year's, and in the daylight, he'd come to his senses? But he had proposed, had really asked her to marry him, not just hinted at it. And she'd said yes. Still, the waiting nearly killed her.

She got up and looked through the leaded-glass window in the dining room door into the dark street, then went into the study and sat down at Charlie's desk — Pearl's now — playing with an ore sample that Pearl used as a paperweight. She wandered back into the parlor and stood rearranging lilac branches, although she could barely see the blooms in the light that seeped into the room from a street lamp. It didn't matter, because Susan had never been much at arranging flowers. She bent and put her face to them, taking in the scent.

And then Joe was at the door. She hadn't heard him come up onto the porch, and she gave a sigh of relief. He knocked instead of using the bell twist, which gave out a screeching, metallic sound that would have made her jump.

"What are you doing in the dark?" he asked.

"Thinking about you."

"About last night."

"Yes."

"I've been thinking about it, too. You're haven't changed your mind, have you?"

She shook her head, then asked, suddenly apprehensive, "Have you?"

"Not on your life." He led her over to the love seat, and they sat down. "Is your mom still away?"

"She'll be back tomorrow."

He put his arm around her and kissed her, then moved to the love seat across from her. "I guess I ought to ask your dad for your hand? You don't think he'd turn me down, do you?"

"I doubt it. And if he does, we'll elope, like my parents did. Father's coming out in August. We could announce our engagement then and get married in June, after you graduate."

"I don't want to wait that long. I was thinking more like Christmas."

Susan hadn't turned on the lights, and she stared at Joe in the dark. She'd always planned to be married in June, with the reception outside, around the gazebo. But she thought of the Christmas she had just spent in the Bride's House, of the evergreens and poinsettias and candles, and she put the palms of her hands together, her fingers at her lips, and decided that would be the most beautiful wedding she could imagine. "Perfect. Oh, Joe, that would be perfect."

"It's not too soon?"

"Are you crazy? I don't even want to wait *that* long."

He reached for her hands and squeezed them. "Me, neither." Then he turned serious. "About last night. I mean . . ." He glanced down at their hands. "It's not that I don't want to, you know, sex. I just think we ought to wait. We have a whole lifetime. I guess I'm just old-fashioned or something." He grinned. "I think girls are the ones who are supposed to give this speech."

"But you and Peggy . . ." Susan couldn't finish. She didn't understand why he would have sex with Peggy and not her.

"Peggy and I what?"

"You know."

"Had sex? Are you crazy? I've never cared about Peggy that way. Peggy's the kind of girl who'd try to trap a guy. I'm not that dumb."

Susan stared at him in the dim light, thinking no, Joe wasn't that dumb. How could she have been so stupid as to believe Peggy? And then she wondered, If she'd known the truth about Joe and Peggy, would she have tried sooner to stop Peter?

Susan avoided Peggy after that, because she did not want to tell the girl of the engagement. Except for telling Pearl, who was overjoyed at the news and promised Susan could have her grandmother's wedding ring, Susan and Joe agreed to keep their engagement quiet until Frank arrived and Joe could go through the formality of seeking his approval. Then they would announce the engagement at a party before school started. In the meantime, Susan and her mother would go to Denver to pick silver and china patterns, to engage a caterer and musicians and arrange for flowers. "We'll go to Daniels & Fisher to see about a gown. My own wedding dress came from there, although it was twenty years old when I got married in it," Pearl said.

Susan did not want Peggy clouding her happiness, so she did not seek her out, although she also felt sorry for the girl. After all, from the time she was a girl, Peggy, too, had dreamed about marrying Joe, and she would be hurt and disappointed, angry at the news.

Eventually, the two young women did run into each other, however. "You've been avoiding me," Peggy said. Then before Susan could deny it, Peggy added, "Well, I don't blame you. That was sort of a dirty trick."

"What are you talking about?"

Peggy gave a mean-spirited laugh. "You know what I'm talking about."

"No, I don't." Susan was uncomfortable and said, "I have to get going."

"Hey, I'm sorry. I know Joe doesn't care about you, but you were so snotty. I thought you'd realize what a jerk he could be when he didn't show up."

Susan was confused. "I have no idea what you're saying."

"Sure you do. The note. I wrote it. I put it on your car."

"What note?"

"Hey, don't be embarrassed. I said I was sorry." Peggy didn't look the least bit sorry. "How long did you wait at the cemetery, anyway?"

Susan looked at the other girl, stunned. No wonder Joe had been surprised when she'd shown him the note. He hadn't written it at all, just pretended he had when he was confronted with it. But it had turned out well. He had proposed because of that note. If they hadn't gone to the cemetery that evening, Joe might not have proposed at all, might have put it off or changed his mind. So Susan ought to be grateful to Peggy. "You wrote it?" she asked.

Peggy laughed again. "You probably waited there in the graveyard half the night for him, then had to walk home by yourself. I bet you haven't spoken to him since."

"You wrote the note?"

"Are you deaf?" Peggy looked smug. "I told you I did."

"How odd. Joe never told me." Susan mulled something over for a moment, then could not keep herself from saying, "Then I have to thank you. Joe proposed that night. We're getting married in December."

In August, Susan came home from hiking to find Pearl waiting in the parlor, a telegram in her hand. "This came for you," she said.

Telegrams were hardly a novelty. Pearl received them all the time. "I opened it by mistake. I'd thought it was for me," Pearl said. She stood and handed the folded yellow paper to Susan, who read it and looked up, stricken.

"Peter's dead," Susan said, as if Pearl hadn't already read the telegram. "Oh, Mother." She began to sob, and Pearl put her arms around her daughter.

"I'm so sorry."

"He was such a nice guy."

"Yes, he was."

"He wanted to get married, but I couldn't."

Susan sat down on the love seat and Pearl went into the kitchen for a glass of water, handing it to her daughter then sitting down next to her. "You can't be blamed for not loving him. You are marrying someone you really love. I'm sure Peter understood."

"But I never wrote him about Joe. I knew I had to, but I kept putting it off. I feel so

527

awful, Mother. There's nobody to mourn him. He'll be forgotten."

"No, we'll make sure he won't be."

Later that day, Pearl wrote about Peter, included his name and where he was killed. The column began, "America's freedom is bought at the cost of its young men. One of those men is Peter Fanshaw, an airman, who gave his life to protect our way of life." It was a column about how the blood of America's young protected the country's freedom. The column was picked up all over the country and later included in anthologies. It was considered one of best things that Pearl Dumas Curry ever wrote.

CHAPTER 18

The days were shorter now, the nights cooler. The lilac blooms on the bushes had turned brown, and the poppies and yellow roses were dead. The wild asters were dots of purple among the grasses. Susan had hiked up Guanella Pass by herself, had followed the road, then turned off into a meadow of aspen trees. The leaves were still green, but they would change color soon.

She threw herself down under an aspen and began to cry great racking sobs of unhappiness. She couldn't stop. She lay on her stomach, her hands clutching at the dried grasses until the tears stopped and she gulped for air. Then she sat up and beat her fists against her stomach, as if to dislodge the life that was growing there. She stayed in that place for a long time, until the wind came up and she began to shiver. It was almost dark when she stumbled down the road and made her way back to the

Bride's House.

"Your father just telephoned with his flight information. He gets here a week from Tuesday," her mother called. "I've been so busy I didn't fix much of a supper." She came out of the study and went into the parlor, where Susan was slumped in a chair, her hair windblown, her eyes red. "You're dirty. Did you fall?" Pearl asked after she switched on a lamp and saw Susan's tearstained face. She sat down on the love seat next to her daughter. "Are you hurt?"

Susan put her hands over her face and turned away. How could she tell her mother? Pearl had such high standards. She was known as a literary icon of morality. She'd be ashamed of a daughter who was having a — what did they call it in Georgetown? — an off-child.

"What is it?" Pearl asked. She slid over on the love seat and took Susan's hands from her face. "Did you hurt yourself?"

Susan shook her head.

"Is it something else?" Pearl thought a moment. "Did you and Joe have an argument?"

"It's me, Mother."

"What?"

"I'm pregnant," Susan blurted out the words and stared at her mother, not knowing how Pearl would react. She might walk out of the room, tight-lipped, or she'd get angry in the controlled way she had, her voice cold as ice, telling Susan what a disappointment she was. Or she might humiliate her by calling Frank and telling him, letting him know his daughter was no better than a tramp.

Pearl sat there a moment, digesting the news, her face as serene as always, covering her feelings. Then she reached out and put her hand on Susan's arm. "We'll just have to change the plans and move up the wedding," she said softly. "You'll be married right away, something quiet, before Joe's school starts. It's not a calamity. You're not the first bride to change her wedding date."

Susan shook her head. "You don't understand, Mother."

"Of course I understand. You can still have a lovely ceremony, something dignified. I never liked big weddings anyway."

"That's not it, Mother."

Pearl frowned. "Not what?"

Susan took a deep breath and looked away. "The baby isn't Joe's. It's Peter's."

The two of them did not say much after that. Susan cried, and her mother held her. Pearl asked if Susan were sure, if there were a possibility the baby was Joe's, but Susan said she had never slept with Joe, only Peter. "I couldn't even seduce Joe," she cried. He'd know the baby wasn't his. And she couldn't marry Peter, because he was dead.

Susan closed her eyes then. She had never been so weary. She stood and walked to the staircase, stopping with her foot on the bottom step. "The Bride's House," she said bitterly, wincing at the words. "I was the only one of the three of us who was going to be married here. Now look what I've done. You and Grandmother" — she nodded toward the picture of Nealie in the parlor — "you both must be ashamed of the unholy mess I've made."

"You mustn't say that," Pearl told her, but Susan didn't hear her. She held on to the rail, pulling herself up the stairs, then went into her room, collapsing onto the bed and falling into a deep sleep. She didn't wake when Pearl went up a few minutes later to put a quilt over her. Susan slept as if she'd been drugged, although when she awoke, she was still tired. The memory of the day before wrapped around her like a swirl of wet leaves, and she dreaded what she had to do. For her sake as well as Joe's, she would not drag things out. She got out of bed and sat down at her dressing table, taking out a sheet of paper.

At first, she thought she would simply write a note saying she was going away because she'd made a mistake and didn't want to get married. But Joe was too decent for that. She couldn't make him believe she'd dumped him. He deserved the truth, although it would bring pain to them both. She picked up her fountain pen and wrote slowly:

Dear Joe,
    I am pregnant with Peter's baby. Under the circumstances, we can't get married. I'm sorry, because I love you. I hope you can forgive me.

                                                    Love,
                                                    Susan

She dressed and went downstairs then and found her mother, who had not slept at all. She had made coffee and cinnamon rolls, the ones Susan had loved as a girl, made them from a recipe in Lidie Travers's hand-written cookbook, which was held together with a rubber band. Susan sat down at the table, breaking apart a bun but not eating it, letting the scent of cinnamon hang in the air. "I wrote Joe a note," she said, handing the paper to Pearl, who read it and set it on the kitchen table.

"You're going to write him?" Pearl asked.

"I have to let him know."

"In a note? Don't you think he deserves to be told in person?"

Susan thought that over, then picked up the note and crumpled it, dropping it onto the table. "You're right. I have to tell him." She put her arms on the table to cushion her head, trying not to cry again.

After a time, Pearl went to the window. "The leaves will be early this year. The aspen usually don't turn until the last week of September. I love the colors, but when I was young, they always brought me a bittersweet feeling, because they portended winter." She stared out the window a little longer, then sighed and turned around. "Don't tell Joe just yet. There are some things I want you to see and to think about. I've set them out on the desk in the study. Come with me." Pearl picked up the cups and the percolator.

Susan followed her mother into the other room and saw that the wallpaper beside the desk had been cut away, revealing a hole in the wall that she hadn't known was there. On Charlie's desk was an open strongbox, empty now, its contents spread out in some sort of order. Pearl sat down behind the desk, while Susan took the chair in front of it, curious, although she couldn't imagine what the papers had to do with her situation. Why would her mother pick this time to tell her family secrets?

Pearl studied her daughter for a moment, then asked, "First, do you know what you want to do? There are doctors we can talk to, maybe in Europe."

"You mean an abortion? Is that what you think I should do?"

"It's not what *I* think. It's what *you* want."

"There are homes. I could say I'm spending the next two terms studying abroad," Susan said, her voice laced with irony. "That wouldn't fool anybody."

"You could still marry Joe."

"And have him find out a month later I was going to have a baby? He can count, Mother. He'd know it wasn't his. I know you mean well, but you don't understand." Susan glanced up at the portrait of Nealie. "Neither of you."

"You're wrong. We understand better than you think. That's why I opened your grandfather's strongbox." Pearl pushed aside her cup. "He hid this here," she said, indicating the box and the hole in the wall. "I saw it once. I think he intended that. Last January, when I came back to Georgetown to

535

settle his estate, I took it out, and what I found inside stunned me. I'm still shocked. I wanted to destroy everything in it, but I couldn't. He'd kept these things for such a long time. Besides, I'd thought maybe someday long after I was gone, you'd find them. But now is a better time for you to read them."

Pearl picked up two documents and handed them to Susan. "These are your grandparents' marriage certificate and my birth certificate. Look at the dates."

Susan took the papers and read the names scrawled on them. Then she studied the dates and looked up. "Grandmother was pregnant when she got married?" She felt a sudden connection with the woman who looked down at her from the portrait.

"Pregnant brides aren't exactly a phenomenon of your generation." Pearl smiled a little. "Not only was she expecting, but she did not marry my father."

"What?" Susan stared at Pearl. "Are you saying that Grandfather wasn't your father?"

"I didn't know until after he was dead. I'm still trying to cope with it." Pearl raised her chin and looked out the window for a moment. "Read this." She handed Susan an envelope that bore a New York City postmark and the year 1881. It was addressed to Charles Dumas. Susan removed the handwritten note.

Charlie, your terms are acceptable. I won't see her ever again, and the child may be considered yours, but I think it will be anyway if you marry her. Enclosed is the bank draft, and I have made arrangements to purchase the house and transfer the title. It will be done by November 25 at the latest. I want her to have it. God knows, I wish it had been different. I love the girl. At least, tell her I kept my promise to take care of her.

Will

"Who's Will?"

Pearl held up her hand. "I think there were other letters between the two of them, but they must have been destroyed. This answers your question." She handed Susan a rolled-up deed, which was brown spotted with age, the gold ribbon that had held it tarnished to a brass color.

Susan unrolled the document, spreading it out on the desk and holding it down with ore samples. It was the deed to the Bride's House, and at first glance, she saw nothing unusual about it. The document with its ornate handwriting was pretty enough to be framed. There was the legal description, the date, November 23, 1881, and the name Nealie Bent.

"Grandmother owned the house?" Susan asked.

"It looks like it. I wonder if she knew," Pearl mused.

No price was listed on the deed, and it was almost as if the house had been given to Nealie, not sold to her. Susan studied the document but saw no other significance in it. She shook her head. "I don't understand."

"Look at the seller's name."

Susan's eyes swept across the page until she found it — William K. Spaulding. "Will Spaulding? Father's partner? My godfather? He sold Grandmother the Bride's House?" Susan remembered Will Spaulding as a kind man who had given her a ruby ring and a fur muff one Christmas, when she was very young. He had died shortly after that, leaving her a generous trust fund.

"Gave it to her is more likely." Pearl handed Susan another letter, running her hand over it as if reluctant to part with it. "This explains everything." A single word was written in a shaky hand on the envelope: "Will."

When Susan opened it, an uncashed

money order for $500 made out to Nealie Bent dropped out. The handwriting in the letter was messy, and Susan read each word out loud.

Dear Will

They say Im going to pass on and won't live out the day so I take pen in hand to tell you so youll know. I wisht youd come back. I kept looking for you Will. Charlies a good husband and he bought me the brides house. He never blamed me about having your baby. He acts like shes his, so you dont have to worry about her. I named her Pearl. Sometime maybe when you come back you can see her but you won't see me because Ill be dead. I love you even though you didnt keep your promise. I forgive you.

Nealie

Susan dropped the letter onto the desk and stared at her mother, who had tears glistening in her eyes. "Will Spaulding was your father?"

Pearl nodded. "I had no idea until after both of them were dead, of course. But I believe it's true. I see him in you." Pearl swallowed hard. "I don't recall ever meeting him when I was a child, but when your father introduced me to him after we married, he seemed familiar. So maybe I did."

"He paid Grandfather to marry Grandmother?"

"I don't know if that's really the case or if Papa simply figured out he could get money out of Will for something he wanted to do anyway, which was to marry my mother. He always did drive a hard bargain. I do know Will was sorry later on that he hadn't married her himself. He once told your father he'd had a chance to marry a girl he loved and didn't and had regretted it ever since. That's why he encouraged your father to marry me."

"But Grandfather loved you."

"That's the odd thing, isn't it? He loved me so fiercely that he didn't want me to ever leave him. I guess it didn't seem to matter to him that I wasn't his flesh and blood. It was enough to know I was my mother's. You should know that is possible." She held Susan's eyes for a long time.

"Are you saying I should marry Joe anyway, and he'll love the baby?" Her grandfather might have managed that, but Joe Bullock? It didn't happen twice in one family.

"No, I'm just telling you how it happened

with my mother and me."

Susan thought a moment. "How did Grandfather get the letter? Wasn't it ever mailed?"

Pearl shook her head. "No, you'll read about that in a minute. I wish I could have asked Aunt Lidie, but of course, she died before Papa did, before I found all this."

Susan reached across the desk for her mother's hand, and the two sat silently for a moment, before Pearl said, "There's one more letter for you to read." She poured coffee into Susan's cup. "I'm going for a walk, but first I want to tell you something. Your father and I were secretly engaged when I was thirty. When your grandfather found out, he threatened to disinherit me, and your father asked to be released from the engagement, because he couldn't support me. He was afraid we'd live in poverty, and he said he wouldn't do that to me. I believed him, but later I found a receipt for a fifty-thousand-dollar loan Papa had given him — that's how I learned about this box; Papa left it open so that I'd come across the receipt. For years, I thought Frank had been bought off. But then he came back and said he had used the money to make enough to meet Papa's conditions for marriage. It took nearly twenty years."

Pearl sat silently for a moment, and Susan watched her, hoping she would continue. But she didn't. Instead, Pearl stood. "I believe I'll walk down to the park. There is one more letter, one that Aunt Lidie wrote to Papa. You can read it while I'm gone. All of this" — she swept her hand across the papers on the desk — "might help you make a decision. That's why I opened the box. That's why I showed you these things now."

Susan watched her mother put on a coat and a scarf, then go out, watched through the curtains as Pearl stepped onto the dirt street and walked quickly in the direction of the park. She turned to the envelope Pearl had left on the desk. It was addressed to Charles Dumas, and when Susan opened it, a cablegram fell out: "PACKAGE ARRIVED SAFE. ALL WELL. LT." That doesn't explain anything, Susan thought.

She opened the last letter, written in Aunt Lidie's cramped hand and dated July 15, 1913, and read it slowly so that every word was clear.

Dear Charlie Dumas,

I guess you understood my wire yesterday that Pearl was delivered of a baby. Both mother and child are satisfactory. Pearl begun her labor at six in the

542

evening and the baby was not born till half past six the next morning. The baby is a girl and weighed seven pounds, six ounces, and has fancy hair. Pearl held her in her arms and fought to keep her but she knew there was no choice but to give her up. I thought I'd tell her the baby died a little later, and that would ease her, but there's already enough lies. The child — Pearl called her Faith, although who knows if the name will stay — went to a watchmaker and his wife who have no other children. I arranged things with them when we arrived, Pearl leaving the details to me. They seem to be good people and say they will raise her as their own. I paid them the amount you settled on, and they know they don't expect more. You needn't worry about blackmail, because we are staying here under false names, so they don't know who Pearl is. I think they wanted the child for itself, not the money. It helps me to think so. Pearl does not know they were paid.

Charlie, it does not sit easy with me that we deceived Pearl. She believes me and her have pulled the wool over your eyes, and she's made me promise a dozen times never to tell you why we

took this trip. It would kill her to find
out you know about her off-child. She
thinks I wrote she had the influenza, and
the doctor ordered bed rest, and that's
why we're staying here such a long time.
When I told you in Georgetown, I did
not know what else to do. The poor girl
was so upset I feared she'd throw herself
in Clear Creek. You asked me when it
happened, and I said I did not know. But
now, I believe it must have been in
Denver the day they visited the capitol.
Maybe he took her back to his lodgings.
I remember she was awful flustered that
evening.

She does not ask about the baby, but
she has always been one to keep her feelings to herself. She is all right in body,
but she grieves bad. I don't know if she
yet pines for Mr. Curry. She doesn't talk
to me about him, except to ask one time
if she should have informed him of her
condition. I said she should not, although I am not so sure now. I ought to
have told Mr. Curry myself, and it wor-
ries me plenty that I did not. I know you
wouldn't have liked it, would have fired
me for it, but it bothers me. I could have
given them the chance to be together,
but I held my tongue. It wasn't right that

Mr. Curry didn't have a say. It's not good keeping secrets.

Like I say, I don't know if I did the right thing telling you either. It brings to mind me giving you that letter Nealie wrote on her deathbed to Will Spaulding. I've turned it over in my mind all these years whether I ought to have mailed it to him. Maybe I should have read it first. But that's done, and maybe it's best you burned it. We have enough deceit now that I won't worry about the past.

Lydia Travers

P.S. You can make your plans to join us now.

Susan sat back in her chair, her heart beating hard, her throat dry. Her mother had had an illegitimate baby, a child born twenty years before Susan. Like Susan, her mother had been pregnant and unmarried. She set the sheet of paper on the table and picked up her coffee cup, but her hand shook so that she returned it to the desk without drinking. She stood and went to the long front window, looking out, but she could not see her mother. How many times had Pearl stood in that very spot, staring at the same mountain, thinking about her first daughter? And then Susan thought about herself. What would she feel if she gave up a daughter? Would she ever get over it? How could she?

Agitated, Susan walked around the room, touching the spot where the strongbox had been hidden, depressing keys on the piano, then playing a chord with one hand, picking a withered leaf off a flower stalk that sat in a vase. She went to the window a second time, but Pearl had not returned. Abruptly, Susan grabbed her coat and went out. The sun had touched the snow on top of Sunrise Peak, but Susan didn't notice the mountain as she walked into a wind that blew dirt and dead leaves down the street, until she reached the park and found Pearl huddled on the steps of the bandstand. Susan sat down beside her, and in a moment, Pearl reached out her hand and clutched Susan's.

"How could you give her up, my *sister* — Faith?" Susan swallowed when she said the words.

"I didn't have a choice."

"Did you ever see her again?"

Pearl shook her head. Her scarf had come undone, and she retied it. "Your father didn't know, of course, not then. I told him on our drive to Denver, just before we married. He hired a detective in Paris, but the

546

home I'd gone to had been torn down, and there had been the war."

"How awful, Mother."

"The worst part was giving her up, then wondering all those years whether she was still alive. During the last war, I was afraid she'd fallen into the hands of the Nazis somehow or had starved. I guess we'll never know."

"I'm so sorry." Susan put her arms around herself to keep out the cold wind. Then she gave a short laugh. "We're a fine family of women, aren't we, every one of us pregnant and not married."

Pearl smiled. "I'd thought of that irony." She stretched out her legs. "My mother married a man she didn't love so that she could keep her baby. I gave mine up, and I've regretted it ever since. And I wasn't fair to your father. I should have told him. I had you read those things so you'd know we understand, my mother and I. Maybe we can help you decide what to do."

"The only choice I have is between giving up the baby and tricking Joe into marrying me, and both of them stink."

"There's another," Pearl said.

Susan frowned at her mother.

"You could let Joe decide," she said softly.

"You mean tell him and see if he still

wants to marry me? Who would do that?"

"Your grandfather."

"Well, Joe isn't Charlie Dumas."

"You'll never know if you don't tell him."

"I can't, Mother. I'd be too ashamed."

Pearl stood then and drew her coat around her. "You have a few days to decide. It's cold out here. I don't want you to get chilled." She held out her hand to Susan, and the two walked back toward the Bride's House holding hands.

Susan refused to see Joe after that. When he phoned, Susan said she had the flu. He stopped by the house, but her mother told him Susan was in bed, which was true. She barely left her room, spending her days crying and looking into the mirror, wondering how she could have made such a mess of her life. Joe brought a bouquet of purple asters he'd picked in the mountains, but Susan still wouldn't see him.

"You can't hide forever," Pearl told her daughter.

"I can't face him."

"You have to, Susan. It's not right. You're treating him shabbily. He deserves better. You haven't much time now."

Susan nodded slowly. "I know." She was sitting in the dining room in her bathrobe, looking through the shutters at the gray day. Although it was still August, snow had fallen on the high peaks, and the wind that blew down from them brought a chill. The house was cold, and despite the heavy bathrobe, Susan couldn't get warm. She nibbled at an apple, but she wasn't hungry and put it down. As Susan sat there, miserable, trying to decide what to do, the doorbell rang, and Pearl answered it. "Yes, Joe, she's up." And in a second, Joe was standing in the doorway.

"Hey, how are you doing?"

"About as lousy as I look." Susan's hair was uncombed, and her eyes were red.

"You don't look that bad to me. I thought maybe fresh air would do you some good. Why don't we go for a walk?"

"I don't think so."

"Getting out of the house would be the best thing for you, Susan," Pearl said. "You get dressed, and I'll entertain Joe for a few minutes." Susan shot her mother an angry look, but Pearl insisted. "Go on."

Her mother was right, Susan thought. She might as well get it over with. So she went upstairs and washed her face and combed her hair, then put on a heavy white wool sweater and jeans. The jeans were already tight.

"You look even better," Joe said, when Susan returned. He took her hand, and they went out onto the porch and down the steps, Pearl watching from the doorway. They didn't talk as they made their way down Taos Street and into the park. Susan sat down on the steps of the bandstand, while Joe leaned on a rail beside her. "I've been doing some thinking," he began, and Susan wondered if he knew somehow, if *he* would be the one to break their engagement. She was relieved. He'd say he'd changed his mind, and she wouldn't have to tell him about the baby, and she would be gracious, saying she understood.

She closed her eyes and waited, and when he didn't continue, she asked, "About what?"

"Getting married." Susan took a deep breath, but before she could reply, Joe continued. "I've been wondering why we should wait until Christmas. I don't know about you, but I'd rather not have a big wedding. Heck, I'd elope, but you probably wouldn't like that. So I was thinking we could get married at your house when your father gets here next week, and then we could go to California while I finish my senior year. What do you think?"

Susan didn't answer. She stared across the

dead grass in the park. A few aspen leaves had turned yellow and had blown into the corners of the bandstand. It could work, she thought. She wasn't that far along, and Joe might wonder, but there were plenty of babies born at seven months, and he'd never know for sure that the child wasn't his. Joe and Peter resembled each other, so the baby might look like Joe. Even if Joe found out later, he'd have to accept the child. He couldn't divorce her, because a divorced politician had no future. She weighed all that in her mind, and then she turned to Joe. "I can't."

Joe looked crestfallen. "You don't want to marry me." It was a statement instead of a question. He turned away, sadness on his face.

She wasn't being fair, Susan thought. It wasn't right to let him think she didn't want him, and so she said, "I can't marry you because I'm pregnant with Peter Fanshaw's baby."

At first Joe just stared out across the rooftops to Sunrise Peak, and then he turned to her and said slowly, "And you can't marry him because he's dead."

Had she let him know that Peter had been killed? Susan couldn't remember. He'd probably read her mother's column. Everybody had.

"Your mother told me about him," Joe said. "And about the baby."

"My mother told you! She had no right!"

"She knew that. She said it was an awful betrayal and that you might never forgive her. Then she told me she wished someone had betrayed her like that. If that had happened to her, your mom said, her life would have been so much richer. I'm not sure what she was talking about." He shook his head, then grew serious again. "Your mother said that no matter how wrong it was of her to tell me, she wanted to give me a chance."

"A chance?"

"To marry you anyway."

"Even though the baby's not yours?"

Joe nodded.

"And you'd still marry me?" What Joe said didn't make sense. "Why?"

"Because I've never loved anybody but you, and your mother said you felt the same about me." Joe sat down beside her and took her hands. "When she told me, I, well, I have to say I didn't take it very well. I was hurt. But I thought it over, and I don't want to give you up. I got to thinking that you have to deal with the surprises in your life, with the things you don't plan, and make the best of them. You know, like the note

Peggy put on your car. I hadn't planned to ask you to marry me that night, but that note made it seem like just the right time. And it was." He smiled and added, "Peggy told me later on what she'd done, as if that meant our engagement didn't count." He grew serious again. "I figured the baby was just a bonus. Somebody has to give that kid a home. You're its mother. And I'd sure like the chance to be its father."

"But don't you want —" Susan stopped when Joe put his hand over her mouth. Then he brushed the back of his hand across her cheek.

"From now on, this is my child, too. Someday, maybe you'll want to tell it about its father, but we don't have to talk about that now." He stroked her cheek. "Let's talk about the wedding instead. So how about us getting married next week?"

"I'd like that."

"Good going."

Joe left Susan at the Bride's House just as Bert Joy pulled up. "Your mama called me to do some work," he said.

"I think maybe she wants you to paper over the wall in the study."

"Oh, that again. Okay, then." He followed Susan into the house, where Pearl waited with a roll of wallpaper in her hands. "What've you got there?"

"Wallpaper. You've done this before, Bert," she said. "I want you to put that strongbox back inside the wall and paper it over."

"Why don't you folks just get a safe-deposit box?"

"Tradition," Pearl told him.

Bert headed for the study, and Pearl turned to Susan. "You're looking a little better." She searched her daughter's face.

"A lot better. Joe and I are getting married next week, as soon as Father arrives." Susan closed her eyes, and tears seeped from under her lids. "It's going to be all right."

They heard Bert whistling in the next room, and Pearl said, "I think maybe there's something you might want to add to that box then, before it goes back into its hiding place, something you might want your own daughter to discover one day."

"You think the baby's going to be a girl?"

"There's a fifty percent chance," her mother replied.

Susan laughed for the first time in a long while. "There's nothing for me to add. I threw away the note I wrote to Joe."

Pearl removed a paper from the pocket of

her apron. It was wrinkled, and she ironed it with her hand. "It's up to you."

Her eyes clouded, Susan stared at the paper. "This is a house of secrets. I suppose one more won't hurt. Maybe one day, I will tell my child — my daughter — about her father."

"And right the wrongs of the past?" her mother asked.

"Were they wrongs? Or were they only secrets?" Susan pondered that for a moment with no answer. Then she picked up the note, went into the study, and laid it inside the strongbox, adding her story to those of her mother and her grandmother. Placing the note there gave her a continuity with the two women who had shared both her shame and her joy.

Bert Joy tapped the box into place, then he cut a square of wallpaper and swiped it with paste, fitting it over the box so neatly that the women had to look closely to see the patch. "Okay, then," Bert said to himself as he picked up his tools.

Susan walked him to the door and watched him get into his truck. She stayed on the porch, staring out at the mountains, which were obscured by clouds. Sealing up her secret with those of her mother and grandmother was a way of putting the past behind her. Now, she could think about the future, a future with Joe Bullock and her baby — *their* baby. The clouds drifted away then, and a ray of sun penetrated, touching the tower of the Bride's House — her house, hers and Joe's, because no matter where their lives took them, this would be their home, this house that had sheltered three generations of women of her family, this house where she would be married.

She breathed in the cold mountain air, catching the scent of the wet pines, and although she knew it was late for their blooming, Susan thought she could smell Nealie's lilacs, too.

ACKNOWLEDGMENTS

There really is a Bride's House. It may not be as magnificent as the one I wrote about in *The Bride's House,* but it is an elegant place, one of the finest homes in Georgetown, Colorado, when lumberman Charles Bullock built it in 1881. But when I entered it 125 years later, the house was a derelict, its paint scoured off by the wind and snow, old cars parked in the yard. The inside had been stripped of its charm, the parlors and foyer turned into a single room, a part of an old house propped up against one side to serve as a bedroom. Raccoons lived in the tower.

My husband, Bob, and I toured the house one summer afternoon in 2007 with preservation architects Kathy Hoeft and Gary Long, who saw beyond the grime and destruction to what the original house had been — and could be again. When he glimpsed the walnut staircase, Gary raised his arms and exclaimed, "It's a bride's house!" At that moment, Bob decided to buy the place. I decided to write a book about it.

I am grateful to so many people who undertook the three-year challenge of returning the Bullock House to its nineteenth-century splendor. Thanks to Don Buckley for entrusting us with his family home. Kathy Hoeft lovingly restored the house's Victorian integrity while meeting our own needs. Dave Grasso and Ann Sill oversaw the rebirth of the Bullock House, working with two dozen other craftsmen, including Art Boscamp, Mark Ackerman, Patrick McKendry, and Gene Rakosnik. Elaine St. Louis selected the colors and decorated the interior, giving the house warmth and personality. Landscapers Bryan Lee and Jennifer Klaetsch replaced weeds and junked cars with a Victorian lawn and garden. You people are artists, and your work will stand for another 125 years.

While I knew that restoration of our Bride's House would take years to complete, I expected *The Bride's House* to go much faster. No such luck! The book, too, took three years, and I would have dropped the project if it hadn't been for the literary craftsmen who are my lifeline — Danielle

Egan-Miller and Joanna MacKenzie, my loyal and supportive agents at Browne & Miller Literary Associates, who talked me through draft after draft, and Jen Enderlin, my editor at St. Martin's Press, whose unerring instincts always make my work better. Buff Rutherford shared a lifetime of Georgetown stories, including the ones about the tire and the snake. Happy trails, Buff. Bruce Harlow answered a barrage of questions about the Air Force, Korea, and the 1950s, and Arnie Grossman gave unwavering support, as he always does. Thanks to both of you for fifty years of friendship.

My love to Bob, for embarking with me on this remarkable venture, and to our children, Dana, Kendal, and Lloyd, and our grandson, Forrest. The Bride's House, whether you like it or not, is your legacy.

Join Sandra's *Piecework* subscriber's list for her quarterly newsletter and information on her appearances.
Go to www.sandradallas.com and click on "Newsletter."
You can also find Sandra on Facebook by going to her website and clicking on the Facebook link.
And welcome!

ABOUT THE AUTHOR

Sandra Dallas is the author of nine previous novels, including *Whiter Than Snow, Prayers for Sale,* and *Tallgrass,* as well as two works of nonfiction. She is a former Denver bureau chief for *Business Week* magazine and lives in Denver, Colorado.

The employees of Thorndike Press hope you have enjoyed this Large Print book. All our Thorndike, Wheeler, and Kennebec Large Print titles are designed for easy reading, and all our books are made to last. Other Thorndike Press Large Print books are available at your library, through selected bookstores, or directly from us.

For information about titles, please call:
  (800) 223-1244

or visit our Web site at:
  http://gale.cengage.com/thorndike

To share your comments, please write:
  Publisher
  Thorndike Press
  10 Water St., Suite 310
  Waterville, ME 04901